CROSS A WIDE RIVER

Paul R. Stevenson

REAL WEST
FICTION SERIES

Sunstone Press • Santa Fe • New Mexico

To Helen
She believed in me
and I loved her

FRONT COVER: "Restin' Up" by Don Schairer
from the Sunstone Notecard Collection

First Edition

Printed in the United States of America

Library of Congress Cataloging in Publication Data:

Stevenson, Paul R., 1920-
Cross a wide river / Paul R. Stevenson. -- 1st ed.
p. cm.
I. Title.
ISBN: 0-86534-117-6 : $13.95
PS3569.T4565C7 1989
813'.54--dc19
88-12301
CIP

Published in 1989 by SUNSTONE PRESS
Post Office Box 2321
Santa Fe, NM 87504-2321 / USA

CONTENTS

CHAPTER 1
NEW BLOOD

Malcolm McCleod tilted back in the leather lined chair and blinked pudgy eyes at the two lean men sitting across the library table. He hadn't spoken for some time. They seemed not at all ill at ease waiting for him to start the bargaining again, or to accept their terms. McCleod idly fingered the solid gold fob at the end of the heavy gold chain which crossed his ample belly. Not since he left his native Scotland had he encountered such hard-headed bargaining as these two unreadable mountain men, who sat so relaxed in the chairs across from him. McCleod thought of how cruel and bitter the long war, so recently over, had been to most people, reflected on how he himself had fought to keep together the good life he had made for himself in the Mississippi Valley. When he was just a young boy, he had heard of the tremendous opportunities in the westward undeveloped lands of the United States of America. When his parents died, young McCleod had gathered all the family fortune, then had gone to England where he purchased twenty head of shorthorn heifers and two yearling bulls. He had lived with those cattle every moment of his life as he had had crossed the Atlantic in the hold of a clipper ship. He made his way to New Orleans, thence up the Mississippi on a river boat. With the help of two brawling, strapping stable hands, he had been able to bring his precious cargo all the way to the new, bustling river port of St. Louis, in the territory of Missouri. He acquired two full sections of hillside and river bottomland where, with backbreaking work and tender care, he built one of the finest herds of shorthorn cattle ever assembled anywhere. All through the war years he had been able to supply beef to the armies of the Union. Yet, he had maintained the purity of his breeding stock to the point that his fame had spread to all points of the union. The two men across from him had traveled all the way from the territory of New Mexico to buy bulls from his now vast herd; they were offering to pay in gold.

McCleod knew that he would not let them ride away without the prizes they had come for, yet he was determined to let them know that the blood they were buying was not going to come easy. He looked hard at the younger of the two, then said in his heavy Scotch burr, "I do na mind selling good animals when I know that they wi' not be wasted . . . but I canno allow my beautiful bulls to become beef fer some damn injun, o' be bred out til they become the stringy, skinny-assed lot ye have in yer brush covered wilderness. I tell ye again, Mr. Bolt, I dinna bring these bovine all the way from England to have 'em bastardized back to nought." McCleod's nerves began to tingle as he started the bargaining over again. The truth of the matter was that he really felt strongly about his cattle. He wanted to be certain that they would be appreciated as well as dearly paid for. His appraisal of these two from the West had left him with the good feeling that, here were men who would value his prize stock enough to fight for them every inch of the way. This kind of man he could appreciate.

The Scot hoisted his bulk from the chair and said, "Come wi' me to the feed lot again and let's look at these fine boys ye are trying to steal from me." He motioned with his fat, muscular arm to the outer door. Wes Bolt rose from the chair and stood to his full six foot height. A black servant handed him his flat-crowned hat which he pulled down close to his eyebrows. Wes was dressed in the finest style of the times. He had spent the greater part of one full day buying just what the salesman at the big St. Louis store had said was right for a gentleman. There was no mistaking the lean, muscular hardness of his lithe body beneath the new material of his expensive suit. Forty-five years rode easily on Wes Bolt, the age lines were just beginning to make themselves apparent on his handsome face. As he moved toward the door, the older man beside him uncrossed his legs, stood up and gingerly stretched one knee out in front of him. He moved silently across the room, for he wore Navajo moccasins on his feet. The rawhide bindings were laced to silver conchos on the side, and the tops were almost to his knees. Viejo was somewhere past sixty, but nobody had guts enough to remind him of it. What hair he had was snow white, but he held his body erect as he limped toward the door. He tried to ignore the pain of the old wound where an Apache lance had found him just above the knee.

The three men stepped out of the warmth of the spacious, comfortable house and started out into the bone-chilling fog of the Missouri morning. Viejo hunched his shoulders and tried to ignore the cold that seemed to seep into the very depths of his wiry frame. Wes Bolt couldn't help but remark about the damp weather as he thought of the sunshine of his beautiful mountain home in the territory. "I'm damned if I have been so cold in a long time . . . and I ain't seen the sun since we left Kansas. I got to admit though, that rain and fog makes the grass grow high." Wes' gaze wandered over the lush grass pastures of the Scotsman's fenced-in range land. Fat cattle wandered aimlessly in the bountiful feed or lay down in scattered groups chewing their cuds in blissful contentment.

McCleod spat tobacco juice through the fence rail at thé ear of a fat cow lying near the footpath. "Ladies like tha' un can give ye calves that sell five to one over any other kind of beef. Besides, they will fatten out twice as heavy as your range stock, and on the same amount of feed. Though I hate to give an Englishman credit, they really started a breed when they come up with the shorthorn. The northeast of England is a long way from here, but ye can bet yer best horse that the breed has improved since they been in my care." The three men had been walking rather briskly and were rapidly approaching the pasture where the Scot had a prize herd of yearling and two year old bulls. "Ye a' wantin' to take twenty o' 'em, an that wi' about clean me out for this season, but I like the cut o' ye two and I want to see ye be the owners of the finest bulls in the country." McCleod let down the bars of the rail fence so they could get nearer to the young stock eyeing them curiously. Viejo could bridle his excitement over the prospective ownership of the animals no longer; he exploded with a loud "God almighty! I ain't never seen such a bunch o' beef in all my borned days!" The calves stood solidly on their short legs, some lowered their heads in mock challenge. They were in full coat for the chill winter. The wetness of the fog glistened on their roan and white coats. They were compactly built, with rectangular bodies, lean shapely heads and small, short horns.

McCleod folded his hands across his expansive midsection, his eyes glowed with pride as he surveyed the results of his patient recording and breeding process. "These are just lads now . . . but just gi' em a little time to grow to be men, and they will breed anything that walks in front o' em and the result will look just like Papa!" He laughed deeply at his own frail joke, slapping Wes on the back with a resounding thud. "Now when ye take them to yer wilderness be sure not to let the range bulls interfere wi' em, fer they are lovers, not fighters. They'll make sons and daughters so fast ye will na have room for em." The older man looked the Scot squarely in the eye and said, "They damn well better. At the price yer askin! They are gonna make calves if I hafta hold em up to their work." The Scot rumbled in laughter again, but sobered quickly as he realized that now was the time to close the sale. He said sharply, "I'll let ye take yer choice of the twenty, ye pay me in gold at the bank in town tomorrow. I know I'll curse myself fer being a weak kneed spendthirft but I'll take yer offer fer just two dollars per head more, fer makin me stand in the cold more than once to show em to ye." Wes Bolt knew that the price he was asking per head for the prize stock was an outrageous one, but they had ridden over a thousand miles to get just what he was looking at, at the moment. "You got your price, Mr. McCleod," Wes said, extending his hand for the grip that would make the deal binding on them both. "Let's go to the house then, and I'll treat ye to the finest Scotch whisky in America!"

The three men entered the big house again, McCleod summoned the servant to bring whisky and water. While they enjoyed the luxury of the imported spirits, McCleod busied himself with the bill of sale for the blooded shorthorn calves he had just sold to Wes Bolt and his father, whom Wes always called by the Spanish word Viejo, or old man. The Scot carefully recorded the bill of sale, the number, and age of each of the bull calves which were branded with a small burned mark on the hide of their hip and a number burned into the left horn. "Now be ye interested, Mr. Bolt," McCleod said, "I can tell ye that it is a good system to burn the horn of the cows each bull breeds with a like number on her horn. That way if ye are to keep yer stock on the upgrade ye can keep a record in a manner that will let ye rotate yer breeding stock to separate parts of yer range each year. That way Papa don't see his own daughter, and run the line out in a couple of years. I canna urge ye strong enough that the matter of accurate records is the only way to make a start of seed bulls to bring yer herd up to the beautiful animals ye can be proud of.'' Wes listened intently to the Scot, once in awhile interjecting a quiet, ''Yes, sir,'' or a short ''uh, uh,'' but he never missed a word of the lengthy lesson in how to raise prize shorthorn cattle.

As the March morning wore on, the fog began to lift. The landscape outside took on a beautiful, serene grandeur which Viejo could appreciate. Stately oaks and hickory trees that surrounded the house, came into bold focus as the sun began to brighten and warm the rolling wooded hills, and grassy meadows of the Mississippi Valley. The old man had not been this far east in a long while. The sight of the glistening, and seemingly endless expanse of the wide river, held him in silent fascination. His thoughts dwelled on the possibilities for some of the broad expanses of wasteland in the country he was used to, if they just had some of this water, which to him seemed to be going to waste. He watched intently as huge river boats with rolling black smoke spewing from their stacks, passed on the wide water, saluting each other with several loud blasts of their steam whistles. Just what boats of that size could be carrying was too much for him to comprehend. He made a silent resolution that he and Wes would take a ride down to the river docks before they left so that he could tell Clemmy all about it when he got back to his beloved Rancho Feliz in the valleys of the Sangre de Cristo. At the thought of Clemmy, a contented tender feeling crept over the old man and his mind began to wander over the years he had been married to Eliza Clementine. The Scotch whisky had sufficiently warmed him, to cause him to doze in the comfortable leather-lined chair.

McCleod had finished with the lecture and was putting the finishing lines in the bill of sale. He leaned across the desk, aimed a stream of tobacco juice at the brass spittoon on the floor. ''It be none of my business now that ye ha em Bolt, but I got a very lot of curiosity as to how ye aim to get these animals all the way to the New Mexico territory. I ha never been west o' here, but I been told that there is a gigantic lot of prairie and mountain tween here and Santa Fe. Not to mention the Indian wars that are now on. I hear tell the army is hard-pressed to keep the ranchers and settlers out there, with hair on their heads. Besides, them redskins love beef and they would na rest if they heard ye had the best in the world. What's more, if ye plan to drive them bulls, it be so damn far, their short legs will be so wore off, their peckers will drag the ground before ye get there." Wes chuckled at the Scot's humor. McCleod himself gave forth with his rumbling laughter at the mental picture he had drawn for the journey of the bulls. Viejo stirred in his chair, trying to pretend that he had just been resting his eyes. After the Scot had enjoyed his joke to the fullest extent, Wes said, "No, Mr. McCleod, we don't aim to drive em. We plan to buy four big freight wagons in St. Louis tomorrow. With four head of Missouri draft mares to each wagon, we can haul six of em in each. The last will have only two, but will have room left fer sacked oats in case we run short o' feed when we leave the populated areas. We'll haul em by train from here to Dodge City, then take the Santa Fe Trail south to our place. There, I'll meet my boys with a herd of young heifers they are driving up from Texas. I got three young sons, McCleod; they can out-ride, and out-shoot double that many." Wes' voice took on a note of pride as he referred to his sons. "Besides, there is a boss vaquero with em who could eat the fires of hell if he was called on to do it. Me and Viejo will be at the Citizens Bank tomorrow at ten in the morning, at which time ye can deliver the bill of sale. We will have the bank credit yer account with the right amount of gold. Ye hold our animals in a separate pasture fer us until we send our hands to pick em up with the wagons. We would be obliged if ye can work it that way, Mr. McCleod."

The Scotsman pushed himself to his feet, extending his big hand again. "I'll have yer horses brought to the gate and I'll be waiting in town fer ye tomorrow." The hovering servant took his cue from the statement, scurried away to do his boss' bidding.

The morning was not long in coming since they were both early risers. Wes and Viejo tried to work off their impatience by eating a leisurely breakfast, then walking up and down the busy streets of what to them, was one of the biggest cities in the whole world.

Opening time for the bank was nine o'clock. Viejo did an overdone share of grumbling about people wasting half their lives, and too damn much of his, by not getting up when the sun rose to start their day. Breakfast at the hotel seemed to drag. They talked at length about the leisurely life of city folk, opposed to theirs on the ranch in far-off New Mexico territory. They had already booked passage on the next train for Dodge City, which would carry their precious cargo a great deal closer to their destination than they could hope to make in long days of driving wagon teams across the prairie.

They left the hotel, joining the throng of people on the street; it seemed that the whole world was going in different directions. Wes, vigorous man that he was, could not help but notice the slender, beautiful young girls, some of them dressed in the latest fashions. His mind wandered in a fantasy of wondering what one of them would be like in a man's bed. A grin creased his weathered face as he thought of Mama who was holding down the everyday routines of the vast ranch in the territory, while he and Viejo made the trip to the east for the new stock. He chuckled to himself when he remembered the shameful things he had bought for her in a little shop, where he was sure no one would ever see him again. He was so embarrassed, he could hardly wait for his purchases to be wrapped and handed to him. He could hear Adelia now, scolding him for wasting good money on such shameful things as he was taking to her. He also knew that she would not be able to wait to try on the lace-trimmed corset and silk stockings in the privacy of their own room. He was looking forward to her scolding in eager anticipation. He could picture her kindly broad face framed by a halo of beautiful brown wavy hair. Her ample bosom had fed his three stalwart sons and her work-worn hands had helped him with many a chore that should have had the strength of a man. The girls were pretty, but to rancher Wes, nothing could take the place of good hard-working stock. The help that she afforded him made her far more beautiful to him than any that could parade before his eyes. His mind wandered back to their Georgia home, where he and his beautiful Adelia had married in what seemed so many years ago.

The winds of war were just beginning to blow across the land as slave owners, and those who would free them, were beginning to take sides and engage in bitter debate. Viejo, or Poppa John, as he was known in those days, would often say, "If the North and the South have a go at each other, I'm pullin up stakes and headin for the territories to the west; the further west, the better." The holding of slaves, to him, was just not worth fighting over, so he had done just that. Wes looked over at his aging father and thought, "Well, Viejo was wrong a lot of times, but right a hell of a lot more than he was wrong."

When the bank opened, Wes and Viejo were standing by the door waiting. They were most anxious to get their business over with so they could start back on the long journey to the dry and beautiful climate of the New Mexico mountains. The purchase of the young bulls, wagons, feed, and horses had just about depleted their precious supply of gold and they were gambling their whole lives' work on the combined efforts of Wes and Viejo in St. Louis, and the boys with the herd of stock coming up from the hill country of Texas.

CHAPTER 2
APPRENTICE

John Bolt had heard about free land in Georgia when he was in the last part of his teens. He made a vow to own some of that land, even if it killed him. It almost did!

He was the son of a shiftless horse trader and his frumpy wife, who had never wanted John in the first place. His presence only slowed them down in their wanderings up and down the Atlantic seaboard. He would often feel the lash of his boisterous Pa. At times when they thought he was asleep in the wagon, he would hear the trader slap his mother around, telling her that the brat wasn't his'n anyways. The only thing he could say for his mother was that she had seen that he had plenty to eat, and he grew with a strong lean body. He had to learn, at an early age, to fight for what was his, and sometimes things that weren't.

When John was twelve, the rag-tag wagon with three horses abreast and four tied behind, made its way to the waterfront area of Savannah. They made camp by the river, and the old man started taking on a load of Jamaica rum as fast as he could buy it from a sidewalk vendor, then pour it down his profane throat. John shuddered, for he knew that the mean streak would start to show at any minute. It came almost at once. ''Woman, has the brat finished feedin' and waterin' the horses?'' ''No, he ain't, cuz there's a bunch of em. The poor tyke is hurryin' as fast as he kin.'' ''Them horses gotta be in shape if we gonna get anythin' fer em. Now git his ass movin' fore I kick one of his slats in.'' John scurried as fast as he could; it wasn't fast enough; the horse trader grabbed him by the back of the neck, cut him across the bottom with a leather strap from the harness hanging on the side of the wagon. The pain was so intense that John struck out with his small hard fist; he hit the man squarely in the nose. "God damn . . . now ye don it, ye broke my nose." He had reeled back against the wagon, the blood running freely between his dirty fingers. "Now I'm gonna give ye the hidin' ye been deservin!" John wanted to run, but knew he had nowhere to run to. He felt the bit of the leather line as it crossed his legs, then higher at his groin. Unmercifully the leather bit like a coiled snake across his slender body. He began to scream in agony. The woman came to his rescue. "Git offa him fore ye kill him." Ye been right all the time ye son of a bitch, ye ain't his Pa, and if ye hit him again I'll kill ye. So hep me, I'll wait my chance then I'll kill ye." The screaming declaration from the woman seeped through his rum soaked brain. He staggered off to wash his blood soaked face in the nearby stream that trickled into the river. John crawled into the wagon where his mother applied a mixture of hog lard and sulphur to his cuts and welts. That night, he made a vow never to take a beating like that again.

Sometime after dark, he heard voices from the direction of the campfire. The whisky voice of the man said "I know some places on the waterfront where they'll pay a pretty figure fer a strong whelp like that un, and by God, after today, I aim to collect fer his hide. That youngun got a mean streak in him as wide as yer fat ass. He ain't gonna be with us another day of his life. Them ships need cabin boys, an' he'll be a good un, after they teach him how, an' they got ways of teachin!" John's eyes grew wide with fright. His thoughts ran wild. What if they sold him to a slaver. He had heard waterfront tales about the ships which brought the blacks to be sold in the markets. He whimpered a little at the thought; then he heard the woman say, "He ain't yers to sell, I told ye. He belongs to me, an' I be the one to see that he have a chance to live to be a man. I take him tomorrow to see if I can find someone who take him to apprentice. They pay fer that too, ye know." "Ye damn well better get a good price, er ye might as well sell yer own ass right along with his. I aim to get somethin out o' him. After all, look at the money I been out, feedin' him since ye brought the squallin' idjit into the world. Ya didn't fool me none, when that dandy come tradin' to the wagons when I was in Mobile that night. I screwed him on the horse deal, but he had done screwed you. He got the best of the bargain cause I have had ta feed his bastard all these years. I should uh throwed ya out when I first suspected it."

John was exhausted from the beating, but slept only fitfully, wondering what would be his fate on the morrow. Not a word was said the next morning as they breakfasted on fried corn pone, and fatback salt pork. John noticed that his helping of black molasses was a little more generous this day.

After the horses had been fed, and the breakfast skillets were cleared away, his mother came to John, placed her hands on his shoulders, saying "Johnny, we gon' take a walk down into town to see what we can see." John, for the first time, saw tears come to his mother's eyes. She even held his hand as they left the camp, headed for the already bustling Savannah waterfront. "Ya ain't gonna sell me to no slaver, are ya' Ma?" John could not disguise the quiver of fear in his young voice. "So, ya heard last night? Well, Johnny, I borned ya, an' I aim to see that ya have a place where they be good to ya. I know a man, used to be a sailor man, but he on dry land now. He got a heart as big as a whale, he be good to ya."

The day was just beginning on the waterfront. The night catch of fish was being unloaded, John's nose wrinkled at the smell. Wagons loaded with cotton bales were waiting their turns at the gangplanks as the gang boss chanted, the black bodies strained to unload the bales from the drays, to get them on board the ships, bound for who knows where.

John again recoiled in fear at the thought of being forced to board one of the tall masted vessels. He wanted to run past the loading ships to another part of town. As he trudged along by his mother's side, he felt a wave of dread at the thought of leaving her and being taken in by someone he didn't know. He felt as though he wanted to vomit, but he knew he would be scolded for that, so he begged his mother to release his hand so that he could go behind one of the buildings to relieve himself. He ran to a spot beneath the wooden docks, then peed into the Savannah River. He thought to himself, that's about all I amount to in this world, pee in the ocean. Nobody cares if I live or die. He remembered the tears in his mother's eyes as he made his way back to her side.

John and his mother ambled up the dusty street; they both seemed reluctant to reach whatever their destination was. The morning heat and humidity began to build, it became oppressive. John paid scant attention to the endless strings of wagons, mules, and oxen which filled the street with their stink, flies, and noise. There were slaves everywhere. Some were under the watchful eyes of an overseer, while others seemed to know their jobs and were doing them with no direction at all. To John, this was the scene all up and down the eastern seaboard. He had been in every dirty village and bustling city from Washington to St. Augustine. He watched the sweating bodies of the half-naked blacks, wondering how one man could own another. He raised his eyebrows at the thought. Oh well, everyone who had enough money to buy them was doin' it, so it must be alright. Such was the attitude of the South in those days. John had not yet learned the full impact of man's inhumanity to man. He would live to see some horrible examples.

His mother started across the dusty street. She hoisted her long skirt to the tops of her high-buttoned shoes, then charted a zig zag course between the numerous piles of horse and oxen manure. A sleezy looking mule driver, walking beside his team, made a remark about hoisting the skirt higher. She started to tear into him with a string of profanity when she remembered John. She checked herself in embarrassment, mumbling something about a man hadn't ought to talk to a lady like that. The dirt was hot on John's bare feet, but since he had never owned a pair of shoes in his life, his feet were not really in too much discomfort. He didn't think he would like to wear shoes or boots anyway.

As they walked along the street, the shops and stores began to thin out. John noticed, off to his left, an open-faced shed with smoke drifting out of a metal chimney extending above the back of the sloped roof. He recognized it immediately as a blacksmith shop, and metal work shop. John had seen enough of these since his wanderings with the horse trader. He had watched the trader have his trading horses shod, then heard him beg, and haggle to see if he could get out of the price quoted for the smithy's work. His last resort was always try to trade some horse, or mule for the work; one which he knew would not bring much a price on the market. One thing, thought John, the good of this will be that I will be away from him for the rest of my life, however short my life may be.

As they neared the open shop, the woman started talking in a low, intense voice. "John, we gon' see Antonio Larkin. Now, he ain't got no woman . . . leastways he didn't have un the last time I seed him. If Tony decide to take ye on as apprentice, then ye gotta kind o' make do fer y'sef. Ye a big boy now, and can do a lot o' things what maybe other tykes yer age don' know how to do. Jes try to remember all I teach ye, lak yes sir, no sir, an pass the black-eyed peas ef ye please."

John tried to remember what she might have taught him that might help him to be an apprentice. In the first place, he didn't know exactly what an apprentice was. He had remembered his mother saying that the work was going to be hard. He was used to hard work, so it couldn't be much worse than he had already done. At least that was the reasoning from his immature mind.

They were getting close, he could hear the occasional ring of a hammer on the steel anvil. Several horses and mules were tied to the trees which shaded the smithy. As they drew near enough to feel the fires of the forge, the heat of the day seemed to become even more oppressive. He could see the intermittent glow of the fire as a young black boy lowered and raised the long handle of the bellows which fanned the charcoal to a white heat. A huge black man, naked to the waist, stood with his back to them. He held a horseshoe in the fire with a pair of long handled tongs. At another forge stood a tall well-built man with black curly hair. His shirt was open to the waist. He wore baggy canvas trousers, which reached about halfway between his knees and ankles. He wore heavy shoes with a leather strap across the instep, fastened at the side with a shiny brass buckle. John took him in at one glance, but his eyes could not leave the shoes with the brass fastener. The man had just taken a huge iron hinge from the forge, and was beginning to shape it on the anvil. He would tap the glowing metal lightly as he bent a flat protrusion around a hinge pin. He was so intent on his work that he didn't see the boy and his mother until they were quite near him. His mother said in a nervously quivering voice, "Tony Larkin?" The man looked up, a smile creased his ruggedly handsome face. "Yes, ma'am, what might I do fer ye?" John noticed his clean white teeth, and the wrinkles around his brown eyes. "Don' ye remember me, Tony? . . . It's Hilde from up Boston way." The boy could see recognition spread over his face as he said, "Hilde! It be you. Ye have changed a bit!" His big hands went out and took her by the forearms to pull her closer. "Where in glory be have ye been keepin' yerself?" "It's a long story, Tony, an I want ye to spare me a little of yer time for the tellin'. By the way this here is my tyke, John." "Didn't know ye had one, Hilde." He reached down to tousel the boy's hair. John thought his hands might have been made of horn, they were so hard. The smile was reassuring, so John held his ground. "How be ye, lad?" "Good sir, I reckon." John began to realize that this was the first time he had heard his mother's name. The horse trader had always just called her woman. He would remember this moment forever.

The man said, "Ye look hot, laddie . . . git yerself a drink from the barrel yonder, then we'll go find some shade under yonder tree." The boy welcomed the invitation, for he was thirsty. They walked a short way to a bench under a large tree. As they sat down, his mother said, "Tony, I gotta talk to ye private like, cause I gotta ask a powerful favor." The man winked at her. "Ain't that the way we usually talked, Hilde?" The woman smiled behind her hand, to hide a broken front tooth. Tony motioned to a small house just a short distance away. "There's me quarters, Hilde, we can talk there, if the boy'll wait here fer ye." "Wait here, Johnny, I'll try not to be too long." Yes, Ma'am." John saw the man put his arm around his mother's waist as he guided her toward the house. The child apprehensively watched his mother disappear through the doorway, then he turned to the shop to watch the giant black man do his work.

Other customers were lounging, or squatting in the shade of the trees as their animals were being shod. When the man turned toward John, the child recoiled, he almost took flight. This was the ugliest man the boy had ever seen. His shiny black face was heavily pock-marked. He had no teeth in front, and scar tissue made his lips appear as though they had been pounded on a rock. The cartilage of one ear had been thickened, it hung down as though it was an effort to hang onto his head. He was scarred from his throat to his beltline, and John knew that he had tasted the whip.

The man took a horse shoe in the tong walked over to a big mule standing hitched to a high rail. The big black man leaned against the mule's flank, then lifted its hind foot as though he dared the mule to kick. The animal's hoof had already been shaped and rasped, so the big man tried the steel shoe on for size. When he was satisfied that all four of the shoes were bent to the right configuration for each hoof, he began to nail them on. He drove the sharp steel nails through the pre-formed holes in the shoe, through the outer rim of the hoof. When all the nails were through, he nipped off the ends and bradded them over. Rivers of sweat were running off his shining skin as he labored. John had never seen anyone who could perform this task so fast. When the giant had finished the mule, he quickly led another to the hitch rail, tied his head up high. He didn't say a word to anyone, just kept working at top speed. The young negro boy had slacked off the up and down motion of the bellows, and found a place in the shade.

Every now and then John would glance toward the little house, imagining what was happening between Tony and his mother. A twinge of fright shuddered through him as he wondered again what was going to happen to him. John became so fascinated with the untiring efforts of the black man, that the passing of time was hardly noticed. The sun grew hotter, the blast of heat from the forges caused him to move away from the open shed, further into the shade of one of the tall trees. He covered his face as protection from the flies, then dozed. The occasional loud ringing of the hammer on the anvil would awaken him; he would look toward the house. He noticed that the black boy was back at his task on the bellows handle, and the smithy was pouring water over his bald head for relief from the humid air that surrounded them. Presently, his mother emerged from the doorway, followed closely by Tony. As they approached him, his mother nervously smoothed her skirt over her round hips. "Johnny, we had a long talk, me'n Tony did, and things goin' to be real good fer us." "Don't coddle the lad, Hilde, git on with what yer have to say. Send the lad to me when yer ready. Remember, yer promised to stop by and see me next time yer in Savannah." The big man patted her on the rump and winked at her as he sauntered away toward the shop. The woman sat in the shade with her only son, putting her arm around him to draw him close to her. Johnny was ill-at-ease, for he wasn't used to affection.

"Things is nice, Johnny. Tony has agreed to take ye on as apprentice. That mean he gon' feed ye, buy ye clothes, and fix a nice place fer ye ter sleep." Hilde began to whimper as she hugged the boy's shoulders, rocking gently back and forth. "I ain't got no choice, Johnny boy, I got ter leave, but I tell ye shore, I come back some day an git ye, John boy. Then we live in a fine house, maybe even buy ourself's a servant to wait on us, and do our work fer us." Tears were pouring down her face now, dripping off her chin. She mopped them with the back of her hand, and loudly snuffed her nose. "Damn that trader . . . damn him to hell. The no good horse thief is gonna beat me cause I dint git no money fer ye. To hell with him anyway. Leastways he cain't whup ye no more." Hilde planted a teary wet kiss on the boy's mouth, and tried to hold him closer to her ample bosom. John wiped his face with the sleeve of his shirt. This was the first time he could remember having been kissed.

Hilde got up from the ground, brushed back her unkempt hair, again smoothing her dress over her hips. "Ye stay, Johnny, soon's I leave ye go over to the smith shop, tell Tony ye ready to go to work. He gon' teach ye all kinds of wonerful thins ye can do with iron. Ye'll make fancy doors, winders, an all sorts o' beautiful decrations. Be a good boy, Johnny." She turned quickly, stumbling toward the dusty road. He wanted to scream for her to wait for him. He wanted to grab her around the waist, beg her not to leave him with a stranger. He had a big aching lump in his throat, and couldn't keep his chin from quivering. A wave of despair washed over him as he threw himself to the ground, covering his head with his arms. He couldn't seem to choke back the sobs that wracked his small body, nor stifle the agony in his small aching breast. Presently, he felt a hand on his heaving ribs. "Come wi' me laddie, we'll find a cold cup o' water and a biscuit. Then we'll make some talk. Twon't be so bad, laddie, I promise ye that. Go pour some water over yer face. I not be accustomed to a big man like ye, blubberin' like a bull calf."

The mere suggestion that he was a man caused John to stand up and square his small shoulders back. "Ye aint' gonna see me cry no more!" He never did, at least where someone could see.

John walked with the tall man to the shelter of the small house. As they entered, he was surprised to see that everything was clean and neat. All utensils seemed to have their own place and articles of clothing were hanging from wooden pegs in the walls. "Ye'll see that I keep things ship-shape here, lad, so will ye." John had never heard of anyone making a point of being clean before. He really didn't see much use in it. Tony crossed the room, then opened a door at the back. John could see that it was a woodshed. The roof evidently leaked and he could see wide cracks between the boards of the outer wall. "This be yer quarters, lad. Not much now, but after some fixin, ye'll be able to live. It be summer now. Fore the wet and cold weather starts, I'll be teachin' ye to work with tools, and yer can make yer own comfort. First thing we'll make is a outside winder, so's ye can breathe."

It really didn't look that bad to John, especially since he was used to sleeping in a cramped space in the back of a wagon, or under it. "Fore the day be over, John, ye get Tobe and Roof to help ye make a bed. Plenty of straw and corn shucks 'hind the shed. Chuck 'em in some burlap, ye'll sleep like a new bornt babe." John didn't have to worry about where to put his clothes. He had on all that he owned, one pair of pants and a cotton shirt. Tony threw two tin plates on the table, then served up big hunks of corn bread. Over this he poured black sorghum molasses from a crock jug. John was hungry, so he ate with gusto, washing it down with water. There was very little conversation during the meal. Tony did say, "I be takin' ye to git ter know Tobe and Roof. They be mine, and some day I will be tellin' ye how I come by 'em."

After the meal was over, Tony washed the plates, and threw the water into the yard. "Now set, pay attention, fer I aim to tell ye only onst. I know my trade. I went to sea when I was no mor'n a bit bigger'n ye. I reckon I sailed to all the ports in the world, lad, and I made a practice ter keep me eyes and ears open. I lernt fancy iron grill work when I was in a long stay in the port of Genoa, that be in Italy. I can heat-weld a pice o' metal so ye cain't see the seam. I mean to teach yer me trade, lad, but yer be earning yer keep in the bargain. I expect hard work and I will take no sass from the likes o' ye. If ye figger ter be real bad, lad, I take the back o' me hand ter the side o' yer head." John recoiled a bit, which brought a smile to the face of the man. Again, the boy was fascinated by the straight white teeth, and the kindly expression of his dark eyes. "I be the product of a Irish sailor pa, and a Portagee ma. The British were bearin' down hard on the Irish when my pa were a wee lad. His folks bound him out to the skipper o' a fishin' craft out o' Portugal. Accordin' to the tales he told, however Irish sailors is bad liars, he married the prettiest Portagee gal on the coast. That was o' course after he was full growed and decided he did not want more o' the sea. He set up a fish buyin' shop in a small port and started about the business o' making a passel o' younguns. I be the youngest o' the lot. I had enough o' the stink o' fish by the time I be fourteen. I went to Lisbon, signed on with the tallest masted Portagee trader in the harbor. I was signed on as apprentice to the carpenter and blacksmith. He were a mean ol' Portagee, but he know his trade well. I learnt as fast as I could. I minded my own affairs, an' if I were forced to fight, I fought to win. I never provoke no brawls, an' I mean to learn ye to be the same way. I be Antonio Larkin, I be proud o' me name and me sel'."

Tony stood up, and John could see the ripple of his hard muscles. He noticed that Tony's belly was as flat as a board. "Yer body be a precious gift ter ye, lad, take care o' it the best ye can. I aim ter see ye git plenty ter eat, an by Jupiter yer gonna stay clean. Ye'll wash yersel' ever night. If'n ye don't ye'll sleep wi' the mule which draws the delivery wagon. I mean ye wash from head ter toe. Start tonight by washin' them clothes ye got on. Ye'll speak ter me with yes, sir, an no, sir, and if ye please, sir. When ye think yer big enough not to call me sir, then I'll call on ye to prove it."

John was wide-eyed at the rapid flow of instructions. He felt sure he was to absorb it all at one session, or be severely punished for his stupidity. The horse trader had derived a great deal of pleasure out of telling John how stupid he was. This had begun since the child had learned to talk. By the time he was twelve he was convinced that he was the slowest person in the world. Much to the contrary, his mind was razor sharp, so he retained a great deal of what he was told on a first time basis.

Anthony Larkin headed for the door, then motioned for the boy to follow. The path to the blacksmith shop was well worn, branching off only to a privy which sat nearer to the house.

"Ye'll be meetin' Tobe and Rufus, I call him Roof, and I want ye to know that yer ter treat 'em like people and not like property. Tobe don't speak too good, mostly mumbo jumbo. I reckon he cud learn if he was a mind ta, but he don't seem ter give a damn. Importin' slaves ain't really legal in America no more, laddie, but it be done anyway. Slavers park 'em on the outlyin' islands and bring 'em ashore here in the big ports as though brung in on one o' them hell-ships. Tobe be a bad 'un at that time, they had chains on his feet ter keep him controlled. I bein' a smith, had a job o' separatin' the irons from their feet and hands when they were sold. Tobe wuz half-starved at that time, but he still be a big un. A trader from the interior bought him, an' wanted me to put a neck iron on him so's they could control him when they wanted to take him away. Tobe's leg irons be fastened to a big stake in the ground. The trader sent three other blacks to hold Tobe whils't I put on the iron and chain. He waited fer 'em, till they got real close, then he looked like the hinges of hell as he tore inter 'em. Rufus bein' just a lad, had no chanct at all agin the likes of Tobe. He was lifted high into the air and flung agin the walls o' the stockade. He lay where he fell an didn't stir. We all reckoned he was dead. The other two didn't do much better. Tobe had 'em on the ground, bleedin' afore ye could say saints presarve us. When that big black stood up to his full height, I could see that he had been sorely abused. He hadn't healed from the whip which had been liberally applied since he was captured. They had smashed his face; his big lips were still bleedin. He still had cuts on his head, from where they had laid him low a few times. He stood naked, filthy as any hog. I kin still recollect the stink o' him!"

"The trader said, 'Looks like I bought me a real outlaw. I'll break him or kill him.' That cracker be a real expert with the blacksnake and he laid it to Tobe til I was sure he was nothin but a big pile of black, bleed'n flesh. I told the trader, 'B'fore ye kill him, what will ye take fer yer investment?' 'That's an outlaw smith. He'll kill any man don't know how to handle 'im. Face it he may never be broke. He done kilt thet boy over thar . . . he were a good 'un, too. Never give nobody no trouble a'tall'."

"Tobe was beginnin to roll in the dirt, an' make all sorts o' sounds in his throat. I know he was sufferin' the torment o' a thousand demons in his body. B'fore I know what I said, I had offered the slaver a hundred dollars fer him. He took me up on it, quick like, an I was the owner of a huge pile of bleed'n man. I quick put the neck and hand irons on him 'fore he had a chanct to get back on his feet. The slaver said, 'Bury that oter'n over thar, an I knock five dollar off'n the price.' I went over where Rufus lay; I could see he was still breathin'. 'He ain't dead yit, mister!' 'Might's well be; he is some busted up, an I ain't got no way to wait him back to life this fer from the plantation,' 'Gi' me his papers, an ye keep the five,' I said. Well I bought 'em. I loaded 'em both in my wagon, an brung 'em here ter my shop. I could tell Rufus had a broke laig and his ribs was stove in. I splinted him, made him as comfortable as I could in the mule shed, then I tied Tobe to thet big tree by the shop, put hog lard an sulphur on most o' his bleed'n carcass. I got cool water, an washed his head, an poured some of it down his throat. When he open his eyes, I still di' na know if he were thinkin kindly on me, er if he would kill me if he could git them big hands on me. I left him tied, an made sure I give him plenty o' food, an water every day."

"On the second day, I went behint him and took off the neck iron . . . he seemed to say thank ye, by noddin his head back an forth. I bathe him down wi' buckets o' water, then I put more salve on his hurts. I took the hand irons off the same day. I would talk ter him gentle like whilst I was doin' me work, an he seemed to respond. I went ter take the leg irons off. I figgered if he went crazy wild agin, I just have ter kill him. I walk right over ter him, put out my hand; he took my hand, an got up off the ground. I wuz shur the fight wuz about ter start. He jes stood an nodded his head back an forth. He was talkin in the same strange tongue and pointin' ter the leg irons. I took 'em off, then handed him a pair o' me pants fer him ter hid his nakedness. I ain't never had to speak harsh to him even one day since that time two year ago. Rufus had mended some an' I took Tobe in to see 'im. I could see the pain in his eyes as he bent over an put his big hands on the boy's shoulders. He rubbed gently, as if ter say, 'I sure be sorry fer what I done ter ye'."

Tony and John had long since reached the shop, and had stopped in the shade of a tree while Tony finished his narrative. "I don' hold with slavery, laddie. I seen it in all parts o' the world, an all it is, is men wantin' other men ter do their dirty work, an hold absolute control o'er other men an women. I see men sell their own daughters on the Chinee coast, an I see mostly one race want ter dominate t'other. The good book says that slavery goes way back yonder ter the beginnin o' time. That don't make it right, jes cause some folks thinks it does. Old King Neb, way back yonder in the Babylon days, helt the Hebrew prisoner, then the Romans had all manner o' servants which were all slaves. Agin, I tell ye, John boy, I cannot abide one man ownin' another. I have papers which says I own these two. If I made 'nother paper an' turn 'em loose, then some slaver would have 'em 'fore the ink were dry on the paper.

Besides, I ain't never learned to write anyway. One day they be free, John boy.

"We be greatly criticized if we tell everyone how we feel 'bout slaves. After all, we be citizens o' the South and this is the way people live here. I give Tobe and Rufus so many hours o' work every day, 'cept Sunday. Extry work they do, the pay goes inter a special savin' fer 'em. One day they be able ter buy ther way ter the North where them Quaker folk say all slaves should be free. Let's go talk to 'em. Now Tobe don' talk too good, but he will understand."

John slept soundly that night, secure in the belief that he had at last found where he could make a place for himself, at least find a word of encouragment now and then to sustain him in his efforts to learn a new trade; possibly at the same time please Tony, his new taskmaster.

There were long hot days when John thought the sun stood still in the sky. He took his turn at the bellows handle, learned to clean the forges, and build fires that would be just right for the job to be done. He learned the use of every tool in the shop, the shape and weight of every hammer, and why they were shaped thus. He had to learn to fashion his own tools, then use them for each step in the sometimes intricate iron grill work. Tony was a good teacher, although hard and unrelenting. He demanded perfection in every step of the work, from the pattern to the finished product.

John thought often of the leisurely days he spent strolling along behind the trader's wagon, as they wandered along some new-found road. His interest in his work quickly dispelled any wish to return to such a life. The memory of the trader strengthened his resolve to learn quickly. His affection for Tony grew with each passing day. He tried all the harder to please his teacher. His trade was the only schooling he had, and he often wondered what it would be like to be able to read and write. The opportunity did not present itself, so he dismissed it from his mind. One thing he did learn, however, was his numbers.

Although Tony couldn't even sign his own name, he would drill John on how to keep track of his accounts by adding columns of numbers. During the long evenings, he would sit and talk with Tobe and Rufus about the things they had seen in the world. Tobe could barely be understood, so John would look into his battered face, then pronounce the words slowly. Tobe would try valiantly to make the sounds come out through his scarred lips, just the way John had said them. His missing front teeth didn't help, but John was persistant. Soon Tobe began to be understood a great deal better. Rufus didn't care, so long as he had a full belly and some place to sleep. Rufus was probably about nineteen at the time. He had suggested a few times that it would be right nice if'n they had women to keep them company. John saw little use in that, and didn't pursue the subject.

As Tobe learned to talk, he would tell of his homeland, his voice drifting off as he described the beauty of his wives and children back in darkest Africa. He would never admit that he would never see them again. He told of countless people who had died on the slave ships, not leaving out any of the details of the cruel treatment they had endured at the hands of the slave drivers. They landed in the Caribbean Islands first, and were put ashore to be washed and cared for. This, of course, made them bring more money on the blocks of the markets in the island ports. Smugglers would buy them there, then bring them to the American shore, identify them as having been there all the time. Slave trading, directly, had been abolished for fear there would get to be so many that a deadly insurrection would take place. The law held little authority, the slaves were brought anyway. Tobe had gone along with the flow of wretched humanity until he was shipped to Georgia, where he was put to work loading ships and barges on the Savannah River.

They worked the slaves from first light in the morning, until they could no longer see in the evening. The work never slacked for a moment. It was then that Tobe decided to rebel. He was severely beaten for his decision. They tried all sorts of punishment to get his giant strength back on the gang. Nothing changed the rebellious tower of muscle. The owners of Tobe decided to sell him to the gang buyers from the plantations in Mississippi. They worked them there until they died, and then bought more.

The price of cotton was high, so they could well afford to use up more slave labor to produce the bales of white gold. This was when Tony had rescued him from certain death, for Tobe had resigned himself to die rather than be subjected to further indignities and torture at the hands of the drivers. As they sat and talked one day, Tobe said, "By'n'by, John boy, I go back across the big wottah, ober dere." He waved his big arm in the direction of the ocean. He had heard other slaves tell about the colony of Liberia, established on the coast of Africa. He longed to go there, then leave in search of his wives and children. "By'n'by, John boy, by'n'by." John hoped he could. A twinge of loneliness for his own mother swept through him for a moment.

There were many evenings when John would sleep in the back room of the stable with Tobe and Rufus. Tony would have company, and tell John that he had things to talk about that were just not for his tender ears. She would usually be gone by the next day, so John didn't really have time to give it too much thought. On Sundays, when he had time to himself, he would wander down to the riverfront to watch the giant ships loaded or unloaded. He would hear the strange tongues spoken by the many nationalities and wonder what they were saying.

He got acquainted with riverfront boys of his age who could out-cuss a mule skinner. Some of the language rubbed off on John. The river boys knew the different flags, and the countries they represented. They could even say a few words in the different tongues. Paddle wheel steamers were just beginning to make their appearance on the river, and John would marvel at the complexity of the machinery which made them go upstream without a sail. Great blasts of black smoke poured from their stacks. How they could build a giant machine like that was beyond his comprehension. It must have taken a hundred blacksmiths working for a year to get it done. He remembered Tony saying that one paddle wheeler had been built right here in Savannah, and had crossed the ocean. The horse trader's threat to sell him as a cabin boy crossed John's mind, he shuddered at the thought. He had no desire to cross any ocean.

Savannah, in the year 1835, was a growing, important port on the Atlantic. Huge churches and meeting halls were being built. The magnificent homes of the rich were scattered in groves of oaks along aristocrat row. There were great white columns in front, slave quarters and stables at the back. The whole thing was then surrounded by a white fence, with fancy gates. These were the customers who kept Tony Larkin in business, and many times John would see the fine ladies, accompanied by a slave or two, drive up to the smithy to order fancy wrought iron from Anthony Larkin. Some of these he would see after dark, as they entered Tony's house. When he saw them he would, without question, head for the stable quarters for a night with Tobe and Rufus.

The business was growing and began to prosper. Savannah had come a long way since its founding in 1733 by General James Oglethorpe, then chartered as a city in 1798. The city was laid out with wide regular streets, Bull Street being the main thoroughfare. The city was planned in squares, as protection against marauding Spanish or Indians. The spires of Christ Church could be seen from the blacksmith shop. The two boys wondered if God lived there. Their religious education was sorely lacking, with only a vague reference once in a while to the good book, and the saints to pray to. Tony, their mentor, knew very little about religion himself.

In the early part of his thirteenth year, John was beginning to grow tall. His eyes were bright blue, under long curving lashes. Light hair, and light complexion made his handsome face look somewhat effeminate, although he was far from it.

On one of his trips to the waterfront, he was challenged by a boy about his size, but a couple of years older. "Hey, sissy boy, me and the boys done decided ter let yu jine the River Front Sassiety. Yu shell out four bits and hand it ter me, then automatic yu become a member." John was reluctant to share his hard-earned money with anybody who didn't deserve it. "Ain't gonna pay no four bits ta anybody!" "Then Axel Olsen is gonna kick the shit outa yu." The older boy moved menacingly closer. John thought about Larkin lecturing him about not provoking a fight. With the others cheering him on, Olsen moved in on the frightened John. John's hands and muscles were hard and strong, but in the face of such numbers, he felt a surge of fear go through him. His mouth was dry and bitter. There was no place to run to. "I cain't fight the lot o' ye, but I'll stand up to the best o' ye." Olsen took this as his chance to be a champion. "Yu bilge rats stand off, I'll handle the sissy boy." The others made a circle. Olsen stooped to the dirt and got a handful of horse manure. "I think I better unshine his purty clean face fer him." The manure landed in John's face full force. Rage took over, he tore into the riverfront bully with a vengeance. Olsen found, too soon, that he was no match for the wiry, work-hardened blacksmith apprentice. Olsen began to give ground, trying to cover his face from the hard fists. One of the other boys lunged forward and tripped John. He fell heavily to the ground, Olsen kicked him in the face with his hard bare foot. John felt his nose smash, he tasted blood in his mouth. By then the others in the circle were taking their turn with the kicking fun. John had no chance but to try to cover his vital parts as they all took their turn. When he was weak from the beating, they stripped what little change Larkin had given him from his pockets, spat upon him, throwing dirt and manure from the street all over his aching body. "When Momma fixes yu up, sissy boy," Olsen jeered, "come on back down to the front and jine the club. Be sure to bring more money, though, cuz now the dues gonna be a big pile higher." As they left, John thought he would never be able to get on his feet again. He painfully made his way back to the shop where he knew that his friends would help him pull himself together.

When he reached the shop, big Tobe picked him up as though he were a feather, he held him in his arms. The big man's eyes filled with tears, he began to rock the boy like a babe in arms. "Who done do this thing to ye, John boy? I go to the ribber, I fling 'em all in wid dere face down." The black man began to mop at the blood still oozing from John's nose. He wiped John's face with his hand, then wiped it on the leg of his coal grimed pants. "Fech mas Tony, Rufus, fech him fas." Rufus took off for the house at a run. Tobe carried the bruised boy toward the house. He mumbled as he walked. "Ain't nobuddy gon' hurt my John boy lak dis here. Tobe go down dere and break dey bones." Tony met them near the door, held it wide for Tobe to carry the bleeding, bruised boy inside. Tears streamed down the giant's black face. "I go fine 'em, Massa Tony . . . I go fine 'em." "I'll hear none o' yer talk, Tobe. Ye be gettin us all kilt. Lay him yonder on his own bed, and fetch water to clean him up." John felt his clothes being removed, then a wet cloth being applied to his battered face.

"Ye'll be good as new, boy." Tony's voice seemed to be coming from a long way off. "I bet he lathered 'em good 'fore they tuk him down. Look at the way his hands be skinned up." By now John was spitting blood from his mouth. He ran his tongue over his teeth to see if they were still all there. He tried to talk through his split lips. "Jes lay still, John boy, we be fixin' ye good as new. Then ye got some gang fightin' to learn, an I be the man to learn it tu ye.

I'll learn him ter fix em so's ther mithers won't even know 'em, I will.'' Tony was seething with anger. ''Now lad, sit up, feel if there be any broke bones.'' John felt the agony of a cracked rib, but everything else seemed to be moving alright.

Tony told Tobe to hold John while he straightened his battered nose. ''This be right painful, lad. Bite on this.'' He stuffed a wet rag into John's mouth. As gently as he could he squeezed the bleeding nose back into shape. ''May be some outa line when it heals, laddie, but maybe not too bad. Ye can still smell wi' it.''

John had to miss the hard work of the smithy for weeks while his ribs mended. Tobe had wound a strip of canvas around John to give him something to breathe against, to keep his rib from splintering, and going into his lung. The weather was hot, the bandage made him sweat; he got heat rash under the folds of material. John made himself as useful as he could by helping to keep the house clean, washing clothes and feeding the animals in the stable.

Larkin began to practice a strange ritual which John had never heard of or seen. Larkin called it ''Jujitsu,'' which he translated as ''The gentle art, ''I learnt as much of this as I could when I be on a Dutch trader what was stove in on the coast of Japan. That be a country in the far, far east, John, me lad. While we be reparin' the hole in the ship, and gettin' her ready ter sail agin, I paid a Jap expert to teach me all the moves he knew how, then I practice them fer years. Now I need some time ter git it all in me head agin. The principle be that every part o' yer body be a lever. A lever ter defend yer life wi'. Another part they call 'Judo' will destroy yer adversary onct ye have him at a disadvantage. When we git inter this, I be in shape ter show ye all ye need to defend yersel'.''

After work every day, Larkin would spend long hours practicing the moves and counter moves of the gentle art of self-defense. At first John thought that Larkin's hand positions, kicks, spins and falls were very funny. Then he began to see a pattern of counter moves against an imaginary foe, take place. When Larkin had his body tuned to a perfect precision, he told them that he was ready to begin the classes.

They fashioned a huge mat from cotton they bought at the mill. Although it was strictly against the law to teach slaves to engage in combat, Larkin included Tobe and Rufus in the nightly classes. When all was ready, Larkin removed all his clothes except a cloth which was tied around his waist, then between his legs. He was a magnficent figure of a man, although he told them that he reckoned he was past forty-five.

The training had caused his already muscular body to take on the form of a coiled spring about ready to release. "Now ye listen to me, all o' ye. No man should attack another man unless it be ter pertec hisself, someone o' his friends, er fambly, er ter fill a starvin belly. If'n I find thet any of ye have hurt someone fer naught, then ye must also reckon wi' Antonio Larkin, and the reckonin' may be severe fer each o' us. The object is, if ye feel ye must strike, then strike wi' all yer force, strike where it will count sorely on yer opponent. Jes sit like the rattlesnake, still and quiet, until ye must move, then move wi' lightnin' in yer aim; strike ter make it count. Even warn 'em if ye feel ye must, but don't move til ye know thet ye must cripple yer foe. Do not provoke a fight, run away from it, be it at all possible. Now strip down, all o' ye, and let's git er work. I be startin wi' Tobe, ter show ye thet it ain't all muscle which counts in a close fight."

Larkin explained to the black giant just why he wanted to be attacked. Tobe protested, "Massa, I wudn't hut yo effin ye was cuttin off mah han. I jes cain't do nothin lak dat wif yu, Massa Tony." The master explained again that he wanted Tobe to help with the class by trying his best to get a hold on him. "We be savin the vicious blows till a later time. Fer now, jest try ter get a hold on me, then throw me down ter the mat." Tobe thought that this kind of wrestling would be fun, so he advanced on the lithesome Tony. The big man lunged, Tony gracefully whirled, and went to one knee. Tobe's momentum was increased by a hard pull on his left arm, by Tony. Tony's right leg was extended at just the precise split second, Tobe crashed heavily to the canvas pad. Before the huge man could recover, Tony demonstrated two vicious kicks to his ribs. He stayed the force of the kicks to avoid injury to the downed man. "Be ye gettin the idee, Tobe, thet ye got a body to reckon wi'"? Tobe got to his feet, "I git yu dis time, Massa Tony. I git yu fer sho, and I set on yu belly and light ma cob pipe." They both grinned good naturedly.

Tobe advanced again, this time in a crouch, with his big arms spread to encircle his teacher. John and Rufus thought he was a truly frightening creature, who would have Tony down for sure. Tobe grabbed for Tony, missed, except for a hold on his right wrist. The hold was like a steel vice, but Tony quickly worked against the black man's thumb, spun like a flash of light, and was behind Tobe with the huge black arm extended in a position where Tony could have dislocated his shoulder, or broken his elbow. The demonstration went on for about two hours, until Tobe was thoroughly tired. He had not once taken the advantage of the combat-skilled Tony. Tony then gave each of them instruction on how to fall, just in case the tables were turned in the other direction.

These nightly classes extended into months, with all of the students learning the fascinating art of self-defense, so ably taught by the ex-sailor. They then advanced to the attack. Tony showed them how to administer vicious kicks and recover, splash with their extended hands against vital, vulnerable parts of an opponent. They learned how to find and gouge nerve endings to cause their foe excruciating pain, thus causing him to loosen his grasp. Larkin would repeatedly admonish them to keep their bodies in shape at all times. Not a day went by that the three did not go through the ritual of self-defense and attack, even the lackadaisical Rufus became a real contestant in the games they played.

Their routines were not without bruises and strained muscles. Larkin taught them to scream and yell at the attack. "Ye know jes whut ye be aimin to hit. But yer foe gets all rattled when ye come at him like a wild man. Make as ugly a face as ye can, then yell like a banshee from the fires of damnation."

The scarred, stone-bodied Tobe became a formidable opponent when he learned speed and surprise, as well as using his huge muscled body. Larkin would lecture them by the hour. "Now don' ye never hurt nobody wi' out a cause, and the cause should be a sore aggravation a'fore ye take to him. Cours effin ye be attacked without provocation, kick his balls off, er break his arm er leg fast." John took to the games as though they were going to be a part of his life from now on. Larkin chided Tobe, "Ye scare the beshit outta me, Tobe, an ye need niver move from the spot ye stand in." The giant grinned his toothless grin and said, "Yes, Massa." They all worked as hard as they played; the business became the gathering place for horsemen all over the country. They were of the opinion that Larkin's black could shoe a horse to perfection; also the artistry of Larkin and the young boy apprentice became the talk of Savannah.

John had learned to draw intricate designs, such as vines and flowers, then they would be wrought in iron just about the way they appeared on the paper. When he was still in his early teens, his artistry was in great demand. They all ate well, so John became as lean and hard as a young panther. Rufus and Tobe would go off on dark nights to join a jubilee, as they called it. Some of the blacks who had permission to leave their quarters, would go off into the river breaks where they would meet at a predetermined spot. They built a huge bonfire, and would dance and sing until they were almost exhausted. Some of the men and women would sneak off into the trees to make love. Rufus and Tobe did their share of the jubilee trick, but never told John too much about where they had been. Tony would always admonish them not to get into trouble by fighting over some girl. For one of the other slaves to have provoked Tobe to fight was a rather remote chance. However, Larkin demanded their promise that they would not get into a donnybrook.

John frequented the waterfront many times again, but mostly in the company of Tony. Tony found plenty of diversion in the form of southern belles, both married and single. True to his word, Tony would put money aside for the two slaves, he also made sure that John put away a decent portion of the extra pay that was awarded to him. Larkin figured he never lost a penny on the apprentice, John. He loved him like a son, and watched him grow as the days and weeks blossomed into years. By his early teens, John was tall and handsome. Just a little curve in his nose showed where it had been kicked out of line by the waterfront bully, Olsen. John had indeed made a place for himself.

CHAPTER 3
INDIANS

Eliza Clementine walked along the winding path that made its way from the pasture on the hill to the corral at the back of the crude log house nestled at the edge of the pine forest. It was a lazy summer day, Eliza was enjoying every minute of it. Every now and then she would stoop to examine the beauty of a wild flower along the path. To her, they were God's way of making the world more beautiful for people like her. She thoroughly enjoyed living here on the red land of Georgia near the headwaters of the Savannah River. She had never been more than fifteen miles from this cabin. Another world somewhere was just something that the older folks talked about when the work was over at the end of the day. She had traveled with her Pa one day to the county seat. It had been so far away that they slept in the wagon that night. When they had reached the place where all the people were, she held tight to the fringe of her Pa's shirt. It was a town of at least five thousand people. She was sure they would never find their way back to the security of the cabin near the woods. She had seen the slaves working in fields along the way, rich folks lounging in the shade of the trees near the plantation houses, or engaging in games on the spacious lawns.

Clemmy, as her Pa lovingly caller her, was eleven years old, as slender as the reeds that grew near the edge of the ponds along the road. Her hair hung to her waist, black as a raven's wing. She kept it tied back with a string of wool yarn. The black hair framed a face of simple beauty, large brown eyes, a straight nose, and full lips that when she smiled, revealed rather wide apart teeth. Her skin was very light brown. She had never worn shoes except for rabbit skin moccasins in winter, so her feet were small but hard and calloused. She had on an ill-fitting cotton dress that was tied in the middle with a piece of cotton rope.

Clemmy and Pa entered the General Merchandise Store and a whole new world opened up before her eyes. Food on the shelves, barrels of flour and molasses, harnesses hanging from the rafters, dresses, boots and shoes were on display. There were all sorts of things which Clemmy had no idea what in tarnation they could be used for. They approached a glass counter, there she recognized barber pole candy temptingly laid out. Pa said, "Zeb, put a stick of that there peppermint candy on the bill fer my girl."

The heavy browed grocer shuffled over to the counter to bring out a piece of the candy. "What be yer name, chile?" Clemmy was not shy, although she was still somewhat frightened. "I be Eliza Clementine Bandy, sir. Pa says I be eleven years old." The pot-bellied store keeper laughed, letting a stream of snuff juice run down the corner of his mouth. "She shore mouths off too much for a female, Will, but I reckon when she get old enough to marry, some cracker boy'll shut her mouth fer her." Pa put his arm around Clemmy's head and drew her close to his hip. "You asked her Zeb, and she told you. Her name be Clemmy Bandy alright." "Thet the only youngun ye got Bandy?" "Shore is! Her ma died at berthin' and my wife's maw been lookin' after her fer me. Sides, when ye got a gal lak Clemmy, ye don't need no more." Again Pa patted her head. Clemmy felt that nothing in the whole state of Georgia could hurt her as long as Pa was near. "What else ye be needin' Bandy?" The storekeeper eyed Clemmy again as he asked the question. Clemmy licked the candy, as her Pa intoned the things he would need for the next few months . . . flour, salt, bullets, powder; the list went on as a small pile grew where a black boy stacked them.

Pa cleaned out the wagon bed, for he had hauled a load of fat hogs to the county seat, to barter for the things they would need for the rest of the summer. This was the way of the Georgia backwoods in those days. Soon the wagon was loaded, the lazy mules were headed once more in the direction of their beloved cabin at the edge of the woods. As the day wore on, Clemmy slept on a pallet in the bottom of the wagon.

Will Bandy let his mind wander back to the days of his coming to this part of the country. He was a very young man when he came to his claim of the Georgia land. He had found just the spot he had wanted to call home for the rest of his life. He set about carving his spot from the tough brush and stumps of the Georgia red land. He built his cabin from logs he would cut from the land. A wide chimney was fashioned from stone he selected near the river. This became the pride and joy of the young girl he later married. He hunted in the woods for food he needed to survive on. He killed wild turkeys, deer and wild hogs. He carefully cleaned, then smoked the meat to preserve it for the leaner times he knew would come when winter set in.

As Will Bandy labored, he felt that the forces of nature were all against him at times. He would cut trees and brush, saving the trees in hope that someday he would be able to haul them to the sawmill at the County Seat, for maybe a dollar or two. He didn't even have a mule to help him till the land and pull the stumps. He was philosophical about it though. Every day he would say a prayer of thanks to God, that he was alive and healthy. He watched his farm grow as he burned and grubbed. He would use a hoe to make a hole to plant his crops, corn, potatoes, yams, turnips, and anything else he could get the seed for. His smokehouse was constantly busy as he cured venison and other wild game, which he was able to bring down with his single shot rifle. With Will, one shot was quite enough, his aim was deadly. Little did he know that as winter approached, he would be called upon to share his bountiful harvest with the remnants of a family in the gravest of need.

Will Bandy had joined the Federal Militia when he was just a boy. He grew up in the Shenandoah Valley of Virginia, the son of a sharecropper family. The Federals, at that time, were recruiting young sharpshooters to join in the Indian campaigns, to push the local tribes further back into the wilderness. This they had done, and effectively. When they were mustered out of the militia, each man was encouraged to settle on free land in the states of Georgia and Alabama. The law was that they stake out a hundred and sixty acres, build a house and clear four acres to farm, within a two year time. Thousands took the government up on the free land offer, pushing the Indians off the choice river valleys and pastureland.

Will was one of those settlers. No man, white, red, or black, was going to take what he felt was rightfully his. Bandy and his fellow settlers were the persecutors of the once proud, intelligent

Cherokee tribe. This tribe was descended from the Iroquois. Vast numbers of them lived in Virginia, the Carolinas, Georgia and Tennessee. The Cherokee women were well-known for their comely beauty. They were tall, slender, full-bosomed and intelligent. They began to intermarry with Irish, Scotch and English traders and adventurers.

In the very early part of the eighteen hundreds, the Cherokee became a great nation and they began to build their own civilization. They were bolstered by the Hopewell Treaty of 1785, when the United States had recognized their tribe as a nation. By 1802, the Federal government reneged on their treaty promises, making it known to the state of Georgia that all Indians should be removed from the South, to be settled in other parts of the nation. Naturally, the proud, ambitious Cherokee refused to move. They stayed on their land, suffering at the hands of both the government soldiers and the land grabbers, who were encouraged by the greedy politicians.

In 1828 and 1829, Georgia defied the government treaty and seized the prosperous lands of the Indians. The Federal government decided in favor of the Cherokee. The laws were not enforced, however; Georgia encouraged the squatters to take over the Indians' lands.

Before the takeover began, the stately Cherokee were led by an American Indian halfbreed known as Sequoia. He was also known as George Guess. His mother was a Cherokee, his father, a trader who's name was said to be George Gist. Sequoia devised an alphabet in the Cherokee language, and was a proud leader of his people.

When the great Indian removal began in 1828, Sequoia went with his unhappy people to the new lands selected by the government in the territory of Oklahoma. The great move was forced when Andrew Jackson became President. A word campaign was begun to inflame the populace to demand that the Indians be banded together and moved. False treaties were formed with a few of the tribe who were influenced by money and greed. This made it appear that the whole Cherokee nation was ready and willing to move. Most of them were removed, want to or not. The long trek to Oklahoma began. Hundreds of them died on the long journey. Many stayed behind, to defy the white men who had lied them out of their beautiful farms and hunting lands. Soon they became fugitives, seeking out a bare existence by living in the deepest of forests and swamps. There, they became weakened and decimated by disease and starvation. Their lodges became hovels, made from skins stretched over bent trees. They still held their heads high, though many a farmer or trader who ventured too far in the woods was never heard from again. Those wretched few who remained behind would probably have joined their brothers and sisters, numbering over forty thousand, who were given land in the Oklahoma Territory. There again they formed a nation. As progress proved, there was oil under some of the land, and Cherokee descendents are much the richer for it.

Will Bandy was following a meandering flock of wild turkey, when all at once he smelled wood smoke. He flopped to his belly, crawling to a creek bank. He looked through the brush to a clearing. There he could see a small group of Indians slowly circling around a huge newly formed pile of stones. They were clad only in rags and animals' skins, with just enough flesh on them to cover their bones. A toothless woman with grey in her hair was keening an Indian death chant. She was followed in her circle by two young boys and a skinny young girl. The keening chant made the flesh crawl on Bandy's scalp, as they pranced and chanted. He had seen the death dance many times before in his experience with the tribes of the south. This time a wave of pity surged through him. The chant ended, the old woman placed more stones on the heap. Will could see no other Indians in the encampment; besides, those who were there didn't seem to have weapons. He got up slowly, walking carefully toward the wretched group. They formed a line, the two young men shoulder to shoulder, the women behind. They seemed resigned to accept whatever fate he was ready to mete out to them.

"How do, I be Will Bandy." The farmer placed his rifle against a tree, then showed them his hands with the palms outward. "Ye maybe Cherokee?" The older woman stepped forward to look Will right in the eye, with her gaze never wavering. "We Cherokee, yu maybe kill all us? My man down, he die, he sick two week, he cross big river yesterday. We die soon maybe . . . no powder, no bullet, no food. Yu maybe give old lady tobacco before she die? Yu maybe give little food these young Indians? They no hurt no man." Will started a battle with his conscience. He felt that he should take up his rifle and go home. A long look into those black eyes peering from the emaciated face of the starving woman made him shudder with the thought of dying of such a fate. He had left venison and turnips in a big iron pot on the hearth of his fireplace. He said breathlessly, "Ye come ter my cabin, I will feed the lot o' ye." They stood silently staring at him. He turned and picked up his rifle.

It was a good five miles to the cabin by the woods. He wasn't sure this band of half-starved wretches could make it. When he had crossed the creek, he turned to see if they were following. They had bundled a few belongings into rabbit skin pouches, then, in single file, were tracing his steps. He would look back occasionally to see if they were still making it. Each was on his, or her own feet, walking steadily. When he reached his yard, Will ducked through the front door, to the pot on the hearth. The fire had gone out, the meat and turnips in the pot were a little on the cold side. He had only one crock cup, and a crock plate. These he filled with the stew, then handed them out the door to the woman and skinny girl. He ladled out chunks of the meat with a wooden spoon he had carved from a hickory limb. He handed each boy a chunk of the venison. They all began to eat hungrily. They ate very little however; Will imagined their stomachs were shrunken from long days and nights, with little to fill them. He left the pot of food, turned to go into the house. It was along toward evening then, so Will was sure they would have eaten their fill, taken what was left and vanished into the darkness of the forest. He kept his rifle at the ready, just in case they decided they wanted to take more than the pot of food.

The next morning, just at the break of day, Will rolled over, his eyes open wide. The recollection of the episode of the day before caused him to have a little uneasy feeling. He reached for his rifle, made his way to the door. As the door swung into the room, he took a careful look both ways to be sure they were not ready to pounce on him from the darkness. No sign of them anywhere! He started around the corner and was startled to see them huddled there against the chimney as protection against the crisp fall air. "God, what a pitiful pile of human bones." They were shivering as they slept in the crisp morning breeze. He walked to the pot and saw that it was about empty. They must have gone back to the food several times during the night. He muttered under his breath, "They might just as well be dead. What in God's world will ever happen to 'em? They ain't got no place to go, the winter will kill 'em fer sure. I reckon the good Lord would want me to feed 'em like a stray cat, till they get enough strength ter scratch fer therselfs." The smallest of the boys opened his eyes. Startled, he sprang to his feet, cowering against the rocks of the chimney. "Ain't no fightin' left in 'em, I reckon." Will again showed the palms of his hands in a friendly gesture. The boy relaxed a bit as he nudged the other with his bare toe. He too, came alive, his eyes opened wide in fright. Again Will made the friendly sign to show he was unarmed. "I be Will Bandy. Who ye be?" He pointed to the older boy. "Me Jim Little Owl." The conversation had awakened the women who lay where they were, still in each other's embrace. "Him my son. Other boy, Jim Little Owl, son of my man's brother. This Little Dove, my last woman child. Little Brother, my last man child." The old woman looked with pride upon the three young Indians. "Me, Sun Flower," she pointed to her own breast. "We stay work for you, Will Bandy. We all work hard, make farm look lak big planter place." Bandy was surprised that the old woman knew so much English. She seemed to have knowledge of the farm, also. After all, these were people the whites had pried loose from their own farms.

Will wondered if the girl could talk. To this point, she had never uttered one word in any language. Will really noticed her for the first time. She was, because of her starvation, as he would describe her, "skinny as a willer stick." Her big black eyes were accented by long lashes. The high cheek bones complemented the lovely shape of her face. She was barefooted, with rabbit skins loosely sewn together, serving to cover her hunger punished body. He looked at her asking, "Ye talk, Little Dove?" "I talk WillBanee." She said his name as though it were one word, leaving out the D in Bandy.

Will grinned to himself as he thought of the gossip and criticism he would bring down upon his own head, by taking in four homeless Indians. Nevertheless, he had made his decision. He nodded his head in agreement to their silent entreaty. "Yes, I reckon I do need some help here on this farm. First thing to do is build a place fer ye to git outin the weather." They set about clearing a spot down near the creek for a two-room, crude cabin. There were already plenty of cut logs handy, so Will figured that with everyone helping, the shelter would be up in two or three days. He built a fire in his huge fireplace, putting the girl to watching a haunch of venison, which he had mounted on an iron spit, so that it could be turned occasionally to keep it from burning on one side.

Will felt a surge of real happiness as he watched everyone take to their assigned tasks as though they had been working at them for months. The dirt-floored structure went up quickly. Will even supervised the construction of a rock fireplace at the end of the largest room. Sun Flower began to gather great heaps of moss to use as caulking between the logs. She mixed the moss with clay, then began to force it into the openings between the logs with a flat stick. Their pace slowed well before noon, as the ravages of their recent starvation began to show on them. They still struggled to keep up with the tireless Will. When he saw them begin to stagger as they walked, he called a halt to the backbreaking labor, suggesting that they all sit in the shade of a tree, to be served the roast venison with big slabs of cornbread. This time there was no brake on their appetites; they all ate as though they would never have another chance.

"How in the good Lord's name am I gonna feed this bunch during the cold spell?" he asked, as he looked into the sky. At least he was not alone anymore, making it possible to talk to real folks instead of to himself. After they had eaten, Little Dove took the cooking utensils to the creek and scoured them with sand. They had not been so clean in years.

Will was not inclined to put them all back to work too soon, so they all took a snooze in the warm Georgia sun. All of them seemed to be able to work with a new lease on life. Will noted the progress with pride. By the end of the week, the new shelter on the Bandy place was almost complete. It still lacked a roof and floor, but Will knew that the floor could be added later. They raised the ridgepole for the roof, and added smaller ones for the rafters. The two boys, taking turns on the saw, with Will at the other end, split logs lengthwise, to build a crude board roof. It wasn't beautiful, but at last they had a home where they could stay out of the rain and chill of the winter nights.

As the health of the two boys mended, they became so anxious to help that Will had to hold them back to keep from wearing out his own strength. They built a hog pen that looked like a stockade. Slender pine logs were set in a trench side by side, then sharpened on the top. At one side of the pen, they built a shelter for the hogs that were not yet in residence. One leg of the fence crossed a little branch of a creek, so that they would not have to carry water to feed the swine.

As winter wore on the new family became very talkative. The white man learned many ways of the Cherokee; they learned the likes and dislikes of their new benefactor. Sun Flower told Will that she had had seven sons. They were all gone except Little Brother. She did not know where some of them were. Some of them were dead. Little Dove was the only woman child she had. One other had died at birth. Little Dove had come to her sixteen summers ago. "She good girl, Will Bandy. She do just as Sun Flower tell her do. I teach her many things Indian woman must know. She know medicine in forest. She know how find food when there is very little. She sew rabbit skins, make moccasins for winter. I tell her 'bout men too, Will Bandy. She be good woman some day." Will was embarrassed by the subtle suggestion. He had never had experience with women in all his life, except his mother.

He had known for some time now that when he looked at Little Dove, it was with a new and strange feeling. He could not help but notice how her body had rounded out. On a fast trip to the county seat, Will had bought plain cotton cloth which the women had sewn into straight, long dresses. They tied them in the middle with another long strip of the same cloth. On occasion, Will would look at Little Dove's ankles, which were now the target of his glance. Sometimes when she was working, she would unceremoniously hoist her dress to knee height, to keep it from getting in her way. Her legs were long, slender and shapely. She had firm, high round breasts that seemed to Will, were straining to be released from the confines of the cotton gown. It disturbed him greatly.

As spring came near, Will traded some of the bountiful seed harvest from last year for two bred sow hogs, to populate the pen they had so exactingly built last fall. Before planting time, they were all busily engaged in clearing more land. The brush was cleared, the stumps dug around and pried out. They were then piled to burn.

Will Bandy didn't know that the entire county was whispering about the "passel o' thievin' Injuns" living on the Bandy place. It was the most exciting thing the dirt farmers and their families could discuss. Each narrator would invent just a little more, to add spice to the telling, until people were warning their children to stand clear of the Bandy place, lest they get scalped by the murdering redskins.

Will had been saving for years to buy a pair of mules and a plow. Now was the time. He and the two boys packed as much trading seed as they could carry on their backs in preparation for a trip to the county seat. The two boys were excited about the trip; they nervously chided each other about the things they would buy with the barter goods they had. Besides the back pack, they had made a litter of two poles to carry between them. Each was to take his turn, alternating with the other two. The boys were clad in roughly fashioned buckskins: shirts, pants and moccasins. They wore a band of leather around their heads to keep their long black hair out of their faces. Bandy also had on a pair of moccasins; his were made by Little Dove, who insisted that he wear them to town.

Besides the precious seeds of squash, pumpkin, melons, peas and beans, they had a large bundle of choice animal skins which they had trapped during the long winter.

It was with a great deal of anticipation that they lifted their burdens and headed up the trail that led to the main road. It was very slow traveling on the muddy road, but they trudged along as fast as they could. Weighted down as they were, they were fortunate to reach the edge of town just as the sun began to set. Wood smoke, backyard stables, and various suppers being prepared assailed their nostrils as they trudged down the main street. Playing children, barking dogs, tinkling cow bells and the occasional braying of a mule furnished a strange cacophony of sound that the boys were not at all used to. People began to stare at them, children would run next door to alert their friends to the site of the farmer and Indian boys slipping and sliding in the mud of the street. They made their way through town, camping in a grove of oak trees.

As morning came, they built a little fire to prepare the food that Sun Flower and Little Dove had packed in a skin pouch. They boiled coffee, drank their fill. All three of them were at peace with the world. The farmer, because he had a family to talk to, and the Cherokee boys who had a friend they could trust. Will figured that with the little money he had, coupled with the price for the seed and prime pelts, they would have enough to buy two mules and a wagon.

As they made their way back up the street toward the several general stores, curious people would stare at them, then murmur to others doing the same. Bandy didn't really give a damn. They were his people, he knew them for their worth. They made their way to the wide wooden porch of a big general store which Will knew was operated by Zeb Turney. They placed their burdens down against the wall of the store and started inside. The spit and whittle crowd was already gathered at the store. All heads turned in their direction as they entered the store. Zeb spit a long stream of snuff juice at a cuspidor near the end of the counter. Some hit, some missed. "God damn, Bandy, why you bringin' them damn muddy footed, louse carryin' Injuns inter my store lak this?" Will felt the anger rising as he approached the store keeper. "These here two boys air friends o' mine, Turney. They live at my place, they help me on my farm." "We heered 'bout yu and yer damn Injuns, Bandy. Yu been workin' the ass of the bucks and screwin' the ass of the women." Will could contain himself no longer; he made a lunge for the slovenly store keeper. Every man in the store jumped to his feet, expecting a fight about to start. Zeb dodged, scurrying behind the counter where he was known to keep a sawed off shotgun. Will wanted to go over the counter after him, but felt a hand on his shoulder and heard a calm voice. "Calm down, Bandy." It was a tall stoop-shouldered, grey-haired man, known to Will as Bill Hawkins. Hawkins increased the pressure on Will's shoulder, and he again heard, "Calm down, Boy." Will knew Hawkins to be one of the most respected farmers in the county, so he listened. Hawkins' voice rose a little, "Now Zeb, yo shore owe Bandy a pology. He has been sorely tried by yo and shoulda tore yore haid off." In Zeb's excitement, he had allowed the snuff to dribble down over his chin. He looked totally ridiculous as he mumbled, "Dint mean no harm, wuz jes joshin." The store keeper knew he was in the wrong, he could see business drifting away from his store, after the gossip got around. Zeb wiped his chin with his hand, then extended it to Will in a pseudo-friendly gesture. Will had come to town to trade, so he thought he better get on with it. He wasn't a violent man, anyway. "I got some prime pelts and some first class seed I took from my crop last year." Zeb saw a profit coming his way, so began to be very conciliatory. "Truly, Bandy, if'n ye'll jes ax them Injun boys ter stand over next the door out'n the way, we kin git on with the tradin." The others in the store had wandered back to their various seats, still eyeing the two young Cherokees.

Hawkins stepped around in front of Will to say, "Don't mean no personal offense to you, boy, but there still is a right smart amount of hard feelin' agin them Injuns. Reckon it will cause all of us a heap less troublin' if'n yu'd have 'em stand easy." Of course, the boys had understood every word said by the white men. They had been ready to do battle when they thought Will was in danger. Now they understood that they were greatly outnumbered, so they backed over to the door and stood shoulder to shoulder, as they had when Will had first seen them. He knew they would give their lives for him if the situation demanded it.

Will just looked at them and shrugged his shoulders. Will made out very well with the bartering, so they started out in search of mules and a wagon. Their inquiries directed them to a farm not far down the road, where a shrewd old man engaged them in the business of buying mules. When the bargain was struck, they went to another part of the settlement to buy the wagon and harness for their newly acquired livestock. While Will bargained, the boys stayed to themselves, talking in low tones, trying hard not to offend anyone.

When all was done, Will and Little Owl climbed to the seat of the new wagon, Little Brother hung his feet out the tailgate. It was getting along toward evening so they were anxious to head for home. "Will Bandy, me an' Little Brother need knives." Little Owl was serious-faced as he looked at Will. "We need knives to help you work, to cut bows and arrows to help you hunt." Will thought of the incident that morning and he was gripped by apprehension. "Yu ain't got a mind to carve on anyone, have yu?" Will's alarm showed in his voice. "We make word you, we no hurt no man here. Me and little Brother need knives.'' Will could see that the boys had made up their minds to have knives, however they got them. He could picture them taking someone down in the woods and relieving them of their knives. ''So be it! I got yer word.'' Will got off the wagon and went into the hardware store, where he bought two well-balanced steel knives. He handed one to each. There was no word of thanks, they just assumed that that was the way it should be. They pushed the mules hard on the way home.

Will could not understand why he could not keep his mind from always drifting back to the hauntingly beautiful black eyes of Little Dove. He had traded for a two-foot long piece of red ribbon, stuffing it into the pocket of his buckskin jacket before the boys could see.

They arrived back at the farm well past midnight where they were greeted by the two waiting women. Will thought of giving Little Dove the ribbon right away, but was too shy to present it before the old woman and the boys. One thing he had remembered, was several plugs of molasses flavored chewing tobacco, which he gave to Sun Flower. She had no teeth to chew it with, but to her it was ambrosia.

The boys turned the mules into the new corral, then went to their beds. Every time Will would glance in the direction of Little Dove, it would seem that she was looking back at him. Probably only his imagination, or was it?

Morning dawned clear and beautiful. The family began working at their various chores, the world seemed good. Will had always remembered his religious upbringing, so would never work on Sunday. This being that holy day, they each chose their own leisure. The boys immediately began looking for just the right hickory limbs to carve out bows shaped just to their liking. Their new knives were a constant object of admiration. Will took his shotgun, heading for the lower pasture where he had seen several large coveys of quail. Roast quail for dinner would be an exceptional treat. As he walked along a rail fence row, he heard, ''WillBanee, you wait for me.'' As he turned, he saw Little Dove running after him. Her long straight black hair was loose and flying in the wind. Will's heart beat faster at the sight of her. ''I ain't seen nothin' as beautiful as thet in all my borned days,'' he breathed.

"Maybe God meant for me to have her." She ran smoothly up the path with her cotton dress clinging to her lithe young body.

Will laid his shotgun on the ground, he encircled her with his arms as she reached him. She returned the embrace for just a moment as she looked up into his face. She was panting from the long run. She laughed as she wriggled free from his grasp. "I go with you, WillBanee. I better hunter, I show you birds." Will wanted to prolong the embrace, for he felt all of her beautiful body against him as he held her. Will gently grasped her in his arms again. "I am a better hunter! See, I have already caught a little dove!" "Little Dove maybe no stay caught, WillBanee. Maybe fly away over yonder and not come back." Without thinking, the words came quickly to Will. "I would follow you forever, if you left me Little Dove. I want you with me always." Little Dove bowed her head, pushing against his strong chest with both hands. "You loose me now, WillBanee . . . I want make talk." Will released her as he reached in his pocket for the strand of bright red ribbon. "I brought you something." His hand caressed the back of her neck as he passed the scarlet ribbon beneath her raven black hair. His big work-worn hands shook as he tied it into a bow. He stepped back to survey his artistry. Her face tilted up towards his as her lips parted to whisper, "Oh, WillBanee, oh, WillBanee." Her mood seemed to change quickly as she said, "You walk now, we talk." Will took her hand, starting up the path. "No! Woman walk behind man."

Despite his admonishing to the contrary, she fell in step behind him, they continued along the path. As the grass began to get higher on each side of the track, Will kept a sharp eye out for snakes. This was the habitat of the deadly pit vipers, the copperhead, cotton-mouthed moccasin, and the dreaded diamond back rattler. Will wore high-topped boots or moccasins as a protection against them, but he wanted to be doubly sure, so his eyes never left the ground. He was taking long ground-covering steps as he was accustomed to. "WillBanee, you walk fast. You slow, and I talk." Will laughed. He felt that this was an exceptionally beautiful day.

They descended a small hill to the grassy creek bank. "WillBanee, you listen, I talk." She was even with him now, and he turned to face her. "I talk Sun Flower while you go to county seat. She say I now have sixteen winters, it is time I have a man. She tell me all I need to know, WillBanee." Will's heart started to beat faster as he realized what she was about to say. She stood closer to him, as she looked up into his face. Her eyes seemed more beautiful than ever to Will. The serious expression made him smile. "Do no laugh at me, for I want you be my love man. I be good woman, so not have other woman, WillBanee, I not be good to her." This simple declaration of love from someone as pure in heart as this little Indian girl caused Will's breath to catch in his throat. "There ain't gonna be no other woman in my life until I die, Little Dove." He drew her close to him, then his mouth covered her full parted lips. They never knew such happiness existed in the whole wide world. They stayed on the grassy bank of the brook, in the shade of tall pine trees, and planned their lives together, until the sun had descended on the western horizon. To them, everything was beautiful, the wild flowers, the Georgia sunset, the farm they had worked so hard to improve.

As they made their way back to the cabin, Will watched a mockingbird glide to a tree, climb his way to the topmost branch and begin his trilling springtime song. Will grinned, grasped Little Dove's hand. "That's me up thar, on the top branch o' the tree." The rest of the walk to the cabin was in silence, each wrapped in the ecstasy of newly found love.

When they reached the porch, Will rounded up the rest of the family to tell them the good news about their decision to spend the rest of their lives together. The old woman nodded her head and said, "It be good, Will Bandy. You good man, she be good woman for you." She stood before them grabbing their right hands. She placed the girl's small hand in the work-worn palm of the farmer. "She you woman now, Will Bandy. I her mother, I give her to you." The old woman bowed her head over their hands, softly murmured words in Cherokee, which Will did not understand. She looked up, locked her eyes with those of the man. "She my only woman child, I give her you. You take her your house, Will Bandy." He did.

The next day, Will began to be troubled about their marriage. When he had been just a boy at home, he had heard his mother talk about people who lived in sin, and that their souls were to be damned to hell's fire. He asked Little Dove if she would be married in the manner of the white people. "I you woman now, WillBanee. You no ask me what I want, you tell me. You want me see this white man wedding, we go."

They set off for the home of the preacher, the adjoining farm down the creek. As they approached the house, Little Dove fell in behind Will as she was wont to do. Three coon hounds came yapping at them, as the preacher opened his front door. "God bless yu, Will Bandy. Lord knows I ain't see you here to visit, and ain't seen yer face in the church congregation either." Will was so embarrassed he started to stutter. "Wull ya see, Preacher Rue, I been so busy with my place that I ain't had the time to do much visitin'." "Yu ain't had much time for the Lord, Bandy, yet I see he done blessed yu with a nice farm. Time fer yu to bring some o' yer goods into the Lord's storehouse." Will stifled a chuckle as the old joke about, "You shoulda seen that place when the Lord had it all to himself," went through his mind. "See yu bring one o' them Cherokee with yu Bandy." The preacher nodded toward the girl. "Scuse me, Bandy, I hate to be without my bible in the face o' the heathen. I'll be right back." The preacher turned to go into the shabby cabin. Will bristled at his words about Little Dove being a heathen. "What a heathen, WillBanee?" Little Dove's innocent face turned to him in wonderment. "It means ye ain't never been baptized, I reckon," stammered Will. "What baptized?" Will could see himself sinking deeper and deeper into a morass of explanation which he was not sure he could explain anyway.

They gazed around the unkempt farm as they waited for the preacher to return. Will was determined he would be married the right way, even if he did have to endure the insults of the ignorant, itinerant preacher. When Preacher Rue emerged again, he was followed by an untidy woman who attempted to brush her hair back as she came. "Let me interduce yu ta my wife, Bandy. Clare, this is Will Bandy from the farm up the crick. He brung one o' his heathen with him." Will could hold his anger no longer. "Now see here, Preacher, she ain't no heathen. She is Little Dove, and I brung her here to have you say the words with us to make us man and wife." Rue looked at Little Dove and asked, "You been livin' in sin with this man?" Her puzzled look at him told him that she still did not understand a thing that the preacher was driving at. "Cain't she talk, Bandy?" "She talks, she talks good. We want you to marry us now!'' Rue ignored his impatience. Again he asked the girl, ''Yu give yer soul to the Lord yet, woman?'' Little Dove smoothed the dust of the yard with the toe of her moccasin, then replied, ''Me give everything WillBanee.'' The woman gasped in mock horror at the Indian girl's reply. ''I reckon yu did, Injun girl, I reckon yu did.'' The preacher smirked as he looked the young Little Dove up and down. By now Bandy had lost all patience with the so-called clergy. ''I brung my momma's bible fer us tu put the day down in, and I brung two dollars fer yu ta tie the knot Preacher. Ef all yer gonna do is chide us fer being whut we are, then I reckon we will go hitch up the wagon and head for the county seat.'' The thought of the two dollars heading for the county seat changed the preacher's outlook considerably. ''Now hole on here, Bandy, I jes wanna be sure this chile know what she is doin. Ef she says she will give her soul to God, then I will read the words, and yu'll be married all proper like.'' Little Dove promised to do anything WillBanee asked her to. Will Bandy felt that the childish innocence of Little Dove was known to the Lord already.

Preacher Rue had them kneel in the dust of the yard as he intoned the words of the wedding ceremony over them. At the part about ''Until Death Do Us Part,'' Little Dove said, ''WillBanee know that part already!'' Will squeezed her hand and whispered, ''Yes, my Little Dove, I know.'' When the ceremony was over, Will paid the two dollars, thinking to himself, ''They didn't even ask us into their house.''

As they left the cluttered yard, Will put his arm around the slender waist of his beautiful young wife. ''Jes who be the heathen,'' he mused, ''Jes who?'' They felt they were back in their own heaven as they climbed over the rail fence of their own farm.

There began long hot days of bone-wracking work as they all toiled at the business of making the soil yield a living for all of them. The fruits of their labor were soon evident as the corn and other crops began to flourish. They began to harvest, hauling the surplus to town to trade and sell. When it was all done, one October day, the two boys appeared at the cabin door. Will could see that they had something very serious on their minds.

They were outfitted with new clothes, new moccasins and they had large bundles strapped to their backs. The older boy spoke as they looked at Will. ''We go now, Will Bandy!'' ''Yu don't have to go nowhars! This is yer home as long as yo want it to be.'' Little Owl spoke again. ''Will Bandy, we stay, one day we kill a white man. White man he have something . . . other white man come take, the one who take get kill. People say that alright. He can not take other white man thing. White man come take Indian things, Indian kill, then other white man come hang Indian. They say this dirty thief Indian did not own anything, anyway. They hang Indian up by neck, nobody say this wrong. My father, name Walk In The Sun, tell us of other tribe in far west, across wide water of Mississippi. They roam all over big land of Texas. They ride horses like the wind, they no listen to no white man words, they called Comanche. Me, Little Brother, we listen in the night many time. We hear them call us. We go.'' With this final word and no further farewell, they turned, walking briskly into the woods. This part of the family never saw or heard from them again. The old woman went into the woods; presently they could hear her keening, eerie chant as she grieved the loss of her last man children.

With the coming of a rainy crisp October, Little Dove insisted that Will go to the county seat to buy a cow that would be giving milk by early the next spring. Little Dove told Will, ''Maybe I give you big man to help you in the field.'' Again, Will Bandy thought the whole world was made for him alone. His own child was to be here by spring.

Fall turned to winter, it was one of western Georgia's worst. Old Sun Flower stayed in her own cabin, sallying forth only to help with the ever-present chores. Now there were hogs to feed, chickens to gather eggs from, the cow to tend to, and feeding all combined. Their cabin at night was their haven from the stormy weather outside, protection from the various cares of the day.

The bigger Little Dove grew, the greater the love for her became in the heart of Will Bandy. She was never idle for one moment. Night was the time for mending. Will fixing harness, or some other farm item. She carded wool, mended their clothes, prepared for the coming addition to their family, as well as the regular household chores, such as cooking and cleaning. The days seemed to fly by for the big, plain farmer and the beautiful little Indian girl. They got up, dancing around the room in glee, as they felt the first movement of the unborn child. They were in bed early every night, enjoying the snug warmness of each other. Up with the light of dawn the next day to begin improving their status in the world.

They didn't visit the neighbors, for they felt that their love was great enough to sustain them against any loneliness or isolation. Along toward spring on a rare sunny day, they harnessed the mules, hooked them to the wagon and went into the county seat for Little Dove to visit the doctor. Sun Flower sulked for days afterward, since she felt that this was an insult to her abilities as a healer and help in all cases of emergency.

All was well with Little Dove, according to the country doctor. They cheered Sun Flower with a gift of chewing tobacco. She particularly liked the kind that was pressed with molasses.

One day, when her time was really quite near, Little Dove spoke to Will in a very quiet and calm voice. "WillBanee, I think now you ride one of the mules to town, tell the doctor to come back with you in his buggy." Will Bandy rushed from the house to the corral. There, in his haste, he frightened the poor mule 'til he could hardly catch it for the bridle. Will was finally astride, mounted bareback, he strapped the mule into a gallop as he headed for the main road. Little Dove laughed out loud at the sight. She knew it was a long ride, so she had Sun Flower make all the preparations just in case Will did not return in time.

As night drew on, Little Dove began to feel anxious about Will's absence. Sun Flower knew all the symptoms connected with what was about to happen. All was ready as could be.

When Will returned with the doctor in the buggy, the mule hooked behind, it was well after midnight. Upon entering the cabin, they could see the small face of Little Dove against the white sheet. The newborn child had been placed at her full breast, completely contented. "Yu late, WillBanee!" Little Dove's voice came weakly from the bed. "I brought yu woman child, she fine, she take care of little brother when he come next." Her head rolled weakly on the pillow as the doctor looked beneath the cover. The overworked, tired doctor said, "Go outside now, Bandy. I got work to do." "She is fer shore gonna be alright, ain't she, Doc?" "Go outside, Bandy, let me do fer her." Will retreated from the cabin, pacing back and forth in front of the happy home they knew. The minutes were hours as Will beat a path in the dust of the yard. Sun Flower came out of the door, headed for her own cabin. She retreated as fast as her tired old legs could carry her. When the door opened again, "Bandy, come in now." Will, in his anxiety, pushed the doctor out of the way, going quickly to the bedside. "She wants ta talk to yu, Bandy. I'm sorry, I jes could not stop the bleeding." He was talking as he passed through the doorway. "Jes could not stop the blood."

Will rushed to Little Dove, fell on his knees beside the bed. "Yu gonna be alright, Little Dove," he said reassuringly. "I done said a prayer, an' yu gonna be alright." He took her small, weak hand, kissed the palm, then smoothed a strand of her shiny black hair from across her cheek. "I talk now, WillBanee." Will had to lean closer to hear her words. "I say to you, I love you forever, WillBanee. This is forever. I give you woman child, you love her as you love me." Her voice grew weaker. Will agonizingly whispered, "Little Dove!" She closed her eyes saying, "You listen now. You name her with white people name. When she grow to fine young woman, your people not scorn her because she Indian." Her voice faltered, Will placed his cheek against hers. "She Cherokee, she be good girl for you." Will could barely hear her failing words. "WillBanee, my love man, I cross wide river now." She said no more.

The shock took Will Bandy's body and soul. He kissed her still mouth, saying as he rose, "Yu rest now, my Little Dove, I am gonna be back in a little while." He looked up at the sky and noticed that heavy clouds had drifted in. He walked numbly to the edge of the woods, fell to his knees, doubled his body over until his face was in the grass. "Oh, dear Jesus, why did yu have to take my Little Dove? She was love dear Jesus, jes as yu learned us love." He could say no more as great sobs wracked his tortured body. He heard no answer to his question, just the soft patter of the rain as it began to fall. Even the heavens seemed to be weeping for the beautiful, beloved Little Dove that had fallen on this Georgia spring night.

From back in the woods came the haunting, ghostly death chant of the Cherokee as the old woman wailed out the agony of the loss of her last child, her woman child. Will Bandy buried the Little Dove at the foot of a tall pine tree near the brook. Soon there was a well-worn path to the spot where he talked to her after his chores were done on the long Georgia evenings.

* * *

The mules stopped at the gate. The trip from town had been long. Bandy's wandering mind had covered the whole span of his life with the Cherokee family. The precious thing, besides the memories, that was left to him, was his constant companion, Eliza Clementine Bandy. She hardly let him out of her sight. She spent long hours with the old woman. She learned things that were dear to the heart of the old Cherokee. What herbs were best for certain ailments, what plants were good to eat, the juice of what berries made the best dye. Bandy let Clemmy know that she was Cherokee alright. He made her be very proud of it. She was a happy child, living a very happy life in the shadow of the big farmer, her Pa.

CHAPTER 4
THE SMITHY

A tall handsome eighteen-year-old man leaned over his anvil, working to put the finishing touches on a set of window grilles he had fashioned on a special order. John Bolt sang loudly as he worked. The huge black man at the anvil next to him was keeping time with the rhythm of the song as he shaped a horse shoe which he had heated to cherry red. John didn't realize how the years had flown by since he came to the smithy under the trees at Savannah. He was just twelve then, carrying the weight of the whole world on his small shoulders. Now, he and the black man were both naked to the waist. They each wore a heavy leather apron. The shoes they wore were heavy and ugly, but afforded protection from falling sparks or pieces of hot metal which occasionally fell to the dirt floor of the shop.

The heavy work of a blacksmith had developed the muscles of the young man until they rippled as he moved. His belly was flat and hard. Every movement he made seemed to be as effortless as breathing, he was quick and decisive in everything he did.

The work orders were piled high, as more were brought in every day. Larkin had long since quit the shop, leaving the work to his apprentice and the two black slaves, Tobe and Rufus. They were not slaves in the eyes of Larkin, however; they were all a team now, each man earning his own keep and seeming to enjoy every minute of it. The apprentice had outdone the master as far as the artistry of their trade was concerned.

John drew the plans and executed the work as skillfully as the oldest journeyman craftsman. Rufus, now in his early twenties, was his lackadaisical self, content to be told what to do, and when to do it. He never shirked a duty when it was assigned. Tobe, the giant blacksmith was beginning to show some grey in what little hair he had. He was still a mound of muscle, turning out the work of three men.

Larkin was now banking a generous share of the shop's earnings to the credit of his three valuable helpers. When John had reached seventeen, he was no longer considered an apprentice. He earned a fair wage, free to spend or save his money as he saw fit. He spent some, but saved most against the day when he would head to the west, looking for a farm to buy. Owning a farm and his own livestock had been his dream since he was a small boy following the horse-trader up and down the coast.

Tobe would still sit by the oceanside when the chance presented itself. He would gaze for hours out across the water, dreaming of the day when he would be set free to go in search of the life he knew when he was a very young man in his village in far off Africa. At times the memory of the slave drivers would cross his mind. He would begin to sweat and tremble, sometimes actually feeling the pain he had endured at the hands of the cruel slave traders.

Rufus had fallen in love with a young slave girl who worked as a house servant on aristocrat row. Any time that he knew she would be in the markets doing the shopping for the house, Rufus would be there somewhere, hoping that he would get to say a few words to her, or brush by her as she walked with a full shopping basket. She began to notice him, smiling occasionally as she caught his eye.

One day, when her mistress was preoccupied in a conversation with a group of women of her neighborhood, Rufus sidled over to the girl and said in a very low voice, "Gal, I got tu talk ta ya. I jes got tu!" She looked at him with a scowl. "T'ain't no way proper fer ya ta speak ta me. Besides, my name ain't gal, it be Sally. How come yo have de time ta loaf aroun dis her market? Ain't yo a slave jes lak I is?" Rufus was so overcome by the music in her voice, that he couldn't answer her. He began backing away saying, "Yes, maam, yes, maam." He backed through the door and fell off the low boardwalk into the dusty street. He could hear her low laughter as he got up and ran down the street toward the shop. That night poor Rufus didn't sleep. Every once in a while he would mutter, "She dun speak ta me, she dun speak ta me!" From that day on, they would secretly gaze at each other through the crowds, or brush past as closely as they could; when opportunity presented itself, he would softly say, "How do, Sally." One day when their nearness allowed, she asked coyly, "What yo name, bashful boy?" Rufus thought his heart would stop as he blurted out, "Rufus." Some people turned to stare. Sally was a slave, she knew her limitations, she quickly retreated so she would not draw attention. She turned, looked back at Rufus. The smile she gave him was unmistakable, she felt just as he did.

When John finished the order he had been fashioning, he and Tobe loaded the wagon for delivery. It was quite a long way to the cottage down the river where the order was to be installed. Rufus took his seat on the wagon, clucking to the mules who began, at their own pace, to draw the heavy wagon loaded with the wrought iron grill work. This particular order was to go to the home of Mrs. Jeanine Le Clere, wife of Captain Marcel Le Clere, Master of the Yankee Trader, Gerogia Star. This was the flagship of the Georgia Star line out of Savannah, indeed one of the finest ships afloat in that booming era in the forming of the United States of America. Her owners kept her at sea most of the time, her captain jealously guarding his command; he would not relinquish the exalted position as Master of the finest to any other captain. Therefore, he was at sea most of the time with the ship. The good captain, in his early forties, was already a man of means from his faithful service to Georgia Star. His home in Savannah was in modest taste, in a good neighborhood. Its furnishings were above average in expensive decor. One of the most beautiful of furnishings was his wife, Jeanine. She was just twenty-one. Married to the captain for three years now, but alone most of the time.

Jeanine possessed a classic French beauty. When Captain Le Clere had decided that he would finally marry, he made a trip to New Orleans where he had friends in the shipping industry who introduced him to a host of beautiful and available young ladies from the better French families. He had spent considerably more time there than he had anticipated, for he found that wife hunting was not just the easy task he had supposed it to be. He realized that he had become very exacting in his quest. The young lady of his choice would have to have just the correct face, figure and character that he had outlined for himself. Yes, wife-hunting was a very serious business. When he was at last introduced to Jeanine at a dinner-dance given in his honor, he knew at once that she was the one he had come to New Orleans to find. Her skin had the delicate velvety smoothness of a precious pearl; dark flashing eyes behind long, curving lashes revealed a challenge to Le Clere that he had not experienced in his contact with other young girls in the city. Her figure was perfect in every respect. The cut of her gown revealed a beautiful bosom with little left to the imagination. She had a small waist that blended perfectly into rounded hips. Her beauty was that which he sought.

When his host interrupted the small talk of a group of young people to introduce him, she turned and smiled. At that moment, Captain Le Clere made a pledge to himself that she would return to Savannah with him. Le Clere was so taken by her dazzling beauty that he stammered in reply when she spoke to him. Her voice was soft and quiet when she acknowledged his introduction. She spoke to him in English, with just a trace of French accent. "At last I have met you, Captain Le Clere. You are the talk of New Orleans, you know." Marcel had suspected this but here was the first time anyone had confronted him with the fact. He reddened beneath his tan. "I . . . I hope that what is being said is favorable to me." She was not in the least ill at ease. "Most assuredly, Captain, most assuredly." The music had begun, so Marcel awkwardly asked, "Could I . . . would you . . . may we dance?" She laughed lightly. "But of course, Captain, it would be my pleasure." He held her lightly in his arms, her perfume invaded his senses. He tried valiantly to make small talk about the city, and what her interests were. She answered politely to every question, volunteering considerable information about herself and her friends.

As the evening wore on, Marcel would try to engage other people in conversation, but found himself repeatedly seeking her out. Before they said good night, Marcel asked her if he might call at her home the next day. "How charming of you to ask, Captain. Would about six tomorrow evening be alright?" Any hour of the day or night would have been perfect for Marcel Le Clere. When she started to leave with her companions, she turned to him, smiled captivatingly. "My Capitan, please do not number me among your candidates for your purpose in New Orleans." With this she turned quickly and left the room. Marcel was stunned. All the other young women he had met had tried to impress him with their desirability. This one was trying to discourage him. He resolved that he would not be discouraged, that he would have Jeanine Renault to be Madam Marcel Le Clere. It had not been an easy conquest, but finally she consented and returned to Savannah with him. The honeymoon was a romantic one for both of them. His ship was being refitted, repainted, and made ready for the next voyage. This trip was to be to the Orient, with trading stops in between. Star of Savannah Line knew of the shrewd bargaining ability of their Captain Le Clere. They gave him a percentage of the net results of every voyage; this, of course, was not generosity on their part, they knew that it increased the flow of money into the company coffers. Although this was to be a long voyage, Le Clere was looking forward to it. Making a lot of money was his first love, then came Jeanine.

Before leaving, Marcel had given her adequate money for the budget he had outlined for her. A long list of things for her to do was included. Iron grillwork for all windows of the house was on that long list of keep busy items. For this, she had sent one of her servants who lived in the quarters at the back of the house, to contact the famous blacksmith shop of Anthony Larkin.

The blacksmith had sent his artist, John Bolt, to visit her with designs and sketches of the work they were capable of turning out. When John had appeared at her front door, the servant had admitted him, then ushered him into the library where Jeanine waited. When she turned to greet him, her lovely eyes widened in surprise and disbelief. She stammered, "But I was expecting a much older man. Could you be the designer for the Larkin Ornamental Iron Works?" The beauty of her made John Bolt feel as though he were a clod of dirt that had been deposited on the floor of her library. John looked down at the floor and stammered, "I be the artist fer the smithy, ma'am." He had picked up much of the speech of Anthony Larkin. "Forgive me, wasn't it rude of me to assume that Mr. Larkin would send someone who was not capable of doing the designs which I have pictured in my mind. Besides, my husband had made some crude sketches before he left." John had never in his life been in the presence of such a beautiful creature as this. John's big blue eyes were still focused on the spot on the library floor.

"Mayhaps Tony Larkin shoulda come hisself, ma'am." "Nonsense, please sit down at the table, Mr. Bolt, I will fetch paper and ink." "Scuse me, ma'am, I brung my own. I got a paper I like special, so's I got it with me." John reached into a folder he was carrying, brought forth his drawing paraphernalia. "Ef ye'll jes show me yer husban's sketches, ma'am, I'll get right to work." John wasn't sure he could draw in her presence. He felt that his hands would shake. She handed him the crude sketches made by the Captain. John improved upon them, and began to incorporate ideas of his own. He could picture the expensive cottage done in just the window design he was about to create. She left the room allowing John to finish his design quickly. Before leaving, he carefully measured one of the smaller windows of the house. "Our way of doin' things, ma'am, is ter go back ta the shop and make one winder cover. Ef'n ye like what I done, then yu can buy the whole job." "That will be wonderful, Mr. Bolt. If it is as you have put it on paper, then I know that it will be most satisfactory." John was again ill at ease. He knuckled his forehead, a Larkin characteristic, and quickly strode up the street.

Jeanine smiled as she watched his lean strong body retreat up the winding path. Never, she thought, have I seen such a beautiful male body. She blushed at her own bold thought, she tried to dismiss John Bolt from her mind. The ecstasy of her perfume lingered with John as he made his way back to the shop.

Young Bolt was restless in his sleep that night, most anxious to get started the next day on the production of the one window grill he had designed for Madam Le Clere. The next morning, other work, which should have taken precedence over the Le Clere job, stood waiting while John's skilled hands wrought the intricate designs he had fashioned the day before. This window grill was finished in record time. John would have carried it to the Le Clere cottage right then, if Larkin had not interfered with a rush order which he told John had to be finished that day.

Again that night the vision of Jeanine Le Clere filled John's thoughts. Sensations filled his young mind and body which he was not used to, it troubled him deeply. Rufus had described the sensation of being in love to him, but he dismissed this from his mind. After all, wasn't Madame Le Clere a married woman? Yes, she is, but why does the haunting picture of her face and figure keep coming back?

The next day, about mid-morning, John set off for the Le Clere house, carryng the window grill with him. This design, thought John, would not only beautify the cottage, but serve as protection for the lovely lady who lives there. John's mind was filled with fantasy, born of stories he had heard, as he strode toward his destination. When he sounded the knocker, a grey-haired slave woman opened the door; upon recognizing him, she showed him into the comfortable library. "I go fetch Mistress Le Clere. She were jes not sure you be comin' this day. You jes set, and I go tell her you are settin'."

As she made her way out of the room, John looked at himself in a mirror hanging behind the library table. He had been very careful this day to be sure that he had on his very best clothes. Some of his hard-earned money had been spent on improving his appearance. Today, he was just a little too well-dressed to be a blacksmith apprentice. John waited, fidgeting for what he thought was a very long time. Then he heard footsteps, and the lovely voice of Jeanine Le Clere.

"That will be all now, Meena. I will call you when I need you." "Yas'um, I be in the kitchen." When Jeanine entered the library, John thought his heart would stop. Her softly curled black hair was still down, forming a halo around the ivory skin of her throat and face. Her full red lips were slightly parted, she had pinched color into her cheeks. What a sight! He could only stare. He dared not try to speak. "Good morning, Mr. Bolt. Would it be proper for me to call you John?" He answered too quickly, "Yes'um, I would be pleased if ya would." "I would like for you to call me Jeanine, but since I am the mistress of this house, I suppose it would be improper." John stammered, "Yes, Jeanine, I mean Mrs. Le Clere, Ma'am." She laughed softly and said, "Very well, make it Jeanine, as long as the servants are not around." John felt weak in the knees; although he had properly stood when she entered the room, he now felt that he just had to sit down before he fell. He sank heavily into the chair behind the desk. She smiled at his breach of etiquette, she sat lightly on the edge of a comfortable leather upholstered chair opposite the desk. The smooth line of her thigh was revealed through the expensive gown when she crossed her ankles and lightly brushed the wrinkles from the shining green material of her dress. ''What have you brought me, John?'' She nodded toward the grille work which had been carefully placed on the floor of the library. '' I shorly hope I brung what ya had in mind.'' He lightly lifted the artfully designed grille from the floor, and held it in front of him. This time his large blue eyes locked squarely with hers. His curly blonde hair had been carefully combed. The freckles across the bridge of his slightly crooked nose stood out against the fairness of his skin.

Jeanine could see the ripple of his arm muscles as he lightly held the heavy window screen. ''Oh! How perfectly handsome.'' She was not sure whether she meant the window screen or the young man holding it. ''John, my house will be the loveliest in Savannah when you get it all done. Don't change a thing. Just make them all as beautiful as this one, and all will be perfect.'' A wave of pride swept over John. ''I done it all myself, ma'am. I will even do all the work on the rest, if ya jest give me the chance.''

She rose from the chair, John again experienced the enchantment of her perfume. John could think of nothing else to say, so he got down to business. ''Larkin insists that we git a order on paper, ma'am.'' ''Call me Jeanine, just one time, John. If I don't hear my own name once in a while, I will lose my mind.'' John swallowed hard, blinked his blue eyes and stammered, ''Jeanine.'' She laughed nervously as she explained, ''not even the servants ever say Jeanine. Do you have the order with you?'' ''Larkin would be obliged if'n ya could write one, ma'am. Here are the numbers of the measurements of the winders, Jeanine,'' he said her name again, this time it seemed to come easier. She quickly wrote a note acknowledging that the sample was what she wanted for all the windows of the house. ''Larkin allus wants a deposit on the job, too, ma'am.'' ''Of course, John,'' she reached into a drawer of the table and produced a generous deposit on the job to be done. ''Just for business sake, John, will you sign a receipt for me?'' She wrote the amount and, ''Received of Madam Jeanine Le Clere,'' on a slip of paper, then handed it to John. His face paled, as he felt he was the most ignorant man in the world. He had never even learned to write his own name. He carefully drew an X, with one leg bearing slash marks across the line on the bottom and a square on the top. This to John was ''John Bolt.'' ''Johnny,'' she now seemed even more familiar, ''I did not mean to embarrass you. I did not know that you could not write. A fine artist like you should learn immediately. Please let me help you.'' She took a clean sheet of paper, then carefully inscribed John Bolt in big bold letters. ''With your talent, you should be able to copy this in no time. Here, try!'' John's humiliation was welling up in him like a spring, yet he felt that she was not making fun of him, merely trying to help. He looked carefully at the drawing, took the pen and began the start of the letter J. ''You practice it, John, I will go to the kitchen to see if I can find something to drink.'' She left the room with John watching every step until she was around the corner, out of sight. He began a series of copies of his name on the paper.

When she returned, he had a number of them neatly inscribed across the page. ''It is excellent, Johnny! Keep practicing until it becomes quite natural with you. No one will ever have to show you again.'' She went behind his chair to lean over to inspect his lesson. He felt one of her shapely pointed breasts brush his shoulder as she murmured, ''Magnifique.'' The sensation which went through his young, strong frame could not be described. He wanted to turn and fold her into his arms so that he might feel all of her. She went quickly to the door to indicate that their visit was at an end.

John's feet did not touch the ground as he made his way from the high bluff of the river bank back to the shop under the trees.

There became days of overtime work, while John fashioned the window grilles of the Le Clere house. He had his other work to do, so it kept him from concentrating on the one job he had in mind. No handy work could have been done to better perfection. Every hour was spent with the memory of the beautiful captain's wife. His imgination prompted him to still feel the caress of her firm young breast on his shoulder. Larkin had never lectured him about the ills of taking a married woman. To this bold seaman, all girls of age were fair game, as long as consent was given. Therefore, John's conscience did not bother him a great deal.

Meanwhile, in the Le Clere house there was a constant battle with waves of shame which gripped the beautiful young wife of the sea captain. Her strict Catholic upbringing was torturing her conscience about the way she had reacted to John Bolt. She would admit to herself that she had wanted to make passionate love to him. Then again, she would ask, how can this be? I am married to a fine man, who provides for me and loves me dearly. She had prayed for this feeling within her to go away, and not torment her so. During the day, she was able to cope with it, but at night when she was in the solitude of her own bed, she would ache for the touch of John Bolt again.

Two weeks of intermittent labor had gone into the load of wrought iron which John and Rufus were hauling to the Le Clere house. Rufus was to go along to help with the hard work of unloading and installing the window grilles. The mules ambled along pulling the heavy wagon. John's heart began to pound at the anticipation of once again seeing the first woman in his young life who had really impressed and excited him. Rufus kept up a constant dialogue as they rode toward the river bluff. To John it was just a gaggle of words with no meaning. Every once in a while Rufus would loudly inquire, "Yo heah me, John boy?" John would nod his head, then resume his thoughts.

When they reached the gate of the cottage, John sent Rufus around back to find the slave gardener who lived in the quarters with the woman house servant. It was still early in the morning. The servant came from the back, opened the gate for them to drive nearer the house. "Madam say yo could git rat ta wok soon's yo gits here." John's heart sank when he didn't hear the man say, "I go fech de madam." He had pictured her rushing from the house to greet him when he made his appearance. They went right to work on the installation of the window decorations.

John thought once that he had seen her lovely face framed in the shadows of one of the rooms. As the job neared completion, he began to despair of seeing her at all. He slowed his pace, which caused the carefree Rufus to do the same. The day was turning into evening when Rufus announced that they had installed the very last one. John summoned the slave who was working in the yard. "Will you please go ask the Madam if she would come out to inspect the work?" "She say dat if it come from Tony Larkin, it boun' ta be awrite." Again, John was disappointed that Jeanine had not put in an appearance. All of his beautiful dreams were washing away with the tide.

The sun had begun to set, Rufus seemed anxious to go. The mules were even pointing their ears in the direction of the shop. They, as well as Rufus, knew that the evening meal was at that destination. Jeanine spoke softly from close behind them. "The completed job is even lovelier than I had expected." She had come from the front of the house without being noticed. All at once, John was again on top of a mountain. "Rufus, you take the wagon an' go on back. I need ta stay an' talk to Madam about the pay for the iron work." Unsuspecting, Rufus volunteered to wait at the front gate so John would not have to walk. John leaned near him and growled, "Go now, Rufus." The startled black leaped to the seat of the wagon, clucked the mules into motion. "Come in, Mr. Bolt, so that I may pay you the entire balance. The completed project is most satisfactory."

As he entered the house, he was met by the elderly slave woman. She indicated that he was to follow her. "Madam say mayhap yo want ta wash up some fore dinner." This suggestion caught John completely off guard, as he was ushered into a spacious guest bedroom. A basin of warm water and towels were laid out on a marble topped table at the side of the room. John had never seen such splendor in all his life. He was used to the humble abode of Larkin and company; he and Tony in the house, with Tobe and Rufus in the room at the back of the stable.

John self-consciously removed his shirt and began to wash himself in the basin of warm water. There was even a bar of scented soap. This he had never seen before. When he had finished, he paced the floor like a lion in a cage, until he heard a knock on the door. When he opened it, the servant said, "Madam say dinner is suved now." He followed her to the spacious dining room where a table was simply set. Serving bowls of delicious smelling food adorned the center. The thought of dining with a lady sent a chill up the spine of the uneducated blacksmith.

Jeanine entered the room, dressed in a simple gown which buttoned up the front with shining white button beads. John could not move his eyes from her gorgeous face. She had applied just a hint of rouge to her full lips, and a small amount on her smooth white cheeks. She handed John the agreed upon amount of money for the iron work, then said haltingly, "John, I did hope that you would stay to dine with me. I, I must talk with you." "I ain't never et with a lady, Jeanine!" "Please, John, I will not let you be ill at ease." She turned to the attentive servant. "That will be all, Meena. I will serve, you may tidy up in the morning. Go now to join your man in your quarters.'' Meena bowed her head as she backed out of the room mumbling, ''Yasum, yasum.''

When they were alone, they stood for just a moment looking at each other. She seemed pale to John. Her eyes would not meet his. ''It's been a long time, John.'' They tried to make small talk as they ate the carefully prepared supper. When it was over, they retired to the settee in the living room. The servant had left the lamps lighted. ''I thought 'bout ya ever hour o' the day since I seen ya last.'' John blurted this out, as though it would be the last statement he would ever make. She still looked down at the floor as she nodded almost imperceptably. ''Johnny, I have to tell you that I have done the same about you. It's wrong, Johnny, I have gone to church and prayed about it many times. I can not think about you.'' Impulsively, John put his strong right arm around her shoulders, then lifted her beautiful face so that he could look into her eyes. ''How can this be so wrong? I have had a crazy feeling ever since I left here the last time. Jeanine, I ain't never kissed no woman, but by God I am to try at this very minute.'' He pressed his lips to hers, and she began to yield, as she arched her willing body against his. In fact, she soon became the aggressor. As John picked her up from the settee, he began to walk toward the guest bedroom. Her trembling fingers were unfastening the white bead buttons of the gown as he walked.

The paradise of their love-making was guided by the more experienced Jeanine. John thought that surely he had gone to the heaven he had heard talked about. Before daylight the next morning, John kissed her sleeping face, let himself out the front door, and headed for the smithy. There were wings on his heels, a song in his heart, as the events of the previous evening surged through his mind. Nowhere in this world could there be anyone as happy as he.

He had no more than entered his room, when Tobe summoned him to breakfast. He wondered if he should tell his only family about the beautiful Jeanine. Silence won out over his urge to tell the world about the new love he had found. He would sit at his drawing table staring into space, instead of putting designs on paper. Larkin observed him and smiled to himself. He reckoned the young lion had found some teen-aged girl he was sweet on. ''Pray the saints that this be the only sickness he will ever have.''

The smith looked upon John as his real son. They would sit and talk for hours about things that interested them both. Larkin wanted to buy a wagon manufacturing company, while John still had a dream of owning a beautiful farm with livestock of his own. He wanted to raise horses and cattle. They, of course, would be only the finest in the state of Georgia. Larkin encouraged him in his dreams, all the while urging him to save his money for the day when he would be his own man.

Larkin began to see more and more of one Molly Rafferty, whose father was a wagonmaker with a small business down toward the sea. John had seen Molly. She was a typical Irish girl with auburn hair and good full figure. She was several years younger than the smith, which seemed to make not the least bit of difference. Larkin was still a fine figure of a man, who had done well for himself in this new world.

John had stayed away from Jeanine as long as he could stand to. That evening he put on his finest clothes and headed for the cottage of Le Clere on the high bluff above the river. When John impatiently sounded the knocker on the door, the grey-haired servant came to answer. When she saw it was John she said, "Jes a minute, suh, Madam done gived me a letter for ya." She disappared into the house. When she emerged, she handed John a scented envelope with his name on the front. "She dun say, she cain't talk ter ya. She say it hut huh too much. She cry a lot suh, but she cain't talk atall. Please go now suh, git somebody what kin read ta tell ya what it say." John began to protest but then turned quickly and left the yard. In contrast to the feeling he had when he last trod this path, now his heart felt like lead inside his aching chest. He felt that he knew what the letter said. She had tried to tell him the last time she saw him. He carefully tore it into bits, letting it flutter to the winds. John vowed to himself that he would never love another woman in all his life. Such are the vows of the very young.

CHAPTER 5
FAREWELL MY FRIENDS

During the next few weeks John tore into his work as though he were possessed by demons which drove him to accomplish even more than was necessary. Many times he had noticed Larkin practicing with a pair of throwing knives. The sailor could draw the knife in a flash, throw it with pinpoint accuracy. John thought this sport might be fun. He enlisted the aid of his mentor to show him how to temper the finest steel, then grind it into the spear pointed throwing knives that became his constant companions. The weight of the knives was forward of the handle, with the point and both edges as sharp as a razor. Just as Larkin had shown him the gentle art of self-defense called jujitsu, he carefully taught the young man how to wear one knife on his hip and another down the back of his neck. As Larkin put it, "In this world, ye nivver know when ye might need ter save yer life, or again the life of a loved one. Don't hut none to know how." They practiced for hours, until John could throw with either hand, never missing the target more than a fraction of an inch. The flashing blade would speed to the target with the quickness of a cat. This was a product of his constant practice of Judo.

The knife at the back of John's neck was fastened with a thong at the top of the scabbard, tied loosely around his neck. Another thong was at the bottom, tied around his chest. With his shirt on, the knife was out of sight. The one on his hip was in plain view. Again Larkin admonished him to "nivver hurt a body who did not desarve ter be hurt." John could draw and throw either knife with the speed of lightning. Rufus and Tobe did not join in this new sport, for slaves were not allowed to carry a weapon.

One still moonlit night in the hours of the early morning,

Rufus came to John's room and shook him awake. "Massa John, Massa John, wake up fas, Massa, cuz Rufus got a powerful hurtin' to tell ya bout." John woke up fast, for the urgency in Rufus' voice could not be mistaken. "I dun toll ya I bin goin' to da jubilees. Well, my Sall been sneakin' out ter jine me. We din' mean no harm, Massa John, we jes want ta be togedder. We sing an dance the juba an have a good time. We dun want nobody cept each other, Mas John. She my woman, John Boy, jes mine. She never hol no truck wid no other man. She jes mine. She carryn' my chile now. O Lord God amighty what por Rufus gonna do?"

The slave began to sob. Great tears filled his black eyes and spilled over onto his cheeks. They made shiny rivulets in the moonlight as his shoulders shook with the pain of the ordeal. "Hole on, Rufus, I cain't see whut the hurt is all about. She gonna have yer chile, so what?" It seemed that simple to John. "The hut be that she dun gonna be sole to the cloth mills in Atlanta." This statement hit John like a sledge hammer. He knew how much Rufus loved Sally. "When de folk whot own huh fine out she gwine have a chile, they don't wont Sally in de house. Dey say she look too bad wheh she git big wid de youngun. Some folk come down fum Atlanta lookin fer slaves ta wok in de mills. I gotta go wid my Sally, Massa John, I jes gotta go wid huh. They cain't take Sally an my chile. We betta run to da noth an see kin we fine dem Quaka folk what help da po slabe. Help me, Massa John. All I want in de whole worl is my Sally an my chile."

All at once a light shone through the darkness for John. "Buy her, Rufus! Larkin been saving yore money. Tomorra, find out how much money you got and buy her." "A slabe cain't own no slabe, Massa John." The idea had caused Rufus to stop sobbing and start to plan. "Yo buy her, Massa John." Rufus began to get excited. "Ifn yo buy her, Massa John, then when Larkin set me free, me an my Sally be yours til the day we dies." "Ya kno I don' hold with ownin' no slave Rufus." "But, somebody gotta take keer us, Massa John." "I told ya not to call me 'Massa'." "Yes, Massa John, I ain't gonna say dat no mo." "It'll hold to morning, Rufus, then we have a chanct ta make some plans with Tony. Ya stay in yore bed til we call ya in the mornin'." "Yas, Massa John." Rufus stumbled away toward the stable. John lay and thought about the slave jubilees. The word dated all the way back to the Old Testament book of

Leviticus, where it was recorded that every fifty years the Hebrews were to celebrate by the blowing of trumpets, leaving fields untilled and the setting free of bondsmen. The slaves had a tendency to hang onto certain words and scriptures which appealed to them. They often would place their own interpretation to words and phrases to make them fit their own moods.

The Juba was a dance which featured two or more dancers while the rhythm was supplied by clapping hands, patting their knee or singing a refrain with the word, Juba, often repeated. To the oppressed slaves, being allowed to attend a Jubilee was their greatest entertainment. These facts of the Jubilee were not known to John, but the joy and excitement of such good times were often described to him by Rufus and Tobe. This was their theater, their concerts, their joy, indeed their lives.

The next morning, just at daylight, Rufus was shaking John awake. "Us gotta hurry, Massa John. No time ta lose." They called to Larkin who awakened to listen to the sad tale of woe poured out by the heartbroken Rufus. Larkin was not at all adverse to the idea of buying Sally. "Dem folk whut own huh, dey dun seein' some hard time, Massa Tony. Dey sho take a higher offer dan de one made by da fakory in Atlanta." "Pray the Saints we got enough money to do the trick." Tony didn't know just what the going price for a female house servant was these days. "Sally's mistress ain't all unkind, Massa Tony. Eff I wuz ta tel Sally yo gonna buy her, she tell de mistress she lak ta stay in Savannah." "Go tell her right now, Rufus." No further word was necessary. Rufus took to the road in a high run. He didn't stop until he had reached the quarters of the slaves owned by the mistress of Sally. He told the other servants that Mr. Larkin had sent him to make a higher offer for the girl, Sally, than that which they had been offered.

One of the servants appeared presently to inform poor anxious Rufus that the mistress would indeed entertain a higher offer for Sally. Rufus made dust in the other direction as his spirits lifted at the thought that Sally was to be his. When he reached the shop, he was so exhausted, he could hardly choke out his good news. "Us go now, Massa Tony?" "Well it peers ter me Tobe gets ter sleep wi the mules tonight." They all laughed in relief as they worked frantically to hitch the mules to the wagon.

They left Tobe at the shop while the other three went to bring

Sally home. When they reached the fashionable house on aristocat row, Tony and John were shown into a study at the side of the living room. Presently a man and a woman entered and bade them sit down. They were both nervous in the presence of these well-to-do people. The man was a pudgy, short fellow with a friendly smile. The lady of the house was tall and thin, with a rather hooked nose and sharp features. The man spoke first. "So, ye care to buy our Sally? Well we already had an offer for her. You see, Sally is a very obedient girl. House trained for every kind of serving. We been offered five hundred dollars for her." The woman cut in sharply, "The man said he would go as high as six." Larkin was a good trader himself. "We want the gal awright, we need her as a mate fer one o' our own. We kin go as high as seven and that is about the size o' it." The woman said, "If I bargained with the buyer for the factory, I'm sure he would beat the seven." Larkin rolled the brim of his hat in his hands and spoke slowly. "We been lookin' at a coupla others. I will make one last offer, then we be gittin on back ter the shop." John's heart stopped for fear they would not accept the offer Larkin was about to make. "I go as high as eight hundred." Larkin stood up as though to leave. John hung back, waiting for a reply from the woman. Instead, the man extended his hand to Tony. "You got yourself another slave, Mr. Larkin. Please treat her well, we were very partial to Sally." "We like to be takin her now, sir, ef ye don't mind." "Not at all Mr. Larkin. My lawyer will draw the ownership papers tomorrow and come around to your shop to collect the money."

They were both honorable southern gentlemen, both knowing the others' reputation. They needed no more than the handshake. As an after thought, Larkin instructed the man to make the ownership papers in the name of John Bolt. "John is my son, she is a present." John's heart filed with pride at the declaration by the sailor that he was his son. John would never forget this day, for he would indeed be proud to be the son of Tony Larkin.

Sally's meager wardrobe was rolled into a bundle, then she and the grateful Rufus took their place in the tail end of the wagon. The black man was so overcome with joy that big tears began to roll down his shiny black face. Sally took the corner of her apron and dried his tears. "Don' yo be cryin' now Rufus. We is happy at las. Dear Jeaus in heaven, we is so happy at las." Their love and happiness was an inspiration to them and others, both then and in the future when times were not so good.

That afternoon was spent in building a lean-to on the side of the mule barn. Tobe did not complain, just grinned his happy toothless grin as he carried his belongings to the new abode. Supper that night was cooked by the skillful hands of Sally. They ate like kings. This was, without a doubt, the good life. The younger ones thought it might last forever.

The addition of Sally to the group brought nothing but happiness for all of them. Summer days faded into winter, with Larkin spending more and more time with Molly Rafferty at the wagon factory. Since Larkin held more property, they began to discuss the possibility of moving the wagon factory to the blacksmith site. It was not only to be a business merger, but Larkin had decided that it was time for him to settle down to being a husband. He had asked the willing Molly to marry him. This news was taken by the others with mixed emotions. They felt they were losing Larkin, yet they were glad for his sake. The first thing Larkin determined to do was build a more suitable house for him and his intended bride.

They set to work. All had a hand in the project, so it progressed rapidly. A modest white house soon became the new headquarters for the Larkin and Rafferty wagon factory. The new partnership caused John to be restless. Much of his idle time was filled with the memory of the beautiful Jeanine. He realized that she could only be a passing chapter in his life, so he tried to dismiss the disturbing thoughts and concentrate on the dream of having his own farm somewhere to the west.

Rumblings of secession were beginning to shake the southern states of the United States of America. Political unrest was the topic of conversation everywhere people would meet. Those who could read the newspapers told those who could not, with, most times, the teller adding his own thoughts and observations to the already troubled situation.

Before the wedding, Larkin called them together for a serious talk. "I be tellin Tobe and Rufus, they be free men one day. A goodly sum of money has been saved fer each o' them. I had a lawyer draw their freedom papers all right and legal." He handed each a leather-bound paper. "That leaves only Sally. She be the property o' John. When John see fit, he will do the same fer her. John, ye be man enough now ter take the money saved fer yerself, and buy your dream. It is yours from this day on." The moment was so choked with emotion that no one dared speak. Then Larkin continued. "I be takin Molly fer me wife soon. That will be me life fer now and ever." Rufus stood up. "Make no mind what de paper say, me and Sally going wid John Boy! He gon take keer o' us'n. Shore as de papa say it, some mean soul take dem someday, den we be slaves agin. Please, John Boy, we gwine stay wid yo, ain't we?" His big eyes were pleading. John didn't know what he could do without them anyway, so his reassurance was quick in coming. Tobe said not a word; just stared into the distance. No one disturbed him.

Later that night, they began to make plans. "Let's build the first good wagon fer ouselfs." John could already see a fine team of horses pulling a beautiful sturdy wagon fashioned by their own hands. "It be a good idee, John Boy. Be sure it wi have Larkin and Rafferty burned inter every part and parcel o' her." They all formed a picture of the Larkin-Rafferty wagon.

Tobe asked John that night to help him secure passage back to his native land. They promised to see that Tobe was in safe hands for the journey. With the help of the experienced Rafferty, the wagon soon became a reality. The blacksmith work was done to perfection. Only the finest of first quality kiln dried oak was used. The metal findings were carefully crafted by themselves, the best blacksmiths in that section of Georgia. The wagon bed was rigged with a canvas cover. They didn't know how long they might be using it for a home.

John had been attending horse sales, so that he might have a feel for the prices of the pair of work mares he intended to buy. When it came to horses, he wanted only the very best. That was a characteristic of John from that time on. He finally saw a beautiful matched pair of Percherons. He bargained for, and bought them as his first investment. The wagon was a work of art, it would have cost them much more than they would have wanted to pay. After all, though, it was a labor of love and their own sweat went into it. Harness for the team was another item. John again made a deal for the very best. He brought his prize team home, made a shed for them on the other side of the mule barn from Tobe's lean-to. By now, Sally had begun to grow. John thought to himself, "Soon I be the owner of two slaves when I don' even want ta own one." According to the law, the baby would automatically belong to John Bolt.

John, Rufus, and Sally didn't know where they were going. All they had in mind was that it would be somewhere to the west. They were going to look for a good farm to call home for the rest of their lives. Their plans were many and wonderful, but plans wander sometimes, just as men.

The wedding day came and went. Molly Larkin was firmly in charge of the new house. The sailor's interests drifted from rowdy rough-house bouts with his three companions to being at home every evening with the attentive Molly.

John felt that the time to leave was soon. At his age now, he looked forward to the adventure. When he had arrived here, a small boy of twelve years, he had never dreamed that life could be so good. Passage had already been booked for Tobe on a sailing ship to Liberia. The giant black spent his idle time sitting with his face toward the sea. He would rock slowly to the rhythm of a song he would sing in a low voice. His thoughts were already across the great water.

When the day arrived, they each bought a leather-bound chest for their personal belongings. These went into the wagon. John and Tobe carefully packed their precious metal working tools in oiled skin pouches and tied them up with a leather thong. Carefree Rufus had only his clothes to worry about, even they were a small bundle. Molly pointed out to them that she felt it was a very bad time to be taking the pregnant slave girl on a wagon ride to the Lord only knows where. Sally assured her that she knew all about babies and giving birth. She had had long talks with some of the mammies who had a number of young children. "Ain't nawh tin to it, Miz Larkin. I gonna do jes fine." This was the attitude of everyone who was to go. They made it a point to obtain and stow in the wagon every type of tool and useful item they could think of. of.

By February, the adventurers' preparations were all complete. Goodbys to Larkin were not nearly as sad as everyone had anticipated. All, including Tony Larkin, were anxious to proceed with a new adventure. "May the Saints presarve ye, and the mither o' God keep a watchful eye o'er ye. Now don't be fergittin a thing I have tried ter larn ye. It be a long time, maybe, til we see each other again." He shook the hand of each of the blacks, then quickly embraced John, as he said softly into his ear, "God bless ye, my son." Larkin quickly withdrew, walking toward the house. "Now be gone wi ye." They were indeed a long time in seeing each other again; it was never. That was the way of adventure in those formative years of America.

John climbed to the seat of the new wagon, clucked to the beautiful Percheron mares who stepped out at a lively trot. They pulled their load with ease as they were reined toward the river front. Tobe, his freedom papers in his pocket, was to board the high masted sailing ship in time to catch the morning tide. Tobe rode in the back of the wagon, Rufus and his pregnant bride in the place prepared just behind the driver, the proud John on the high seat. The tug of the beautiful, anxious horses pulling at the reins made him feel the whole world was waiting just for John Bolt to direct it's next turn.

The riverfront was already bustling with wagon and human traffic. Since everything had been pre-arranged by John and Tony a few days before, getting Tobe aboard was to be an easy task. The ship's master had already offered Tobe a job aboard. The huge former slave's ability as a carpenter and blacksmith was well-known on the waterfronts of Savannah.

John stopped the team, set the brake lever to which he secured the reins. The well-trained team stood with their heads high, once in awhile snorting at the strange smells and sounds of the heavy riverfront traffic. They all disembarked, standing in front of the team, to say their goodbys. The huge Tobe took his sea chest from his shoulder, placed it on the ground beside him. The big black man could not look up, he kept his eyes riveted to the ground. John placed his hands on Tobe's shoulders. "I will never forget you, my dear friend. You were always there when I needed you, you always cared when I was troubled." With that, John turned quickly, climbing back to the seat of the wagon. Sally was already aboard. Tender-hearted Rufus could not tear himself away from his long-time friend. Huge tears filled his eyes, streaming down his face. "Oh, Tobe, oh, oh, oh, I got a turble misry in ma soul." Rufus wept unashamedly for the friend who at one time had almost cost him his life. "We gwine go ta happy times now, Rufus. Don' ya cry." The big man clasped Rufus in his arms, as he slowly rocked from side to side. "Don' ya cry no more now, Rufus." He pushed Rufus toward the wagon. Without another word, Tobe picked up his belongings walking for the gangplank of the waiting ship.

With that, John whistled to his team and headed up river, toward his new life. The brothels and honky tonks along river row were already experiencing a good trade. Sally had been taught by her mistress that these places were frequented by the devil. She kept her eyes averted as though the bawdy houses were not even there. Music mixed with raucous laughter was heard from inside, as they passed the open doors.

Along toward the end of the row, John heard the shrill voice of a woman. "Keep yer damn hands off'n me, yo river rat." The shrill admonishing of the woman was followed by a lewd laugh. "I am jes the waitress here, and thet ain't no way at all ta treat a lady." "Beggin yer pawden, my lady." More loud laughter. The shrill voice pierced John's consciousness again. "I shore as hell gonna stob ye with this here carvin knife ef yo don unhand me." They passed on out of hearing with John puzzling to himself. "Where have I heard that voice afore?" It seemed to him to be familiar, yet he could not put a face with the shrill, scolding voice.

As they left the populated area heading northwesterly up the river, it began to rain. John pulled the team to the side of the road so they could roll the canvas down on the sides of the wagon. Then they lowered the wagon cover on one side and walked around behind to begin the other, they noticed a big black man with a sea chest on his shoulder trotting up the road toward them. Tobe had been following since they left Savannah. He was winded, tired from keeping up the steady pace of the young team. He placed his possessions in the back of the wagon, mumbled an explanation. "Ain't got no kin in Aferker by now, no way. Them slavers kitch all o' em when dey tuk me nohow. It were jes a dream, Massa John, an I been thinkin a new farm be better an a dream, anyhow. Kin I go wid ya, Massa John?" John and Rufus circled the big blacksmith like children around a maypole. Drivers of passing wagons stared in disbelief. "You air a free man, Tobe, don be callin me Massa!" "Yas, Massa John, I won' Massa." They all laughed loudly, then resumed their journey to somewhere.

CHAPTER 6
THE CHEROKEE WAY

Eliza Clementine Bandy had just turned seventeen. She was still slender and willowy, but the hard farm labor alongside her beloved Pa had helped to fashion a beautiful young body, full of the vitality of life. Her one-half Cherokee blood made her hair as black as the ravens which frequented the feedlot. She wore Indian moccasins to the knee. She could run like a deer with the long tresses streaming behind in the winter wind.

Clemmy's circle of friends was limited, since the farms were far apart; neighbors would come to visit only once in awhile. She had never cared for the slovenly preacher and his wife on the farm down the creek, so it caused her little concern that she didn't see them. Her Pa was her life and her happiness. They were constant companions, working together as a team. There was always land to clear, chores to do, endless repairs to be made. Her old Cherokee grandmother, Sun Flower, had taught her a great deal about life. They would have long talks in her little cabin by the woods. As the old woman became even older, she began to lose her eyesight, her hearing and her memory. One morning she failed to appear for breakfast which they usually had together. Will and Clemmy were alarmed, so they went quickly to the little cabin. When they entered, there was no Sun Flower in residence. Clemmy quickly crossed the room to a cupboard on the wall. When she opened the door, tears filled her eyes for just a moment. "She don gone, Pa." "Gone, where in tarnation would she go in the middle o' the night?" Will went to the door to whistle for his hounds. "I'll go find her. Twon't take but a little spell. I'll have her back in two shakes o'a lamb's tail." "No Pa, don' go lookin'. She has gone into the woods to cross her wide river. Jes let her be, Pa. She tuk her medicine bag, only she knowed what wuz in it. She also tuk her rabbit skin robe. It is the way of the Cherokee, Pa. She felt she had outlived her usefulness, so she don it her way. We could maybe find her one day in a cave in the rocks, er in a big holler log. It is the way of her people, Pa. She has her terbaccy, and she will know of some yerbs ta chew with it. She jes gonna go to sleep and cross the big river to be with her people." Clemmy's chin quivered for just a moment. "Come on, Pa, I will race ya ta the barn. We got chores to do, an the time is here to do them."

With no crops to look after winter days sometimes became long, so Will and Clemmy would go hunting in the woods. Through the patience of her Pa, Clemmy became extremely adept at the handling of a rifle. As Will Bandy would say, "If'n Clemmy pints that gun at yo, Mister Squirrel, yo might jes as well come over an jump inter the sack." She learned to bring down a running deer with a shot placed squarely into its neck. Wild hogs and turkey were the most excitement for Clemmy. She and Pa would follow the hounds after the hogs, or sit quietly, calling the wily turkeys to them. Her accuracy with both the shotgun and rifle were a pleasure to behold for the sharp-eyed farmer. He thought he was good but his seventeen year old daughter could outshoot him on every turn. When they killed game it was to eat, with nothing going to waste.

Will said, "Know sompin Clemmy, God give us food aplenty, so don' us go and spile this worl by killin off his creatures. Tell yu, little gal, we git up early tomorra, hook a good team ta the wagon, head fer the county seat. Time ya had yerself some new duds, an ah could use me some new things mysef. We work hard, Clemmy gal, gal, les go spen some jes ta make us beautiful." "Oh, Pa reckon ah might could git me a new dress? Maybe one thets bright red, with a big bow at the side?" "Cain't go lettin' my gal git too purty. Some young scallywag might jes ride up this away and carry her off." Will tugged at Clemmy's long hair. The beautiful young girl was embarrassed by her Pa's remark. She had never pictured herself as an attraction for some young man. It was not an unpleasant thought, however. She pretended to be in great pain from the gentle tug on her hair. When he released her, she playfully kicked him in the shin and ran for the house. "Jes fer sayin thet, Pa, we ain't goin ta no county seat." He knew better, so did she. Her eyes were wide with excitement for the rest of the evening.

She was up at daylight, urging the sleepy Will to hurry so they could get to town early. "Pa, I aim ta look at the dresses in all three of the stores in town. When I find the one that is jes right, I aim ta begin atryin it on. An if'n it fits, ya promised, Pa, you would buy it." "Buy it, I will! I don' reckon there is a way ta make ya more purty then ya done are, but ya might jes be the most beautiful in the hull county." They secured all the livestock as best they could and started on the road before the sun was even up. This would put them to town and back in time for the evening chores.

Clemmy's heart was singing as she snuggled close to Pa on the wagon seat this cold morning. As the sun rose, the jays began to glide between the trees, the crows started their raspy conversations, an occasional possum or raccoon would scurry across the road in front of the hurrying team.

They were both reflecting on the beauty of this glorious Georgia morning. How could there be a better place to live anywhere? The young lady was much too excited to sleep on this ride to town. She kept up a steady barrage of words to the farmer. As the sun began to shine on her lovely face, he recalled another face even more lovely. It had belonged to his precious Little Dove, her Cherokee mother. Will had never considered marrying again after he had lost her. His whole life was tied up in this chatterbox on the wagon seat beside him. She was wearing one of the plain cotton dresses Will had bought for her the last time they had gone to town. It was just beginning to be too small for her. Firm, high breasts were very apparent through the material. She had the dress tied in the middle with a piece of braided yarn which she had spun herself. Her feet were adorned with the beaded moccasins made by the loving hands of old Sun Flower, her granny.

They arrived in town at about mid-morning. The livery stable and barn was down at the end of the street. Their team of mules mules would be fed and watered while they waited to go to the boarding house for their noon meal. They had some time to kill so they walked up and down the boardwalks, looking into the shop windows. There were all sorts of fascinating things Clemmy was used to doing without. She saw a big, one-bladed pocket knife which she wanted, but Pa didn't think that would be too lady-like.

There was a store where they sold a host of things used around the house. Pots and pans, huge boiling pots which could be used out in the yard to boil clothes or scald chickens. In the other stores there were rings for her fingers, flowered hats, parasols, the latest from Paris, sunbonnets, high button shoes, just a world of things to excite the mind and eye of a seventeen year old from out in the country. There was just too much to see. As people walked by, both men and women would turn to stare at the striking beauty of the half-Indian girl and her Pa, Will Bandy.

Will was becoming quite well-known in this section of Georgia as one of the best farmers in the whole country. His crops grew better, his hogs were bigger and fatter. Little did they know of the hours of toil which went into this hard-won success.

They had, by now, gone down the side street to the boarding house of Mrs. De Lany. Clemmy was so accustomed to eating her own food that she was sure that no one in the whole world was a better cook than the kindly lady who served noon meals to all who would pay, as well as keeping a group of men boarders who worked in the saw mill.

The lithe and lovely girl was not aware that she was upsetting all the clientele by her simple charm and beauty. Instead of eating, the saw mill hands would just sit and look. Although it did not impress Clemmy, Will was awkwardly aware of it. The meal was replete with fresh home-made bread, ham and gravy, black-eyed peas, and great slabs of pie made from dried apples and blackberry preserves.

They both ate hungrily, Will paid the asked-for price, then they once again headed for the wonders of a day in town. When they reached the porch of the general store, Will said, "Honey, I reckon as how I look right wooly. I'fn yo don' mind atall, I will go to the barber shop yonder." He pointed across the street. "Ya hankered ta pick out yore own dress, anyways. Jes go on in that thar gen'l store an pick out which ever one ya take a shine ta. I promised it would be yorn." Clemmy's eyes widened at the thought of picking out her very own dress. There was some trepidation about going into the store alone, however. She imagined she would feel the piggish eyes of Zeb Turney, the storekeeper, on her every minute she was in the establishment.

This was the biggest general store in the county seat, with rows and rows of dresses to excite the desires of any woman for miles around. "Go on Pa, cept I mayhap won't recognize ya when ya come back out. Thet barber is rat apt ta think he done got holt o' a wooly bar." She shoved Will off the sidewalk into the street. Her moccasined feet caused little sound as she entered the big store. No sound was necessary. All eyes turned in her direction. Once again the town spit and whittle club, sitting around the big cast-iron pot-bellied stove, became silent. Clemmy self-consciously walked past them toward the drygoods section at the rear of the barn-like mercantile. "Gawd almighty thet leetle squaw is gitten ta be a looker." The store-keeper could not contain his leering admiration. He was waiting on a customer, but nevertheless, watched Clemmy until she began to look at what she thought would be her size in the dresses. She would take them off the rack, hold them up, look at herself in the large mirror at one side of the room. She became so engrossed in her selection that the rest of the world just did not exist. She would select a dress, hold it out to look, then hold it against her slender young body. She acted as her own critic for the vision in the mirror. The staring eyes of the men in the store did not impress her one little bit. Zeb Turney had to be prompted several times by other customers about their purchases. He saw that he was ignoring them, so he appointed one of the regular loafers to take over the clerking. He had a more exciting customer to attend to.

Zeb was beginning to show his age, his easy living was apparent in the way his belly spilled over his belt. His hair was grey at the sides where it blended into mutton-chop whiskers. A stubble of beard covered the rest of his pudgy face. His clothes needed washing and hung on his body like the vestiges of a scarecrow. He wore no socks in his brogan shoes which clumped on the floor as he approached Clemmy.

By now, she was so enchanted by the new dresses that she was softly humming a little tune as she looked and whirled. She was not aware of Zeb Turney's existence until she caught a stifling whiff of body odor and snuff. "Lordy," she thought, "we got hogs thet smell bettern' yo do, and they don' even dip snuff." He grinned evilly at her, causing a little trickle of snuff juice to trace that which was already dried in the creases at the corners of his mouth. Tobacco stained teeth showed above his snuff-laden bottom lip.

"Well, ef it ain't Miss Bandy. Yo done growed, honey. Yo

done growed inter a right purty somethin'. Now thet red dress yo got helt up to yore bosum makes ya even thet much purtier. Go put hit on in thet leetle room yonder." She was hesitating for just a moment. After all though, she had told Pa she intended to try on her choice. She went quickly to the dressing room. Zeb ambled close to the door with the hope that she might somehow leave it ajar enough for him to peek. Instead, before she closed the door, Clemmy made sure it had a fastener. She saw the latch was secure before she began to remove her cotton dress over her head. She stood momentarily looking down at herself. She had never enjoyed the niceties of the dainty under tops which the ladies wore. Nature had provided her with a figure that needed no pushing, pulling, lifting or flattening. She put the bright red dress on quickly and adjusted the bow at the waist. She felt that by now, Pa would be there to see and approve of her choice. When she emerged, she noticed other people wandering aimlessly about the store, so she felt a great deal safer than she did when she had retreated into the dressing room.

Turney defeated her, however, when he suggested to the customers that they go to another part of the store to see some new oil lamps that just arrived from Atlanta. When Zeb thought they were out of hearing distance, he turned to Clemmy and put his unwashed, pudgy hand on the back of her arm. "Whut a purty leetle injun I got here." Clemmy pulled away to look him full in the face. "Honey, be nice ter Zeb and thet red dress ain't gonna coss one red penny." Clemmy knew the meaning of his lewd suggestion. After all, old granny Sun Flower knew the ways of men. All men, Indian as well as white. Zeb tried to move his hand to cover one of her shapely young breasts. Clemmy's voice rose, causing all eyes in the store to rivet on the scene. "Git yore filthy paw offen me, Turney. I take no dress fum the likes o' yo, an besides, I cain't stand the stink of yo."

Will Bandy had entered the store, crossed the room in bounding strides. This time he caught Turney before he could retreat to the safe haven behind the counter. Will was shaking with fury. He spun the store-keeper, hit him squarely in the mouth with his hard fist. Zeb fell backward, dragging a rack of dresses with him. He was momentarily dazed by the hard blow to the mouth. Bandy stood with his feet wide apart, waiting for the counter attack. It never came, instead, the store-keeper spat blood, snuff and a tooth onto the board floor. "God damn ya, Bandy. Ya busted out one o' my teeth." A circle had formed about the scene. Zeb looked at the regular crowd, whiningly began to explain. "I dint aim to hurt her none. Sides, she ain't nawthin but a Cherokee squaw." Bandy kicked the sniveling Turney in the fat belly. He squealed in pain. "I ain't no dog, Bandy ya caint kick me like no houn dog. Git outa my store. Don' ever come here again! I'll have the sheriff onta ya. Git outa here, Bandy." Will was not a violent man, so he was quite ready to leave anyway. "Ain't nobody ever kicks us Turneys an gits away with it, Bandy. I aim ter even up one o' these here days. Yo gonna see, Bandy, one o' these days." This threat came from Turney, still on the floor.

As they crossed the threshold on their way out, Will noticed that Clemmy was still wearing the pretty red dress. He threw money back through the open door. They strode down the street toward the livery stable. They walked fast, Will was still seething with rage. They hadn't gone far when Clemmy began to giggle. Will thought she was sobbing, so he looked at her in alarm. When he saw that it was laughter, he grinned. "Yo are a little vixen, Clemmy, yo know thet?" By now Clemmy was laughing loudly as she hung onto Will's arm. "It were really funny, Pa, I kin still see him with his tooth out. He musta swallered half a bottle o' snuff when ya closed his ugly mouth. Did yo hurt yore hand, Pa?" He, too, began to laugh. Soon the ugly incident was forgotten as they began to talk about other things that caught their interest. It was a pleasant ride home. Clemmy was still proud of her brand spanking new dress.

Winter would soon be spring, so they tore into their land clearing project with a vengeance. Will would fell the trees, while Clemmy trimmed the branches. The young pine trees were a crop, the same as other things which grew on the farm. The sawmill paid for them delivered. The brush was piled where it could be burned. Stumps were dug around, and pulled and pried from the ground. The working mules earned their keep as they strained at their traces to do the bidding of the farmer. On the Bandy place everybody worked.

At times they would meet the preacher at the rail fence which separated their two farms. Each time, the conversation would get around to the suggestion that Will should bring some of his harvest into the storehouse of the Lord. "It would be afurtherence o' the good Lord's work, Bandy. Iff'n ya was to feel the burden of the necessary of sharin one o' them sugar cured hams, then thet ud free me up to preach some more to the heathen o' this here county. The Lord's work is my work, Bandy. Don't ye feel it in yer heart ta push mah missionary work a leetle further along? We cud stand ta have some o' them blackeyed peas ta go with it, too. Maybe a sack o' goobers to help keep our body an soul tergether whilst we preach the gospel." The preacher kept eyeing Clemmy who was trying very hard not to laugh out loud. "Thet youngun o' yorn ain't so young no more, Bandy. She air a growed woman now. I an the old woman kin come over tomorra with the cart ta get them things yo promised the Lord." "Sure, Preacher, sure," Will chuckled. He knew when he had been taken in. They turned toward their own house. "Come on, Pa, I'll race ya ta the porch." Clemmy ran like a deer with her black hair flying behind. Will was hard put to stay even near. He was winded when they reached the yard. "Ya took advantage o' a old man by takin' a head start. Thet ain't no way fair." Clemmy threw both her strong arms around his neck and hugged. He was her champion, her grand and glorious Pa; she was his living memory of Little Dove.

Spring began soon. Wildflowers of all description and colors began to make their appearance, bobwhites whistled their mating calls in the rail fence rows. It is a beautiful world which God made in that part of Georgia. The preacher and his wife became regular visitors to the Bandy farm. Will didn't really mind, since the good Lord had indeed been good to him.

One day, when they came to replenish the Lord's storehouse, the preacher's wife went into the house with Clemmy, while the preacher was with Will at the barn. She was a big, angular, unattractive woman, with never an attempt at making herself look a little more presentable. Her sleeves were always full length, while her skirts swept the ground. She helped Clemmy prepare supper, talking as she worked. "Clemmy, don' call me Miz Rue. Please call me by my name, Clare. I need a woman to talk to jes lak you wush I could have ya fer my fren." Clemmy was surprised at the sudden show of affection by the preacher's wife. "Course I want ya fer ma fren, Clare, sometimes the days is awful long with nobody ta talk with cept Pa.'' Clare Rue smiled and patted Clemmy on the shoulder. ''The preacher, he ain't sich a bad un, Clemmy, he really got a heart o' gold. He jes got a way of chidin people too much bout their soul. He really do believe what he preaches. He shore nuf is a good man, an he wants us ta go on the road one o' these days so's he kin help poor loss souls all over the back kintry. I gotta go with him till I die, I reckon. Eff'n the Lord called him ta travel, then we got no say in the matter.'' She looked wistfully out the window toward their own farm. ''I hate like pizen going off, though. Les be frens till the preacher gits his wagon and teams gathered up to hit the trail.'' ''That would be rite nice, Clare, it shorly would.'' From that day forward, they made a trail to each other's doors.

Early summer had started and the backbreaking work of putting in the crops had begun. Plowing, harrowing, planting, listing and cultivating. It was all there to be done, so Clemmy and Pa worked from sunup until sunset. A piece of meadow land near the creek was almost cleared and ready for the plow. They went one early morning to finish up.

Clemmy began to burn small piles of brush, while Pa used a team of mules to drag the trimmed logs to the wagon yard. Will Bandy leaned way over to clasp his hands beneath the butt of a small pine tree which was to be chained with the others. Without a sign of warning, the ugly, heartshaped head of a diamondback lashed from the high grass. Half inch long hypodermic fangs sank into Will's neck muscle, just below his jaw bone. The paralyzing pain caused Will to stand up, he issued an agonizing scream. As he stood, the hugh snake's fangs were so imbedded into his flesh that it could not unfasten. The now frantically buzzing tail almost reached the ground. Clemmy heard the scream, looked up in horror at the tragic scene. Will grasped the head of the deadly viper, wrenched it from his neck, then threw it to the ground a few feet away. He fell forward on his hands an knees, with his hands clasped behind his neck. Great waves of blackness began to engulf him.

''Clemmy, oh, Clemmy, I knowed better an do a fool thing like that. He didn't rattle atall, he just struck.'' Clemmy, in her frustration, found the limb of a tree, then hunted the snake and beat it into a pile of quivering mush. Running back then she said, ''I kilt it, Pa, yo be alright now, Pa. I kilt thet snake with a big stick.'' Agonizing whimpers were issuing from Clemmy. ''Pa, Pa, what can we do? I kin cut it, and suck the blood and pizen, jes lak ya showed me, Pa.'' Clemmy was trying to get the knife from Will's pocket. ''No use, honey, jes no use. I ain't got but a little spell now, so be quiet and listen.'' The big farmer rolled over on his back in the grass. His neck was beginning to swell, speech was an effort with each word. ''Eliza Clementine Bandy,'' he said her full name. ''Yor Ma wants ya to be a lady. Yo been my princess, my life. I don' wanna leave ya, Clemmy, but ya kin jes try to remember all the things me an old Sun Flower learned ya.'' Clemmy had to lean closer to hear him. ''I will see yor Ma now. I will cross her river. Dear God, in the name of your precious son, Jesus Christ, be merciful to me, a sinner.'' This last came in a halting whisper. His big hand brushed the tear-stained face of Eliza Clementine, then the wide river was behind him.

Clemmy screamed until her throat could no longer make a sound. She ran to the house to get one of the comforters from the bed that Will and his Indian wife had shared so many years ago. She returned, covering him carefully, then stumbled in the direction of the Preacher Rue farm. When she arrived there, Clare Rue gathered her into her outstretched arms. ''Dear God, what happened, chile?'' Clemmy weakly waved an arm in the direction of the field in which her precious Pa lay. The woman started screeching, ''Reveren, Reveren!'' The preacher came from the direction of the privy in the back of the house. ''Hurry, Reveren, somthin jes happen to her pa.'' Preacher Rue began to mumble a prayer as he ran toward the women. ''What is it, chile? Yore Pa hurt bad?'' Clemmy shook her head numbly. When the preacher saw the tragedy in her grief-stricken face, he did not need to ask another question. ''How'd it happen, child.'' ''A big rattler,'' Clemmy managed to answer. The preacher looked toward the heavens, ''An the viper shall bruise the heel of man. Them is your words, dear God.'' Rue then placed his trembling hand on the girl's head and humbly asked, ''Kin ya see fit ta comfort us now in our time of great loss?'' Tears began to course down his rugged cheeks.

''Take Clemmy home, now Missus. I aim ta fetch some neighbors.'' He ran to the barn, bridled a mule, mounted it bareback, and rode away at a gallop. As Clemmy, with Mrs. Rue, walked the seemingly endless trail back to the Bandy farmhouse, she could not keep her eyes from fastening on the bright colored comforter in the field of waving grass. The mules had begun to graze contentedly a short distance away. That is the order of God's universe. The living go on doing the things they must to sustain them in their efforts to survive.

Clare Rue did not leave the sorrowing girl for one moment. Neighbors began to gather. A grave was opened beside the pile of stones where the remains of Little Dove lay. A pine board casket was quickly fashioned, all the livestock was looked after. Not a thing was left undone. This is the way of country folk in a time of sorrow or need. They all vowed to return at daybreak the following morning to have a proper funeral for one of their own.

Clemmy didn't sleep at all that night; just sat looking toward the forest where she and Pa had had such good times together. From time to time she would call to him in a little girl's voice. True to their words, the country folk gathered to hear Preacher Rue read from marked passages from the 143rd and 144th Psalms. "Man is like to vanity, his days are as a shadow that passeth away. Hear my prayer, Oh Lord, give ear to my supplications, cause me to hear thy loving kindness on this morning; for in thee I do trust cause me to know the way wherein I should walk, for I lift up my soul to thee." Clemmy heard the words of the Preacher, but her mind was filled with the stories her Pa had told her of her mother, Little Dove. Their's was a love made for happiness on earth. Clemmy now wondered if, in that land beyond the wide river, a white man could hold the hand of a little Indian dove, and walk in the beautiful fields they both loved so well. It had to be so, oh, God knows it had to be so. Little Dove had given her love man, WillBanee, half of her and half of him. Eliza Clementine Bandy fell asleep on the pile of dirt with a marker reading "Will Bandy . . . Died in May, 1839."

The needs of the livestock kept Clemmy busy. There was an endless chain of chores to be done. In between there were the fields to look after. She did what she could, but it was just too much farming for one lonely seventeen year old. Her hands began to look rough and hard. She was not so careful about her appearance as she used to be. Neighborly men began to call at the Bandy farm, some young, some old. Clemmy gave no encouragment to any of them. She would politely, but firmly, refuse their offers of assistance with the labor.

As summer wore on, Preacher Rue finally realized his means to answer the call to hit the backroads to be an evangelist. He firmly believed that he was called to help save the souls of the heathen and non-believer. What he lacked in finesse he made up for in conviction. He had sold his run down farm to a young man from the east of the state. They had paid in cash, which enabled the preacher to have a wagon built much in the fashion of the European gypsy. When they were ready to depart, Clemmy and Clare bade each other goodby at the rail fence which divided the two farms. Clemmy was beyond tears by now. She had cried all there were to shed. Clare Rue hugged and kissed the lovely young girl, she began to weep as she turned to join the Lord's new evangelist on the high seat of the house-wagon. Clemmy leaned on the rail fence, watching three men stripped to the waist toiling in one of the fields. There were two negroes and a blond-haired man. They were at a distance, but Clemmy could hear them chanting as they worked. They were already clearing brush and rock from the field which bordered her farm. Smoke was coming from the chimney of the ramshackle house. "I'll take some things to call on the lady o' the house by an' by. I hope she is a tolerable sort." Clemmy had taken to talking to herself at times now. It kind of helped to dispell her loneliness.

Clemmy made her way down the path to her house. When she reached the yard, she noticed a wagon turn off the main road to enter her gate. She could see a young black man driving the team of mules which approached the house. Clemmy went to the barnyard to meet the approaching wagon. Before he had reached the yard, the negro boy stopped the team, got down, tying the reins to the brake handle. Clemmy walked to the wagon pass-through in the barn to get a better look at the strange behavior of the visitor. She was startled by a voice from the corner of the barn. "Howdy, Miss Bandy."

The storekeeper approached her with his expensive hat held in front of his wide chest. For some reason, he had chosen to dress up for this call. He had even shaved and combed his thinning hair. What Clemmy didn't know was that he had made his way to the barn through the woods. The black boy's instructions had been for him to stop short and stay there. He was not about to disobey.

Clemmy's heart began to beat faster as he advanced. "I come ta make friends, Miss Bandy. I don' hold no grudge agin yo jes cuz I din't like yore Pa. Thet is all in the past. I aim ta offer yo a better then fair price fer yore hogs." He grinned a wide grin, showing tobacco-stained teeth. All except one in the front, it was missing. The wide gap had caused him to affect a lisp when he spoke. Clemmy suddenly saw a vision of the incident in the store, followed by the good laugh she and Pa had had afterward. She inadvertently smiled at the recollection. "I see ya ain't takin too unkindly ta the suggestion Miss Bandy." Clemmy's face suddenly froze into a mask of hatred at the realization that the unwanted visitor had mistaken her smile for encouragment. She retreated backward until she felt the boards of a manger against her firm round hips. She knew she had a pitchfork leaning against one of the log columns near at hand. "Git away from me, ya stinkin pile of garbage." She hissed the words with all the hatred she could command. "Now see here, ya uppity leetle squaw. I come here ta be friendly an by God thet is jes what yo an me is going ter be. After I show ya jes what a man is fer, then mayhap yo wil git a little sense in yore purty head. I kin be a lot o' good hep ta ya. Yo won' never hatter worry about nothin no more." "I ain't worried bout nothing now, ya skunk. Stay away fum me!" Clemmy grabbed for the pitchfork, but too late. Turney was anticipating the move, he had her by both wrists before she could bring the tines of the fork to her defense. He was surprisingly strong, his weight bore her backward until she was bending over the top board of the manger. Her arms were forced behind her, he stood so close she couldn't kick. She spat in his face as his evil smelling breath blasted her senses. He drew his head back in rage. "Now looka here ya leetle injun cat, I ain't the fust man whats been here, an ya know it. Now settle down afore I hatter knock some sense inter ya. I told yore Pa I be gittin even fer what he done ta me, but ef ya'll jes be nice ter me, then I be fergittin about thet." Clemmy's mind was racing for a way to check his advances. She knew that screaming would do no good. It was too far to the nearest neighbor, and the black boy on the wagon belonged to Zeb. She nodded her head in assent, hoping he would release her long enough for her to take flight. She knew she could outrun him. She allowed herself to relax just a little. Zeb took the bait, relaxing his hold on her, except for one wrist. Clemmy nodded toward the house. Zeb grinned his lewd, evil grin and stepped away from her. He looked toward the house in anticipation. Standing before them was a muscular, blond young man. His eyes were as blue as the skies and as cold as steel. A knife hissed through the space between them and imbedded itself in the wood of the manger, between Zeb's legs, just below his groin. The store-keeper looked down at the knife, his pudgy face blanched in fear and utter surprise. A calm voice came to them. "Go ahead, reach fer it ef yer a mind ta. I got another, an it'll find a spot a mite higher than the first one. I don' know jes who ya be, Mister, but peers ta me the lady don' jes cotton ta ya. I get the idee she don' care fer ya atall."

John Bolt balanced on his toes, ready to cripple the would-be lover, if he so much as moved. "Let go the lady's han now, Mister." Zeb released her, beginning to quake in fear. "I din't mean no harm now, Mister," Zeb wheedled. "Me and this her injun gal already know each other. I wuz funning with her. Her an me been friendly afore. No matter what she tells ya Mister, it's the God's truth."

Clemmy was so enraged and frightened she could hardly utter a word. "Ain't no man never touched me, ain't no man never will." With that, Clemmy ran to her house and slammed the door. Young John Bolt told the store-keeper that if he ever saw him in that part of the country again, he would slit his fat throat. Zeb hurried to the wagon, he applied a whip to the team while the black boy drove.

John Bolt and his entourage had made their way leisurely up the Savannah River. They looked at farms for sale all the way. When spring drew near, they made their way to Atlanta. As Sally put it, "Here I is in Atlanta anyways. They kaint have me in the cloth mills though, cuz I got to git on wid de bizness o' havin a baby." Her time had sure enough come, they hired a midwife. The woman was a slave herself, the money for her services of course went to her master. Rufus and Sally became the parents of a son named Wilfred John Bolt. He was the property of John Bolt because his mother still did not wish to be set free. She was so afraid that she would be retaken by some slaver and made to become a slave without rights again. She liked the life she was living with her man Rufus. She knew that Rufus would never leave John Bolt, free or not.

Whenever they felt that they were making too much of a drain on their farm purchasing money, they would set up a temporary blacksmith shop. This was their trade, they had all the tools necessary and the customers came to them.

When spring arrived in the midlands of Georgia, they all became anxious to settle down to become the farmers they had so longed to be. It was late in the season when they finally arrived at the county seat of Cherokee County. They were told of the preacher's place for sale, so they went to see it. They saw a great potential in it, so they made the deal then and there. They paid Preacher Rue for the crops he already had in the fields. In their inexperience, it was a great bargain for the preacher. Nevertheless, they were anxious for him to be gone so that they could put their backs to the task of running their very own farm. None of them, except the preacher, could read. Rue, although taking advantage of the bargain was just as careful as they were about getting their papers all in order. He took them to town to the same lawyer who had handled all the paper work ever done by Will Bandy. It was the lawyer who had told them about the tragedy of Clemmy's father, not sparing any of the details, and expounding upon the beauty of the daughter who was left to run the big farm so lovingly cared for by the farmer. He had said, "The preacher's place can be made to look just like the Bandy place, if you will put the work into it. Please be neighborly, look in on Miss Bandy. See if you can help her to find somebody to do the heavy work for her. There just ain't no way the poor little soul can keep thet place going by herself. She don't cotton to folks much, see if you can let her know that you aim to help. Seems ta me yo got a heap o' help, Mr. Bolt, what with them two slaves o' your'n. That biggun looks like he could move a mountain." John explained to the lawyer that Rufus and Tobe were free men, able to come and go as they saw fit. "The woman, Sally, and her youngun are mine, but I aim ta set em free jus as soon as they want ta be." The lawyer couldn't see the sense of wasting good slaves by setting them free. His was the opinion of the big majority of Southerners at that time. Some talk of freeing all slaves had been circulated in Georgia, but it was bitterly and forcefully opposed.

With their farm securely purchased, they set to work. The first thing Tobe wanted was a blacksmith shop. This would be their extra money and, at the same time, serve them by getting their farm tools into shape for the task ahead. They made the house livable for John, then set about preparing a place to live for Rufus and his family. Tobe was still obliged to set up abode in the barn. Eventually, he would have his very own cabin. After all, this venture was part his.

John had made a lot of effort to contact the girl on the next farm, but it seemed that every time he would get within hailing distance of her, she would change her course, to head in another direction. He had never gotten close enough to see her face. Only the graceful carriage of her straight slender body, the long black hair down her back tied with a bright red piece of cloth. She had seen him from the edge of the woods one day. She thought how much nicer he looked than most of the farm boys who had come to the Bandy farm to offer their services to her since the death of Pa. Had he known that she had seen him working in the field, stripped to the waist, he would have been terribly embarrassed.

John felt that he had waited long enough for a meeting to just happen, so that morning, dressed in his best, he headed through the fields to the Bandy farm. His approach had brought him to the back of the farmyard. As he neared the house, he observed another man approaching from the other direction. John stepped behind a vine-laden tree, then waited to see just what was taking place. He saw the wagon coming in from the road. Miss Bandy had left the house, walking slowly to the barn. John had felt his pulse quicken when he had seen her. Lordy, what a beautiful creature, he breathed. She was quite enough to take a man's breath away. He watched her lean against a post at the wagon drive-through. What could that fat jasper be doin? By now, the other man had emerged from the woods and had come behind the barn. When he saw Clemmy's startled reaction to the heavy-set man, he knew that no good would come of their meeting.

This was when John made his acquaintance to Eliza Clementine Bandy. She had retreated to the safety of the house so fast, that John had not had a chance to say another word to her. He turned slowly, left the barnyard, making his way leisurely back up the path to his own house.

Clemmy, her heart still pounding from her frightening experience, watched him stride smoothly up the path. Never had she seen a man stand so straight, and walk so smoothly. She thought again of the remark the storekeeper had made about having been friendly with her before. Her face flushed hot, tears of frustration came to her eyes. "What will he think o' me? Oh, Lordy, what will the whole county think o' me eff'n thet no good man spreads thet kind o' talk? I ain't never going ta have nothin lak thet to do wit no man." She raised her head with her chin thrust out. "I don need no man! All they be is a heap o' trouble. Peers ta me though thet I need ta buy me a couple o' slaves ta help with the work, and jes be here iff'n they be needed. Pa lef me enuf money, so thet is zakly what I aim ta do. Maybe a woman an a man. Yep, thet gotta be the bes way ta run this place." She strained to see the man in distance as he climbed the rail fence between the two farms.

CHAPTER 7
THE LAND PROVIDES

Georgia was a veritable cornucopia of wonderful things to eat. Fruit trees, peaches, cherries, and a host of wild fruits and berries were everywhere. Steady summer rains caused crops to literally jump from the ground once they were planted. The trouble with John Bolt was that he had not started early enough to get his crops into the soil. The sickly crops the preacher had planted were doing much better under the tender care administered by John and Rufus. Word spread rapidly that the preacher's place was now occupied by a young fellow and his slaves. None of the country folk would concede that the slaves were anything but just that. John grew tired of explaining that they were freedmen, who could come and go as they pleased.

At their chosen farming occupation they were not so well informed as they might be. Their expertise as iron workers and farriers spread quickly. They had set up their smithy between the barnyard and house, near the main road. Their rail fence took a u-shape from the road toward the house, then back to the road. This way they could leave a wide opening for their customers to approach but still not run the risk of letting their livestock out. As they worked for their neighbors, shoeing horses and mules, shrinking steel wagon tires back onto wheels, making farming tools and various other things that were demanded in a farming community, they would listen intently to what their peers had to say about farms, the methods they were using.

At that time in history, cotton was king. Many of the farmers thought that they could grow cotton from now till kingdom come, not worrying about the soil. After all, the land was there to stay. For the most part, plowing was done in the easiest fashion with never a thought to the contour of the land. Cotton was planted year after year. Wasn't it the money crop?

The hot, humid month of June was dragging by. Clemmy had still not brought herself to go to the county seat to buy slaves. She had mentioned to some of the neighbors who called that she might be interested. She remembered that Pa had not particularly been in favor of owning other folks. She hesitated, toiling in the fields to try to keep the crops ahead of the weeds. It was a losing battle. As she worked, she ran the incident of the rescue by the handsome young man through her mind, time after time. She began to feel guilty about not even having said thank you to him. After all, maybe some men were not all bad. Pa was a man, and he was the best human in the whole wide world and Georgia.

One afternoon Clemmy went to the smoke house, selected a large sugar-cured ham from the many hanging on hooks. It was about time to make the acquaintance of the lady of the house on the farm next to hers. A sudden realization came to Clemmy. She had never associated the blonde, blue-eyed man with a woman. Now that the possibility crossed her mind, a feeling of puzzlement came over her. Why did she feel this way? After all, most men she knew about chose to be married at a young age. They needed help to survive the double drudgery of working a farm. Was he married? What kind of woman would he have chosen? "Well, married er not, I gotta go an thank him fer doing what he done fer me." She carefully wrapped the ham, then put it in a sack to make it easier to carry.

It was a sweltering hot afternoon but Clemmy made her way briskly up the path. She climbed the rail fence, entering the pasture they had just begun to clear from an overgrowth of sassafras, wild cherry, and rosebud. The larger oak trees had been left to be plowed around. Their stumps were just too hard to move. Little nagging twinges of timidity began to eat at Clemmy as she approached the cabin. The front door was open. She could see a negro slave busily doing the house chores. A fat black baby cooed in the crib near an open window. Clemmy knocked at the door jamb, clearing her throat to get the attention of the girl. Sally turned and saw her. "My, my, I shore nuff didn't see ya thar, Miss. Oh! Yo am jes as purty as Massa John say." Clemmy felt the heat of embarrassment rise to her cheeks. "Do come on in the house whilst I fetch a cole drink from the well out yonder." Sally indicated a chair, took an oaken bucket from the stand, then headed for the well. Clemmy sat nervously, crossing and uncrossing her feet. She watched the fat, happy child as he batted a string laden with hickory nut shells which was strung across his crib. Clemmy laughed aloud, feeling an urge to pick the child up. Sally returned quickly, offering a dipper of cool water from the bucket. It did taste good. After she had drunk Clemmy asked, "Where might the lady o' the house be?" "They ain't no lady o' this here house Missy. This here is the house where Massa John sleep. I is the onliest married woman on dis here farm. My husban is called Rufus. We live in the cabin yonder." She waved her arm in the direction of the newly constructed cabin. "Tobe, he still sleep in the barn loff. We gonna build his house later. They all been so busy, we jes ain't had time."

Clemmy indicated the sack which she had laid on the floor beside the chair. "I brung this here ham. Pa was rite good at sugar-curin. Mayhap Mr. ah, ah," she suddenly realized she had never even heard his name. "His name be John Bolt, Missy. Sometime we calls him Johnny Boy." Clemmy was shocked. She had never heard such disrespect from a slave. Clemmy stammered just a little. "I would lak ta pay my respec ta Mr. Bolt. After all we air neighbors. I own thet farm jes over yonder." "I know who yo be, Missy. Massa John done tole us all about how he went to yor place fer a sociable call. I don't reckon thet other feller been back?" Sally answered her own question. "Nope. These men here keep a good watch on yore farm since thet day. No siree! Ain't nobody gonna bother yo no more." Clemmy didn't know that she had been such an object of attention. "Wait here, Missy, I run fetch Massa John. They all at the smithy over there." She made a fast exit, lifted her skirt a bit and began to run toward the shop.

Clemmy's attention once again turned to the baby cooing in the crib. She had never seen anything so appealing in all her life. Clemmy took the tail of his little dress and wiped the sweat from his smiling upturned face. They were friends from then on.

A small breeze had come up and Clemmy went to the door to catch some of the cool air borne by it. She saw John Bolt walking briskly toward the house. Suddenly he made a detour into the hickory grove along the creek. Sally come on to the house. "John

Boy, he went ter de creek. He gonna wash up some afore he come on in ta see ya, Missy. Blacksmithin ain't jes the cleanest wok they be, Missy."

The baby began to fuss so Sally went to the crib to pick him up. "This here is Wilfred John Bolt. Ya see, me and Wilfred we belong to Massa John. Tobe an Rufus, they be freemen. They be made free by Massa Tony afore we come ta Cherokee County."

John emerged from the trees, his hair still dripping water, he dried his hands on the sides of his trousers as he neared the door of the cabin. "Howdy, Miss Bandy." Clemmy thrilled at the pleasantness of his low, forceful voice. "It shore is rite nice uv ya ta come ta call." The wetness of his curly blond hair caused a little trickle of water to course down his forehead, then drip off the end of his slightly crooked nose. He self-consciously wiped at it with the sleeve of his shirt. An endless silence descended. Sally broke the spell. "I jes gotta go ta my house now ter feed Wilfred. I got the evenin vittles all done fix. Call me an I come a runnin to put it on de table." With that, Sally left in the direction of her own house. John looked at Clemmy, they both started to talk at once. "Come sit on the porch. It's gotta be a heap cooler out there." John indicated a swing which had been fashioned from willow limbs, then hung by chains to the cabin porch roof. They sat as Clemmy told John of her first encounter with the storekeeper, then the second. John was there for the third. She felt that it was necessary to tell about Zeb Turney in order to make it known to John that all that the hateful man had said about her was a lie. She stammered out her embarrassment as she tried to make John understand that she had never known a man in the way that the storekeeper had inferred. "Don' trouble yursef about that none, Miss Clemmy. I seen his kind from here to Savannah. He is jes the kind that Tony Larkin wuda sed needed hurtin."

For decency's sake, they left the door to the house open as they went inside to eat the evening meal. Sally was a very good cook. The corn bread was flavored with cracklins, young summer turnips cooked with parts of the tops still intact, pie made with fresh blackberries picked just that very morning. They ate like healthy young people do, each trying to tell the other as much as they could about themselves. John went back to his beginning apprenticeship in the shop in Savannah. Clemmy told about the happy days with her Pa when they were just beginning to clear the farm.

Soon, whippoorwills began to call in the tangled rosebud bushes along the edge of the woods. Clemmy looked through the open doorway. "Lordy, I been settin here and did not even notice thet it is gittin towards dark. I gotta be gittin on, Mr. Bolt. Peers lak I jes talked myself inta a walk in the dark." She picked up the sack she had brought the ham in, and started toward the door. John followed her onto the porch. "Miss Clemmy, it would please me mightily if'n yo would let me walk to yore house with ya." Clemmy was not in the least afraid to walk in the open fields and meadows at night. She had done it many times. She particularly liked to stroll in the moonlight, listening to the night sounds all around her. This night, however, she pretended to be just a little apprehensive about the trip through the field. "I ain't skeered at all, Mr. Bolt, but iff'n yore a mind ta, mayhap ya could walk with me at least ta the rail fence."

The stars were bright, with just a half moon to give a little light. John fell in behind her, marveling at her fast walk. She seemed to glide through the fields. Her long black hair waved in the breeze behind her as they continued to talk about the things that interested young people; one a total country girl, while he was a boy from one of the larger cities in the state of Georgia. When they reached the rail fence which divided the two farms, Clemmy did not hesitate. She swung easily to the top rail, stood up and walked along like a circus performer on a tight rope. Her magnificently formed young body was silhouetted against the darkness of the night sky. John caught his breath at the sheer beauty of her. She laughed, "Come on scardy cat, see iff'n ya can walk the rail." John climbed to the rail and began to follow. She ran a few steps then jumped lightly down on her side of the fence. "I kin run on from here, Mr. Bolt." John stepped close to her, catching both her hands. "I ain't gonna let ya go till yo promise not ta call me Mr. Bolt." Clemmy didn't resist his light hold on her hands. She looked up and smiled. "Awright, John, my name is Clemmy." "I ain't goin back now, Clemmy. I jes happent to think thet ya got a heap o' chores to do at yore place yet." Clemmy had been so lost in the excitement of her newfound friend that she, too, had forgotten. John took the lead, heading for the Bandy barnyard.

They worked together feeding pigs, the cow, mules, sheep,

and closing the chicken coops to keep other animals out. When they had finished, they strolled to the porch of the house. When they reached the heavy door, Clemmy turned to extend her hand. John took the small workworn hand in both of his. He gently squeezed her fingers. "Clemmy, I. . .I. . .gotta. . .I wanta. . ." With that he turned quickly, and strode toward his own farm. Clemmy had never felt so excited in all her life. Her heart began to pound as she opened the heavy door to go inside. She closed the door, leaning her back against it. She pressed the panel hard, as though she could lean back into the arms of John Bolt. She hummed a happy song as she prepared for bed.

John's head was in the stars as he made his way back up the footpath. He found himself comparing the half-Indian girl to the glamorous beauty of Jeanine Le Clere. Many times John had thought of his first love. The face of the enchanting French girl became dim to him now. Instead, there was the outline of a lithe-bodied country girl balanced on a rail in the pale moonlight. Jeanine would always be a beautiful memory to John Bolt, but this half Cherokee girl possessed a charm which was just indescribable. As the rail fence came into view, he imagined he could hear her soft laughter as she chided him about being afraid to run the top rail. When he neared his own house, he began to invent reasons why he would have to go back to the Bandy farm very soon. A small red fox crossed the path in front of him, disappearing into a tangle of blackberry bushes. "God made a whole bunch o' purty things, Mr. Fox, yo and her are two o' them." John removed his clothes, fell across the bed for a night of restless sleep.

As the summer dragged on Clemmy did not find it necessary to buy slaves. The path between their farms became a road with a pole gate in between. Since John had not had time to get all his crops planted, they all concentrated on producing a bumper crop for Clemmy. They worked out what they thought would be an equitable exchange. John, Tobe, and Rufus were to furnish the manpower to harvest the crops. Clemmy, in turn, was to furnish them with the seed it would take for the next year's crop.

The huge draft mares John had bought in Savannah were the envy of the county. The pulling power of the powerful matched horses was unequaled in that part of the country. They would hook them to a stump in the field, the well-cared for team would lean into their collars, the stump would begin to move. Hour after hour, the three men would labor in the humid Georgia sun. They would use Friday and Saturday as blacksmith days. Their neighbors soon learned that it was just no use taking things to the Bolt shop on any other day. The skill and speed of the three men working together would soon turn out more work than twice their number. The speed with which Tobe could shoe a horse or mule was just unbelievable. The plantation owners from around the country heard of the fine work of this particular smith, they began to try to buy the huge machine-like black man. John would protest vehemently that both Tobe and Rufus were free men, not to be bought or sold, but to go where they chose at whatever time they chose to do it. As John would get upset over the many attractive offers, Rufus would tell them that he wasn't going anywhere except where John was. Tobe would just grin his toothless grin as he kept on working.

They charged a fair price for their work, but seldom too little. Soon their mutual savings became quite an impressive sum. Since the work on the farms was so demanding, coupled with the extra work of the blacksmith shop, they decided to hire a crew of men skilled in building to come onto the place to build a house for Tobe. Rufus and Sally's cabin was added on to, to make more room for their first baby boy and others which were bound to be there before too many years went by.

A new barn was raised so that John could begin his dream of being a breeder of fine horses. He wanted the giant brood Percheron mares to become the matriarchs of a large stable of magnificent draft horses. He and Tobe traveled to Atlanta to buy a fine stallion of the same breed. All of this purchasing power was made possible by the skill of all three of them in the blacksmith trade. By this time, they could have abandoned the farming and gone strictly into the tool mending and horseshoeing trade. But, their first dream was to have a beautiful farm. They were working toward this end. Their land was being cleared for the planting of fruit trees on the steeper slopes, while they were reserving the flatter portion for the planting of cotton when spring rolled around again.

The southern states of the United States were kings of cotton then. Right here in their own Georgia, Yale graduate Eli Whitney, some time after the year 1792, had invented the cotton gin to increase the production of that crop a hundred fold. Seeds which were separated from the fiber by hand labor, were now separated by the marvel of the Whitney machine. Mr. Whitney also contributed to the horror which was to befall the same state, by the invention of interchangeable parts for firearms. That was yet to come. Now the world was a huge and exciting challenge for those at the John Bolt farm.

Eliza Clementine Bandy was caught up in that same wonderful exciting whirl. By now she had become used to Rufus and Tobe being around her barn and house. They came and went, as the work demanded.

The more often John Bolt came to visit her, the more she looked forward to the next trip. Her heart would begin to beat faster as she saw him striding down the path with that long easy gait which seemed to make him glide, instead of walk. Her horrible experience with the storekeeper, Zeb Turney, as well as her vow to never have anything to do with men, were just about forgotten in her anxiety to see the handsome face of the blonde-haired neighbor.

She had begun to take more care with the combing of her long black hair. She had even had Rufus and Sally take her into town where she bought new clothes. That evening she put on her prettiest white dress, made her way down the path toward the Bolt farm. She knew that John would be on that same path headed in the other direction. She saw him coming. The same exciting feeling caused her blood to race. She ran, just a little so that she would be at the rail fence at the same time he arrived. She reached the fence before he did. Clemmy climbed to the top, balancing on the top rail. She called to John as he quickened his stride to reach her. "I know yore a scardy cat to walk the top rail. The first time yo walked it, yo fell off." The evening summer breeze caused the thin cotton dress to cling to her supple young body. John caught his breath at the sheer excitement of her. Her light brown skin and black hair contrasted with the whiteness of her dress. What a glorious sight to behold. She was laughing at him now. He ran to the fence, took hold of the hem of her skirt, pretending to pull her off the top rail. He noted that she still wore beaded moccasins. John pinched her toe through the finely tanned leather. In an effort to free her toe, Clemmy lost her balance. She half jumped and half fell toward him. Her arms went around his neck as his strong arms encircled her slender waist. Her mouth was near his ear. She whispered breathlessly, "Ya made me bump ma lip on yore head, Johnny Bolt." John gently wound his hand into her thick black hair, forcing her face up toward his. "I aim ta fix thet fer ya, Clemmy Bandy." John lowered his mouth to hers, then Clemmy Bandy became lost in the rapture of her first kiss from a man. Their mouths sought each other hungrily. All the pent up passionate emotion in both of them began to release in the ecstasy of the moment. Could there be anything in heaven to equal the magic of this breathless moment?

Clemmy seemed to lose consciousness as his strong arms encircled her to hold her close. When his embrace became even more insistent, she became just a little frightened. Clemmy turned her head to one side, gently pushed her hands against his strong chest. "Please, Johnny," she whispered. He felt the rise and fall of her hard young breasts against him. Again, "Please, Johnny." "Oh, Clemmy, you precious and beautiful darlin." John could hardly speak. Again, she pushed gently against him. As he released her, she leaned weakly back against the rail fence. John moved toward her in an effort to kiss her again. "No, Johnny, I reckon I could not hold out against another kiss from you. Peers lak I done let it go too far as it be." "We will go all the way to the preacher, Clemmy, iff'n ya jes say ya will." "Course I will, John, yo done know thet. I cain't git ya shut o' my mind even fer jes a little while." "Clemmy, I been wanting to touch ya fer a long, long time. Ever since I walked home with ya fum my house thet night." "I think we have touched about all we are about ta fer awhile, John Bolt." "Clemmy, less go tell the others that we are going to git married as soon as the parson in one o' them churches in the county seat will say the words fer us."

They held hands and ran along the path toward the house that Clemmy was soon to call her own. As they both tried to tell the news at once to the others, Sally began to swish her skirts and sway to a song she made as she went along. "Lawdy, lawdy, lawdy me, there gonna be a big time jubilee."

Plans began that very night for a wedding in September. Clemmy was shy about having a big wedding, but the gregarious John felt that a joyous occasion like the one they planned should be open to all who might hear about it. Through the month of August, when a customer would come to blacksmith shop, he suddenly became an invited guest to the wedding. The preacher from the nearest Protestant Church was to come to the Bolt farm on the first day of September, musicians were hired for the party that was to follow the ceremony. Before the great day had arrived, John and Clemmy went to the county seat to record their names on the wedding license. John signed in the beautiful artistic form so carefully carefully copied in the cottage in Savannah. It was the only word he had ever learned to write. Clemmy painstakingly placed an X on the line indicated for her signature. She had never learned to write even her name. She never did. The embarrassment of the moment did not dampen the spirits of the indomitable Clemmy for very long. She was the proudest woman in the world as she left the county court house on the arm of John Bolt.

Friendly neighbors from near and far had volunteered to bring good food of every description. Georgia could produce about any delicacy there was to mention. Great tubs of sweet corn, whole hams roasted over charcoal fires, huge kettles of black-eyed peas, shelled peas and string beans. There was just about all the different wild game that could be thought of. Wagons and buggies began arriving early in the afternoon. Corn whiskey and apple cider were much in evidence.

After the ceremony, the grand party lasted until the sky was beginning to turn pink in the east. The dancing was in the yard where there was plenty of room. Sally, Tobe and Rufus joined the slaves who had been brought along as wagon drivers and servants. They, too, had a glorious time. They danced to the rhythm of their stamping feet and clapping hands. The off key strains of a banjo and fiddle furnished whatever melody they felt they needed. As the morning put in its appearance, sleepy children were roused from their resting places to be put aboard buggies and wagons for the journey home; some near, some quite far. The Bolt wedding was an affair to be remembered and talked about for months to come.

John and Clemmy had long since slipped away from the celebration to make their way hand in hand to the house where she was born. In the very bed where Little Dove had given her life to let Clemmy live, she again pledged her vow with John Bolt to love and cherish each other until death would them part. They both were sure that nothing in heaven could be greater than their love for each other. This was September 4, 1842.

Clemmy and John lived in the Bandy house, leaving the other farm complex to Tobe, Rufus and the two slaves which now belonged to John: Sally, the happy growing baby boy, and another on the way. Clemmy never got around to buying the slaves she had thought about. John would not have permitted it anyway. The honeymoon was not over, in fact had just begun, when Clemmy discovered that she, too, was as fertile as her Georgia fields. She told Sally of her symptoms. The black girl gave a delighted giggle and clasped Clemmy in her arms. From that day on, Clemmy never again thought of herself and Sally as mistress and slave. They depended upon each other. When Clemmy told John that night, he held her close as he stroked her long black hair. "Clemmy, honey, everything on this here farm is gonna produce." He patted her on the rump. "Yore ever bit as good as them brood mares. I spec they will be ready to foal about the same time you are. Yours won't haveta be branded though. An effen he be a little stud, we might jes as well keep him fer breedin stock, too." "John Bolt, the way you talk is a scandal. We gonna haff ta start goin to church so that when the baby gits here, he ain't gonna be no heathen. He is gonna be brung up right." Clemmy was remembering her Pa saying that her Indian mother, Little Dove, wanted her to be a lady. Clemmy's morals were certainly not anything to be ashamed of, however, her refinements in etiquette were something that had not been a part of her education.

One day Tobe joined John where he was mending fences for the milk cow pasture. His usual mumbling speech was even harder for John to understand, since Tobe would look at the ground and barely speak with enough force to be heard. "What in tarnation is a troublin ya, Tobe? I cain't hear a word yore a sayin." "Ah been keeping some money back, Massa John. I been keepin it back in gold." "Well, hit aire yore money ta keep, Tobe. What's so all fired important about thet?" "I been goin over ta da Rodgers' plantation ta shoe da mules, Massa John." "I gotta keep tellin ya, Tobe, yore a free man ta go anywhares ya got a mind ta." "I knows, Massa John." Tobe began to spread the loose dirt in the wagon road with his bare foot. All at once, Tobe grabbed John by the arm, his big hard hands were like a steel vise on John's forearm. "I gotta ask sompin ob ya, Massa John." "Then ask hit afore ya tear ma arm outen the socket." "Dere be dis gal, she some younger dan me, she look at me more den one tam, Massa John. She look at old Tobe an I don git da feelin dat she see jes what a ugly one o God's creatures I is. She look at me tender lak, Massa John. Some of da odder slaves tell me that da Rodgers family might sell her. Seems lak she ain't never been able ta produce no chilen ta hep bill up dey stock. I wonts her, Massa John. She look at me so kine. Buy her fo me, Massa John, jes lak ya buy Sally fuh Rufus. We use da gold I sabe, Massa John, but dey ain't gonna sell huh ta no slabe. Ask yo missus ta go buy huh and say she be fur er own survant." "Tobe, if you done made up yore mind she is the woman ya want, then me and Clemmy shore as hell is gonna buy her. What name do they call her, Tobe?" "Dey calls her Cissy, Massa John. Do she not wanta stay here wid old ugly Tobe, den jes sot huh free, Massa John, could'n ya do jes dat?" "Yore one of the bess men I ever know, Tobe. She is gonna wanna stay fer shore." "Buy huh soon, Massa John, fore dey sides ta sell huh ta some odder place." "Me an Clemmy gonna buy Cissy tamorra, Tobe." "One more thing, John Boy. Reckon we might git married jes lak real folks? Seem lak dat be da thing ta do." "We gonna have ourselfs another jubilee, Tobe!" "Don' reckon so, Massa John. Don' want too much tenchion called ta darkies, specially a freed man lak me. I jes wan Cissy ta be mine. Please tell huh thet I be good ta huh, Massa John." "We aim ta tell her awright, Tobe. She is gonna stay. Yu'll see. Yes sir, yu'll see."

The Rodgers plantation was one of the best customers of the Bolt blacksmith shop. There seemed to be always an order of some sort waiting to be picked up for the Rodgers plantation. This time, instead of waiting for them to send for it, John had the newly sharpened tools and the mended wagon wheels loaded into his wagon for delivery to the big plantation further down the creek. John felt they needed to make a very good impression upon the rich plantation owner. He put on his best clothes with his high topped boots. He had Clemmy dress from bonnet to shoes.

By midmorning they had reached the gates of the huge plantation. The gigantic white columned house sat way back from the public road. White painted fences surrounded the entire front of the grassed plantation yard. The entrance to the big house was a circular drive paved with bricks. Further down the road, there was a wooden gate which opened to the road leading to the barns and slave quarters. This is the gate which John and Clemmy entered. Field after field of maturing cotton stretched away from the plantation yards, then diminished into the horizon. It seemed to Clemmy and John that there was enough cotton right here on the Rodgers place to supply the entire world. When they reached the barnyard, an aging negro came to the wagon to inquire about their presence there. John knew the overseer, he asked for him by name. "I come ta see Jack Clemmons. I brung his smithy work from my shop up the creek. Tell him John Bolt wants ta see him." "Yass suh. We fotch boss Jack right away. He in da close fiel taday." The old man summoned a half-naked little boy from the shade of the barn roof. "Skeeter, yo skin outen here dis minute an fine boss Jack. Tell him Massa Bolt are here ta talk wid him."

John and Clemmy looked in the direction the little boy ran. In the distance there were rows of slaves, both men and women working in the cotton fields. It was just the beginning of cotton picking time. They could see a figure on horseback sitting in the shade of a distant tree. The old man came back to the wagon to invite the newcomers to step down and go into the shade of the overhanging barn roof. They watched the little boy grow smaller as he approached the horseman. The figure reached down, swung the little black boy to the back of the saddle, then came up the dusty road at a gallop. The delighted little slave boy was hanging on to the saddle shouting in sheer delight. Jack Clemmons was widely known for his ability as an overseer of a big plantation. He made the fields produce to the very last inch of the soil. He had a firm persuasive way of working the slaves to make them strain to his bidding. He was a kindly man who did not believe in applying the whip, except in the most gross breach of discipline. He did, however, often use the threat of selling this one or that one to the plantations in Mississippi. They had all heard countless stories about the fate of a slave sold to the big plantations further west. When a slave was particularly bad, or shirked his duties consistently, then a sale to a driver who come by occasionally in a covered wagon was whip enough for the others who were left behind.

Jack approached Clemmy and John. He lifted his straw hat from his bald head, gave the a big grin. "How do, Miss Bolt. Nice day ta see ya. How do, John. How come they send the boss man ta deliver my smithy work?'' Jack knew the value of a good tradesmen, thus made it a point to be friendly. They visited for a while about the crops and the weather. Finally John came to the point of their visit. ''Jack, the missus is goin ta have a baby fore long, an I aim ta git her a gal ta look after her whilst she ain't too strong. Then a good slave kin serve as a mammy fer tha youngun.'' Jack Clemmons spat a stream of tobacco juice at a crack in the barn wall. His wide friendly grin was even bigger. ''Miz Bolt, from what I hear bout the Bolt farm, John here is gonna need all the hep he kin git. Maybe ya could see fittin ta give him twin boys as a start.'' Both men laughed. Clemmy lowered her head in embarrassment. ''I aim ta try real hard ta keep up with the size of the farm, Mister Clemmons.'' ''I ain't got no say about buying and sellin this here stock. Hit gotta be the decision o Mister Rodgers. Skeeter, skeedaddle ta the house and tell Mr. Rodgers thet me an the blacksmith, Mr. Bolt, wanna talk to him.'' Skeeter took off like his namesake. Clemmons admired John's team of huge mares. He walked up to the head of each of them telling them what beautiful ladies they were. John told him the date they were bred to the same kind of stud. ''Ya got a market fer them colts afore they hit the ground. Mister Rodgers ull pay ya top dollar. Don' offer em till we have a chanct ta bargain with ya.'' Skeeter returned to extend an invitation to them to join Mr. Rodgers on the porch.

As they made their way to the big house, Clemmy became apprehensive and clung to John's arm. When they approached, Rodgers rose from a cane backed chair, nodding to Clemmy. ''How do, Miz Bolt.'' He extended his hand. ''John, how are things at the Bolt place?'' John nervously rolled his hat in his hands. ''Jes fine, Mr. Rodgers, sir.'' John was plainly ill at ease before the rich landowner. The older man reassured him by slapping him on the shoulder. ''Tell ya this, fore sure, you got the best blacksmith in the whole county. If ya ever feel ya need more financin for yore shop, jes tell me, Bolt. Ya could expand into a regular foundry.'' ''Thank ya, Mr. Rodgers, but I jes as soon stay lak I be. We ain't had no schoolin, so jes don think we could handle anything more.'' Jack Clemmons addressed his boss. ''Mr. Rodgers, Miz Bolt is gonna have a baby pretty soon an she needs ta buy one o your wenches help with tha work.'' ''Well now, we got some real fine ones that could do the job jes fine, Mis Bolt. Trouble is, it happens ta be right at the start of the cotton pickin time. We need all the hands we got. Havin to hire some contract labor from out of Atlanta." John felt his heart sink at the decision of the landowner. He could just see the hurt in poor Tobe's scarred face when he had to tell him the news. "Sorry, Miz Bolt. Maybe later in the season, when there ain't so much rush to get the crops in." "My man Rufus and his wife, Sally, been comin over here fer some time now, Mr. Rodgers. They come to make the deliveries. They know of one of yours thet would do jes fine." John thought there would be no harm in trying just one more time. "Her name is Cissy." Rodgers looked inquire-ingly at his overseer. "I'd like ta do some business with Mr. Bolt here, Jack." "She is a big strong wench, Mr. Rodgers. Ya cain't rightly spare her from the fields right now. Howsomever, John is goin ta see his mares foal fore too long, Mr. Rodgers. Them two matched percheron mares ya seen las month down at yore stable. Ya could sell Cissy if'n John would agree to a coupla things. Let Cissy stay here till the cotton pickin is all done. Then give yo first call at a colt." "I aim ta pay fer Cissy in gold, Mr. Rodgers. Whatever is a fair price fer her." "You go along with Jack's idee, Mr. Bolt?" Clemmy spoke up, "Iffen ya let her come ta us on Sunday till they end o January, Mr. Rodgers. Theta way she could start gitten used to our place, the way I want her ta work." "It's a deal, Mr. Bolt." The price was set, the money paid. Jack stepped to the edge of the porch. "Skeeter, run to the field to fetch Cissy. Tell her ta stop at the wash stands and clean up some. Fetch her here to the front porch." "Yes suh, boss, I run fass." Jack Clemmons got up from his chair and excused himself. "There is a heap of work to be done yet today, so I better ride on back ta that field." He backed away from the porch, headed down the path to the stables. Rodgers watched him go, "Good man, that Jack. He kin do more with the workers than any man I ever seen." Rodgers sent a servant for cool drinks and some morning pastries. Before long, a big framed black woman rounded the corner of the house, holding the hand of the now tired little Skeeter. Her head was swathed in a cotton rag tied loosely at the back of her neck. She had no shoes on her feet as field hands seldom did. Her skin was as black as ebony, her large breasts were heaving from the effort of her fast walk on this hot Georgia morning. Sweat trickled down her face. Big wet patches showed where her dress clung to her body. John judged her to be at least six feet tall. She approached the trio on the porch. "I be Cissy, Massa Rodgers." She was obviously frightened at the presence of the master. She had no idea why she had been summoned from the field. She was sure it was something to be dreaded. "I bin a good gal, Massa, I wok haad. I never leave tha fiel, Massa, till it be dak." Cissy bowed even lower, and shuffled her bare feet. "Stan up, gal. You ain't got a cause to make excuses. This here is Mr. and Miz John Bolt. They jes bought you. They gonna send someone fer you next Sunday." The fear and apprehension showed clearly on the anguished face of the big black girl. "Doan sell me, Massa, I wok haada, jes doan sell me." Cissy began to whimper. She did not know her fate. Clemmy felt a surge of pity for the poor girl. "You gonna like it, Cissy. Ya won be no field hand no more. Ya gonna hep me have my baby. I be the wife of the blacksmith up the creek." Cissy looked up in surprise. For the first time she realized that she was not being sold for punishment. She remembered that the giant Tobe was a smith, that his master had a shop some distance up the creek. "Lawdy, oh lawdy, lawdy." "You can go now, Cissy," Rodgers spoke to the now relieved black girl. "Yas Massa," she turned, retreated toward the quarters. "I'll have Jack explain our deal ta her, Mr. Bolt, an I hope ta see ya'all again soon." They both realized the polite dismissal, and rose to go. As they rounded the corner of the great house, John mumbled to Clemmy, "I know he thinks we air jes a coupla crackers, I reckon he is right." Clemmy giggled, really content with her station in life.

The ride back to the Bolt farm was a joyous one as they rehearsed just how they would tell Tobe about the purchase of the woman of his choice. As they turned off the main road and reached the shop, they could see Tobe waiting patiently in the front of the forge area. They climbed down from the wagon, both tried to speak at once. "Ya got the one ya wanted, Tobe!" John playfully slapped the big man's cheeks. "She de one I want, Massa John, now we see eff'in I be de one she lak ta have. There ain't no other woman ever look at me that way Cissy does, Massa John. By an by she maybe care fer old Tobe, too." She did with all her heart!

Every moment Tobe was not working, Cissy was at his side, seeing to his comfort and just plain keeping him company. Never in her life had she been wanted because she was just a person. She made the big ugly Tobe feel as though he were the greatest man in the whole wide world. She did indeed look at him kindly. The greatest pastime she and Tobe could derive from the Bolt farm was to go down to the creek to see if they could catch a bigger fish than they caught the last time they were there. The big creek was not too far from the houses and barns. Along the creek bends there was the ever-present tangle of blackberry bushes, gum trees, redbud, hickory, and elm trees.

Tobe and Cissy got to know every fishing hole on the creek in both directions from the house, as far as they felt like going. That was not too far, for they could catch fish just about anywhere they reached the water. The game, however, was never ending for them. Cissy could cook the catfish in several delicious ways. They all lived off the land, the land was bountiful, so they were spending some very happy days. Tobe had never known such happiness in all his battered life. Time after time he would thank John and Clemmy for bringing Cissy to him. They would have been content to live out their lives in the small cabin on the farm. They worked from sun up till sundown with never a complaint. They felt that the work they did was for them.

After the long cotton picking season was over, Cissy came to the Bolt farm to live, instead of just visiting on Sundays. She was home at last!

CHAPTER 8
TROUBLED PARADISE

John and Clemmy were living their own kind of blissful life in the Bandy house. Although she was beginning to show from the little one she expected, she was still very active with the farm work. She would take a shotgun, then go to the fields to shoot bobwhite quail for their supper. She was so skilled that she never wasted a shot. John would marvel at the way she could fire a rifle with such unerring accuracy that she could shoot a running rabbit at unbelievable distances. Every time Clemmy would make an unusually difficult shot, she would jump up and down in glee.

When the cold rains would come, they would curl up together in front of the big fireplace, dreaming their dreams together. The world just wouldn't dare treat them unkindly. Clemmy would occasionally take a drag or two from John's corncob pipe. It began to happen so often that John would laugh and say, "Clemmy, effen yore gonna burn out my cob pipe by smokin it, jes make one fer yerself and kinly leave mine in ma mouth." She did.

Although John did not learn to read or write, he was a planner. He would map out a course of action, then make it happen. Soon he began to design, then build, stables to house the work and saddle horses he began to trade for and breed. The farm produced their food, as well as feed for the livestock, while the blacksmith shop furnished money to buy the things they had dreamed about owning. John was the planner, the others followed, toiling to accomplish the goals they would set for themselves.

The Bolt farm became the horse-breeding headquarters for that part of Georgia. Never would John sacrifice the purity of his stock in order to produce more. Every animal had to come up to his standard. While other farmers were improving the quality of their homes, the Bolt crew was improving the desirability of the livestock they raised. Steam powered sawmills were being established by then. The prolific timber was being harvested as fast as big crews of slaves and millhands could bring it to the saw. Hickory, oak and wild pecan were in great demand for the construction of wagons and other implements. Sawmills brought more demand for the skill of the blacksmith. It seemed the work was never ending. Tobe and Rufus were forced to expand the shop, to take on other help to turn out the orders which came to them. No matter how they were tempted, they never turned out an inferior piece of work.

Winter rains set in, turning the clay wagon roads into rivers of red mud. Work was at a standstill, except for the endless round of daily chores which the farm animals demanded. It was a matter of fact, a way of life for all of them, so they never had time to think that there were more pleasant ways to spend early mornings and late evenings. On weekends, they would all get together at one house to talk and sing into the early morning hours. The negroes knew ballads and spirituals which had been passed on to them from the slaves at the neighboring plantations. The religious songs would take on the flavor of hero worship ballads. "Joshua fit da Battle O Jerico, Jerico and de walls come a tumblin down. Go down Moses, down inter Egyp lan, tell ole Pharo let mah people go. Ezekial saw de wheel way up in da middle of de air, da little wheel run by faith and da big wheel run by da grace o God, Zekial saw da wheel way up in the middle of da air. Roll Jordan Roll, roll Jordan roll, I wanna go to heben when I die to see ole Jordan roll." Verse after verse of the different themes would roll off their tongues as though they lived every minute of the mental picture they painted. They would all harmonize as they kept the rhythm by clapping their hands while stomping their feet. When the rhythm was particularly good, Rufus and Sally would get up to dance their own version of the Irish jig. Sally was big with her second child, while Clemmy was getting uncomfortable with her first. Being pregnant did not faze the ever active Sally. On the other hand, it seemed to weigh heavily upon Clemmy. Although she felt terrible at times, her love for the handsome John Bolt grew with every passing day. She had thought that no man could ever replace the love she had held in her heart for her Pa. He was still there alright, but now John

Bolt was in her thoughts during every waking hour, also many times during her sleep. The brood mares were about to foal. John would light his lantern and go to the stable in the barn at odd hours of the night to look after them. They were his second love. They would gently nuzzle him, vying for his attention. John would pet them, talk to them as though they understood just what he was saying. After all, weren't they a big part of his dream.?

One morning John, with Clemmy by his side, went into the barn stable to find a stud colt pulling at the teats of his mother. John had not been needed at all. They rushed to the mare and colt to get a better look at the first foal produced on the Bolt horse farm. They shouted and laughed, frightening the bewildered little colt. He didn't stay frightened for long, the lure of the warm milk he was having dispelled all his fears. A few days later, another fine stud colt made his appearance in the barn. John had wished that it might be a little filly. Suddenly, with a pang of regret, John remembered that he had agreed to sell the first foals of these huge mares to Mr. Rodgers at the big plantation. Well, after all, a man's word was his bond. Tobe and Cissy were inseparable. They had been a good bargain after all. The mares would have other colts, while his old friend's happiness was of utmost importance. Rodgers had seen fit to charge John top dollar for Cissy. John grinned as he thought that now he had something that Rodgers would have to pay dearly for. After all, he was to raise them to sell anyway. They were livestock and had to be thought of as just that. Rodgers, on the other hand, dealt in human beings, he felt that they too were livestock. Cissy had been nothing more than a fine work animal to him. To him, there were three distinct kinds of people in the fine state of Georgia: slaves to be bought and sold; the poorer class of Georgia cracker; then there was the class of plantation owners, bankers, merchants and other property owners. This was the educated class which ran for political office and won. Customs and traditions of the old south were dictated by this class, it was ground into the minds of all who dwelt there, black, white, rich or poor. The fine minds of the middle and lower class whites were often wasted on this concept of southern gentleman, southern lady. Only those with the determinaton to succeed would be able to really assert themselves. John and Clemmy Bolt, along with all the people associated with them, were in that group. Rows of horse barns were added to the farm buildings. John saw his dream growing, coming true. Bolt horses, as well as Bolt blacksmith work, became known throughout that part of Georgia as only the very best.

Rufus never questioned the spending of the money he would earn as his part of the great effort. Tobe began to save portions of his by having John change it into small gold coins. No other person on the farm, except Cissy, knew where it was hidden. He often said, "It gonna be used some day agin bad times which is sho nuff shore to come."

Plantation owner Rodgers became very active in Georgia politics in those days. He had been elected to the Georgia legislature. Even though John Bolt was very young, he was looked up to by all the working, smaller farm class. Rodgers would often ride over to the smithy when he had a string of horses to be shod. The main reason for the ride was to visit with John. This young man's quiet, but forceful opinions could always be counted upon to represent the true thinking of the farmer class. He and John could never see eye to eye on the question of slavery, although John was now the owner of three human beings. Sally had presented him with another property in the form of a second healthy child. John made it known to everyone that as soon as he felt they would be safe on their own, he would promptly set them free. As this opinion became known across the farm roads and villages, there was a lot of hateful gossip directed toward him. Even the lowest cracker in the county could not, in his wildest imagination, see the sense of freeing a slave. It seemed the more uneducated they were, the more they felt that they must have something to look down upon. The lowly slave was it. John became known among the low have-nots as the "nigger-lovin Injun breeder." Clemmy was still not accepted into any society. After all, wasn't her Ma a full blooded Cherokee?

The Bolt farm could well afford the attention of a doctor. John, accompanied by Tobe, had ridden into town to make arrangements for the services of the best there was to be had. Despite the careful instructions of the doctor, Clemmy constantly felt bad. During the last days of her pregnancy, Cissy never left her side, night or day. Clemmy would never complain of the pain she was experiencing, although it was obvious to all who were close to her. Her face was drawn and pale. Her big dark eyes constantly reflected the fear she felt for the life of herself and her unborn. On the last day of May in 1843, Rufus rode their best saddle horse at a run to fetch the doctor. He arrived at the farm well before the baby, then decided to stay until the event took place. Clemmy was not feeling at all strong. A special room was prepared for both the mother and expected child. Big, strong Cissy was a constant comfort to everyone involved. "Dis here gonna be a boy, I say. Miz Clemmy carry him jes right fer to be a fine boy. Ain't no reason ta fuss, ever thing gonna be thout no trouble. De good lawd say dis here man chile be ready ta be borned, and borned he gonna be." Things did not go just as easily as Cissy had predicted. The doctor worked with all his knowledge and experience to save Clemmy and the baby. Wesley John Bolt made his appearance into the world early on the morning of June 1, 1843. He was a fine strong baby, crying lustily. Cissy took over, caring for him while the doctor spent all of his time with the failing Clemmy. John remembered how Clemmy had told him of the death of Little Dove, her mother, at the time Clemmy came into the world. A cold chill gripped the heart of John Bolt, he began to pray. "Dear God, I don' know much bout how ta talk ta ya. I din't have much chance ta larn about tha teaching o Jesus. Only'est thing ah kin do is ask thet ya spare ma Clemmy. She wants nothin but good fer everyone, God. She had sitch grand plans fer tha chile. She wants him ta have schoolin, God. Clemmy allus done what she think be right, God. Clemmy be'in half Injun don't make no difference, does it, God? She loves everybody no matter what they be." John had sunk to his knees in the barn lot. Soon he was joined by the giant Tobe and tender-hearted Rufus. They placed their tear-stained faces in the dirt and prayed with the only words they knew how. When Sally's oldest boy rounded the corner of the barn, he saw them there still on their knees in the dirt. "Momma say, da docta an Miz Clemmy wanna see Massa John." John sprang to his feet, he ran for the house. The other two were close behind. He rushed into the house to see the tired Dr. Rollins sitting in a chair in the living room. "She is fine, Mr. Bolt, jes fine. She is restin now and better that you not disturb her, but I feel that she is gonna be well an strong agin fore too long." The weight of the world rolled from the shoulders of the new young father. Tobe and Rufus began to chant, "Thanky Lord, thanky

Lord.'' They ran to tell everyone who would listen that there was a new boy on the place and Clemmy was fine.

Dr. Rollins again began to speak to John. Tears of joy were coursing down John's face. ''Wench, bring that boy here so his Pa will be able to get a better look.'' Cissy quickly complied with the shouted command. She came to John placing the bundled baby into his waiting arms. Of course, John held him as the most fragile of objects. ''I prayed, Doctor, yes sir, I prayed real hard fer this to be alright.'' ''Sometimes that is the way son, only God can be the final word. Now I gotta find me a whole hog to eat, and a place to sleep.'' Sally had the meal already on the table; the doctor and John ate heartily. Dr. Rollins went into a bedroom to sleep, John tiptoed into the room where his precious Clemmy was sleeping. He could see her breathing easily with the rise and fall of her full breasts, telling him that she was alive. He wanted to touch her. He spoke softly. ''Clemmy, we ain't had no larnin. Thet cain't make no difference, though, in how a man an a woman love. Ya tole me bout Little Dove crossin the big wide river. Reckon it jes weren't yore turn. I be so grateful ta God fer thet, Clemmy. Reckon hit makes no difference ta the good Lord how he be worshipped neither. Jes so's we know he be there, no matter what form he may take. Little Dove was Injun, but I low as how God were there ta cetch her han when she reached tother side. He lowed me ta keep ya, Clemmy and keep ya I will till it be my turn.'' John's tears fell on Clemmy's hand. He thought he saw a faint smile crease the corners of her full lips. He whispered. ''Sleep now darlin'. Our son gonna wanna talk ta ya bout dinner fore long.''

John left the room, and he too fell into an exhausted sleep. Wesley John Bolt had his first meal from the breast of the slave girl, Sally. It made not one bit of difference to that hungry baby what the color of the container might be. Clemmy quickly gained her strength, taking over the care of the newborn son herself. It was indeed a happy day at the Bolt farm as the first thin clouds of a horrible disaster for the nation were just beginning to gather on the horizon.

Another forge was added to the blacksmith shops; more stables added to the ones already there. John began to concentrate on the breeding of fine saddle horses as well as the magnficent work animals which grazed in the Bolt pastures. Everyone had all he or she could do to keep the work done. There were, however, times for fun and singing. John and Clemmy were now being invited occasionally to the big Rodgers plantation for dinner or an evening visit. They were well aware of the barrier of acceptance kept tightly drawn between them and the great southern society. It was difficult to get Clemmy to make the calls, but John and Mr. Rodgers were becoming good friends, always finding something to talk about. Still divided, however, on the subject of slavery. They had learned to just avoid the subject when they were together. It was becoming more and more evident that Rodgers was dealing with the seditious talk of rabble-rousers at the state level. He dismissed them as just a bunch of damn yankees down from the north to make trouble.

Great strides of progress were being made in Georgia, and the rest of the southern states. It seemed that the bountiful harvests, along with the manufactured goods would never cease. Steamboats were beginning to appear on all the rivers which would allow the shallow draft of the paddle wheels. Steam was now being harnessed to the maximum. Giant engines ran the sawmills. The forests yielded pine and hardwoods of several sought after varieties. The main buildings at the Bolt farm began to expand. In fact, they took on a look of elegance. Not a full-fledged plantation, just a prosperous farm. In the long twilight evenings when the whippoorwills began to call, Tobe and Cissy would stroll hand in hand to the creek. Each had a cane pole over a shoulder. Tobe carried the bait. Sometimes Cissy would walk ahead so as not to smell the stink of the concoction Tobe called fish food. He would mix bran with animal blood. "Simetimes jes a tech o garlic ta fotch out tha flavor." This evening Tobe said, "We gonna git old granpa fo sho." "Tobe, yo done a fishin fibber, thar haint no granpa fer as yo concern. Ever time yo cotch a big un, ya sa, 'no, thet haint ole granpa, thet jes one o his little boys'." Tobe slapped her on the ample behind. "Yo gonna see one o these days, Cissy. I gonna cotch the bigges catfish that ever swim in dis here creek. He gonna have whiskers all da way down to he tail. Maybe when I looks he in da eye, I say ta him, 'Howdy dere granpa! I been gonna git ya fer a long, long time.' Iffen he be a good spowt bout it and jes smile, den I take da hook outin he lip an push dat ole feller back in da creek. After all, he gotta make some mo o dem chilen o' his'n so's we kin fry em up nice an brown." They were content to just sit quietly on the creek bank, watching the muskrats and otters play along the reedy banks of the slow moving stream. Muskrats would swim near, then dive and disappear beneath the water at the edge. "See der, Cissy, dem muskrat gotta hole down here neath da bank. Dey digs up tords da tree roots, den dey make a big room, full o dry grass. Dey got a happy life, cept fer dem marsh hawks, er dem big black moccasins which is allus tryin ta eat em fer suppa. Da critters do jes lak folks, seem lak. Allus sompin ta take da happy outa living."

As darkness fell, they carried their catch of blue channel catfish toward their humble cabin. Tobe didn't tell her often of his love for her. She just knew. There were times when he would stare into the distance as though he could see beyond the life he was living. Cissy never interfered when Tobe was in such a mood.

The months stretched into years. The young of the farm grew strong and healthy. Young colts would frolic in the pastures beside the full-blooded mares which were the pride and joy of John Bolt. He would often tell Clemmy, "Nothing cept the finest, Clemmy. Effin hit caint be the finest, then hit jes caint be." Although they wished for their family to grow, for some reason Clemmy was unable to become pregnant again. Sally's oldest boy, Wilfred, was never far from young Wes. He had appointed himself the constant keeper of Wes Bolt during his early toddler stage. Both little Wes and the older black boy were with the horses throughout most of their formative years. Wes was riding by himself by the time he was five. Wilfred constantly on guard to see that he didn't fall. Wilfred had the happy disposition of his mother and father. By the time he was twelve, he was one of the best grooms in the country. John had taken on the Arabian line for his choice of saddle breeding stock. Wilfred would race the fastest ones in the shows at the County Fair. He appeared to be a part of the horse as he would coax the last ounce of speed from his mount. Many blue ribbons came to the Bolt farm, for both racing and showing. Plantation owners from miles around would buy the foals before they were even dropped. Both the draft animals and riding breed were the finest in northern Georgia.

Although Clemmy had never made an effort to take on "book larnin," as she called it, she nevertheless made sure that the education of young Wes was not neglected. John still kept his body in perfect shape. He insisted that everyone on the farm do the same. He, Rufus, and Tobe would still go through their judo routines. John felt that here was a perfect conditioner. Tobe would grumble about being much too old to take part in such foolishness. The others knew that if his big hands ever closed on them, the struggle was over.

Wes was a well-formed, handsome boy who had taken on the curly hair of his father, except that it was black to match the darker features of his half-Indian mother. His eyes were large and brown. One eye tooth slighly lapped over another to mar the perfection of his strong white teeth. He had never known a day's hunger, nor had he ever wanted for the love of other human beings. He was the object of worship of both his father and mother.

Sally kept the farm supplied with children. Now there were four, two boys and two girls. Wes learned quickly in school so he was the recorder on the farm. Everything which needed to be recorded was carefully written down in a leather-bound book. John was justly proud of this stock record book, although he could not read what it said. Wes would also read from the Bible, particularly the Book of Psalms which Clemmy dearly loved. As he would read, Clemmy would repeat the verses after him. Verse after verse was committed to memory. Clemmy's desire to memorize would heighten her son's ability to read. There was no person on earth more proud than Clemmy, that her Wes could read a book. By the time he was in his early teens, the storm clouds of a horrible holocaust were gathering on the not-too-distant horizon.

There came a man named Yancy, a smooth and even-tempered man. The Democratic Convention was to be held in Charleston in the spring of 1860. William Yancy was insistent upon the things he wanted for the nation. There were other marchers in the ranks, such as John Brown, Theodore Weld and others. There were ministers such as Charles G. Finney who spread the word of abolitionism like a plague which was running rampant and dividing the United States of America. It was a time in the land when people liked to listen to speeches. The more hell and brimstone spewed forth by the orator, it seemed, the more popular he would become. President Buchanan was trying desperately to walk the middle ground. This middle ground was fast eroding away to a fine line. When April 23rd, Convention time, rolled around, it seemed that a great wall of tension began to hang over the beautiful, peaceful, typically southern city of Charleston.

The sun sparkled on the waters of the bay. The prosperous city of about 50,000 gave way to the thickly forested rolling hills of the countryside. As the steamboats would arrive with more delegates from the north, they would gaze curiously at the crowds, always looking for a friend or ally. Charleston would have been a bonanza for the Bolt blacksmith shop. Iron work was the style of the day. Iron filigree and railings outlined the wide porches. Trimmed fences looked in upon flowering backyards. Is this the setting for a confrontation which would result in the loss of thousands of lives on both sides of the slavery controversy? The lines were already drawn. The decisions were already made. The Democratic party was in sympathy with slavery, both northerners and southerners. The Republicans were gathering to back Seward of New York, his innuendos concerning conflict were widely known. Senator Stephen A. Douglas of Illinois, a man whose expert political maneuvering had placed him in a most prominent position, was a scheming professional politician who was opening the doors for the fire storms which were to cover the land.

Charleston was not exactly the setting in which the Douglas faction would have chosen to fight. There was a very strong representation which was determined that Douglas would not win a position of prominence. For example, delegates were sent from Georgia, who were to declare vehemently that Douglas would just not do. Northern Democrats proclaimed loudly that they were fighting the South's battles. At this point, a Mississippian rose to declare loudly that 'Mississippi is able to fight her own battles and if not with the union, they could do it without the union.' Fire-eating secessionists from the South mingled with the throngs to spread word that the South was a cotton empire without the need of a north which was determined to do away with their means of progress, the slave. It was an idea, yet an idea which most southerners feared. There were, however, born and bred southerners who were to become violent abolitionists. Hinton Rowan Helper was one of those. He not only spoke violently against the system, he advocated that the slave owners themselves be treated as criminals. Not that Helper was so fond of the negro slave, he just had that sort of personality which inflamed people. He enjoyed this ability to the utmost. He had written a book, *The Impending Crisis of the South: How to Meet It,* which he published in 1857. By 1859, the book began to become an irritant to the whole nation. The book advocated that every southerner become an abolitionist. It was within this seething cauldron of political strife that young Wes Bolt was striving to become a man. His father, John, was finding it harder and harder to maintain his right to free the number of slaves which came under his ownership.

Wes was breaking a colt which had become his favorite. This special colt was two years old. The only blemish to mar the beauty of its magnificent sorrel coat was the Bolt brand low on its left hip. The colt carried his head high, true to the Arabian bloodline. John had not thought him to be of stallion quality so had gelded him at one year. His striking beauty, coupled with his ability to outrun every colt on the farm, had caught the eye of both John and Wilfred. They named him "Big Red," they began to handle him in the breaking corral before he was even old enough to mount. By the time he could hold the weight of Wes and the saddle, he was so tame that he never once offered to misbehave. All he needed was training. This, the two boys set out to do.

Wilfred rode an older, well-broken saddle horse while Wes rode along side. A bossal halter on the colt kept him well under the control of the groom on the older mount. One Sunday afternoon they rode to the general store in town; work for the colt as well as a chance for the boys to get away from the farm. This was a regular Sunday afternoon with people strolling around the town, or gathering in groups to discuss the latest politics or fashion. Young boys gathered to watch the proper young ladies pass by on the other side of the street. Although Wes knew most of the boys, he had never had a cross word with any of them. In every group there will always be a challenger. Wilfred knew that blacks were not allowed inside the store. He stayed with the horses while Wes went inside to buy refreshments. When he returned to the hitching rail, he handed Wilfred two of his sweet buns he had purchased. Ike Bently, followed by four or five other teenagers, suddenly appeared. "Hey thar, Bolt, how come ya give nice buns ta a nigger? Ain't we'uns good enough fer the high an mighty Bolts?" Wes turned in surprise, "Sure, Ike, I just didn't see you standing there. I'll go in an get some more." By now it was plain that Bently and the others were looking for a fight. Wes was just as determined to avoid one. Bently took the other buns from Wes, threw them on the ground stepping on each one. "Now thar ain't no way we aim ta eat no sweet buns like them, after we hafta see your nigger hog em." Wilfred started to dismount. A shiver of fear for the well-being of his friend ran through Wes. Nothing would suit this bunch of bully boys better than for a slave to strike one of them. He said quickly, "You mind the horses, Wilfred, don't you get down no matter what." Bently moved closer. "What ya got in mind now, Wes? Jes cuz yore Ma is a breed Cherokee, don't make you no warrior." The others laughed. Wes knew of the discredit to his mother caused by just this type of bigoted talk. "You have slandered me, Bently, but you just ain't going to talk about my Ma that way."

By now a small group had assembled around the two young roosters, as one so aptly called them. Wes removed his hat, throwing it up to Wilfred still on horseback. Bently elaborately rolled up the sleeves of his shirt, then started the balled fist gyrations of a fighter. This was a first fight for Wes, he knew it would take all he had to best the heavier Ike Bently. Although he had never actually taken part in the judo routines performed by his father, Rufus and Tobe, he had been a spectator many times. He tried now to recall the swift moves executed by the skilled combatants. Wes raised his hands, waiting for the attack he knew would come. A tight circle of grownups and boys alike had formed around the two contestants. A hard-balled fist swung, just brushing the top of Wes's head. He had ducked under the blow, spun quickly to one side. Bently crashed into the ring of spectators. They quickly pushed him back into the ring. This time Bently rushed in low, butting Wes in the belly with his head. The wind went out of Wes in a mighty grunt. He crashed to the dusty street, weakly gasping for breath, when he saw Bently lift a foot to kick him in the face. He moved aside weakly. A gash was cut in his cheek as the rough shoe descended into his face. The pain caused him to recover, he quickly regained his feet. Bently rushed again. This time Wes had picked a spot to hit. It was Bently's nose. The heavier boy crashed backward. He rolled over to his hands and knees. The blood gushed from his ruined nose. The rage inside of Wes had not subsided, so he grabbed Bently by the hair, hauling him to his feet. He started to smash his fist into the face again. Bently covered his face with his forearms begging, ''Please don' hit me no more, Wes. I was jes funnin. I din't mean no slur bout your Ma.'' Wes held his fist at the ready, just in case this was a trick from Bently. When he saw all the fight was gone from Bently, Wes snarled through his teeth. ''Never let us Bolts hear no kind of talk like that ever again.'' He seemed to be addressing the rest of the crowd, as well as the beaten Bently. ''The most sacred thing in this world to us Bolts is my mother, Clemmy. We will fight you into the ground if we hear one word.'' Blood was streaming down the front of young Bolt's shirt from the cut on his bruised cheek. The crowd dispersed in search of other entertainment. When Wes looked back at his friend Wilfred, there were big tears of rage and frustration streaming from his big black eyes. ''Is it allus gonna be this way, Wes? Will I allus hafta jes sit an see another man fight my fight?'' ''Maybe not always, Will, maybe not always.'' Wilfred got down from the horse to help Wes make his way to a watering trough where he could wash away some of the blood. He had wet a handkerchief from his pocket. Wilfred was doing a very painful, clumsy job of dabbing at the bruised face. ''Watch it, Wilfred, I ain't no horse. Take it a little easier.'' ''Da blood gotta come off, Wes. Den we gotta fine some medicine some place.'' Wilfred tried again, this time more gently.

A soft female voice addressed them from behind. ''Excuse me, Wes, are you hurt really bad?'' They turned quickly to see a full bodied young lady standing a short way from the horse trough. Wes recognized her immediately as Adelia Rodgers. He had seen her many times before but had never had the nerve to speak to her. After all, her folks owned the huge plantation just down the creek from the Bolt farm. ''Pa is in the Cotton Buyer's office there,'' she pointed behind her, ''he says you had better come into the office where he can have Doc look at your face.'' ''It ain't nothing, Adelia,'' Wes was embarrassed. He put his hand over his swollen face. The blood was still oozing from the cut below his cheekbone. ''Please come in, Wes, I would like for you to.'' He looked at the kind expression in her green eyes, he lost sight of the world around him. Rather heavy brows and long lashes helped to accentuate those eyes which were set in a wide face. A pretty mouth was complemented by straight white teeth. An abundance of chestnut brown wavy hair framed this kindly face, tumbled about her shoulders, then reached her waist. Adelia was just a bit self-conscious of being a little overweight. Her natural beauty so far outshined this one small flaw that no one ever noticed. She extended her hand, Wes lightly touched her fingers. He would have followed her to the end of the earth at that moment.

Wilfred tied the horses, then retreated to the shade at the store side where other black grooms were waiting for their masters to decide to return home.

Even at that time in the history of the south, the slaves were beginning to talk in low, guarded voices about the day when they would all be free. Some rabble-rousing secessionists had even promised them that they would be living in big houses, and riding the fine horses they now must care for. Some were content to live as they were; in others the fires of freedom were burning deep inside. A volcano of hatred ready to erupt.

Wes followed Adelia into the Cotton Broker's office. Mr. Rodgers had already sent for Doctor Rollins who was just putting the finishing touches to the bandages on the nose of one Ike Bently. Wes was ushered into the back room of the Cotton Broker's office. The place was nicely furnished for the comfort of the clients who patronized this particular broker. Cotton buying was a keenly competitive business. Foreign mills were buying all the south could produce.

Wes was ushered to a chair where he sat nervously on the edge. Rodgers, now developing a pot belly from his easy living, spoke to Wes in a fatherly manner. "Wes, your Pa is one of my very best friends. I hated to see you get into that brawl. I suppose after hearing your speech at the finish of it, that you gave that Bently trash all that he deserved." Wes fingered his right hand where the knuckles had swollen from the hard use they had had. "Yes, sir, Mr. Rodgers, sir," Wes let his eyes wander back to where Adelia was standing near the doorway. "Well, I aim to tell John Bolt what a fighter he has for a boy. I was right proud of you myself, Wes." Dr. Rollins came in, carrying the ever present black bag. He bent Wes's head back for a better look at the laceration below the cheek bone. "Ain't too much damage, boy. Somebody should tell you though, that fist fighting can be real hard on handsome faces and store bought clothes." He probed the wound with some kind of medicine which Wes thought must be made with fire. "Ain't so bad it won't heal in a few days, Wes. You may always have a scar there, but pray to God that this will be the worst wound you will ever have. Go on home now and tell John to send me two dollars fer my time and trouble. Next time, move your face outa the way of young Ike's boot." The doctor chuckled as he slapped Wes on the shoulder and headed him for the door. Wes wished that the time could be extended so that he might get one more chance to speak to Adelia. Instead, he left hastily, striding for the rail where the horses were tied. He didn't wait for Wilfred, he just mounted the colt, reined toward home in a gallop. Big Red wanted to run but Wes held him back with heavy pressure on the bossall. the feel of the way the colt would run let him know that he was mounted on the best horse in the world.

Wilfred had to extend his mount to catch up with Wes and the big red colt. "You hole dat colt down now, Wes, he jest a baby, we shore ain't wantin ta hurt his legs none. De bone in his body is still soff. Hole him down." Wes reluctantly reined the colt to a walk. "Wilfred, when Big Red grows some, don't you ever try to mount anything that will out-distance, or outrun him. There just ain't no such a animule." Wilfred's shiny black face split in a wide grin. "Tain't the hoss what'll decide a race twix you an me, Wes, it most likely be the rider. When yo grows into yor britches some, den you challenge Wilfred to a race." "Beat you any day, Wilfred, beat you any day." They finished the trip to the Bolt farm in a fast trot. When they reached the gate, Wes was very tired from trying to hold the big red colt back. He knew horses, in this one, he knew he had the best their farm could offer then, or later.

When they went to the house, Wes's face, on the left side was swollen, black, and blue, also hurting with each step he took. When he entered the living room, Clemmy saw him, her eyes opening wide with fright. "Wes, baby, what has happen to yore face. Thet new colt throwed ya, din't he? I tole yo not to ride them unbroke colts. Leave em fer Wilfred and Rufus. Lordy, chile, set down, lemme see bout yore poor face." "It wasn't the colt, Ma. Beside I ride as good, or even better than Wilfred. He ain't that much older than I am, you know!" "Cissy, go fetch his Pa, I want him ta see how bad hurt this boy can be fum them horses." Wes stood up, taller than his mother. "Ma! I told you it wasn't a horse.

I might as well tell you, I had a fight with Ike Bently when me an Wilfred went to town." "Ike Bently is bigger'n you, Wes, I outta go drag him out an horse whip him my sef." Clemmy's voice had risen in her indignation at the thought of someone hitting her baby. John had entered the room to hear the last part of Clemmy's declaration. "What is this here bout Ike Bently?" Clemmy started to explain. John held up his hand for silence. "Let Wes tell the story, Clemmy, looks like he used his face fer a choppin block. Yo got a story to tell, Wes, so git on to it." "Pa, you told me not to hurt anyone unless he was going to hurt me, or someone I love very much. Well, Ike was doin both. He threw the sweetbuns we had bought on the ground because he said white folks were not supposed to watch a nigger eat. Then he called Ma a squaw. It was a fair fight, Pa, an I whipped him good." Wes straightened his shoulders back and looked his father in the eye. They didn't speak for a long interval. "Good Wes! That there is jes what I tole ya. Reckon me an Rufus better show you a few ways ta keep yore face outin the way of tother feller." John, who seldom showed affection to his boy, put his arm around the only son he would ever cause to be conceived. "Yore gittin ta be a man now, Wes. Yo be playing a man's part fer some time now. Stand up strong fer whut yo think be the right thing ter do. Stand strong, and fight ter win. Git ready fer supper now." As Wes left the room, John sank into his favorite easy chair seemingly deep in thought. Clemmy knew this mood, she sat quietly working on some sewing which needed to be finished. They ate their evening meal in silence. Each was occupied with his or her own thoughts. The fight was long dismissed from the young boy's mind. Instead there stood a image of a smiling young girl. Her flawless complexion framed by a tumble of wavy chestnut hair. Clemmy was still seething with anger over the Bently affair. That bully had bruised her boy. Sides thet he had spoke of her as being a squaw. Clemmy half smiled to herself. Well after all wusn't she half squaw? Jes the nasty mouth way he done that speaking. John could not erase the vision of the big, kind-hearted Larkin. He had said, "Doan' be hurtin no man lest he needs it. Fight your own fight, John boy. Fight to win." John thought of his childhood as compared to that of Wes. John's companions had been the blacks, Rufus and Tobe. They were still just as brothers to him.

All the turmoil about slavery, the south breaking with the north, just a host of things which churned in the mind of John Bolt. He thought of plantation owner Rodgers. A good man, but miles apart from John on the question of one man owning another. If the south was going to fight some unknown people in the north because the man in the south wanted to own other men, then John Bolt wanted no part of it. They had subscribed to an Atlanta newspaper which came about a week or so late. John would have Wes read it to him from front to back. Then John would think about the heated tirades of the Atlanta editor concerning those meddling damn yankees and the trouble they were brewing. He also would listen intently to the stories of the wild frontier, the gold rush stories of California, stories of the cattle barons who were settling in the vast territories to the west. All of the adventure stories held a great fascination for both John and Clemmy. They would talk for hours about the vastness of the lands, descriptions of the endless buffalo herds, the plains Indians who depended upon them for survival. They were still young people. Clemmy's hair was still as black as the night while John was beginning to show premature grey at his temples.

This evening Clemmy sat close to John in his easy chair. "How come ya ain't no worry type, John, yit there still is silver in the yaller? I wonder effin yore Pa was grey-headed when he wuz as young as you be? She snuggled closer to her husband as she tousled his curly hair. "Ya know, Clemmy, onliest Pa I ever knew was Larkin. I done give ya the story o the horse-trader. I doan even remember what he looked like. I do recollect the wanderin though. We used ter roam from one end of this land ta the other. Sometime I kinda git tha wander fever agin, Clemmy." "Ya know thet I ain't never seen nothing cept this here county John." Clemmy was pensive for a moment. "I sometime paint a picher in ma mind bout the things Wes reads bout. There sure be a heap o things in this here worl which we ain't seen, John. Mayhaps one o'these here days, we may jes git inter a wagon, an head fer the skyline, jes lak thet Preacher done." John patted her behind. "Clemmy, you do carry on. Thet Preacher didn't have nothin to leave. Jes look at all we would be leaving behind." John waved his arm in a half circle. "Cain't hurt us none, jes to jaw bout it, does it, John?" Clemmy pressed closer as she looked up into his eyes. She adored him.

"Tell yo one thing fer sure, John Bolt. Iffen ya ever wuz ter say ta me, 'Clemmy, let's go harness up and head outen here; then I wouldn't cross words one secon. I will foller John Bolt to the jumpin off place." She laughed. "Jess fer this evein, though . . . how bout follerin me?" She left in the direction of the bedroom. He did not have to be coaxed. Clemmy was still a desirable woman.

CHAPTER 9
YOUNG LOVE

Just as the sun rose the next morning, Wes was back at the stable with his favorite colt. He, along with Wilfred, had already done all the feeding chores. Wes was anxious to get on with the training of what was to be his and only his horse. Big Red was never to know the feel of another man in the saddle. Neither was he to know the feel of a bit in his mouth. The strong long legged colt was to have a steady workout every day from now until he was thoroughly trained to the words, and knee pressures, of his admiring rider.

This pretty morning, for some unexplained reason, Wes reined the colt in the direction of the Rodgers plantation. Wilfred gave Wes his big toothy smile. ''Why yo spose dat crazy hoss got a mine to prance pass that Rodgers place? Reckon he want ta show off a bit, thinkin mayhap da head groom put an eye on him fer ta buy.'' Wilfred laughed heartily. ''Yass suh, he got in his mind ta be a Rodgers plantation hoss.'' ''Hush up, Wilfred! Even the jay birds ain't listenin to ya.'' Wes slapped Wilfred's mount on the rump. It gave a leap, almost unseating the unsuspecting groom. Both mounts leaped to a run in just no time at all. These young men were laughing, shouting at the top of their lungs. The zest for living was a part of both of them. Wes began to try to check the colt. The hackamore was a sturdy halter with a rough braided rawhide band which fit across the colt's nose. Wes began to haul back on it, teaching the young horse the word 'whoa' at the same time.

From there on past the Rodgers plantation, they rode in silence. Wilfred admiring the beauty of a Georgia sunrise with the stirring about of dozens of species of birds, squirrels, and the scurry of other small animals in the underbrush. Wes had his thoughts filled with the vision of the plantation owner's daughter. Since his first close encounter with her, she had never left his mind, waking or sleeping. He, of course, had guided his horse in this direction in the hope that he might catch a glimpse of her as he rode down the road, past the stately white fence which was the front border of the huge plantation. As they rode, Wilfred nudged his mount into a gallop. "Come on hoss, if Wes feel he gotta show off, den he might as well look good." Although Wes tried to be casual about looking toward the big house, he still didn't miss a thing which was moving. He thought he saw the flash of a bright blue dress near the end of the veranda. It could have been anyone, but Wes imagined it to be Adelia. It just had to be. They rode well past the Rodgers mansion before they turned to start back up the same road. Wilfred was keeping up a steady chatter about the colt being in a nervous sweat. When they wanted him to turn left, Wes would exert pressure with his leg on the right side. Right, was the same routine. To help the young student get the right idea, Wilfred would crowd him with the trained mount. He was beginning to get the idea that the new pressure meant that he was to turn in the direction indicated.

As they again came near the archway of the big front gate at the plantation, Wes began to look. This time he saw a vision of loveliness in a bright blue dress approaching the gate from the direction of the house. Adelia was being trailed by a house slave. It would just not have been proper for her to have gone to the gate by herself. The servant stayed a discrete distance behind, but was there just the same. The swaying of the blue dress caused Big Red to point his ears in her direction, snorting and shying away as though he thought he was in real danger. Wes had to concentrate on his mount so closely that he could not enjoy the beauty of her walk toward him. Wes felt more nervous than the colt. He threw the halter reins to Wilfred, dismounting at the same time. The sudden move by his rider caused the colt to shy even more. Wes Bolt was dumped headlong into the dusty road. He jumped up quickly to try to hide his embarrassment. By now, Adelia had reached the open gate. She gave a little cry. "Oh! Wes, are you hurt?" "No, I just caught my toe as I started to dismount." Wilfred was trying valiantly to surpress waves of laughter which kept trying to overwhelm him. He rode on down the road where he could really enjoy the mirth of the moment. Adelia began to brush the dust from Wes's shoulder. The side of his sweaty face was caked with dirt where he had landed. A little twinge of pain shot through his already injured cheek. "Oh! Wes, you started your poor face bleeding again. Come to the house. Moses can clean your face, and put on another bandage. It seems that every time I get to see you, you are getting hurt some way. I hope I am not a bad influence. Maybe I have put the evil eye on you like some of the slaves say." She giggled. Her laughter was like the music of a thousand violins to Wes. He just looked. Adelia had her hair tied back with a blue grosgrain ribbon. The glowing natural softness of her complexion accented the expression in her eyes. She took his hand again, turning to go to the house. As they walked, Wes looked down at the plainness of his clothes. This was the first time he had ever felt ill at ease about the way he looked. His clothes were neat, but the rough cloth of the working class. He was thinking this as she was saying breathlessly: "Wes, I want to see you more often. I know it is shameless of me to say it, but there is just no other way for it to happen. I know that you would never approach me, for some silly class reason. I have to say this before we reach the house. Mother would not hear of it, I know! Please Wes, don't let that make any difference to you. I know how proud you are." She released his hand as they neared the plantation house. "Whether you think I am a bold hussy or not, I will have Tilly take me for a drive tomorrow afternoon. I will be at the meadow by the creek at about two o'clock. I will have to take Tilly with me," she indicated the girl behind her, "but that will be alright, won't it, Wes?" Young Bolt couldn't manage a word from the excitement welling up within him at the prospect of seeing this beautiful girl in a place where he could talk to her.

As they entered the living room of the plantation house, they were met by a stern-looking Mrs. Rodgers. She was a plump, overdressed lady in her late forties. She respectfully listened to her daughter introduce Wesley Bolt. "He fell from his horse, Mother, he needs Moses to tend to his face." "Very well then, if that is what he needs, take him around the house to the kitchen. I will call Moses, he will meet you there, young man. I will see you in the sitting room, Adelia." Mrs. Rodgers turned to summon the servant. Wes felt out of place. Adelia turned to look at Wes. An apology was plainly written in her kind, lovely face. Wes shrugged his shoulders, followed Tilly around the house to the kitchen where an aging negro house-servant cleaned, then re-bandaged, his face. At the same time Wes was receiving his first-aid, Adelia was receiving a very disapproving look from her southern society mother. "Adelia, how in the world did you pick up that trash? Why, I was just mortified when I saw you walking so close to him" "Momma! He is not trash' His folks have built one of the most prosperous farm and blacksmith businesses in this part of Georgia. Wes Bolt is one of the most polite boys I have ever talked to." "Well! You are not to talk to him any more. Adelia, what in the world, and Georgia, would our friends say if they thought my daughter was being friendly with a poor boy whose mother is half Indian. She is, you know!" When Mrs. Rodgers saw that Adelia was being really hurt by her tirade, her voice took on a shrill note, she continued. "Don't you ever bring trash like that into our living room again." Tears began to fill Adelia's eyes. "Momma! Please don't say anything bad about Wesley Bolt. He really is a very nice man." "Man, your foot! He is still not dry behind the ears and a cracker boy who was brought up by negroes, and a half squaw." Adelia dared not say more, for fear her mother would restrict her to her room on the following day. As it stood now, she was sure that her mother would not imagine that she would sneak off to the meadow by the creek, just to talk to this young man she yearned to be near.

She began to cry, then turned to leave the room. Mrs. Rodgers was still muttering about the younger generation not minding their elders. Hadn't she made a special effort to see that Adelia was introduced to the highest of Georgia society? She had made it a point to invite several eligible young men from prominent plantation families to spend the weekends with Adelia's brother, Kerry. Kerry was a typical southern gentleman, two years older than his sister. He had been spending the last years of his education at the military academy in Virginia. He was his mother's pride and joy, to say the least. Mrs. Rodgers was sure that Kerry would marry one of the very best of the fine family girls of Georgia. After all, his father was in the state legislature now! "This Rodgers family just doesn't appreciate all that I am doing for them. Only the very best was good enough for the Rodgers plantation. They could now buy just about whatever they wanted, and if necessary, she would buy a southern gentleman husband for her daughter. She will be so grateful to me when she is finally married. I just must make sure that she has no more contact with the likes of that Bolt dolt. Adelia's trouble is, she is just too tender-hearted. She sees good in just about everybody." Mrs. Rodgers made a mental note to talk to Mr. Rodgers about Adelia that very evening. Not that Rodgers listened too intently to everything she had to say.

Wes left the plantation, running up the road toward Wilfred and the mounts. As he drew near, Wilfred started to ride on up the road as though he didn't know Wes was on his way. Wes began to yell. Wildred put the horses into a trot to stay ahead. When Wilfred finally took pity upon Wes, he reined the horses to stop. The winded Wes came to the end of his run, then he tried to pull Wilfred from the saddle. The black boy was laughing so hard, he almost fell to the road. "Scuse me, Wes, I was shore yo had decided ta jes live at the Rodgers place. When ya lef me, ya look lak I wuz fersook, fer shore." Wilfred was still laughing as he gave Wes a leg up to mount the still skittish colt. They galloped the rest of the way home.

The rabble-rousers in both north and south were grinding out the vitriol of hate. The Democratic convention had wound up in sheer chaos. Some southern states were determined that Douglas would not be the one to get the nomination. He was a fellow who was trying to give too much comfort to the abolitionists. After all, hadn't he made the statement that if he were elected president, he would consider secession an illegal act? Abraham Lincoln had won the nomination for the Republicans. His was an easy victory at the convention in Chicago. The Democrats, in the turmoil of their convention at Charleston, had placed two candidates in the field. It was this plurality which gave Lincoln the presidency at election time.

After the conventions, one southern state after another followed the lead of South Carolina, began to leave the union. Mississippi, represented by Jefferson Davis, made its decision to leave the union as a matter of principal. Davis, in his farewell speech to the convention, tried to explain the sadness which was weighing so heavily upon his heart. They were all noble gentlemen with an ideal. Each guided by the conscience of his upbringing. There was but a very small minority of actual slave owners in the United States at that time. Others followed the lead of the rabid few who preached that the northerners were trying to make all the people the same social standing as the lowly slave. Poor, middle, and rich, had to feel that they were superior to something. Even Lincoln had favored trying to devise some sort of plan to ship the unwilling slave back to his native land. Audiences were easily assembled, as thunder and lightning orators took to the soap boxes to say their piece.

There was a convention called in South Carolina to dissolve the union of South Carolina, and the other states, of the United States of America. South Carolina became an independent state, or nation, whichever it was preferred to be called. So went the chain of events, on, and on, like a tremendous avalanche of destruction. It was to a background of these troubled times that Wes Bolt rode to the big-eyed girl who had stolen his heart. The girl, Adelia Rodgers, drove a pony cart, with the black girl, Tilly, on the seat beside her to act as chaperone. She hurried the pony with a light stroke of the whip. After all, she was determined not to be late. They dismounted from the cart, tied the pony securely.

"Yo Mammy tole ya not ta get nowhar close ta that po white trash whut wuz at tha big house yisterdee." Adelia turned upon the poor unsuspecting Tilly. "Tilly! Don't you ever let me hear you say a thing like that about Wes Bolt again. I have never hit a slave in my life, but I swar if you ever again do that, I will strap you." Tilly could see that her little Missy was spitting fire. "Yes, Miss Delia! I ain't niver gonna say a mumblin word bout Mr. Wes. Niver, niver, niver. Doan yo go too near of him, Missy. Better yo strap me, dan ta have yore Mammy take all da hide offin me."

Adelia could see Wes by now, riding like the wind on a beautiful Arabian mare. Her heart skipped a beat at the sight of him. He was so tall, strong and rugged. None of the other men she knew could make her feel the way she felt right at this moment. Wes was showing off just a little as he brought the mare to a sliding halt. He tied the animal to the rail fence, climbed over, running to where the two girls were standing, he took both of Adelia's hands in his. "You did come. By golly, you did come." "Of course I came, silly. It was my idea, wasn't it?" Wes could smell the scent of lilacs as he stood close to her. He wanted to gather her into his arms, but he didn't dare. Tilly discreetly wandered on toward the creek, stopping now and then to pick a wild flower. The black girl smiled to herself. She knew that they were in love even if they didn't.

Wes and Adelia held hands as they slowly walked the rest of the distance to the creek bank. They sat for a while tossing pebbles into the water. Not saying a word, they just enjoyed the closeness of each other. Finally Wes said timidly, "Adelia, you know that you shouldn't see me, don't you? I don't have to be hit over the head to know that your Ma don't care for me one little bit." "It's true, Wes, what are we going to do? I simply must see you!" Wes couldn't keep his distance no more. He turned to her, folding her in his strong arms. She lay back on the grassy bank. Her long wavy hair forming a halo about her innocent young face. Wes could feel her heaving breasts through the thin cotton shirts he was wearing. He pressed his lips to hers in the first kiss he had ever experienced from a girl. He couldn't help but think how awkward he must be in the presence of this rich and lovely young woman.

The ecstasy of the moment engulfed both of them. The grassy bank of the this Georgia creek suddenly became an altar upon which they were both willing to place all their love. Suddenly Wes realized that the whole world had not stopped, to become heaven with that one kiss. He remembered Tilly had wandered down the creek. Now he was wondering whether or not she had seen what had taken place between him and Adelia. His eyes began to search the timber at the edge of the creek bend. Adelia laughed. "You silly Wes, Tilly has gone, she won't dare come until I call her. Besides, she will be deaf, and dumb, when it comes to telling Mother anything that I don't want her to." "Your Mother seems to be our greatest problem, Adelia. I wonder what she will say if she finds out that I have seen you alone like this? How can it be wrong for me to want to be with you, Adelia?" I have just as high a moral character as some of the richest men in the county." "Even higher, Wes, besides it isn't any of the rich men of the county, or state, for that matter, whom I want to see. I have watched you, and thought about you since we were in grade school, Wes Bolt. You never even looked at me, cause I was the chubby, little, rich girl. Well, I'll tell you this, Wes, I intend to keep on seeing you just as long as you will let me. Yes. One of these days I will just have to go into the house, to tell my Mother and Father that I have been seeing someone I care a great deal about. They will just have to get used to it." Adelia put her arms around Wes's waist, pulled him close. She looked up into his face. "I love you, Wes Bolt! Can you understand that? I love you!" The sudden realization that his beloved Adelia felt the same way about him as he did about her, gave Wes a tremendous thrill. He bent his head to kiss her again. "Adelia, I want you to be mine, but I just don't want you being hurt by your family. Our family has a great deal of pride, too, especially Ma. She is half-Indian as everybody is so quick to point out, but she is really a beautiful lady beneath her rough way of talking. Ma just believes that a woman's place is wherever she is needed by the man she is married to." "Clemmy is so lovely, Wes, that I think Mother is really jealous of her. Then, of course, there is a the silly class distinction line which Mother thinks can never be crossed. No matter what anyone says. I intend to have you, Wes Bolt; I will be chasing after you until I catch you." "Now isn't that a most shameful way for a well-brought up lady to talk?" "I know it isn't right, Wes, then maybe you don't really care for me the way that I care for you." Wes put his hand over her beautiful mouth. "Don't talk that way. Don't ever talk that way again. There has never been anyone else in the whole world, that I have ever thought about the second time, it has always been you, Adelia. I have just never had the nerve to even go near you. I was afraid you would scorn me. I just couldn't have stood that from you. I would have been so ashamed that I would have left the country." "Wes, I love you. I love you so much that I can't think of anything else. I know that we are both quite young, but I also know that we can live just as good a life as anyone ever did." Wes drew her even closer to him, stroking her long wavy hair. "I want you, Adelia. I am almost twenty. We could go into town to see the Preacher at your church." "That won't do Wes, he would send someone as fast as a horse would run, to tell my Ma and Pa. There is only one thing for us to do. That is go right into the lion's den." She kissed him on the neck. "After all, when they see how much we really love each other, then, they just can't refuse to let us get married just the way we want to." "Your Ma has never even talked to me, but I know this for sure, your Father scares me half to death." "Really Wes, he is blustery, he will shout at both of us, but Mother is the one who will really cause the trouble. She thinks that if I don't marry one of the fine old families of Georgia, then the Rodgers family is going to go straight to hell. Sometimes I think that her society is a religion with her. Wes, don't let her frighten you. There will be a barrel of tears, weeping and wailing, along with a great deal of high-pitched screeching about me marrying trash." She felt the muscles tighten under Wes's shirt. "Please, Wes, you know I love you. Don't let her get you so upset that you will begin to think that we are all the way she is. It is just that she has been a rich society lady all of her life. She just can't believe that there is another way of life beyond the way she and her friends plan things."

Tilly came back up the creek. Trying to be as inconspicuous as possible, yet she was beginning to feel uneasy about the length of time they had been gone from the big house. "Please, Miss Delia, we jes gotta be gittin on back ta the big house. Yore Ma is gonna take a hickory limb tuh me, fer sho. She tell me all the time ta watch over you like a hawk. Now ya jes gotta go on back wid me at this very instance." "Go on to the cart, Tilly, I'll follow you right away. I promise you, I will." As Tilly crossed the meadow toward the rail fence, Adelia pressed her young body against Wes Bolt as though she were trying to actually become a part of him. She kissed him on the lips, moaning contentedly as she did so. The young man's mind spun with the thrill of the total abandon of the girl he loved. He placed his hand over her firm young breast. Adelia pushed away . . . "Now you just remember that Wes Bolt. Go home and think about what we have been talking about. Please talk to Clemmy and John about us. Oh, I do hope that they will not object to what we are about to do. We will be married, Wes, even if the whole county tries to keep us from it."

They walked slowly back to the road, where they kissed once again, promising to see each other very soon. As they went their separate ways, their minds were filled with the thoughts of how to broach the subject of their intended marriage to their respective parents. The telling didn't prove too great a task for Wes, as after dinner he announced to Clemmy and John that he had very important subject to discuss with them. "Well now, whut be so important thet it gotta take both me an your Ma ta listen?" John was in a teasing mood. Clemmy listened intently. "Go bout that telling, son, yore Pa jes cain't understand thet you be a growed up man, now. I know it gotta be a real big subjec fer ya ta be so all fired serious. Now yo jes go right ahead an tell us, Wes, honey." "Well, Ma and Pa, I might just as well say it and get it over with. I have found the girl I intend to marry." Clemmy's big black eyes grew wide with surprise. John smiled, taking a long drag on his cob pipe. Clemmy spoke quickly. "Ya ain't never tole me yo was seein a soul, Wes. There ain't no gal fer miles around here that be fit fer yo. Give yerself some time, boy, look around and fine a real purty and sweet one. Yo cain't jes go out one day, an come back with the idee thet yo found the woman yo gonna spen the rest o yer life with. None o these cracker gals around here got tha class o Wes Bolt." "Clemmy, why don't ya let Wes tell his story? He ain't had a chanct ta open his mouth." Clemmy realized, all at once, what she had been doing. "I reckon I do sound jes like a ole hen with one chick! Sorry, Wes, go right on an have yore say. I do remember Clemmy Bandy makin her choice right off, without even a second glance at any other man. Course she had the very finest of the crop fall right inta her lap." John delivered this sentence with a sly grin. "How a handsome gent like me ever wanted ta marry a skinny little injun gal from thet broke down farm up the creek?" Clemmy playfully kicked at John. "Ya wuz the luckiest man in all of Georgia, John Bolt. Now, Wes, git on with yore serious talk." "Well, Ma, it ain't no cracker gal, as you call them. This happens to be Adelia Rodgers." John dropped his cob pipe, batting furiously at the scattered live ashes. "God almighty, boy, what you sayin?" "Mr. Rodgers is your friend, isn't he, Pa?" "Shore is, but I had no idee ya was sweet on his only woman chile." Clemmy was speechless. Wes hurried onto explain. "I have been loving her secretly for a long time, Ma. We have only been together three times. Only one of those times I was alone with her. She says she loves me, Ma. She says she loves me more than any one o those rich plantation men. She told me so, Ma. I have kissed her, an we know we love each other." All of this came from Wes in one breath. Clemmy looked at him for a moment, then walked over to him and took him into her arms. "I am afraid you are headn' for a big hurt, son. Yo know whut her ma thinks o us Bolts. We are awright in our place, but she wants us ta stay right there, in our place. She ain't never gonna let ya have thet little gal, Adelia. I seen her lots o times, son, I cain't blame yo none for wanting a wife like her. Ever time I seen her, she has always been real sweet ta me an your Pa. She be a real nice chile. It's her folks whut ain't never gonna let you be one o them. As her ma would say, we jes ain't their kind." Clemmy was holding her only son close to her as she stroked his hair. "We be a proud fambly too, Wes! How yo gona hole still fer her Ma sayin thet ya ain't fit ta be the husbin o her precious Adelia? Ya jes gonna have to take your lumps yourself, Wes, cause this here be one time I doan aim ta hep. Effin ya want her bad enough, then yo will jes go take her. I got mine an I aim ta keep her.'' John put his arm around Clemmy's middle, he drew her close to him. ''Go git you one jes as good as your own Ma, Wes boy. She will hafta be one damn fine women ta measure up.'' ''I know that, Pa, and that is exactly why I intend to have Adelia Rodgers for my wife. I intend to tell them tomorrow.'' With that, Wes left them and went into his own room. When he had gone, Clemmy threw her head back, placing her hands on her hips. ''Effin he be a mind ta have her, John, then I tell yo fer shore, Wes Bolt has got the guts ta go inta the nest o that ole she bear an take that chile ta be his'n.'' John looked at Clemmy. What a beautiful woman she still is, he thought. Clemmy's pose brought out all the curves of her graceful body as the defiance in her eyes flashed like sunlight on a placid lake. ''He's a man now, Clemmy, let him take what he is man enough to have. Besides, this may be our chance to light a shuck fer the fer west jes like we been plannin fer a long, long time. We could take what we want and leave the rest to Wes, Rufus, and Tobe. You and me would jes be leavin our part to Wes. He been tendin to all the book work since he wuz fifteen year old, anyways.'' ''John, ya sound plumb serious bout this goin west thing.'' Clemmy could hardly believe what she was hearing, yet it gave her a sort of thrill. ''Clemmy, think about it, we could take the Larkin wagon. Ain't like we be headin west without a thing ta our name. It be still the best wagon ever built. Me and Rufus, an Tobe, built it by hand. Ever piece wuz made to last a lifetime.'' John's voice began to take on excitement as he began to make his dreams into plans. ''We could hitch another wagon on ahint the Larkin wagon. We could take six big draft mares to pull it. Then we could take a young Percheron stud, my white Arabian stud and a couple o good mares fer you.'' Clemmy's eyes began to shine as as the plans began to unwind before her. They talked on into the night.

Wes was so nervous that night that he hardly slept. When he did sleep, he would dream that his precious Adelia was being taken away from him by an angry mother and father. He got out of bed early the next day. When he tried to awaken Wilfred, he got a stream of protests that it was the middle of the night, that Wilfred was not love-sick at all. "Git away fum me, now you go ride that red colt. Mayhap he kin take some o the nervous outin your insides." "I'm worried, Wilfred. You just don't understand. I could lose her. That would be like losing my life. What am I going to do. Wilfred?" "Wull I ain't shore bout you. I be jes shor bout me. I aim ta ketch me bout thirty winks more o sleep. Then I will set aside some time ta worry for ya. Now get outen here an let me git jes a liddle sleep fore Poppa holler fer me in the mornin." Wes reluctanly left Wilfred, then went to the horse barn where he saddled the big red colt. That young animal was anxious to try his speed on the hard packed dirt road. Wes let him run. Lordy, he thought, this is like riding the wind. The colt took great leaping strides. Wes could feel the strength flowing through this magnificent piece of horse flesh. Wes was convinced that Big Red was the fastest, strongest horse the Bolt farm had ever produced. Time went by as he rode over the red clay roads of Georgia.

The morning was well along when he rode past the smithy at the front gate of the farm. Tobe and Rufus were already hard at work, getting out the last orders of blacksmith work which had come the previous day. Wes got down from his horse to watch the giant Tobe go about his work. The good food prepared for him each day by his ever adoring wife Cissy, was putting a pot belly on his already enormous frame. Tobe's hair was snow white by now. Wes thought the scarred ex-slave must be getting along in years. It didn't seem to slow him down in his trade.

There were already horses and mules tied to the hitch rails waiting their turn to be shod. The slaves who had brought them were huddled in a group under the shade of a giant oak tree. Their talk, this day, seemed to be more animated than usual. When Wes wandered near the tree, leading the colt, the conversation ceased, several of them spoke to him in a much too friendly way. "Mornin, Massa Bolt, yo sho lookin fine ta day." Wes was sure they had been passing on the gossip of the politics they heard from the soap box orators in the town square. Politics, and talk of slaves being free, were far from this young man's mind. A young boy of about fourteen left the shade of the smithy to approach Wes. "Scuse me, Massa Bolt, Miss Adelia sent me ta search yo out. She say fo me not to give this here letta ta no other soul." Wes felt his heart begin to beat faster. "Member Massa Bolt, I guv it rat ta yore han." "I'll remember, what is your name?" "I be Caesar, Massa. Miss Adelia say fuh me to hurry. Now she gonna be mad wid Caesar. Yo wusn't here when I come. I come a long time ago, Massa Bolt. Hones I did." "Don't worry about it, Caesar. I will tell Miss Adelia that you tried real hard to find me." The slave handed him a small perfumed envelope. "I bes be gitten on back now, Massa. She gonna wont me ta tell her effin yo got the letta." The black boy took the reins of a mule which was tied to the rack. He mounted bareback, then rode off in the direction of the big plantation. Wes felt his hands shake as he opened the small letter. It began, "My most precious one." Wes was so thrilled that he tried to take in every word all at once. "I want you to come to the front of the big house by three this afternoon. Both Mother and Father will be here. Father rode in last night from Atlanta where he has been attending a meeting of the legislature. He does not seem to be in too good a mood, but we cannot wait forever. I have told them that they must be there to listen to what I have to say. I told them that it was the most important thing that I would ever say to them Mother is in such a tizzy. She is sure that I am going to tell them that I have decided to marry that awful Fredrick Hanks from Oakdale. This is going to be the greatest surprise of her life, isn't it, Wes?" Wes felt that butterflies in his stomach again as he thought of the reaction of the matriach of the giant Rodgers plantation. "I will need you to stand right beside me, my darling. I am more afraid than you are. We will face them nevertheless. If they deny us, then I will find a way to go with you. We will be together for the rest of our lives, my love. Hurry to me now, my precious Wes. I love you . . . Adelia." Wes turned to run to the house. He would look his best for this encounter. As he threw the reins from his mount to a groom at the barn, he thought of the biblical story of Daniel in the lion's den. Daniel had an angel of the Lord to deliver him. Wes thought, I wonder if I have started praying too late to get the same kind of help. He rushed into the house where Clemmy scolded him. "You are way early fer yore lunch, Mister Bolt. Ya know we ain't in the habit o feedin nobody till after twelve o'clock. Yo know hit ain't thet time yet." "I am not hungry, Ma, I am going to ride over to the Rodgers place. I won't be home all afternoon." Clemmy smiled. She knew the reason he would be gone.

Wes prepared a tub of hot water which he sat in the middle of the floor in his bedroom. He got into the wooden tub, scrubbing himself from head to toe. He scrubbed his work-hardened hands, until they were red. As he got out of the water, he glanced at himself in the mirror on his dresser. He blushed as he wondered what it would be like to stand naked before the beautiful Adelia. Maybe she wouldn't even like him. If any woman would admire a flawless young male body, then there would be no reason for Adelia to find him anything but desirable. Wes stood just over six feet tall, weight one hundred and seventy-five pounds. Hard farm work had caused him to develop heavy shoulders and a flat belly. Although he was not aware of it, Wes lacked nothing at all when it came to masculine perfection. He dressed hurriedly in his best shirt, trousers and boots. He combed his hair with meticulous care, although he knew that it would be rumpled by the wind, long before he reached the Rodgers plantation. His haste in getting ready left him with plenty of time to make the short ride to his destination. He would ride his father's white Arabian stallion. This magnificent animal was admired by horsemen all over that part of Georgia. The stallion was snow white, with black stockings up to about his knees. His flaring nostrils were black as well as shades of black around his great dark eyes. When the horse was ridden into any populated area, heads would turn in admiration. He sought out John to ask permission to borrow Aladdin. Everyone on the Bolt farm called him "The Lad." Wes felt that if he were mounted on The Lad, he would create the impression that he was every bit as good as any man in the whole wide world. John slapped him on the shoulder. "Some reason er tother, Wilfred has done got him under a saddle. He is ready to ride out. Hold him on a tight rein, son. Be sure that you turn him over to Ezekiel when you git to the Rodgers' place. Thet boy is most as good as Wilfred when it comes to groomin a horse. I won't worry bout him with Zeke looking after him." Wilfred was holding The Lad in the breezeway of the barn. He led the animal out the double doors into the sunlight. It was a standing rule on the Bolt horse farm that no man ever mount a horse inside the barn. The Lad pranced, tossing his head at the expectation of running free on the open road. Wilfred wrinkled his nose at Wes when they came near. "Man yo smell lak a whole shock of roses done fell on yo. Have yo turned to a gal?" Better let me ride long wit yo. Somebody gotta take care o yo." "I'll take care of myself, Wilfred. Hold The Lad steady while I mount." John Bolt's heart swelled with pride. He took the stallion out the front gate at a fast trot. "Wilfred, yonder goes two of the most important parts o a man's life. T'other part is his mother, Clemmy." Wilfred respectfully nodded his head. "He be part of me, too, Massa John." "Don't call me Massa, Wilfred. You know better." "Yes, Mister Bolt, yo ain't my Massa, but they jes caint be no better man den yo is." John put his arm around the black boy's shoulders. "One o these days, Wilfred, things might change. We possibly won't see it, but it could change." John turned to walk toward the horse barn.

It had been a long night for Adelia, too. She had lain in her bed rehearsing just what she would say to her parents when Wes came on the following day. The frightening thought that Wes might not even come had entered her mind. That thought was quickly dismissed, replaced by the more worrisome thought that a horrible scene would be enacted in the living room of the Rodgers' plantation. Her father was greatly bothered by the turn of political events at the state capitol. Growing unrest from the northern states had invaded the very stronghold of the south. Rodgers felt that the political burden was his alone to bear. He sat that night, drinking too much good Tennessee whiskey. He thought once in a while about his family. His son just graduated from the academy in Virginia. If war came, what could happen to him? His once chubby little daughter, Adelia, her sweet affectionate nature had always been such a pleasure to him. Now she said that he and Mrs. Rodgers must listen to something most important to her and the entire family. His wife was so sure that Adelia was going to announce her intentions to wed the dashing Freddy Hanks from the Oakdale Plantation. He really didn't like Freddy. The boy drank too much, he would also think of the Hanks boy as a spoiled brat. Oh well, Adelia was a woman now. I suppose she has gotta marry somebody sometime. Rodgers sat at his desk in the bedroom. His overweight wife was already snoring contentedly. This woman had never known a moment of privation in her entire life. Rodgers had married Sophia when her brother had invited him to their plantation in the southern part of the state. She had been sheltered all of her life. Even he had indulged her in her pursuit of social standing. She was good at her quest. The Rodgers family was the society leader in Georgia. Rodgers was pretty well in his cups by now. He could picture his wife sending half the slaves on the plantation with messages to other families, announcing the impending marriage of their daughter. Yes, Sophia would relive her own marriage in the great event she would plan for her daughter.

The stallion pranced sideways in his desire to show Wes that he was a tremendous runner. If Wes had loosened his hold on the reins for just a second, the magnificent animal would have bolted into a dead run. By now, Wes could see the front gate of the plantation. The white grandeur of the great big house shone in the afternoon sun. How could a girl from a place like that ever think of him as a husband? Wes knew that there was no doubt in his mind that he wanted her. He was prepared to face the devil himself if it were necessary to have Adelia for his own. He rode boldly up the drive toward the hitching posts at the front of the veranda. The ebony black groom Ezekiel left his gardening at the front of the house to take the reins of The Lad as Wes dismounted. Adelia had watched him ride in. Her Mother was busy with the house servants. She had already begun the preparation for the upcoming event she knew was about to be announced. Adelia's Father dozed in his easy chair. A sheaf of papers were held loosely in his hand, resting on his ample belly. The Lad whinnied loudly, in anticipation of being led to the mares in the Rodgers' barn. The call of the stallion caused Sophia Rodgers to look out the front window. "It's that Bolt creature! Surely he knows that he is not welcome here. Particularly on this of all days." Adelia didn't wait for the house servant to open the front door. She went quickly to open it for Wes Bolt. She grasped Wes's hand, and propelled him into the cool shade of the big room. "But he is welcome here, Mother. He is the reason I have asked you and Father to be here this afternoon. We have something to tell you. Please sit down, listen to us." Mrs. Rodgers remained standing. The opening of the door had caused the plantation owner to open his eyes sleepily. "Well, it's young Bolt. Things alright at your place, Wes?" The frightened, would-be groom, grasped hungrily at the friendly voice in the gloom of the big house. "Yes sir, Mister Rodgers, we are all just fine. I rode The Lad over. Thought you might like to see him." by this time Rodgers noticed Adelia holding tightly to the young man's hand. The impending announcement was already made as far as he was concerned. An awkward pause was broken by Adelia. "Mother, Father, you both know Wesley Bolt. He has something to say to you both." Adelia had taken the easy way out. She had placed the burden of the subject squarely on the shoulders of her intended. Mrs. Rodgers was beginning to recover from the shocking realization that the announcement was to concern Wes Bolt and Adelia not Fredrick Hanks of Oakdale. "Adelia, I order you to your room. I will not listen to a word from this, this, Bolt person. If I must say it plainly, he is not welcome here. Now young man, leave this house; do not ever be so rude as to approach us again." Wes looked lamely at Adelia. She squeezed his hand. "Go ahead, Wes, say it. Say it loudly if you have to, but say it," "Mr. Rodgers, and Mrs. Rodgers, I am here to tell you that I am going to marry your daughter. I mean I am here to ask you if you will consider letting your daughter marry me." Adelia interjected. "No! What he said at first is what he meant. I am going to be Mrs. Wesley Bolt. I am going to be his wife as soon as we can make the plans complete." Mrs. Rodgers grasped a small silver bell to summon the house servants. When the slave appeared, she indicated Wes with a sweep of her arm. "Escort this man to the front gate, see that he goes through it, and don't ever let him enter these premises again." Her face was red with anger, perspiration began to bead her forehead. Suddenly Rodgers stood up. "I know this young man, Sophia. I know his folks. I ain't goin to be ashamed one minute to have him in this family. I have seen him fight at great odds for the sanctity of his good name, and the defense of his family. Thank God, woman, that Adelia is going to get a man who will stand on his two feet and fight for what he believes in. I say by God, Adelia can marry him when she has mind to." Sophia Rodgers pretended a swoon, then sank heavily into one of the overstuffed chairs. Rodgers nodded to the servants to revive her. Then he watched as his daughter threw her arms around the young man's neck, kissing him full on the lips. She then ran to her father. "Oh, Daddy, you did just as I knew you would." She kissed him several times on the face. "Poor Mother, I do hope that she will soon understand. She must! Wes Bolt is going to be my full life. From this day on. I am so happy I could just cry." Wes was still standing in a stupor. He still could not believe that it was over. He had won with not nearly the agony he had anticipated. After the smelling salts had been liberally applied to Mrs. Rodgers, she recovered enough to be escorted from the room. She turned to her husband, "Mr. Rodgers, you have humiliated me and the entire family. I shall never speak to that person as long as I live." "That is your choosing, Sophia, not his. I hope you will change your mind." She left the room. Rodgers held out his hand to Wes. "Congratulations, Wes, you two make your plans. If I can help to make you happy, just call my name. I'll be here to help either one or both of you. I hope I have a whole nest of grandchildren to fuss over." Wes looked at the floor, Adelia giggled, patting her Father on the face. "Wes wants to be married soon, Papa. We want to go to live at the Old Bandy Place. We will fix it up into an envious farm, Papa. You will be so proud of us. Oh! Papa, I am so very happy. Yet I am sorry for Mama. Can't she see that this marriage is meant to be? We love each other so much, and Wes is from a very fine family." "You are right, honey, I can't agree with John Bolt about his slaves, but that is another thing. He don't ever give me any trouble about mine. Your Ma and Pa are strong people, Wes. I admire him. Now you and Adelia go make your plans. I got a lot of work to do, with too little time to get it done." Adelia gently kissed the bashful Wes. "Go now my darling. I will come to the Bolt farm tomorrow morning. We can go to the Bandy place to see how we can fix it up. I do so want Clemmy to like me. I want her to help me plan our wedding." The young people went to the front porch to have The Lad brought around. They kissed again before Wes swung lightly into the saddle. The stud wanted to run. When Wes turned the corner where the driveway met the road, he loosened the reins, calling for the stallion to show his form. He leaped forward in great ground-gaining strides. Wes felt the exhilaration of the ride as he rode for his home. He thought, one day I will race Wilfred. I think my Big Red can outrun The Lad. This would be a race that the whole country would want to see. The stallion covered the ground with such little effort that the Bolt farm came into view in a very short time. Wes thought, next to Wilfred, I am the best rider in the whole half of Georgia. Maybe I am even better than Wilfred. The race will tell. He slowed the Arabian as he turned into the lane past the blacksmith shop. He dismounted at the shop to tell Tobe, and Rufus, that he was 'bout to be married to Adelia. Rufus, gave out with his ever-present laugh. "Yo jest haint big enough in the britches yit boy. Yo go on up ta the house, tell Clemmy yo need to chaw a few more sweet taters afore you be man enough ta get hitched up with some young filly. I've knowed yo since yo was jes this big." He measured with his big hands. "No sir, yo haint hardly grown nuff ta be no husbin yit." He laughed again, slapping his leg with a few resounding whacks. Big Tobe enjoyed the show. He just grinned his toothless grin, nooded his head. No two young people in the world were as happy as Wes Bolt and Adelia Rodgers. They spent every minute of the time they could manage together. Their plans were many. Late fall had set in; November 6 was election day. The inevitable had to happen. Abraham Lincoln was elected the next President of the United States. There was tumultuous celebrating in the streets of the northern states, while most of the southern states took on a somber attitude. The parading and cheering in the south was directed at constant moves for cessation from the union. Men of intense purpose can compel their less aggressive fellows to follow along with them. Lincoln, as the elected, strove valiantly to find words that would calm the troubled waters. Men in the north who had put together an anti-slavery ticket, had put the match to the tinder. The cotton state empire was ready to bolt from the union without an act of provocation. Jefferson Davis, in his home in Mississippi, was gravely concerned over the turning of events.

It was during these troubled times that Wes, along with his totally devoted fiancee, Adelia, set about making plans for a wedding in December. The gala event was to take place at the Bolt farm. John and Clemmy made sure there was a full day of celebration. All hands turned out to ready the old Bandy homestead to be inhabited by the newlyweds. When all was ready, it was, without a doubt, a peaceful and inviting place to come home to.

CHAPTER 10
IT AIN'T MY WAR

It was a cloudy, misty December 2nd in 1860 that saw the only Bolt heir take a wife. This was just two days after Congress had convened. As of yet, no southern states had resigned, except South Carolina. All others had representatives there in hopes that some sort of a compromise might be worked out. The sixty-nine year old outgoing President Buchanan could not manage to please either the north or the south. He just wanted to keep things cemented together until the end of his term.

Who wants war? Isn't it always the cause that everyone wanted to remain at peace. Then what is the propellant which directs men to drift ever onward in the face of destruction? Six hundred thousand men were going to die as a result of the speeches, inflaming oratory, and debating which was the constant scene. One hundred and seventy old, but noble, men were selected to say whether the union of states would be torn apart. Reasoning was something that the immediate speaker had, not what the one who had just spoken had shown. These elected, good men, came together on December seventeenth in Columbia, the capitol of South Carolina. They were the states' best men, from all walks of life. How could they be wrong in what they were about to do? They were the leaders. Too many would just follow. They did not meet to talk about cessation, they came to accomplish it. They voted to separate the palmetto state from the rest of the union. They, in turn, asked the rest of the slave-holding cotton states to join with them in the formation of the confederacy of slave-holding states. The administration in Washington knew that the situation in Charleston was inflammable. They set about fortifying the garrisons which commanded Charleston harbour. The snowball was headed on the downhill run, straight into the mouth of hell. Fort Sumter was still in federal hands, but when fired upon, it became the match that touched off the war, war that came to the brink of destroying greatest nation greatest nation in the world.

During this turmoil, Clemmy and John Bolt started to act upon their dream of heading into the great western territories. They mapped their course with the greatest of care. John felt that he could build a big cattle and horse ranch in the territory of New Mexico. They had had Wes and Adelia read them every scrap of information they could find about the vast lands to the west of Texas. They had bought every map that had been printed about the route they felt they would take. Without a doubt in the mind of either one of them, they were determined to head in that direction. After all, they reasoned, Wes needed a start in life. This was their chance to go, to leave him to build on his own dreams.

John went to the county seat to have a lawyer draw up the freedom papers for each and every one of the people on the Bolt farm who were still under his ownership. When he returned, he and Clemmy asked them all to come to their house. They would break the news, then have the whole crew help them get started on their new venture. Clemmy was even more excited about the prospect of traveling halfway across the continent than John. Her dark eyes would shine with excitement when they would talk about the thousand and one things they felt were necessary to take. They wanted to be away shortly after Christmas.

The evening they were to make the big announcement became a festive occasion. A huge dinner was prepared. Everyone was there. Rufus and Sally now had, besides Wilfred, two daughters who were in their early teens, and one little boy. Cissy was busy with the food preparations, while Tobe just sat quietly, listening to the small talk of the day. When the meal was done, John raised his voice. "Now listen to me all o ya. Everbody in this house now be a free person by the law, well as by the fack that we here on the Bolt farm have allers considered everybody free. I went ta day, ta make it all correct by the each an every one o ya is named an described in them papers." He handed the packet to Rufus. Guard these with your life, Rufus, don' let no man take em from ya." "Twernt necessary no how Massa John. We ain't nevah felt lak we wuz yor slaves. We jes feel lak it were the happy life livin here lak we uns do. We has allers been free as ary bird." John cut in, "Rufus, now the hull worl knows it." He then handed the papers for Cissy, to Tobe. "These are the freedom papers for

Cissy." Great tears filled her big dark eyes, then spilled down onto the cotton apron covering her big bosom. She could only hold onto one of Tobe's arms as she swayed, moaning, "Lordy, Lordy, oh Lordy." Tobe patted her greying hair with his huge hand. His big heart so overflowing with happiness, that he dared not try to speak. "Now all o you listen ta whut I got to say." John felt an urgency to confirm their suspicions that he, and Clemmy, were getting ready to travel to the west. All already knew, but they just didn't want to believe it. The announcement came very shortly. "Now listen everybody!" John commanded their attention. "Bein thet Wes got hisself a new wife, he gonna need ter git a new start in life. Me and Clemmy been thinkin on going west fer a long time. We figger we got things in pretty good shape here at the farm. Now we wanna see jes whut might be over yonder." John swept his arm in a wide arc to the west. "Wes been readin bout thet fer us, goin on a long time now. Afore our time be done, we feel lak we wanna be a part of sompthin bran new. Ain't lak we be leavin here broke, er leavin you folk in a bad way. We aim ta take everythin we feel lak we want. We aim ta take our part o the best there is on this here farm." Clemmy would nod her head in agreement to the points John would make. "We aim to cross the big Mississippi at Natchez. Then on across Lousana ta cross the Red. Then on cross Texas. We aim ta travel up a river called the Pecos. When thet river turns to a little creek, then rat thar is the place were me an Clemmy is gonna stake out our place. All thet New Mexico territory was got by the United States after the endin of the Mexican War. Jest recent, the government want folks, jes lak us, ta go out ther ta make ourselfs a place. The more o us thar is, te better the govment is gonna like it. It's everthin east o Californy, west o Texas, an south o the Arkansas River clean ta Mexico. Out o thet, me an Clemmy want a hundred sections of the best there is. Ain't thet right, Clemmy?" "It's whut we want, alright," she agreed, "We gonna hate ta leave all o you. Mayhap some day, when we git settled, ya could come out thar. Even we might come back here." Clemmy was beginning to feel the pangs of parting. Tobe stood up. "Massa John," . . . John cut in sharply. "Yo ain't got no Massa, Tobe! Ya hain't had one in a long, long time." "Yas, Massa John, whut I start ta say wuz, me an Cissy, we ain't got much o nothin ta do here no more. I reckon ole whiskers, over in da big creek, hain't gonna miss bein cotched no ways. Me an Cissy, we gonna go wid ya, Massa. I been lookin atter yo since yo was a liddle tad. Hain't no reason ta quit now. Cissy tuk keer o Clemmy when she was birthin Wes, remember?" John was tempted to take the big man and his wife with them. Then again, Wes was going to need some looking after, too. John looked at the floor for a long time without speaking. Finally . . . "It be so, Tobe. Me and Clemmy air gonna sore need ya. Then on tother hand, Wes's gonna need some lookin atter, rat here in Georgy." Wes started to protest. John raised his hand to silence him. "Tobe, me and Clemmy gotta know thet you be lookin out fer Wes an Adelia. Rufus done got his hans full jes raisin his own fambly. We want ya to stay here, Tobe." Tobe bowed his head. "Yas, Massa," he motioned for Cissy to follow. They left the room quickly. John knew that the big man's heart was soft as butter. Tobe didn't want the others to see his emotion. "It gonna take all o us ta git us ready for the trip." John started the planning again. "We figger thet Wes and Adelia might move over ta our house." Wilfred spoke up to volunteer his services to look after the Bandy place. They talked on into the evening. When the fireplace coals had died down, Wes put his arm around Adelia. They started for the door on their way to their own comfortable cottage built by a grandfather Wes had never seen. They talked as they walked through the crisp fall evening. Wes seemed saddened as they strolled. He began to speak, "Grandfather Will was married to a full blood Cherokee Indian woman named Little Dove, she is buried not far from our house. He was a true pioneer. She was from the inhabitants of this great land. Pa was the son of an itincrant horse trader. I guest it was just inevitable that they would one day feel the wanderlust and start on a treck some place. Ma is really a bundle of dynamite done up in a pretty package. She is the perfect mate for Pa." Wes fell silent as he looked up at the starlit Georgia night. Adelia gently squeezed his arm closer to her soft body. Her low soothing voice was like music in the night. "Wes, my darling, don't be sad about them going. You know it is just what they both want to do. It isn't as if they were being forced out of their home by some unforeseen circumstance. They seem like two children on their way to a circus. Let them go, feeling that they have our blessing. It will ease the burden of parting. After all, Jesus will provide for them. In the sixth chapter of the Book of St. John, it tells how

Jesus fed a multitude on just five loaves and three small fish. Also, in the bible it mentions the manna which fed the people in the wilderness. All we have to do, Wes, is have faith that God is going to look after them, and He will." Adelia drew her arm around his shoulders, turning slightly so that her breast was against him as they walked. She had another idea bout how to deal with his premature loneliness. "Wes, my love, we are just going to have to live our own lives now. From the sound of the news we read, we are all going to have our rivers to cross, just the same as Clemmy and John." They had reached their cabin, going inside. Adelia quickly undressed, then stretched her full height to place her arms about Wes's neck. She shivered a little in the cold room. She began to unfasten his clothes after she had kissed him soundly. "Let's think about the problems of the Bolt farm, and the whole world tomorrow, Wes. Right now, let's get into that warm, soft feather bed." They made love with complete abandon until they were both ready to sleep the night through.

Back at the Bolt farm there was talk way up into the night about the impending loss of their beloved Clemmy and John. Sally cried the whole night through, and could not be comforted. The ever happy Rufus was himself saddened by the prospect of not having John with him any more. After all, they had been together since Rufus was a mere lad. John was less than twelve years old.

The plans were made, the course was set. Everyone began to elaborate on the preparations to see that John and Clemmy left the farm with nothing but the very best. They chose six of the young work mares to pull the heavy wagons. The prize work stallion was to go along, too. Three prize saddle mares, and The Lad, were to be mounts for the two adventurers. The blacksmiths carefully constructed a long flat oak chest, bound with metal, to hold the precious tools which John had learned to use at a very young and tender age. His blacksmith and carpentry tools were carefully selected from the myriad of hand-made specialities in the smithy. What he didn't already have, John knew that he could fashion what he wanted, if he could find the steel to work with. There were no precious furniture heirlooms to clutter the wagons. Neither of them had any. They had heard of the hardships endured by the Gold Rush of Forty Nine, the Land Rush of the late fifties. Now Clemmy and John were trying to profit by the mistakes of others. The fitness of his precious horses was always the prime concern of John Bolt. The six young mares he had chosen were big and strong. They began to work them to harden their muscles. Some of them were barely broken to harness. Still, John knew each of them by name, and took pride in them all. Their harness was new, they were carefully shod by the never tiring Tobe. These were special, they got the best. They had oak bows made for the wagons, cotton canvas covers made to cover their precious cargo. Clemmy tried to think through what they would need to sustain them for several years. She knew that they could supplement their clothes with the skins of wild animals. Her old Granny, Sun Flower, had taught her well how to sew a fine seam with a sinew made of animal gut.

The first wagon bore their personal effects. The second, their tools, feed, and a coop of chickens which Clemmy vowed were to go with her all the way to New Mexico territory. Last of all, there was an adequate supply of gold coins carefully built into the floor of the lead wagon, just below the seat. This was undoubtedly one of the finest rigs ever to head for the promised lands in the far west. The thrill, and excitement of all the preparations kept them working at a fever pitch. They had little time to regret their decision to begin a brand new life. Wes was the only one who could possibly have changed their minds. He felt he shouldn't try.

Special casks with metal bindings were fitted to the sides of both wagons. They had heard about people running out of water on the long hot treks through the desert portions of the trail. Extra wheels were slung beneath the beds of the vehicles. Choice packets of seeds were sewn into canvas bags, then packed into a large wooden box for safety. The tailgate of the rear wagon was made into a kitchen cabinet of sorts. There were compartments and cubbyholes for all sorts of utensils. After the bed of the front wagon was loaded, a bed for sleeping was made over the crates, and boxes, which would not have to be moved until they reached their destination.

Early on the morning of December 5th, 1860, John and Clemmy said their sad farewells, climbed to the wagon seat, then set out for a brand new life in the territories to the west.

By now, John Bolt's hair was almost all grey. Not from age, but some quirk of body chemistry which caused it. The statuesque Clemmy sat beside him, her hair, still the color of a raven's wing, blew in the cold morning breeze. They waved to the sorrowful group as they headed out the drive, past the smithy John had work ed so hard to establish, then turned the team of beautiful horses to the left. Clemmy then lighted her corn-cob pipe, puffing contentedly, each of them wrapped in their own thoughts. If the weather held good, they had determined to make at least twenty-five miles each day. That weather, however, did not cooperate. A cold steady drizzle began before the day was half gone. Soon the red clay roads were slick and muddy. The horses struggled to keep their footing. All day long they toiled. By nightfall, although they had tried to stay under the wagon cover, they were both soaked to the skin. They made camp by the road. If it had not been for the heavy clouds, they could have seen their own farm back in the valley from whence they had come. Making camp was no small task. They had to make a rope picket line for the mares, separate the stallions, since they were ever ready to do battle. It was dark when they crawled into bed, unable to make a fire to cook their supper. They were awakened the next morning by one of their roosters crowing from his coop in the back of the trailing wagon. John lifted the wagon flap to look out. It was still raining hard. "Wonder what in hell thet fool rooster thinks he got to crow about?" Clemmy laughed. "He jes anxious to get ta whar we be going. He got a lot o work to do afore he can claim he is doing his part to settle the west." Clemmy began to run her fingers through John's greying hair. She kissed him on the face, neck and chest. "We ain't got no business goin out in ta that rain now, John." John slapped her firm behind. "It ain't gonna stop rainin no time soon, Clemmy, We got work ta do." "Lordy, effin a little rain cause you ta be thisaway, John, I shore hope the sun gonna shine afore we reach the New Mexico territory." It was John's turn to laugh. "Yo are a terrible woman, Clemmy! Yo are down-right sinful, an thet be a fact." Clemmy pressed her willing body against him. "Then jes leave me here, John. Maybe you could find yo one of them full blood squaws out on the prairie." She knew he would never leave her. In fact, he didn't even leave her to go tend the horses until the sun was almost up.

They began their way through the Smoky Mountains toward northern Alabama. In some of the towns they camped near, they were told of possible horse thieves on the more thinly populated part of the open roads. Part of their preparation before leaving the farm was to purchase two rifles and two pistols each. The newest repeating models were part of their gear. Clemmy also had the ever-present muzzle-loading shotgun. John carried the throwing knives he and Larkin and fashioned so many years ago. One on his hip, the other down the back of his neck. Their last wish was to encounter trouble, but they were prepared for it just in case it encountered them. They slogged along, with the weather staying bad for several days. They made their way steadily westward. Their destination, for the moment, was the northern terminus of the Natchez Trace, the Highway of Commerce established by the early French traders who founded Mississippi and Louisiana Territories. Their chosen crossing point for the big river was to be Natchez. They planned to be transported across the wide water by steam-powered ferry boat which was carrying a steady stream of settlers going to Texas, and the great beyond. As they drew nearer the heavily traveled way, they began to encounter other lone travelers. There were groups of three or four wagons. Different families who had picked up all their belongings to head for the promised land beyond the western sunset. Most of them were very friendly folks. Clemmy and John would visit the various camps to exchange gossip and experiences. On many occassions, John would share his knowledge of blacksmithing with some unfortunate traveler who had broken some precious part of his equipment.

As they neared the thickly forested portion of the well-traveled Trace, they heard more and more stories of renegade slave bands who would prey upon the hapless travelers who were unable to defend themselves. The stories of horror and cruelty took on more and more terrible dimensions. The further The Trace led them into Mississippi, the more the northbound traffic. It was practice for river commerce to be carried on by the building of huge wooden barges, in the northern areas, then floating them down the rivers such as the Tennessee. Even smaller rivers would carry the barges during the rainy seasons. Produce would stand at the docks until a barge would take it aboard bound for the Mississippi. When the produce reached its destination, it would be sold, barge and all. The lumber from the craft would be used in some sort of construction at it destination. Boat crews would then make their way over The Trace, back to their northern origination point. At this time, however, small steamers were beginning to replace the land travel. Their shallow craft, coupled with paddle wheels either at the back, or side, made them ideal for river navigation.

Congress, under its power, had established post roads along The Trace. Treaties were made with the Choctaw and Chickasaw Indians to let the traffic pass without disturbance from that quarter. Highwaymen were still the big worry.

Clemmy and John found themselves part of a train of about eight wagons. They just drifted together without any organization. When the timber and brush began to thicken on each side of The Trace, they stopped to hold a council. The head of a family from Tennessee, Jeremiah Brown, was chosen as the Captain of their small group. He had had some soldiering, so they felt he might be the most knowledgeable about how to hold off an attack, in the event there happened to be one. The joining with the other wagons slowed the Bolt's progress considerably. The extra precaution was worth it, however. They couldn't stand the thought of losing even one of their precious horses. People everywhere could tell at a glance that the stock they had with them was the finest to be owned. They received constant offers to buy one or several of their animals. All offers were declined. They intended to have them all in their new ranch home at the end of the trail. Many a roving eye took in Clemmy's proportions, too. The look of John Bolt discouraged any advances they might have had in mind. At evening time, Clemmy and John would talk with travelers going in the other direction. They would receive news of the trail, plenty of talk of an impending war with the Yankee north.

This was winter in Mississippi. There was hardly a day that the sun put in an appearance. Rain fell in torrents. Roads beame a quagmire of straining animals and men. This kind of constant pulling was beginning to tell on their beautiful matched team of six mares. At times. John would harness the working stallion. He was called upon to do his part. In the particularly sticky places, Clemmy and John would each saddle one of the riding horses. Ropes were attached to the saddle horns, then they, too, were called upon to lean into the work as John would urge the draft team to greater effort. There were constant streams to cross. Miles and miles of cane breaks would stand on either side of the well-traveled road.

One morning Clemmy remarked, "Mississippi is an Indian

word for 'Father of Waters.' I know for shore, John, we air gonna grow webs betwix our toes." They each wore moccasins which Clemmy had fashioned before they left Georgia. At night they would place them on sticks by the fireside in an effort to dry them out before they put them on the next morning."Shore as hell be on fire, Clemmy, them hosses gonna grow duck feathers. They ain't had a dry minute fer days. Fer the first time, I be thinkin we started out to travel this road at the wrong time o the year. As fer as we got to go, my love, I reckon bad part might jes as well be on this end as tuther." Clemmy was always philosophical. Twenty long, grueling days had gone by since they left their comfortable home in Cherokee County, Georgia. They were now in the middle of Mississippi at Carthage.

They left the road to give their horses a much deserved rest. After some haggling, they made a deal with a local farmer to let them pasture their animals on lush green grass not too far from the main road to Jackson. The days were still grey. After camp was established with a canvas fly at the side of the lead wagon, they prepared the first really good meal they had had since starting. "Reckon we jes as well set here til Christmas day passes." This was Clemmy's idea. "Caint be no harm in thet, Clemmy. The team need a good rest, an so do we." They built fires to dry out their wet belongings. Their cotton clothes were washed in lye soap, the smell of which never left the garment. At least they were clean again.

The other part of the train they were in, had pushed on when they decided to take their break. After all the company of the others in the train, they were beginning to be just a little lonely. This cold winter was getting close to Christmas. They had too much time to wonder what the rest of the family was doing. Were they being missed? Were they all well? Out of the silence, Clemmy said, "Wonder eff Adelia be pregnant yit? I never had time ta think on it, John, but we could be grandparents in jes no time at all." A wave of loneliness swept over Clemmy at the thought. Tears came to her big dark eyes. "There was a lot o things we didn't have time to think on, John." He put his arms around her, drew her close to comfort her. "We could go to town to get some Christmas gifts, but to tell the truth there jes ain't nothin we need." "John, so long as I kin be right next to you, there ain't no better gift in the whole wide world and Georgia." "We be in Mississippi now, Clemmy, our world is gittin bigger all tha time." On the twenty-third, another wagon pulled off the road to make camp a short distance away. It was a family from Virginia. Man, woman and four kids.

The Millers said they were bound fer Texas. They had kin there who was goin ta help make a place fer them near a town named Waco. Clemmy was overjoyed at the opportunity to have the three little girls, and one boy, to fuss over. It eased the pangs of homesickness which had a tendency to gnaw at her. It also gave Clemmy a chance to go with Mrs. Miller to town. The two men could look after the campsites. The chance to buy small gifts for the children was a thrill Clemmy was truly grateful for. They walked into Carthage, going to a general store. As they shopped, they could hear conversation everywhere about the possibility of war with the north.

Jefferson Davis of this great southern state was emerging as a strong leader for the southern faction. That honored gentleman certainly didn't relish the thought of war, or even the division of the states. But after all, he was a child of the south who must stand for his principles. The owning of slaves to work the vast cotton fields of Mississippi was the life-blood of these people. How could a few near-sighted northerners, who had never owned slaves, nor understood the situation, condemn those who did? A surge of fear went through Clemmy as she thought of her own son, Wes, having to march off to war with the Yankees. Something was sure to divert the impending doom. After all, people don't just start killing each other. When it was her own safety which was concerned, Clemmy held little regard. When it was someone who was dear to her, it was another kind of cat altogether.

They bought their small treasures of nuts, fruit, and even candy. This was going to be a joyous Christmas after all. Christmas Eve in the middle of Mississippi was a foggy, cold night for the travelers. They made the best of what they had. The canvas fly at the side of the Bolt wagon was the altar for their services that night. The fire had gone down to a heap of glowing coals from the hickory and oak they had used for fuel. Clemmy, John and the Miller group gathered in the shelter of the warmth to sing songs, to hear the Christmas story told over again, as it had been for hundreds of years in the past. Mrs. Miller read from her bible to make the scene complete. When the Miller children had gotten sleepy, Clemmy helped the mother bed them down for the night. Clemmy asked permission to kiss them all goodnight. She then promised that Santa was shore as shootin gonna be there afore the sun rose in the mornin'.

The women then went back to the fire, where they filled cotton socks with candy, apples and oranges for each of the little ones. Even the men joined in the fun. When it was time for the older ones to say their goodnights, Clemmy and John stood alone by their fire. Clemmy fervently asked God to watch over her only son, Adelia and the rest of the family they had left at the farm. "It were a choice, Clemmy, so we made the choice ta hit tha road fer the west. We haint been gone a month yit. Tonight, though, hit shore seems to be a year." Clemmy could tell that John was beginning to feel some regret for leaving their comfortable lives behind. She opened his coat to place her body closer to his. "John, honey, ain't no use in gittin so broke up bout leaving now. We have each other, an so far we have seen a whole passel o new things. I love ya, John, I allus will." John kissed her forehead as he felt her snuggle closer. They crawled into their warm bed, they could hear the bell of a church in Carthage tolling the coming of Christmas Day.

That glorious day saw the sun come through for the first time in a long series of rainy days. It was a most welcome sight. The two familes had become close friends. The holiday afternoon was spent preparing to hit the open road the following day. The Miller wagon was not nearly the quality John Bolt had put into his. It was pulled by four medium sized mules of varying ages. When John put his six matched grey Percheron mares on a line that evening to inspect their hooves, Miller exlaimed. "Bolt, I ain't never in all my borned days seen a team o horses as beautiful as them." These Percheron draft horses were the offspring of great herds which were imported from France in about 1838. Each weighed well over one thousand nine hundred pounds. Their massive shoulders accented the rest of their compact, blocky bodies. The muscles in their shoulders, loins and thighs easily adapted to the powerful contractions needed to draw heavy loads. The stallion was even larger than the mares. The Bolts were justly proud of thier livestock. All seemed ready for the following morning. That night, when they strolled over to the Miller camp, Clemmy made the suggestion that they join for the trip on to at least Natchez. "Yo know, John, two men is better'n one when it comes to fightin them mean mudholes in the road." "Reckon yo be right, Clemmy, Miller can help me with the stock, an I will hep him effin his team gits stuck." Clemmy heaved a sign of relief. She really had wanted to see these children make it on down the road.

The next morning at first light, John had Miller set the pace. This new arrangement was bound to slow them down, but were they in that big a hurry, after all? The roads were better now with the sun out to dry them. The low areas still were giant mudholes. Trees, brush, and cane had been chopped down, then placed across the holes to help bear the weight of the wagons. There was traffic in both directions. Slaves in ragged clothes were in attendance on many of the great drays hauling produce. Some going this way, some going that, as it always is. Men were much the same as livestock with some of the owners. There were wretched creatures hunched against the chill of winter. Others were well-fed, singing as they walked beside their teams or rode the high seats. As many as ten mules would be hitched to one wagon. Getting the animals to perform in line was a skill that only time could teach. They crossed the Pearl River on barges fashioned for that purpose. They were huge flat-bottomed barges with a heavy fence around the perimeter to tie the livestock to. The horses, and mules, were blindfolded to keep them from seeing what they being led on to. Wagons were placed in the middle with the loads evenly distributed to keep them from tipping the barge. The excitement shone in Clemmy's eyes. "Lordy, what a river! I ain't seen thet much water in all ma whole life!" The bargeman laughed. "Jes wait till you git ta the mighty Mississippi, lady. Now that thar is a wide, deep river." A small paddlewheel steamer came alongside the barge to nudge it across the river. The blindfolded horses snorted, pointing their ears at the clanking monster which was getting too close for comfort. The trip was uneventful. John was sure that the fee had placed a drain on the dwindling money supply of the Millers. This was great concern to the Bolts now that they had adopted this poor, but proud, family. Great flocks of ducks, geese and other waterfowl would darken the sky at times as they got closer to the great waters of the river. Clemmy would take her shotgun after they made camp, she laced on rawhide leggins as a protection against snakes, then walked to the marshes near the road. One or two shots would harvest enough geese to feed the whole group. She did the hunting, while John tended the horses. She approached the camp carrying three large Canada geese. "John, ain't it a blessin o the Lord that folks ain't never goin to run outa wild stuff ta eat?" There be enough waterfowl here ta feed the whole worl." Actually there only seemed to be an endless supply, as time would tell. Clemmy had furnished enough meat to feed both families again. She and John both felt a great concern for the hard-working Millers. Clemmy kept the baby, just two years old, with her every moment she could. Linda was a beautiful child with hair the color of gold, eyes as blue as a summer sky. What a contrast they were! She and Clemmy rode on the seat of the lead wagon, as John drove the six working mares. Linda was the little girl Clemmy had always wanted.

The closer they came to Natchez, the more traffic there was on the road. This was more human beings than Clemmy and the Millers had seen in all their lives. Slaves were driving mule teams, slaves were driving the fancy carriages of the rich plantation owners who, for one reason or another, were obliged to travel on the muddy road. Huge, high-sided cargo wagons loaded with produce, unloaded from river steamers, were on the road with a thousand and one destinations. John was raised in Savannah, so was not so totally impressed with the crowds, the noise of a densely populated area. Clemmy would catch herself staring, the mule skinners, and even the dressed up gentry in the fancy rigs would stare back at her. They were held in awe at the beauty of this dark-eyed lady on the high seat of a covered wagon. Many would tip their hat and smile.

Houses along the road became more plentiful as they neared Natchez. When the damp weather and fog cleared one afternoon, they could see the city on a distant bluff, overlooking the mightiest river known to this part of the world. Clemmy gasped in wonder. She could hardly speak. "Lordy, Lordy, John, whut a sight ta see! This be one o that sights I hadda see in my life-time." Barges, and steamers, made their way through the patches of fog which clung tenaciously to the river surface. "Lordy, John, where in the world are all them people goin? Looks lak as big as them river steamers is, they would jes sink down to the bottom o all thet water." John, too, was impressed with the immensity of the father of waters. It was soon to be fought over by mighty armies locked in a death struggle to control the importance of its traffic. They pushed on to the outskirts of the old, much renowned, Natchez. Magnificent two-story houses rose from the shelter of moss-festooned oak trees. Streets began to be paved with brick to keep them from being a sea of mud. Just as the Miller wagon and team was a typical example of the masses struggling westward, the Bolt outfit was so impressive that people turned to see them pass. The work horses were prancing in their harness, the saddle stock would shy away from unfamiliar scenes along the tree-lined streets. They were hailed time after time with the query, "Do you wanna sell some of them horses?" Of course, John's answer was always the same. Miller halted his team to ask the way to a spot where they could rest their stock for a day or two. Directions were given to a spot only a short way from the river's edge. It seemed that all the wealth of Mississippi was concentrated right here in Natchez. They rented a pasture fenced by zigzag rails. Miller turned his mules loose in the enclosure. Next came the work mares. They ran and bucked in their new-found freedom from halter and harness. The stallions could not be turned loose, so were fed grain from a feed bag fastened over the tops of their heads. It was a constant problem to keep them separated.

Although it was the dead of winter, Natchez was still a beautiful sight. This location on the bluffs above the father of waters was chosen by the Spanish for its situation on alluvial ground as high as two hundred feet, in places, above the river. It later came into the possession of the French. Then the French were replaced by the British. In 1779, the Spanish took the city, they were, in turn, crowded out by the constant streams of American settlers crowding to the west. Natchez then became the capitol of the newly organized territory of Mississippi. Deals were made with the Natchez Indians to allow the settlers to pass peacefully through the Natchez Trace. It became a great roadway to the west. Other tribes to the east had also been bargained with. Even now, Natchez was a railroad terminal of the Natchez Central, and the Mississippi Central. Wooden jetties were built out into the river so that the steamboats could constantly load, and unload, their diverse cargoes. Huge gangs of slaves sang in unison as they strained to unload trade goods, then reload with bales of cotton. Cotton and slaves were the lifeblood of Mississippi. For this reason, Jefferson Davis was one of the first to lead his state out of the union.

Impending war was the topic of the day for those who had time to stop to talk. It was in this whirlpool of humanity that Clemmy and John tried to keep their minds directed toward their goal of a big ranch in the New Mexico territory.

They stayed by the river . . . resting their animals until after the first of the year 1861. The war talk was deepening. More states were withdrawing from the union. At this point they were wavering between turning back, and going on, to find their dream. They made extra money, by letting their two stallions stand at stud. There were plenty of offers to pay, from the plantations adjoining the city. They could have made Natchez their home if John had wanted to start the livestock business again.

One evening when John returned to the camp from one of his trips to a nearby plantation, he saw Clemmy standing by the rail fence looking out across the broad expanse of the greatest river on the northern continent. She was very still, with her head held high. Her black hair was glistening in the evening rays of the sun. John approached, spoke to her softly. "Evenin' darlin!" She didn't stir. He went to her side, putting his arm around her shoulders. He could feel her shivering. The light coffee color of her beautiful face was streaked with tears. "Now what in the whole state of Mississippi could make my love cry like this?" She turned her tear streaked face toward him. Her big dark eyes were deeply troubled. "John . . ." her voice caught in her throat. "It's sich a wide river thet I feel lak we air leavin this world we are in. I got a powerful hurt in my breast, John. Bad times is comin an I feel lak we air gonna be needed sorely at the farm." He held her closer. "Mayhap, they be a heap of trouble comin to everybody now, Clemmy. We larnt Wes the way to be a real he-man. He be one! Ever man gonna haff ta stand on his hind laigs, honey. Wes will do whut be right fer the farm, an our people. They gonna stan by him till they die. There ain't no tellin jest whut they might be called pon ta do. I know this, my precious one. I don't want no part of a war thet causes men to fight over the right ta own another man. Now don' look backards, honey. We got the outfit all ready to move again. Tomorra at first light we go on board a ferry boat which is gonna take us all cross thet wide river ta Luziana. This ain't the same wide river ole Sun Flower allers talked bout, honey. Tha one she spoke of, there weren't no crossin back.'' Clemmy enbraced John tightly. ''Maybe there ain't no crossin back fer us either, John.'' She sobbed softly. They walked slowly back to their campfire where Clemmy had their supper boiling in an iron pot. She leaned her head on his shoulder. ''John, honey, I ain't never goin ter say 'turn back' again, no, never!'' He didn't hear those words from her for the rest of their lives.

There was a lot of hustle and hurry the next morning as they loaded their horses, wagons, and mules aboard the big river steamer. The Millers, along with Clemmy, never ceased to wonder how there could be such a ship that could take all of their horses and wagons at one trip. Mrs. Miller likened it to Noah's Ark. The children were wild with excitement as the steamer began to move away from the loading jetty. Sooner than they expected, they were in Louisiana. The unloading process was hastened by slaves owned by the river boat captain. They were trained in every move they made to get the paddle wheeler headed back across the water to Natchez.

The day was still young when Clemmy and John turned west, away from the greater population center. They no more than got under way, when it began to rain again. Great torrents of cold rain came down, drenching them to the skin. Miller got a bad sore throat, he began to cough. The cold spread to his wife, Margie, as well as to the little ones. Their progress was slowed to a crawl by the endless rain and mud. It seemed that the entire state of Louisiana was a sea of water.

All through the Delta area, there was one swamp and bayou, after another. The high ground was sugar plantations. The swamps yielded furs taken by the muskrat trappers who would pole their one man pirogues through the reeds and hummocks from dawn to dark. This was the trappers' season. They were making the most of it. Some would come to the camps at night to ask for coffee or tea. They were not at all welcome guests, since the stink of them would linger long after they had left.

One particularly bad night, the Bolts took the children into their wagon. Margie Miller had her hands full just trying to tend to the needs of her husband who now was running a high fever. John himself started coughing as he made his rounds tending to the horses. The Millers were hard put to keep going. In the mornings he would struggle with the mules to get them into harness, then, through the horrible weather of the day. Margie would drive them on through the rain and mud. The Bolts could not spare a team, since they were pulling the wagons which were heavily loaded. Even the magnificent work mares had to strain and heave to keep going. When they thought they had experienced all they could endure, they noticed a decided change in the countryside. They began to pass through rolling hills that caused the roadways to improve considerably. Blue sky appeared. Then Margie Miller stopped her team, got down from the seat where she knelt and said a prayer of thanks for their deliverance from the ordeal they had just gone through. They camped again to allow themselves to recuperate from the ravages of the heavy colds they all had. They were afraid that Miller would have pneumonia if they tried to press on. All needed a rest, anyway. Clemmy had them drink tea made from some of the herbs she had brought from home. Clemmy knew every potion and poultice known to both the Indians and whites alike. Some of the most vile tasting was supposed to be the most beneficial. All survived in spite of the medicine. They began the journey. Their starting seemed to signal the unrelenting rain again.

A small herd of swamp deer, frightened by something in the cane field at the side of the road, flashed across in front of the Bolt team. The startled leaders reared, plunging out of control Before John could pull them to a stop, they had left the road. The right wheels of the lead wagon sank into the mud so deeply that the wagon turned onto it's side. Chickens, boxes, pot and pans, spilled. Cover bows were broken, the canvas ripped. Rain was falling in torrents, the travelers unloaded the wagon. To make things worse, Clemmy had sprained her right arm when the wagon tipped. They, and the Millers, struggled in mud to their knees in an effort to get the wagon right again. Night fell as black as the inside of a tomb. The animals were all edgy. John would have to quit his work now and then to talk to the tethered horses. The sound of his voice would soothe them for a while. Then he would go back to his back-breaking toil. The work teams were left in the traces where they stood all night. When it was light enough the next day, the work stallion was harnessed. A chain was fastened to the rear axle of the wagon on the sunken side. The rear wagon then was unhooked.

John urged the team to greater effort as Miller drove the stallion at an oblique angle to help right the vehicle to get it onto four wheels again. Most of that day was used to reload the big wagon. Everything was soaking wet. They got underway late in the afternoon and the rain stopped. The sun made a half-hearted gesture to ease their aching bodies. Before dark, they made camp on a high rise of ground. Livestock, as well as the human travelers were totally exhausted. It was over a hundred miles to their next destination, Natchidoches. That is, as the crow flies, and the travelers certainly were not crows. The winding tortuous route they were traveling would cause them to travel over half again that far. All felt that they would never like to see it rain again. The sun began to shine brightly, their soaked bedding was spread over the tops of the wagons to dry. Their canvas was mended. Spirits rose. They began to pass wagons traveling in the direction from whence they had just come. Where were they when help was so badly needed?

Woodsmoke curled from the chimneys of several houses along the banks of a wide, muddy, river. Natchidoches, the oldest settlement in the state of Louisiana was not too far off. It was established in 1714 by French traders. The town still evidenced the character and customs of its founders. The French had made friends with the Caddo Indians. At that time, they were fierce warriors to be reckoned with. Now they were more a sedentary lot, content to trade furs or steal horses from unwary travelers. To be sure, they had watched the Bolt wagons from the time they first entered Caddo country. Here was a prize worth working for. Camp was made near the rolling waters of the Red River. All needed rest again after their bone-wracking journey through the mud of Louisiana. John struck up a conversation with a teamster who was on his way to the south of New Orleans. His great freight wagons were loaded with buffalo hides harvested on the plains north of the Trinity River. There were seven or eight of the men, who John noticed looked as tough as the slow-plodding oxen they were driving. These men wore animal skin ponchos over their rough clothes. It was obvious that they were ready for any eventuality. Each carried a pair of loaded pistols in his belt in addition to a long bone-handled knife. It was a friendly lot. "Whar in thunder be yo headin ith thet string o hosses, neighbor?" The hide hunter had been eyeing the Bolt herd. He especially examined the Arabian stallion. "They jest haint no other hoss flesh lak that there, from here plumb to Californy." The hide hunter patted the stud on the front shoulder. The Lad was not accustomed to the smell of a hide-hunter. He stamped his front hoof. At the same time he gave a snort, shook his head. The hide-hunters all laughed. One said . . . "Mort, he don't seem ta like the smell o ya." They all had to examine the work teams, admire the work stallion, as they wondered what it would be like to own horses like these. Mort addressed John again. "Tell ya sompthin', Mister . . . ah . . . Bolt," John informed, "I be John Bolt." "As I wuz sayin. Keep a sharp eye from here to tother side o te Sabine. If ya don't, some Caddo is gonna be riding the fanciest hoss in the whole state o Texas."

CHAPTER 11
TEXAS

After a brief stay, the travelers ferried across the Red River, then made for the pine woods for the crossing of the Sabine River into the state of Texas. There was more travel on the roads now. The going was easier for everyone but the Miller family. The mud roads of Louisiana had proven too much for two of the older mules. They went lame so badly that they had to be shot, then left by the roadside. Circling flocks of turkey buzzards made short work of the flesh, while the bones joined those of other animals which had met the same fate on the long treks to the new horizon. The remaining two mules could barely haul the loaded wagon. Miller pulled them to a stop to rest every so often. The stops made John and Clemmy very apprehensive. They had sighted lance-wielding Indians running through the pines along the shoulder of the road. They were waiting their chance for a horse to stray to one side, or the owner's guard to be down just enough for them to loosen a halter, then scare the horse into the trees. John called a halt to make a better plan to continue the journey. There was a bitter cold north wind blowing. The women built a fire to prepare a hot meal while the men talked. "Miller, them mules o yor'n jest caint make it from where we be right now, to thet Waco country. Them hide-hunters say it be good two hunert mile to whar yo be goin." Jake Miller nodded his head sadly. "We gotta rest them mules now an then, John. I know you want to be in the New Mexico territory by the early spring so's yo can git located fore the next winter sets in. Jes pull on out now, John. Me and the woman and kids ull make camp here for a few days, then roll on fast as we kin." "Jake, them Caddo would be eatin mule meat fore two days went by. The rest o yer stuff could wind up in some Injun hut somewhere to the north o here. We come this fer together, Jake, me and Clemmy aim ta see ya with yore kin in thet farm land at Waco. Help me harness the stuf." John slapped Jake on the shoulder. They harnessed the huge Percheron, then rigged him to pull on the tongue of the Miller wagon. When they were ready, John said . . . "Take the rear now, Jake. Them mules is gonna git some rest whilst they work."

The two smaller Miller children had now begun to expect to ride in the big lead wagon with the Bolts. The older children had their tasks. They were to keep a sharp lookout for the ever-present Caddo, lurking in the brush or pine woods. These Indians were determined to get away with one or more of the coveted horses belonging to the Bolts. They knew that trading these horses would make them much wealthier than they were then. Blue-eyed Linda was riding on the high seat beside Clemmy. "Ya know, youngun, I pray ta God that I might have one jes lak yo." Clemmy hugged the child who was bundled against the cold wind. "John, I ain't never complained bout not having any more chillen. I shoulda had a passel o em so's you could have some help with the stock. I know this has been a turrible strain on yo." John didn't answer, so Clemmy glanced at him from the corner of her eye. He was looking straight over the horses' heads. There was smile on his face. That face had taken on a ruggedness from the constant outdoor work. His blonde hair was almost all white now. His frame was still as lithe and muscular as ever. "What a handsome man," she thought. "Wonder whut he be thinkin on? John, you listenin ta me?" "Shore am, Clemmy, whut did you say?" She playfully pinched him. "I known yo never hear a word I say. What ya thinkin on?" "I wuz thinkin bout Wes and his fambly at the farm. He had a big pair of boots ta fill, Clemmy. I know he filled em." They both fell silent again as the wagons rolled on westward.

They began to pass remote farms and ranches which they could see nestled in the valleys away from the main road. More and more traffic was on the road now. They would greet each new face with a cheery conversation as they passed. By 1861, Texas was beginning to be quite thickly settled, by frontier standards, anyway. There was a huge influx of settlers who would arrive at the busy gulf ports. They then made their way inland in search of just the right spot to satisfy a long established dream. Those dreams did not come true for a great many of them. Many dreams turned to ashes and defeat by the tribulations of the raw new land.

Our travelers began to enter the rich blackland farming area along the beautiful valley of the Brazos, the Miller destination, Waco, was just about two days away. Travelers on the track going in the other direction were most anxious to give directions to the road weary adventurers. Farms were now more plentiful along the rich bottom land of the river. They topped a rise in the road, from where they could see the village of Waco. The Miller family was shouting with glee at the sight of their destination. They had finally, with the help of the Bolts, found their home for years to come.

Jake Miller suggested that they camp outside of town while he made inquiry about his kinfolk. Clemmy and John agreed without hesitation. They, too, were happy to see some sign of civilizaton. It was decided to take turns going into the general store to replenish their supplies. The Millers had very little money left. Jake was not reluctant to watch the livestock, while John and Clemmy went into town. He told John . . . "Ask about muh kinfolk so's yo kin see iffin they be livin in this part or the kintry." "Reckon we kin hep ya to make camp, Jake, then me an Clemmy will mosey on in ta see bout supplies. We need to see iffin we kin buy some grain for the horses." They left the camp, with Clemmy promising the children that she would have a look see iffin she might find some barber pole candy. A small list of other items was told to Clemmy for the Miller family.

The townfolks seemed just about as anxious to talk about the traveler's experience as they were, to hear the latest news of what was going on in the world. The general store-keeper introduced himself as Silas Rollins. He wanted to hear an account of their entire trip. His greatest concern was what the rest of the south was thinking about the possiblity of war. Texas was split wide open in trying to make a decision about joining the confederate states which were forming an alliance. Rollins said, "Sam Houston is in favor o jinin the rest of the south in the break with the other states over the slavery question." Bout as many other folks is agin Texas jining with anything." They had fought hard for their independence, so they thought they should just stay that way. John spoke slowly as though he was choosing his words carefuly. "We be horse breeders, an we decided ta head fer the New Mexico territory. We hear tell there be plenty of land out yonder. . . jist fer the takin." Rollins rolled his eyes toward the ceiling. "God a mighty, folks. . . ya got a long and lonesome way to travel yit. There be a right smart o cheap land right here in the Waco kintry." Other shoppers began to edge closer to hear what the Bolts had to say. This was, in effect, just like a newspaper to them. Word from back east, even two or three months old, was better than no word at all. John spoke again. "That be a right nice thought, neighbor, but I reckon we done made up our mind ta stay on the trail till we git to the spot we chose." Clemmy began to busy herself with the buying of supplies. She was being waited on by Mrs. Rollins, who was most anxious to be friendly. Since there were several people gathered in the store by now, John thought this would be a good time to mention their friends. "We teamed up with fambly fum Tennessee a while back on tha trail. Their name be Miller." John raised his voice enough for all to hear. "They be lookin fer kinfolk in these parts." Rollins looked up from putting a chunk of oak into the cast iron stove. "Well, Mister Bolt, there is a fambly o Millers across the river about two day ta the north. Got theirselfs a sizeable herd o longhorn cattle. There are some hard working boys in the Miller bunch." "Our friend's name be Jake, and he mentioned a brother here who is called Delmer." Rollins spat tobacco juice at the fire, then nodded vigorously. "Thet is shore ta be Del Miller awright. He ask us ta keep a sharp eye peeled fer his kin. Where be they, Bolt?" John waved his arm toward the meadow at the edge of town. The genuine friendliness of these Texas people had begun to impress both Clemmy and John. The Bolts inquired about grain for their horses. A big heavy-bodied farmer named Jenkins said that he had had a fair corn crop that year and was willing to sell John enough to supply his stock. They shook hands over their deal, then the Bolts shouldered their supplies for the walk back to their camp at the edge of town.

At the fireside this night, the conversation lasted well into the late hours. The Millers were excited about joining their family, the Bolts were anxious to load their horse feed at the Jenkins' farm, then push on up the river. The prospect of having a home which was not rolling on wheels was real joy to the children. It was getting along toward the end of February, and the wind was damp and cold. Daylight would see them rolling for the river crossing. The loading of the corn into the second wagon was underway when Jenkins mentioned recent Indian trouble to the west. As he panted and worked at the grain loading, he told them of Comanche attacks in the hill country. "Them devils range all the way from up near Cisco, to the desert country of Mexico, on the other side of the Rio Grande. There is only three ranger companies to keep them red demons in check. That is one tribe which don't mind takin on help from any outlaw or renegade injun which might ride their way. In the south hill country, there is Mexicans an injuns from split tribes which rides with the Comanche. They trade off the goods they steal and the prisoners they capture to some o the big ranchos in Mexico. They call em Comancheros, an they are mean enough ta kill their own grandma. If them Comanche see these fine horses, they shore as hell gonna try ta take em from ya. You folks better wait up till spring, then jine more wagons west. Better chanct ta fight them murderers thet way. Rangers cain't be ever where. They got to help the ranch folks too. The rangers try to keep em moving but them Comanche is bout the best horsemen in the whole world. Them braves is on a horse afore they be weaned from their ma's tit." The big man blushed and stammered as he noticed that Clemmy and Margie Miller had been listening to what he was saying about the Indians.

With the loading done, they were back on the well-traveled road north in the beautiful valley of the Brazos River. Well-kept farms showed themselves along the way. Cattle and horses grazed in fields which seemed to be held together with row after row of rail fence. The Bolts rode in silence with pangs of homesickness washing over each of them. They traveled all that day in a northwesternly direction, stopping now and then to chat with a passerby to inquire about the Miller ranch. Most of the valley residents knew the Miller family, reassuring them that they were on the right road to their immediate destination. The horses and mules were urged on just a little faster than usual. There was a grey overcast to the skies keeping the temperature cold and miserable. No storm broke, however, so the miles seemed to melt away. They were directed to turn left at the next well-traveled road. They made camp reluctantly that evening as darkness fell. By the first light the next morning, it was hit the road again. A well traveled wagon road branched to the left away from the river. Frontier Texas was a lovely sight to behold. Herds of white-tailed deer mingled with long-horned cattle grazing in the open meadows. Great flocks of wild turkeys would rise and fly a short distance to the protection of oak trees and brush on the hillsides. The Millers felt that they had reached the promised land, the Bolts were about ready to agree. Thoughts were crossing their minds about getting some of this Texas land to make a home of their own. They topped a ridge from where they could see the rolling hills of central Texas stretching away to the horizon. Clouds of woodsmoke were visible, dotting the scene as busy farmers took advantage of the winter months to clear more land for the plow next spring. Camp was made again after they were directed to turn to the left where the creek crossed the main road. Early the next morning, one of the Arabian mares was saddled so that the Miller boy could ride on ahead to announce their coming. Russ Miller felt like a king as he urged the sleek grey mare into a gallop. By early afternoon, the slower moving wagons were met by a group of seven horsemen coming to meet them. The small Russ Miller rode further behind where a spring wagon loaded with women and children hastened to catch up. Jack Miller's oldest brother, Del, rode at the head of the pack, his grey hair and beard streaming in the cold wind. They were all roughly clad in mostly home-made clothing. Each wore the extra high heeled boots typical of a western rider. The high-heeled boot was designed to keep from sliding through the stirrup. Leather chaps and vests were protection against the limbs of trees and brush they rode through.

When the riders reached the wagons, the older man inquired: "Is this here the Miller outfit?" John waved his hand to the rear where the Millers were straining to see their kin approach. The horsemen dismounted, the anxious family got down from their perch in the front of the worn-out wagon. The brothers greeted each other with a warm handshake and embrace. Del spoke again, "These here are my boys." He called the names of all six of the men of varying ages. "The girls is in the buckboard with the ma." "We been a heap worried bout ya since it has been over a year now since we got word thet you was bringing your family out here to be with us. We found a good spread for ya, Jake. We all aim to help you get set up." By now the spring wagon had arrived with the Texas Miller women aboard. Everyone was trying to talk at once. The children endured the kisses of the older people, the women all shed tears. The Bolts sat silently watching the scene. Clemmy's lovely dark eyes also filled with tears as she thought of her own people back in Georgia. It all seemed so far away now. Margie

Miller hastened to present her friends to the whole family. She was quick to add that if it hadn't been for the Bolts, they would still be back in the mud of Louisiana. John and Clemmy were welcomed into the circle, they all hurried to the comfort of the huge log and rock building that was headquarters for the Miller bunch. Fields had been cleared in all directions from the ranch buildings. The only trees left standing were giant pecans. Fences were poles which were trimmed when the fields were cleared. Everywhere a person looked, there were signs of the industrious labor demanded of his family by Delmer Miller. Horses grazed contentedly. Milk cows and sheep were kept in another big pasture in the bend of the creek. Clemmy thought, this is what hard work can do, an me an John aim ta have a even bigger spread when we reach New Mexico.

There was plenty of help to handle the Bolt horses that evening. The greatly admired stallions were housed in special stables while the mares were put to pasture with the others and the geldings. Most of the talk around the great Miller table that night was about the fine horses brought by the Bolts. Supper was like a banquet to the travelers. There was beefsteak, potatoes, gravy, black-eyes peas, corn bread, dried apple pie and pecan cookies. Before the meal began, Margie Miller prayed fervently . . . "Lord Jesus, thank you fer bringing us out o the wilderness to this place o plenty." Margie read from the twenty-fifth psalm . . . "Unto Thee, O Lord, do I lift up my soul, O my God, I trust in Thee: let not mine enemies trumph over me." Clemmy committed the words to memory and repeated them often from that day on. Jake and Margie Miller again expressed their gratitude for the generous help they had received at the hands of the Bolts. Supper was a festive affair. Everyone was trying to get acquainted all at once. One of the older Miller girls remarked at how pretty Clemmy was. Clemmy, plainly embarrassed, focused her attention on her plate. Mrs. Miller asked . . . "Where does your dark complexion come from, Mrs. Bolt, are you Italian or dark French?" Clemmy raised her head. "My mother was Cherokee." A shocked silence filled the room. It was plain that prejudice against Indians of any kind was very apparent among these people. They had all seen families which had suffered at the hands of cruel Comanche. Del Miller broke the silence. "It don't make no never-mind who Clemmy's ma was. She is one o us now an I don't aim ta have it any other way.'' The conversation started again, but half-heartedly. When Clemmy was with John alone that night she wondered aloud. ''How many miles do we have ta travel, John, afore folks won't swaller their tongues when they hear that my Ma was an Indian?'' ''There will be a place somewhere, someday, Clemmy. Jes remember, there ain't no woman in the whole world and Texas that is loved the way you are loved by me.'' When they lay in each other's arms, she was sure of it.

The balance of the month of February was spent at the Miller ranch. In exchange for provisions, John made his stallions available to the Miller family's mares. The Arabian for their saddle stock and the huge Percheron for the work animals. Their sons and daughters flourished for years in that part of central Texas.

March saw Clemmy and John anxious to push on. John allowed his own mares to be bred. He wanted them to all have colts before the winter set in again. After they were bred, keeping them separated from the stallions was no longer necessary. Before they took the trail again, Delmer Miller instructed them to keep two of their fastest saddle horses ready to ride, in case they were attacked by a band of Comanche and had to run for it. It was good advice, although Clemmy and John knew they would fight to the last to save all of their precious livestock. Del tried to discourage them from going on west at all without the benefit of a ranger escort, or other wagons to strengthen their chances of survival against a roaming war party. Some of the Miller boys had ridden to the west as far as Ford Claibourne, so they carefully described the route Clemmy and John should take. These same stalwart young men who were so enthusiastically showing their new-found friends how to get through the hill country of Texas, would later join the Texas regiment to fight on the side of the confederacy. Some would never return to these beloved rolling hills and meadows. The wild Mexican longhorn cattle they had so painstakingly gathered, would once again become wild and unattended. The dark clouds of war were to touch everyone. With the horses all freshly shod, the wagons in excellent repair and spirits high, the wheels rolled westward again. Clemmy could not hold back her tears when she hugged and kissed the blue-eyed Linda goodbye. The baby could not understand why Clemmy cried. The route wound through the hills and valleys, but ever westward. They had figured to be in ranger and cavalry headquarters of Ford Claibourne within fourteen or fifteen days. One of their landmarks was the Colorado River, easily recognized by the red silt it carried from the red prairie land to the north.

CHAPTER 12
BLOOD OF HER BLOOD

The wind turned stinging cold as they began to cross the flat lands of the river valley. The oak forests of the hill country had begun to give way to mesquite and prickly pear cactus. Suddenly, as if from nowhere, four riders appeared at the edge of a mesquite thicket to their left front. The travelers had been forewarned not to hesitate in this kind of situation, but to go into action immediately. The buffalo robe-clad figures were, without a doubt, Comanche. Clemmy took the reins, then John dropped off the other side of the wagon, running to the rear where the second wagon was hitched. He quickly dropped the wagon tongue, yelling go, as he did so. Clemmy laid the whip to the team, galloped them in a circle to come back along-side the trail wagon. Their eyes constantly searched the brushy areas in search of more Indians. The four they had seen began to separate to ride in a circle. John spotted three more to their right. They, too, were at a wide interval with their ponies forced to a slow gallop. The teams were quickly unhitched, then placed between and wagons. While Clemmy secured the horses between the wagons, John began to fire at the circling warriors, they had begun to sound their war cries as they rode. John and Clemmy took up posts at opposite corners as preplanned. The range was still too great for accuracy. John took careful aim, then saw one of the ponies stumble and fall. The unhorsed rider was quickly swept up by the brave immediately behind him. The downed horseman swung aboard with the agility of a circus performer. The seven braves had now completely encircled the wagons. Their first objective was to kill whites, the second was to be the proud owners of these fine horses. At a signal from one of the Indians they turned toward the wagons, then came head on at a run. They fired as they rode. Four had single shot rifles, the other three bows, arrows and lances. This time, John squeezed off a round that left one of the ponies without a rider. The others turned and began the circle again. This time closer. Neither John nor Clemmy had ever fired at a human being before. Their hearts were racing like the hoofbeats of the Indian mounts. Arrows and bullets whacked into the wagon beds. Clemmy waited until a brave had released his arrow when he rode by. This time she selected a spot somewhere in the middle of him and fired. She saw him rock back and forth in an effort to stay on the horse. He then rode to the mesquite thicket but did not reappear. The brave riding double, slid to the ground to run into the thicket. He came out, riding the wounded brave's horse. The Comanches pressed in closer. One released a terrifying scream as he forced his pony to a run straight toward Clemmy's position in the back of the wagon. He saw her rise to fire so he slid to the opposite side of his mount, with nothing showing but his foot above the withers. He held his rifle in one hand, looking under the pony's neck, to fire point blank at Clemmy. When she saw the maneuver, she fired quickly at the foot above the withers of the horse. The moccasined foot disintegrated as the heavy lead slug tore into it. The body of the brave hit the ground with a thud. He made a feeble effort to rise, so Clemmy fired again. This time he lay still. John had fired too quickly and missed his shots. The braves pulled away to the protection of the brush. There was a quiver of fear in John's voice as he called . . . "Clemmy!" "I ain't been teched, John. I got one down back here. Then that makes three we put out o the fight." A long figure walked from the protection of the brush. His hands were high in the air in a signal that he was not armed. Despite the chill in the air, he was clad only in his moccasins and a breechcloth. The other three Indians showed themselves as the unclad one signaled to John to meet him in a clearing ahead of the wagons. John hesitated, then called Clemmy to the front to cover the three while he went to see what the lone brave wanted. John was more than confident that he could handle one man. When Clemmy had all guns loaded again, her rifle at the ready, John strode forward to meet his adversary. They stopped about fifteen feet apart. The muscular brave's long black hair was unkempt and tied back with a red band of cloth. There were self-inflicted scars on his cheeks and his face was twisted with a hatred John had never seen before. He glared at John as he spoke. "I speak your tongue, white hair. I learned it at the same time I learned to hate white men. I am not Comanche, I am Cherokee, you are looking into the eyes of

Owl.'' A slight chill ran through John. The Millers had described this one as a particularly ''cruel devil''. ''There are only two of you, yet your woman fights like a she-wolf. You have more guns than we and you have beaten us for the time. You have caused Little Brother to cross the wide river, and for this my knife want to taste your blood slowly.'' At the mention of the Indian named Little Brother, sudden flash of recognition came into John's mind. ''These were the two Cherokee boys who had left the Bandy farm years ago to go in search of their own fate. Clemmy had killed her own uncle, Little Brother.'' The Indian voice droned on . . . ''I will have more braves, soon, then I will hunt for you, white hair. I will find you and cut you into little pieces. This I promise Little Brother.'' With that, the Cherokee named Owl contemptuously turned his back on John Bolt to stride back into the protection of the mesquite ticket. That night they camped in a bend of the Red River. Neither John nor Clemmy slept a wink. Clemmy was never to know the identity of the first Indian she had killed. The next day they pushed their teams hard so that they would be within the protection of the soldiers encamped at Fort Claibourne, later to become San Angelo.

Their stay at the fort was highlighted by a visit from the Commander of a ranger company, Mr. Mel Turner, who wanted a full report on the incident with the Comanche. John and Clemmy described the attack in detail. John evaded the name of the Indian he had talked with until the Ranger excused himself to return to the Plaza. John walked with him to where his horse was tied to a huge mesquite tree. ''Ranger, I reckon yo would be interested to know thet one o them injuns was named Owl. He be a Cherokee from Georgia. My wife killed another Cherokee named, Little Brother. This here Owl then swore vengeance on us. He claims he is roundin up more o his friends, the Comanche ta foller us and kill us all.'' John had evaded the fact that the two Cherokees were really relatives of his own wife. The Ranger took out a twist of tobacco, bit off a chunk. After chewing for a moment, he spoke in a soft Texas drawl. ''We know Owl alright, Mr. Bolt. I am huntin him myself. I aim ta be the jasper which puts a bullet in that bad un. He ranges all the way from Abilene, ta the back side of the Edwards Plateau at Uvalde. He is welcome in the camps of the Comanche as well as the Lipan Apache. He knows I'm pressin him hard. One o these days I'll cut his sign and then I aim to kill that bad injun. Iffin Little Brother is dead, then that is one less bad devil fer me ta worry bout. I tell ya, Bolt, ya shoulda killed him right where he stood. Flag o truce er no. His favorite trick is burnin people after he ketches em. With this damn war thets brewin twix the north an the south, them murderin devils is going ta have a free hand with the good people who already have ranches in this part o Texas. If they is a war, them soldiers at Fort Stockton and Fort Davis is gonna have their hands full o some other kind o fightin. They got us rangers spread so thin now that we ain't hardly a fightin force. There are jest three companies o us ta handle all the state o Texas. That includes fightin them outlaws as well as the Comanche and Apache. The bad uns kin drift in an out o Mexico almost as easy as going to church. Mexico has its hands full o them Frenchy rats now. They are havin their own revolution." Ranger Mel Turner fixed his gaze on the southern horizon, gave a deep sigh before he spoke again. "Where you and the missus headin, Bolt?" "We aim ta start a horse and cattle ranch in the north part o the New Mexico territory. Do you know thet country?" "Yep, I rode to Santa Fe onct. Beautiful land and mountains as high as the moon. Ya got some dangerous prairie to cross afore ya get thar, Bolt. Me an five rangers is ridin fer the Pecos as soon as we kin git away. Maybe four er five days till then. There is four other wagons rollin thet way at the same time. They will turn southeast at the Pecos, where you folks branch ta the north. We will ride escort as fer as the Pecos. If'n I was you folks, I would hole up here in Fort Claibourne till ther kin be more wagons goin ta the north. Whatever ya do, be sure your ready fer a long dry crossin. It be over a hunnerd and fifty mile fum here to the Pecos, and there is damn little water twix here and there." "We'll be ready, Mr. Turner. I reckon we won't wait fer no other wagons, though. Me and Clemmy done come this fur. We gotta push on so's we can git a place established afore the next winter comes." Turner spat a brown stream as he swung aboard his horse. "Have it your own way, Bolt. I can't nurse the whole damn state of Texas. I'll tell ya, though, them other wagons is gonna hold you up. They ain't got the teams you got. There be a passel o dry washes tween here an the Pecos. Sand in some is fearsome deep." With that he galloped away without looking back.

Grazing was scarce near the settlement, since other wagons before them had need to graze also. They dug into their supply of grain to give the horses strength to start the long haul to the Pecos. Other travelers had told them that it was over a hundred and fifty miles of rock, sand and mesquite brush. It was now the last of March and the weather was holding so nice that the Bolts thought they had already reached ideal conditions. The other four wagons lined out on the road to the southwest of town, so Clemmy and John joined the prarade. The six rangers looked like riding arsenals. Each carried two rifles, two pistols and a knife at the belt. Two were of Mexican descent. All were weather-beaten, they wore clothes to protect them from the thorny brush which was part and parcel of this wonderful country. Two pack mules completed their meager train. The accurate firepower they represented though, was widely known to marauding Indians and outlaws alike. John and Clemmy were in high spirits rolling along at the end of the line of wagons. It was a well worn trail which had been used for years to link the east with the west. One trail would continue on to the west toward Fort Stockton, the other to the north of Pecos crossing. The other four wagons were to veer south and east back into the Edwards Plateau. The air was briskly cold, but the skies were the bluest our travelers had ever seen. Huge coveys of giant blue quail would run from one patch of brush to another in their quest for fallen mesquite and weed seeds. Clemmy took her shotgun and gathered enough of the quail for she and John as well as the Rangers. They traveled through rolling hills. Giant oak and cottonwood trees grew along the dry river beds where now and then they would get a glimpse of a herd of deer making its way through the undercover. The prairie grass was almost as high as the horses' bellies in spots. It was dry, and rustled in the wind, with the seed pods at the top taking on the appearance of a wheat field ready for harvest. Clemmy spoke in wonder "John, all in the world this part of Texas needs is more people. There ain't no way a person with a gun could starve in this land o plenty." The camped that night in a huge clearing. The rangers cautioned them to be very careful with fire. The grass and brush were dry as tinder. There was a great deal of visiting that evening. Stories of the past and of the future dreams were traded with men and women alike as they sat around a campfire. There didn't seem to be a care in the world. The next day, the mesquite gave way to catclaw bush and prickly pear cactus. Patches of sand were encountered much more frequently now in the valleys, while the hills were covered with flint hard rocks which jolted the travelers to their very bones. When they tried to cross some of the dry river beds, wagons became stuck in the sand. Other teams would be unhitched to help the hapless wagon to resume its place in the line. No sooner would they traverse one draw when they would come to another which required the same patience and power as the last. At these slow intervals, the Rangers would leave their pack mules with the train, then scout toward known ranches in the area. They were combing the country for any reports of Indian or outlaw activity. They found none in this seemingly forsaken stretch of Texas. Now and then they could see off to the north, the endless flat plains of the Plano Estacado, the stake plains of the Texas panhandle.

They made precious few miles this day. That evening, they all made camp with the livestock in the center of the circle. Extra guards were posted against the possibility that thieving Indians would swoop down to stampede the horses, mules and oxen. Strayed animals would then be gathered the next day to become the proud possession of some war party. A stiff breeze made the cold air much more uncomfortable that evening. By morning, the wind had risen to gale force as grey clouds began to scud across the sky from the northwest. How could the beautiful weather of yesterday be so disagreeable today? Some of the party knew the capricious weather of the west and advised Clemmy and John that they thought there was going to be a real duster on the way very shortly. Not only was there cold, the wind flung choking swirls of sand which stung the eyes of human and beast alike. The wagons and riders pressed on in the teeth of the storm which had just begun. The dust and sand prevailed all that day, into the night. A dry, fireless camp was made, with the stock trying to drift with the wind. Extra guards stayed in the saddle all night to keep them bunched up. By morning the skies had taken on a dirty blue cast, with sleet slanting in with pushing force. Clemmy and John, along with other wagon people, wanted to stop to make camp. They were urged on by Ranger Turner. They were expected to meet another patrol at Val Verde, far to the south. They were determined to be on time. Women and children were bundled under the protection of the wagon canvas. All that is, except Clemmy Bolt. She took her turn with John. First driving the team, then in the saddle at the rear of the train. They had to make sure that none of their precious horses broke loose from their hitches at the sides and back of wagons. Hour after hour they plodded on in the grip of the Texas norther. By nightfall the sleet and snow had stopped. The skies from all directions took on a blue grey haze, the temperature plunged to below zero. The wind had subsided enough by then that they build huge fires of mesquite and brush to keep them warm. The stock stamped and snorted their displeasure at the biting cold. The slowness of the other wagons tried the patience of the Bolts who were anxious to press on. Mel Turner stopped at their wagon camp to talk to them. "Better stay with us as fer as the Pecos anyways. This storm is gonna drift some herds of buffalo to the south and the Comanche and Tonkawa are gonna be driftin with them. You only met a small band afore, God help you iff'en ya meet a whole driftin party." A shiver of fear ran through Clemmy. She tried not to show it.

The weather cleared the next morning and the warm sunshine was a welcome sight. Twelve days after they started, they began to see a break in the rolling hills with the broad expanse of the sage-covered Pecos Valley spread out before them. Water was getting low in the barrels of the wagon train, making the anticipation of plenty the uppermost thought in their minds. The winter sun raced them to the valley, then sank in a glorious red glow in the high mountains to the southwest. All were eager to get under way the next day. They were up with first light, the wagons rolling by sun-up. Turner and one of the other Rangers rode along-side the Bolt wagon. Turner spat, then waved a leather gloved hand in the direction of a knob hill to the left of the train. "We call that thar hill, Preacher Hill," Clemmy and John could see the charred remains of a wagon near the crest of the round hill. A lone mesquite tree raised its bare limbs skyward near the fire-scarred remains. "There wuz a damn fool preacher an his woman come this way a number o years ago. He wuz preachin hell fire an brimstone to every soul who would listen. Stayed some time back in Fort Claibourne. Good souls too. Everbody liked them. That preacher told all the folks he was called by the Lord ta teach salvation to the savages of this country. They come this way by theirselves. Trouble wuz, the

Comanche didn't know they wuz the ones the Good Lord had told the preacher about. Them devils musta caught em down here. The ranger patrol whut found em said they could see where they made their way to the top o the hill. Their fancy wagon wuz burned to cinders, they was hangin head down from the limbs o thet big mesquite. Them devils had built a fire under them folks and then left em ta die. The Comanche most likely stayed around fer a while ta hear the last scream. Now ya see why we keep huntin an shootin them savages.'' The ranger reined his horse sharply, the rode to the head of the train. He wanted to caution the leaders not to go near the river brush until the area had been thoroughly scouted. The faces of Clemmy and John became masks of horror as they both realized that the main actors in the horrible tragedy had been Preacher Rue and his wife. The woman who had been Clemmy's friend when she had so sorely needed one, back in her youth, just after the death of her beloved Pa. Clemmy became sick at her stomach, heaving over the wagon wheel. John tried to comfort her, but was in no condition, himself, to be of much help.

CHAPTER 13
TURN NORTH

The party made their way to the banks of the Pecos, where they camped to water their livestock and make what repairs needed to be made before pressing on in their predestined directions. The wagon going west would pick up an escort at Fort Stockton. From there they would be in the company of soldiers all the way to El Paso on the Rio Grande. The other three bound for the Edwards Plateau would have the watchful eyes of the Rangers looking over them as they headed southeast. Clemmy and John would go it alone on their way to the New Mexico territory to the north. Ranger Turner instructed them as carefully as he could. "Don't travel along the river. Them devils kin hide in the salt cedar along the banks. They would be on you afore you knowed which direction they come from. Stay on the wagon road along the foothills. The land flattens out soon an will stay that way almost to Pecos crossin. There is a Mexican farmin village there. Stay on the east side till you git thar, then cross over an stay on the west bank all the way ta civilization in the New Mexico country. Try ta hook up with other wagons on the way. After the Comanche, there be the Mescalero Apache. Some mean injun, they air, too. Git some company soon's you kin." With that, Turner tipped his hat and rode off in the direction of the retreating wagons to the south. John spoke with conviction. "Thet man is one hell of a feller. I do hope he finds that Comanche we met up with, afore the injun finds him. Good luck, Ranger." Clemmy echoed, "Good Luck." The ranger had told them that they had over a hundred miles to cover. They were anxious to get on with the task of reaching Pecos crossing, a spot to gain importance as a stopping place on the Goodnight Trail from Texas. The big team stepped out at a lively pace. They, too, seemed happy to be away from the slow-moving four wagons which had been ahead of them all the way from San Angelo. The air was clear and crisp. The spirits of Clemmy and John Bolt began to rise as their wagons rolled to the land of their dreams. They began to pass scattered piles of buffalo bones, then once in a while small herds of the animals making their way to a drink from the waters of the Pecos. The land flattened out when they entered the edge of the great plains of Texas. Off to the north they could see a huge dust cloud. The rangers had told them that a great dust cloud would mean a great herd of buffalo. They became nervous and apprehensive as they imagined the dust also signaled the approach of a large band of fierce Indians. The day wore on with nothing more sighted except prairie wolves and coyotes feeding on the remains of the downed buffalo. Some of the carcasses were still rotting and stinking. They could well understand what a smell it would have been if it had been hot summer instead of a short time after a freezing cold spell.

Before they drew their wagons side by side to make their evening camp, they began to watch two bundled riders approach from the rear. John mounted his stallion, going to the rear to act as a rear guard in the event the riders were unfriendly. They drew the wagons to a halt, bringing the front end of one around to the side of the unhitched trailer. Before the riders came within rifle shot of the wagons, they made a great show of the fact that they were not Indians. They wore buffalo robe mackinaws with a scarf tied over their ears. They raised both hands high into the air and yelled . . . "Haloo the wagons. Can we come in." John waved his carbine in a motion for them to approach. A man with a grey streaked beard spurred his horse into a trot as he neared where John stood his ground. He rode up, removing his hands from heavy buffalo skin mittens. "Howdy, . . . name's Kincaid, Tim Kincaid. Yonder comes Ram. Don't know his other name, jest call him Ram." John eyed them suspiciously. "Name's Bolt. John Bolt." "We are a couple a hide hunters. We done our job here an the wagons is done headed fer Abilene. Me and Ram was ridin fer Pecos crossin. Fum there we aim ta mozy on over El Paso way." The second rider was a pimply-faced youth with a scraggly red beard. Both the men were unwashed. John could smell them from where he sat on his horse. Pimple face said in a high voice. "Howdy."

John nodded. Kincaid continued, "we been out fer a spell now and I guess we don't look like we wuz goin dancin. Probably smell a mite too. Let us share your fire fer a spell. We could set downwind. We don't aim ta trouble ya none, but we sure could use some coffee. We run out bout a week ago. Besides we seen some Comanche out younder a way." He nodded his head to the northeast. John remembered the friendly hide hunters they had visited in Natchidoches, Louisiana. Then, too, the threat of the Indians and possible help all the way to Pecos crossing made him consider it a good deal. John, still not too sure of himself, waved a hand to where Clemmy had already started a fire. "Come on in. We got some extry coffee. Could even have some hot corn cakes ta go on top." Ram bobbed his head approvingly. They got down from their horses, took off their saddles, then tied the animals to the side of the wagon.

The sun had begun to set, making the air feel cold. The hunters came to the fire on the downwind side where they began to warm themselves. They fetched their saddles, threw them near the fire, then helped John with the other horses. Clemmy busied herself with the preparation of the meager meal. Her black hair glistened in the firelight. The beauty of her lithe body was unmistakable, even bundled against the cold as she was. When the men came back to the fire, the coffee was poured. They settled down for an evening of talk. Kincaid began to tell of their latest hunt. The firelight made the pimples on Ram's face stand out even worse than they were. His loose lips sucked at the coffee, which had been poured for him. He would unconsciously scratch his crotch as he drank from the hot cup. Clemmy spread a heavy quilt on the ground for her and John to sit upon. Clemmy sat upon a bedroll. John crossed his legs and sat straight-backed, facing the hide-hunters. One of the horses behind Kincaid shied nervously. John leaned his head to one side to see what was troubling the horse. Then without further warning, a green salt cedar club descended upon the side of John's head from out of the dark circle of the firelight to their backs. The heavy club almost tore his ear off as it descended on his shoulder. A great blackness with spots exploding red began to engulf John. With his last conscious moment, he straightened his body with a vicious kick at the midsection of Kincaid. Blood spurted from his split scalp as he fell forward into the darkness. Pimple face lunged across the fire to cover Clemmy's body with his. She fell backward off the bedroll, then she smelled the stink of him close to her face. She began to fight like a cornered she-mountain lion. Her clawing fingers met only the resistance of the heavy buffalo hide poncho the loathsome man was wearing. She tried to kick, but the body was between her legs which were bent over the bedroll. A voice came to her ears. "Goddamn Lopez, where the hell you been? I thought you aimed to wait all night. Go finish that son of a bitch, then help me tie this fightin squaw to the wagon wheel. Where the hell is Kincaid?" Clemmy heard the accented voice of a Mexican. "I tink Kincaid got a beeg bell-ache. That guy keek heem in da tripas before he die." "How do you know he's dead? Go finish him, Lopez." "No juice to make de trouble. I break his pinche head good. All his blood and brains spill out." Clemmy began to scream. A dirty hand went over her mouth. The horses began to rear and snort. She tried to bite the filthy hand, but couldn't. Then she felt a rawhide loop go around one of her wrists. She was jerked cruelly toward the wagon wheel, a filthy bandana was stuffed into her mouth. The other wrist was secured by pimple face. Both hands were tied to the lower spokes of the wagon wheel, her feet were left free. As the stinking Ram stood up, he reached inside her heavy wool coat, ripping the bodice of her dress down to her waist. Filthy fingernails raked her tender skin. She tried to kick, but the effort only succeeded in exposing her legs beneath the heavy folds of her long skirt. Lopez let loose with "Eeyaee man, Chingada. Have you ever see a woman like thees one?" They could hear Kincaid begin to vomit in the darkness. Pimple face laughed. "Peers lak ole Kincaid got a hankerin to jine us at the party." Ram began to throw off his clothes, despite the bite of cold spring night. He stood over Clemmy, a high-pitched giggle coming from his throat. Her only defense now was to repeat, in her mind, the twenty-fifth psalm which she had committed to memory. "Unto Thee, O Lord, do I lift my soul. Oh my God, I trust in Thee. Let me not be ashamed, let not mine enemies triumph over me. The sight of the naked hide hunter standing over her, sickened Clemmy to the very depths of her soul. Pimple face seemed to be oblivious to the biting cold of the wind. He spoke to the Mexican again. "Good God, almighty, Lopez . . . where in hell did thet white haired jasper ever find a squaw like this here un? He won't mind eff'en I muss her up real good.'' He giggled again. Lopez growled. ''Git to the yob, you idioto.'' Clemmy prayed . . . ''Dear God let them kill me now.'' She thought again of her beloved John, the only man who had ever made love to her. Tears filled her eyes. Ram slobbered on his chin. ''Fust off, I aim to chew on her a bit.'' When he went to his knees, they heard a loud thump. The expression on his face turned to stark surprise, then twisted in agony. He coughed and a great spurt of blood covered Clemmy's face and breasts. His body fell heavily forward, the hilt of one of John's throwing knives glistened in the light of the dying fire. It was deeply imbedded squarely between Ram's shoulder blades. Lopez fell backward into the dark, yanking desperately at his pants which he had started to remove. He screamed . . . ''Kincaid, que paso? What's going on?'' There was no answer from the otherside of the fire. Clemmy heard boots on the hard ground, then hoofbeats of a horse which was being spurred to a run. Suddenly Clemmy saw John half crawling, half falling toward her. She tried to scream, but the dirty rag was still in her mouth. John's white hair was matted with blood, his bloody right hand gripped the handle of another balanced throwing knife. With his last ounce of strength, John cut the rawhide thong from Clemmy's right wrist. He pitched forward on his face in the dirt, then lay still. Clemmy snatched the rag from her mouth screaming, ''John, oh dear God, John don't leave me now.'' She tried to reach him with her free hand, but could not. She grasped the hilt of the knife between the shoulder blades of the dead hide hunter. She yanked hard, the knife came free. She then cut herself loose, moved to John so that she might cradle his still bleeding head in her lap. She began to rock back and forth, softly singing the same lullaby she often sang to her son when he was a baby. Although she was still in shock herself, she kept looking apprehensively toward the darkness. There was an underlying fear that the Mexican would return to finish them both. It grew colder, she knew that she must get John into his bed in the wagon or he would surely die. Clemmy fastened the buttons on her own coat, then she dragged the 185 pound John to the front of the wagon. ''Dear God,'' she prayed, ''Ho'm I goin ta git John up inta the high bed of the wagon?'' She got robes and quilts from the bed to make him as comfortable as she could on the ground. Clemmy then built up the fire to heat water to wash away the blood. With her scissors, she carefully clipped away the silver blonde blood-matted hair from around the gash in her husband's head. After cleaning the gash, she began to painfully stitch the scalp back together. When she would insert the needle, John would moan and call her name. All the time, she was talking to him to assure him that she was alive and right by his side. By midnight she was done. John began to shiver violently, he mumbled unintelligably. Clemmy walked to the edge of the camp. As she leaned against the wagon box, she looked up at the bright Texas stars. "They ain't gonna beat me, Lord. My man is gonna live, ain't he? Then how could I let em beat me? He gotta have me here when he comes to. I'll be here a fightin, Lord. Jes lend me a hand now an then." Tears creased her beautiful cheeks, she felt them grow cold as they dripped from her chin. Clemmy went back to the fire, where she used the last of the hot water to wash away the blood from the hide hunter which had splashed over her face and breasts. She felt dirty all over. Even a cake of lye didn't seem to wash away the taint feeling. She then made a bed beside John, where she slept fitfully until the morning light started to show. She then brought one of the great work mares around, forced it to lie down. It was a super human effort for Clemmy to drag John over and place him on the broad, flat back of the gentle horse. She did it, then coaxed the mare to her feet. From the back of the mare, Clemmy lifted him into the bed of the wagon box. The horses were all in bad temper, they had no water the night before, therefore they were not in the most cooperative mood as Clemmy fed them before beginning the day's trek. She knew she would have to swing down to the river bank to water them. This fact added to her anxious feeling. She strapped a pistol around her middle, then loaded her shotgun with buckshot. She felt she would give a good account of herself no matter who or what the odds were.

The Pecos River was broad and shallow at the point where she reached it. After testing the bottom, she drove the wagons and team right into the river. There they could all drink with out having to be unfastened from their lead ropes. When Clemmy reached the wagon road again, she drove her team without mercy. When one of the mares seemed to slack abit, Clemmy would yell it's name and crack it on the rump with the long whip. She didn't like to do this, but she felt that if their lives were to be saved, she must.

At midday she stopped to rest the horses. John had a fever and was still unconscious. Clemmy bathed his face with water, then made him as comfortable as possible in the jolty wagon. She saw not a soul on the vast prairie all that day.

The fast pace was beginning to tell on her team, she forced them on in the twilight. She made camp at dark. There was the constant chore of feeding and tending to her stock. When she was done, she crawled into the bed beside her injured husband. "The good Lord would jes have ta look after things this night." She was so weary she could not keep her eyes open. Before dawn, she was awakened by the howling of prairie wolves in the very near vicinity. Clemmy sat up, startled. She grasped her guns and went outside the wagon. Was it really wolves, or was it Comanche getting ready to make their attack at the first light? She circled her precious charges and tried to peer into the waving prairie grass for a sign of something moving. She felt no fear of the wolves but Indians, bent on stealing her precious horses, were another thing. Dawn showed no change, so the task was repeated again. Feed, harness, tie, then start the wheels rolling again. Clemmy would remember this as the greatest effort she would ever be called upon to make in her lifetime. The pull of the heavy leather reins made her arms and shoulders ache. The wind began to rise at about mid-day. She was in for another blinding dust storm. This time she was forced to snap leads into the bridles of the lead team, Then walk ahead of them to keep from losing her way in the blinding dust. That night Clemmy was so tired that she was forced to let her team stand in their harness. The bits were un-snapped so that the tired teams could eat from a feed bag. The supply of corn was getting low. Something good had to happen to her soon.

When first light showed the next day, Clemmy forced the horses to take the bit again so that she could get under way. At about midmorning she heard John say weakly, "Clemmy water, give me water." She cried his name as a surging wave of happiness swept through her tortured body. John's eyes were open, showing bright blue below the white of the bandage about his head. She halted the team, lifted John's head and shoulders in order to give him a drink from a canteen which swung from the wagon seat. "Ya made it honey . . . I knowed ya was too ornery to let scum lak thet kill ya." Great sobs wrenched from her as she stroked John's ashen cheeks with her work-hardened hands. John lay back weakly. "Ya sleep now, my darlin. I know we air gonna make it jes fine now . . . jes fine." Clemmy climbed back to the seat of the wagon where she lighted a corn cob pipe which she clenched in her white teeth. Her fatigue seemed to melt away so she began to sing loudly. That night she made broth from cooked dried meat and corn meal. John ate heartily, complaining that his head ached. Three days of beard covered his face. He was well enough now to ask with great concern. "Clemmy, be ya alright? Did they hurt ya? I tried hard to keep em from touchin ya." "Ya, won, John, they didn't get a chance at me. We left two o em layin on the prairie. Tother rode off in a big hurry. I untied their horses and rove on the next day."

When they camped that night, they both thought they could see the dim glow of lights far to the north and west. "We should be gittin close ta Pecos crossin by now. John, we gotta find someone to help when we git ta some civilization. I did'n realize how much the Miller family helped us till we tried it alone. There be a reason why folks bands together in wagon trains, John. When yo wuz so bad off, I had the loneliest feelin a body could stand. Anyway, God did not allow mine enemies to triumph over me." John was still pale and drawn. His head ached constantly. Clemmy changed his bandages to look for infection. There was none, fortunately. "I reckon I been a great burden to ya, honey. I shore intend ta help ya tomorrow." "Ain't no use in talkin thet way, John Bolt. Jes havin ya her with me again is all I need. Rest all ya kin. Cain't tell when I might jes have a reason to call on ya fer somethin." Clemmy held him close to her, enjoy the feel of his muscular body against hers. "Peers we ain't got no friends out here, John. Only people who want to take what we have. It is a strong an hard country, John. We gotta be jes as strong and hard as it is, or we will be destroyed." John stared into the darkness, making a resolve to do just as Clemmy had said. He was going to be hard in a harder land.

Just as it turned light the next morning they were both awake. Clemmy set about getting breakfast. She almost ran through her routines this morning. John would try to help, but was so weak that he would find himself hanging onto the side of the wagon, or leaning against one of the horse for support. When they were ready, they climbed to the wagon seat. The day dawned in a glorious color-changing display, as only it can, on the great expanses of the plains of Texas. Vast herds of pronghorn antelope which had come to the river to drink, would bound away in their great distance consuming strides. The curious would turn to look at the strange intruders in their domain. Coveys of great blue quail would scurry from one clump of mesquite to the next. They threaded their way through mounds of blown sand with clumps of the thorny mesquite growing on top.

By midday they began to see small fields of dried corn stalks in patchy cleared areas along the river. Small adobe mud houses attested to the fact that human beings did exist in this land after all. Clemmy mounted one of the saddle horses and rode to one of the places on the river to ask for directions. The people spoke only Spanish but made her understand that Pecos crossing was still further to the north. This night they went to the river bank to camp. The clear cold water of the Pecos River was a lullaby for them, they bundled against the chill of the cold wind which seemed to constantly blow. It was getting along toward the middle of April now, the travelers felt an urgency to reach their destination in the New Mexico territory not too far east of Santa Fe.

Pecos crossing was a cluster of adobe houses. There was some semblance of a main street which lay roughly in a north to south direction. Children, chickens, dogs, and pigs wandered at will, with everyone seeming to know whose property they were. Small flocks of goats were herded along the river banks where the grass grew particularly lush. Swarthy complexions and black hair attested to the fact that most of the citizens of this crossroads stopping place were of Mexican descent. From here, the road out of Abilene traced its way on to the west with the next destination, El Paso. The road Clemmy and John had just traversed continued on to the north along the east bank of the Pecos to its headwaters in the Sangre de Cristo mountains of the New Mexico territory. They resolved to stay here a few days to rest their teams before pushing on up the river. Camp was made near the river in a clump of leafless cottonwood trees. A small cluster of adobe houses was just downstream. By now, John had regained most of his strength, but still suffered the headache of his injury. They made rope picket lines to tie their horses to. Clemmy rode one of her sleek Arabian mares to act as a herder for the other horses which they turned loose to graze on the lush grass of the river banks. John set up a forge to reshoe the whole lot of them.

They took their time, resting in the long afternoons. Water was a bountiful luxury, so Clemmy took the opportunity to wash all their clothes and bedding. Almost every afternoon saw another dust storm. They wondered if this was to be for the rest of their lives. After the experience with the mud and water of Louisiana, though, it was not hard to bear. There were plenty of visitors to see their horses and to just inquire about what was going on to the east of them. It was indeed a lonely place, any gossip of other places was a welcome event. Other wagons from the road east began to camp along the river banks. It was almost like having neighbors again.

A week went by and our travelers began to become restless to start again. Evening was coming on, the glow of sunset was on the mountains to the west. They heard the scream of a woman come from the circle of mud houses. One was a huge Mexican with a wide leather belt around a big expanse of belly. They both wore the garb of the typical Mexican vaquero. High topped boots, mounted with large roweled spurs. Each wore a pistol at his side. Clemmy and John were startled to see the big man half dragging a young Mexican girl by one arm. She was crying, trying to fight him off with her other hand. The big man only laughed. An old lady emerged from another one of the huts. She took a stick to beat at the vaquero's legs. He laughed, grabbed the stick from her, then with a vicious stoke, he hit the old woman across the breasts. She screamed in pain. A young boy of about seventeen came running from where he had been herding a band of goats down by the river. He flew into the big man with the fury of a wildcat. "Turn her loose, Vasquez! I weel keel you!" A flailing fist caught the big man on the nose. Blood spurted as he cursed in pain. He turned the girl lose, she scurried into the house. By now John and Clemmy had drawn near the scene. The big man felt his nose. He made a lunge for the boy. The young one spun to one side and started to run. The other man leaped to his saddle to ride the boy down. When the horse bumped him, the boy fell into the dust. Vasquez walked up to him to administer a vicious kick. The toe of his boot put the boy's left arm out of action. The boy leaped to his feet, then grabbed at the knife at the big man's belt. He missed and fell to the dirt once again. Vasquez drew the knife, making an expert slash at the boy's face. The blade hit just in front of his left ear, then laid his cheek open to the point of his chin. His teeth could be seen through the now crimson wound. He drew his arm back to strike again. A blade flashed in the evening sun, embedding itself deeply in the heavy right arm wielding the knife. The knife flew from his limp fingers. He cursed, trying to draw his gun with his left hand. John crouched, balanced the second knife ready to throw. A shotgun held firmly by Clemmy, was leveled at the head of the man in the saddle. John advanced to the big man, calmly pulled his knife from where it protroded from the right arm. He then motioned for the two of them to leave. They did, with Vasquez muttering in Spanish, "One day I will kill you for this, Gringo. Yes, I swear by the grave of my mother, I will kill you for what you have done to Pedro Vasquez." The men rode quickly toward town, then people began to cautiously spill out of the doorways of the mud huts. The girl ran to where the boy was, now on his hands and knees in the dirt. The blood from his face was making a stain in the dust. She crossed herself repeatedly and softly said the boy's name over and over. "Carlos, oh Carlos, precioso, what have they done to you?" John asked, "Is there a doctor here in Pecos?" A woman answered, "No doctor here, señor, only doctor in Big Spring. He come here sometime to help with the sick." Clemmy went to the bleeding youth. She said softly, "I will help you." He nodded his head, "Thank God, he understands English," she thought. Clemmy motioned for some of the men to help carry him to her wagon. There she went to her medicine chest. She found laudanum which she forced down his throat to ease the pain. When it had taken effect, she packed the inside of his mouth with a clean cloth. Then she took her needle again which she had used such a short time before, began to cross stitch the face so that it would heal. It was a crude job, by surgical standards, but at least it put him back together again. The wound would leave a disfiguring scar which he would carry to his grave. The girl introduced herself as Consuela Martinez. Carlos, it turned out, was her brother. She explained to the Bolts that she and Carlos were the children of a mule driver who worked for a freighter on the Big Spring to El Paso road. He was killed by Indians when they were small leaving them to be brought up by their grandmother, after their mother had left with another man. The old woman lived in one of the huts on the banks of the river. Her two sons worked on a rancho to the southwest.

It was a restless night for all. They fully expected the stormy Vasquez to return. Evidently he had had enough during this encounter. Here was the third man in John's life who had threatened to kill him one day. Consuela explained that the bully Vasquez had wanted her for a long time. He had told others that one day he would be just drunk enough to go and carry her off to his place. The day he chose, turned out to be a bad one for him. Carlos was in terrible pain when the narcotic wore off. He suffered in silence. When the bleeding had subsided enough the next day to remove the rag from his mouth, he took John by the hand, looked into his eyes, the first words he was able to speak were, "Thank you, Viejo." The name became popular in all circles later on.

The next morning they discovered that two days hence, other wagons would be leaving for Fort Stanton, so they decided to make the last leg of their journey with company. Before they departed, Consuela timidly asked if she and Carlos might go along with them. She promised that they would work very hard to earn their keep. Clemmy embraced the girl. "Yes, yes, oh yes, Consuela. We want you and Carlos to come with us." This was the help they had wanted!

Five families left Pecos crossing on a dusty, blustery morning. Rolling north on what was later to be called the Loving, Goodnight Trail. Their next destination of any consequence was to be Santa Rosa, beyond the big bend of the Pecos River called the Bosque Redondo, the Round Thicket. This Bosque, or brushy area was to become the unwanted home of the Navajo and the Mescalero Indian tribes. Fortifications were placed all over the New Mexico territory at that time. Each one of these locations was to be named for the general or commanding officer in charge. Fort Stanton was about sixty miles north and west of Bosque. When Clemmy and John would tell the other wagon travelers of their journey from Fort Claibourne to Pecos, unescorted more than half the way, the others were amazed that they were able to make it at all. The plains and mountain tribes were so fierce at the time, that they attacked at will, with very little resistance from the soldiers at the thin line of forts. Each one of these white man strongholds was manned by no more than two hundred dragoons. The soldiers were poorly mounted besides having too much territory to look after.

New Mexico territory at that time, stretched all the way from the staked plains east of the Pecos, to the Colorado River. The two greatest tribes of warlike Indians were the Apache and the Navajo. The Apache were aggressive, carrying the war to the white man while the Navajo would emerge from the canyon vastness of the central New Mexico plains, raid ranches of sheep and cattle, then retreat to the vast canyons and mesas to the San Juan River area. The War Department in Washington could spare little in the way of men and material for the lonely additions to our fast-growing nation. The impending war with the south made it impossible to decide how much would be sent where. Even now, top ranking officers were resigning their posts to take side in the great struggle which was yet to come.

Warm sunny days with crisp cold nights seemed to be the general rule as the wagon train made its way northward. The road along the Pecos was well-traveled. They passed the little village of Eddy, then on to the Peñasco River Valley. Ranches were already being established in these areas. Vast herds of sheep were being tended on the plains around Roswell. When the wind blew, the prairie grass would take on the appearance of a gigantic yellow sea. The slow progress of the train with some wagons drawn by oxen, caused them to reach Bosque Redondo a long three weeks after they had left Pecos Crossing in the state of Texas.

Carlos had been critically ill for the first few days as he rode in the jolting wagon. Clemmy would change his bandages regularly, then carefully wash the used ones to be used again. John had recovered from his ordeal sufficiently to look after his precious horses. The driving of the team was left to Clemmy and Consuela. Not much driving was required as the well-mannered mares held their place in the line and accustomed themselves to the slow pace of the ever northward movement of the new-comers. The vastness of the prairies stretching away on either side of the Pecos made them wonder if they would ever see a tree again. The long hours sitting on the wagon seat with Consuela gave Clemmy a chance to learn hundreds of Spanish words, then to begin to put them together into sentences. Consuela was a patient teacher while the pupil learned fast. After the eighth or ninth day, the swelling had gone down considerably in the horrible face wound young Carlos had suffered. He began to talk in his half Spanish, half English style. He tried to express to Clemmy and John just how happy he was that he and Consuela had been allowed to join them in their quest for a place to settle. He vowed that he and Connie would never leave Clemmy and John as long as they were needed. They never did. The healing of the wound had left one side of his dark face with the appearance that he was constantly smiling. Even the small scars left by Clemmy's crude stitching would always show. The first time he looked into a mirror, he remarked, "Aye que guapo, Carlos, you handsome devil. You are alive for which you may say gracias to Viejo. He gave my life back to me. If he should ever need me, I hope I will be there to help him."

Around the campfires at night the entire discussion would be about the impending conflict which everyone felt would come. It seemed that people were on the move everywhere. Mostly toward the east. Texas had voted to secede early in January. Colonel Lee left Texas for Washington, D.C., where he was ordered to report, and where he promptly resigned his commission in the United State Army. Jefferson Davis knew the role he was to play as he made his way to Richmond. Abraham Lincoln hurried to Washington, where he was desperately trying to hold the union together.

Like particles of steel drawn to opposite poles of a magnet, people of all walks of life were scurrying to their own political destinations. The cold night winds blasting across the prairies of eastern New Mexico would soon reach the hot tempers of Charleston Harbor, but would be unable to cool the determination of the men there, to fight other men just like themselves.

When the wagon train reached the Bosque on the banks of the Pecos, each wagon owner chose a spot of prairie where his stock could get some grazing. Thickets of salt cedar and mesquite covered acres and acres of the big bend in the Pecos River known as Bosque Redondo. This area in the territory was to become infamous in the near years to come as the encampment of hordes of Navajo and Mescalero Apache Indians who were mercilessly rounded up in their homelands then dumped in this forlorn place. This was to be General Carleton's idea of an ideal place to keep the wild Indians and harness them to the ways of the white man. As it proved later, it was a near annihilation for the Indians placed there.

Clemmy, John and the two Mexicans, Carlos and Consuela, awoke the next morning to bitter cold winds out of the northeast.

The sky had turned to a sullen grey, light snow flakes were driven with painful force into the faces of the travelers. After their breakfast, Carlos saddled one of the Arabian mares so that he could watch over the others as they grazed the dead prairie grass. Both stallions were left tethered to the wagons, their turns to graze would come later. Clemmy, Consuela and John were huddled behind a canvas fly, trying to keep warm at a fire they had built. The sound of riders approaching caused John to stand up to look around to see who they were. Four troopers, part of a contingent from Fort Stanton, rode into the campsite, got down from their mounts. John immediately noticed the poor condition of the cavalry mounts. They were skinny and badly used. The troopers were roughly dressed in the traditional blue with yellow striped pants. They wore home fashioned buffalo robe great-coats to try to ward off the north wind. As they approached the fire, a tall bearded man took the lead. "Howdy pilgrim! Me and these troopers here are makin the rounds o you newcomers ta see if there might be some horses fer sale. Quartermaster has authorized me to pay top dollar fer each mount, broke er not. The Army is willin ta pay ya hunnert and fifty dollars per head, seein as ya got some prime stock. We done looked em over." The tall man spat a stream of tobacco juice into the fire. His gaze fastened on Consuela and Clemmy. "Them your squaws, pilgrim?" John's jaw muscles tightened. His face went white with anger. Clemmy put her hand on his arm. "Who be yo, mister?" Clemmy looked the man in the eye. One of the troopers bowed at the waist, then addressed the trio. "Allow me ta interduce Lieutenant Ike Bently. Lieutenant, mind yer manners now cuz I jes presented ya to royalty." The tall man laughed, leering at the women. "Them is royal squaws awright, Wilkins. I kin tell jes by lookin." By now, John had recovered his composure. He stepped around the fire to be closer to the cavalry officer. "Ya done stated yore business now, Lootenant. We ain got no hosses fer sale. These is all breedin stock which we aim ta keep." "You talk like ya come right outin the cotton patch, pilgrim. I reckon yer one o them southern gentlemen which we aim to whip real good." John said evenly, "We didn't come all this way out here lookin fer trouble from the Army. Now jes leave us be." The officer's practiced eye once again surveyed the two stallions tied to the wagons. "Quartermaster don't allow me ta jes take horses, pilgrim. Iffin they did, these would already be on the way ta the stable. When this here war with you rebs breaks open, an it is shore as hell gonna do jes that, then I am ta find these horses fer a requisition.'' The troopers were gathering up their reins to mount their horses. Bently turned to ask. ''Where ya headin fer, pilgrim? I got a feelin you ain't seen the last o Lieutenant Ike Bently.'' With that, the troopers rode back in the direction of Fort Stanton. The cavalry camp itself was a little more than a group of mud huts laid out at the edge of the vast staked plains beyond the Pecos.

The travelers stayed camped for two days while the snow piled to a depth of six inches. The wind drifted the white blanket like a furrowed field. John and Clemmy felt they had never been so miserable from the cold in all their lives. After the third day, the sun shone through the clouds causing the snow to begin melting. The prairie around the fort, where the grass was all used up, had turned to a sea of mud. The wagon train was ready to move again by midmorning. They were to have a cavalry escort as far as the Mission of Santa Rosa. Traders out of Mexico had established a route from northern Chihauhau, along the Conchas to a crossing on the Rio Grande. There, they fanned out into the Indian country to trade salt, tobacco, knives, shotguns and gunpowder to the warring tribes. There were laws to oppose the sale of guns and powder to the warriors, but the cavalry was spread too thin to prevent the movement of these merchants of death. These one or two wagon traders were just about the only people not being harassed by the Kiowas, Comanche and Apache. Rifles among the Indians were scarce at that time, but the dreaded escopetas, shotguns, were deadly at short range. Most of the troops were armed with sabers, single shot rifles and a pistol. Mr. Spencer's repeating rifle had not made its way this far west as yet.

The wagon train spread out over the prairie, then set a course north by northeast up the Pecos River. Off to the west the travelers could see the blue ridge of the Manzano Mountains which divided the Pecos and Rio Grande Valleys. The goal for Clemmy and John was still somewhere near the headwaters of the Pecos. As Carlos regained his strength, the chores of traveling were made much easier. He took turns riding the three Arabian mares. When he was in the saddle, he felt that he was the greatest caballero in the whole world. These horses were to become the most exciting part of his life. As they neared the Mission of Santa Rosa, John was riding along side the slender Mexican boy. Carlos said, "That Lad is the most beautiful caballo in the whole world, Viejo. One day maybe I own a horse like that. Then I win all the horse races in the whole New Mexico." "Stay with me, Carlos, when the colts come, you pick the one you want from the Arabian mares. They be the sons of The Lad here, ya know." Tears of emotion came to the boy's eyes. "I never leave you anyway, Viejo. My life is your life to do with as you choose. I will take the colt and I will make you proud of me." With that, he reined the mare sharply, riding toward the head of the train.

The terrain had become rougher, outcrops of volcanic rock topped some of the small mesas. Santa Rosa was a crossroad with a well-worn track stretching from east to west. The western leg was a trail all the way to California, the other stretched endlessly into the prairies of the great staked plains of Texas and Oklahoma territory. There was much talk around the campfires for the next two or three days as the land seekers discussed their various destinations. The telegraph did not extend into this part of the nation as yet. It would be a long time in coming.

News of the splitting of the union came from riders who had just come in from the east. Declarations of loyalty were made by some, while others, such as Clemmy and John, just remained silent. The war talk brought back to John's mind the threat made by the dragoon lieutenant about requisitioning horses. John spread the word with the troop which had accompanied the wagon train, that he was going to the gold fields in the mountains west of Denver. John wanted anything but trouble, yet it always seemed to seek him out. He had reasoned that the establishment of his ranch near the Santa Fe Trail would be a great asset to his efforts to sell his products to the stream of immigrants pouring westward on the several branches of the trail. Their destination, therefore, was Las Vegas, the Meadow. Fort Union had been establshed in that part of the New Mexico territory to keep the Indians in check.

They swung their wagons westward for about three days, then took the road northward toward their chosen location. Las Vegas was a bustling stopover on the Santa Fe Trail from Fort Dodge, Kansas. The starkness of the prairie had given way to a forest of piñon, juniper and cedar. Low mountains with wide grassy valleys in between made this part of New Mexico one of the finest ranching areas in the entire west. Spanish settlers with special dispensations from the King of Sapin had made this their promised land. Great grants of land were the rewards the Spanish royalty made to the settlers brave enough to face the fierceness of New Mexico. The only link of communication at that time was the long trek by wagon and horseback, down the winding Rio Grande to the Pass of the North. There the trail left the river, made its way down the center of Mexico. After the acquisition of the vast territory by the United States of America, some of the huge land grants were broken up into smaller ranches. In some instances, the breaking up of the grants was done by land dealers who didn't really have the right. American land offices for the most part ruled in favor of the new settlers instead of the original holders of the grants. A land dealer in Las Vegas was most anxious to show John an abandoned ranch of six hundred and forty acres.

Clemmy, with the brother and sister, stayed with the wagons and horses while John rode to the northwest to look at their future home. He was impressed. The remains of a rock house nestled near an outcropping of bluff at the foot of a mesa. A bubbling spring gushed from the base of the cliff, then made its way toward a small stream that meandered through the valley. Rolling hills of grassland interspersed with clumps of scrubby timber stretched away to the horizon. The majestic snow covered Sangre de Cristo mountains were the backdrop to the northwest. This was home to John, without looking any further. He made a down payment in gold and agreed to pay the balance when it was proven in Santa Fe that the land was really his. The six hundred and forty acres was to be a mere start to the vast holdings he would later acquire.

It was past nightfall and bitter cold when John rode back into their camp. "Clemmy, my girl, we are home!" He could hardly contain his excitement about the new-found heaven where they were to live for the rest of their lives. Consuela and Carlos shared their happiness, for they had never known a home of their own. There was little sleep that night, the start was early, for the ranch was a full day away. The air was clean and crisp with the cold.

Patches of snow lingered in the shady places. This was the last of April. Spring was on its way. Their timing had been good. Clemmy rode along side John mounted on one of the mares. They reflected on the hardships of the long journey they had just completed. Pangs of loneliness plagued them both as they thought of their comfortable farm, friends, their son and daughter-in-law in far off Georgia. That night's campfires were built near the walls of the soon to be restored rock house on the Bolt Ranch of New Mexico.

When the sun rose the next morning, the endless toil of building a ranch had begun. They had been warned to be on the constant alert for roving bands of Jicarilla Apache who were now on the war path, constantly driving off horses and sheep belonging to the Mexican farmers in the valleys of the Pecos. Carlos was given a pistol and rifle then instructed in their use. He took to this new-found defense with a will. Before long he was an expert with the rifle as Clemmy herself. Then he began to practice constantly the fast draw of the pistol. It was to serve him well many times in the future.

Little did these now ranchers know, that just twelve short days into April, the United States of America would be blown apart as General Beauregard of South Carolina ordered the attack on Fort Sumter in the Charleston Harbor. The southerners soon overran the defenses of Major Anderson and the War between the States had begun. News of the actual declaration did not reach the New Mexico territory for days afterward. All New Mexicans were required to take an oath of allegiance to the Union. This included Clemmy and John who were under some suspicion, having just recently left the State of Georgia. Suffering and heartbreak had just begun.

CHAPTER 14
THE JOINERS

Excitement and war fever were running high on this twelfth day of April in North Georgia. Not a soul on the Bolt farm was unaffected by the rapid preparations of a country at war. The Bolt blacksmith shop was pressed into service to shoe as many horses and mules each day as was humanly possible. Men, women and children, black as well as white, bent to the task. All available horses on the farm were purchased by the Confederacy. At that early stage in the conflict, the confederate money was honored in any transaction. Jefferson Davis had taken the reins of the government, while politicians such as State Senator Rodgers ruled their own districts with an iron hand. Recruiting stations were set up in every town and village, with all southerners of any means being urged to join up, bring their own mounts to fight the hateful Yankee.

Wes Bolt, although still quite young, was a recognized leader in the county in which he lived. He knew that regardless of his circumstances as a farmer, he would be called upon to join and fight. Adelia, now four months pregnant with their first child, felt that her whole world had come to an end. It was after supper, Wes had just voiced what they both knew was coming. "I have to go, you know. There just isn't any other way. I am a southerner and the south is at war." "Why couldn't they have left the south alone, to do as they wished with their slaves?" "It was just not up to them to tell us what to do." "I wish now that we had gone with Ma and Pa, out to the New Mexico territory. God how I wish I knew how they are doing. I sent letters to the Postmaster in Santa Fe. They can't either one read, though." Adelia, anxious to avoid the war subject, quickly interjected. "They are both very intelligent, Wes, they will have someone read the letters to them. Then they will get someone to write some in return. We will hear from them soon. I have been praying every night that we would hear. Her big hazel eyes filled with tears. "Wes, the baby is on the way. Can't you wait until after the child is born? Don't even think of leaving me now." There was agony in her voice as she held him close. "Someone has to look after the farm so that the troops can have food and horses to draw their wagons." Wes tried to comfort her although he, himself, was troubled. "I saw your Father the other day. He is sending his overseer, Jack Clemmons, to head a cavalry troop. Seems he had a commission with the British cavalry in India before he came to America. Men of his experience are sorely needed. Mr. Rodgers has applied for Clemmons' commission as a Lieutenant in the cavalry being commanded by J.E.B. Stuart . . . I gotta go, Adelia, you know I do. Everyone expects me to." "Well, I don't expect you to. I think it is a stupid waste for you to go off to war and leave this beautiful farm." "Now, darling, you know that Wilfred can run this place as well as I can. With Tobe and Rufus to keep up the smithy, this place will run like a clock as well as produce tons of stuff for the effort." That night, Adelia cried herself to sleep in his arms. The next morning at breakfast she said, "I know you have to do what you think is right, Wes. I will behave myself while I help all I can to hold things together here." Wes called all hands together to tell them he had decided to ride off to war. The men were determined to go with him. It took a lot of persuasion to convince them that their place was right here on the farm. Sally began to cry, then was joined by the smaller children. Her two young daughters clung to her as they tried to comfort her. Her oldest child, Wilfred, put his arm around her as he announced loudly. "I aim to go rat long wid Wes. He ain't got real good sense an somebody gotta take keer o him." Sally wailed. "Whut a darkie lak yo gonna do in a wah?" Yo cain't carry no gun, Wildred. Go long wid dat crazy talk." "I is goin, jes da same. Wes goes, I go. Somebody gotta take keer o dem hosses. Dey ain't no soul in the whole state o Georgy whut know bout horse lak I does. I be a goin!" The white haired giant, Tobe, put his hand on Wes's shoulder. "Let da boy go, Massa Wes. He be a big hep ta ya." Wes turned to Wilfred. "Saddle Big Red and one for yourself, Wilfred. We will be ridin to town this morning." With that, Wes turned on his heel and motioned for his wife to follow him. "Delia, honey, this is going to be real hard on both of us. Maybe harder on you than me. You are the one who has to hold things together here while us fools go off to fight. There is no way it can be easy for you, honey. You are used to a good life. Maybe we can whip the tar out of them Yankees and get back home before it's time to get the crops in." Adelia was through with her crying. "We need you here, my darling, but you are such a good man they just couldn't do without you. I will pray to God to look after you and bring you back to us."

Wes and Wilfred left the farm at a fast gallop. When they reached the county seat, they went directly to the recruiting area. There they found Lieutenant Clemmons trying to enlist fifty horsemen to be sponsored by the Rodgers plantation. Wilfred was allowed to go along as a livery tender. He was denied a uniform, however, he was still content to just be with his lifetime friend, Wes Bolt.

Two days later they were riding northward behind the hard bitten Lieutenant Clemmons. He had began to make troopers of them the day they signed their names to the enlistment roster. The war had come, thus far, like flashes of lightning on the outskirts of an ominous storm. There was street fighting along the frontiers. Untried, restless, and afraid guards and pickets would fire on innocent people. The grinding battles of destruction were yet to come. To the northerners it was still a giant game in which they were going to punish a wayward south. To the southerners it was deadly serious business. They, too, had misjudged the enemy. The first battle of Bull Run or Manassas was shaping up. General Lee was firmly in command of the armies of Virginia. He was thought by the north to be mild-mannered man who would be more prone to negotiate than to fight. The northern invasion force was commanded by General Scott. His district commander was General Irvin McDowell. A badly mixed collection of militia regiments was to bring them to one of the most infamous defeats in military history.

Lieutenant Clemmons' troop of cavalry had a mere three months to train as horse soldiers before the first bloody battle. Clemmons proved an able officer with discipline his watchword. J.E.B. Stuart, to be the greatest cavalry commander of all time, believed in the merits of the individual trooper, thus he had his commanding officers train the troopers to stand alone. General Beauregard had been sent up from Charleston to become Field Commander of southern forces. He, too, was a firm believer in the use of a fast moving cavalry. The flamboyant Jeb Stuart moved his cavalry units in effective reconnoitering movements which kept the enemy guessing just how many troops they had to face. Post riders would shuttle from one unit to the other with dispatches from the commanding officer. Since Wes Bolt was mounted on the fastest horse in the unit he was chosen as one of these dispatch riders. The shuttling of these fast moving cavalry troops helped to keep a large Union Army idle in the valley of the Shenandoah. The bravery with which Lieutenant Clemmons maneuvered his charges brought him a commission as Captain of a company after the Battle of Bull Run. The Union troops were so badly defeated that they withdrew across the Potomac to the nation's capitol. Whether or not the south could have pressed its advantage at that time and won the war, is still a matter of conjecture. Most military experts agree that the Potomac was too great a barrier for the southerners to cross. They consolidated their positions, however, then began to train in earnest.

Wes received a letter telling him that his first son would be born in August. As most soldiers do, he read the letter so many times, folded it and re-read it, that it was worn out. In the quiet times that he was allowed to himself, loneliness gripped his heart like a cold steel hand. He would lie, picturing every line and feature in the face of his precious wife. Why couldn't this war be ending instead of just beginning? Because of farming, and the country life that was peculiar to the south, most of them could naturally ride a horse. Even shoot from one while riding at full gallop. It took the northern cavalry a year to learn to be even passably efficient. Skirmish after skirmish was won by the valiant southern horsemen. All the south rejoiced in the feat of James Ewell Brown Stuart circling the entire army of McClelland during the June campaigns.

After the Battle of Seven Pines, Wes was assigned with his unit to the 9th Virginia Cavalry under the command of Colonel W. H. F. Lee. Other units brought the force to an ominous twelve hundred men. It was Jeb Stuart's plan to move this unit in a flank of the Federal Army at Ashland. Then move to the rear as they crossed the Chickahominy River near Sycamore Fork. Then they were to move over to the James River, make a dash back to the Confederate lines in Herrico County. Three days' rations were prepared, every man was issued sixty rounds of ammunition. Boots and saddles were sounded, the men swung aboard their mounts. Wes felt a thrill as he looked back along the columns of riders.

The first night's encampment was near Ashland. The next morning there were no fires allowed, the men mounted to ride in silence. The column Wes was in was on foot, leading their mounts up a steep hill. They came face to face with a force of Federal Cavalry drawn up in a column of four. Captain Clemmons ordered Wes back at a run to notify General Stuart that the enemy was covering the road ahead. The General scribbled on a dispatch pad. "The orders are simple son, tell the Captain to clear the road." Wes urged the great red gelding to his utmost speed as he made his way back up the hill. The Captain, anticipating the order, had already formed his company into a line. Wes screamed the order to the Captain as he handed him the dispatch. The Captain merely nodded to the bugler to sound the charge. With drawn sabers they crashed headlong into the federal force. The great strides of the big red horse had taken Wes out into the front. His first encounter would haunt his memory for the rest of his days on earth. Wes picked his man, reined Big Red into a collision course. The blue clad trooper's saber was pointed straight at Wes's chest, while Wes had raised his into the air for a downward stroke. Big Red crashed into the northern mount with a thud. The smaller mount started down as Wes chopped at the rider with both his hands through the sword hilt. The off balance rider could not recover, his saber arm was severed at the wrist. The enemy crashed to the ground weakly waving the stump of his once strong right arm. Wes recovered in time to slash the throat of another rider bearing down upon him. The northern column was turning tail, riding for the woods on either side of the road. From there, they retreated in disorder toward Old Church. Wes heard assembly and rode back toward the rear. He could see several of his comrades lying in the dust of the road. Some wounded, one not moving. Corporal Hennessy lay at his horse's feet. A Yankee saber had been thrust all the way through his chest. Captain Clemmons was bleeding from a saber slash to his ribs. Prisoners were being rounded up and sent to the rear. Wes saw the trooper without a right arm being tended by a fellow prisoner. Wes leaned from the saddle to vomit into the dust. As the Captain was being bandaged, Wes heard him command, "Corporal Bolt, take charge of your squard." It was a battlefield promotion.

The Federal forces were unable to make a stand at Old Church, so the Confederates, at the urging of General Stuart pushed on. Men and mounts were at the point of exhaustion. By the end of the second day the full haversacks of the men had been almost emptied. The horses were badly in need of forage, Stuart pressed the men harder. By now they were well in the rear of McClelland's army. They rode steadily, with several confrontations which were quickly put to flight by the charge and rebel yell. At one point, a wagon loaded with Colt revolvers was captured. Since the southerners were poorly armed, this was a prize, indeed. They rode on to Tunstall's Station on the York Railroad. There they tried unsuccessfully to capture a troop train, the southern cavalry lined the tracks and fired down upon the unsuspecting blue coats, killing and wounding many. Later on, some stores were taken to refresh the men. The horses were still without any nourishment. The southern column, after great difficulty, crossed the Chickahominy River on a bridge contructed at the orders of General Stuart. The bridge was then burned to prevent pursuit. The jaded horses and men were pushed on to the James River, there they reached the Wilcox plantation where great fields of clover provided feed for the weary horses. The animals were refreshed, the column pressed on. The men were now falling asleep in their saddles. Richmond was a mere twenty-five miles away. Stuart had taken advantage of every mistake of the enemy and so resolved to ride right on along the James River into Richmond. They even passed close enough to see the masts of the federalist fleet anchored in the James River. Stuart's troopers were not challenged. They rode into Richmond in triumph, having ridden a complete circle around McClelland's Army.

In September, an order came down that all the troopers who owned their own farms were to be given a thirty day leave to go home to tend to the crops. With his leave papers in hand, Wes hurried to tell Wilfred to saddle up and join him in the ride to Georgia. Wes could read the disappointment in Wilfred's eyes as he shook his head. "Ain't no use talking ta me, Wes. This be an order for the land owners only." "But Will, you own part of the farm same as I do." "Go tell thet ta thet Mississippi Colonel who tunk up the whole idee. He ain't gonna see no darkie which owns land. Da saddle done on Big Red. You ride him hard, but take keer o him. I be right here when ya git back." Wes embraced his friend, then swung to the back of his fast traveling Big Red. He covered forty to fifty miles per day, always careful that his mount was in good shape.

When he rode into the lane at the smithy, a great shout went up from the people working there. They all tried to talk at once, to tell him that his son, Matthew, had been born just one month before. He hurried to the house, where they all wept with joy. "Adelia, God made some beautiful things in this world, and you and my son are the most beautiful of all." She embraced him. "Wes, don't leave me again. Just stay here with us. You can work so hard here that you could feed a hundred soliders. Can't they see that?" He smoothed her silky long wavy hair as he turned to go to find Sally to tell her that her son, Wilfred, was not allowed to return with him. She took the news with a bowed head. Then she said, "Don fret none bout Wilfred, he be a good soldier, ain't he, Massa Wes?" "The best in the whole Army, Sally. I just couldn't do without him."

The days flew by, before long Wes was obliged to ride for the north again. When he returned, things were not the same. Captain Clemmons was no longer with the outfit. He had caught a minnie ball in the hip at Manassas Junction while he was riding a reconnaissance for General Jackson's cavalry. To make things worse, search as he may, he was unable to find Wilfred. He was told that Wilfred had been requisitioned to a labor force to help build fortifications. This disturbed Wes constantly. He tried every way he could to find his friend, but in the confusion of war he was unable to trace him. After all, he was still not considered a member of the Armed Forces.

Wes was involved in battle after battle, being forced to see his comrades replaced by raw recruits, some of them mere boys fresh from the farm. A letter arrived telling him that he would be a father again before too long. Adelia tried valiantly to keep the bad news of the poor condition of the homeland from Wes. The Yankee blockade was so effective that it had a strangle hold on the south. Only the gallant seamanship of some of the blockade runners was keeping the cotton going to the mills of England and war material funneled back into the southern war machine. Adelia sent a newspaper story from Savannah about the exploits of one, Captain LeClere who was said to be able to outmaneuver the Yankees on every voyage. His exploits at sea were the talk of Georgia. However, it had been some months now since the Captain had been heard from, he was presumed lost at sea. His widow, Madam Jeanine LeClere still had hope that he would return, but she knew too well that her hopes would not be rewarded. Here was another valiant soul, a forfeited pawn in a lost cause. This year, Wes, now a Sergeant, could not be spared from his duties. His next son, Mark, was to be a year old before his father would see him.

As the sun rose on the morning of April 29, 1863, General Stuart advised General Jackson that Hooker had crossed the Rappahannock at Chancellorsville. All day long there were skirmishes. Charges and counter charges. Jackson's troops forced Hooker's men to withdraw from the plank road and retreat toward Chancellorsville. One of the greatest battles of the Civil War was about to begin. Jackson and Lee had conferred during the night, the advance of the Confederate Forces began at daylight. Wes was assigned to courier duty. His big red gelding had come through previous battles with hardly a scratch.

As the lines started to advance they became ragged and broken in spots where the brush was so thick the men could not struggle through it in line. The attack on Hooker's flank seemed to be a grand and bloody success. Wes was carrying a dispatch from an infantry captain to General Jackson's headquarters. The battle had swung to the east, and night was falling. Artillery shells began to fall into the road ahead. Wes reined the gelding into the trees on the side of a steep hill. He had been spotted on the road, the artillery men, thinking Wes was the point of a cavalry troop, had continued to lay down a steady barrage. Wes tried to make his way to the top of the hill. An artillery round struck the top of a dead pine tree further up the slope. The dead pine top flew through the air like a javalin, it struck Big Red fully in the chest. penetrating into the cavity where his great heart would beat no more. The striken animal screamed in agony as it fell to the hillside. It happened so quickly, Wes could not throw himself from the saddle. The heavy animal crashed to the ground with the rider still astride.

Now it was the rider's turn to scream. His left leg was pinned beneath the dying horse he loved so well. He called the horse's name. "Big Red, Big Red, please get up." He felt the great body quiver, then move no more. Tears of pain and anguish came to his eyes. He could hear musketry just over the hill. It was getting louder. God, would he die in a Yankee prison with a broken leg? He tried to dig his way clear, to no avail. He felt his hand digging in the warm blood of the stricken horse. He lay back and prayed. He thought of the child-like faith of his precious Adelia. She said she had asked God to bring him back to her, safe. Would he be safe? Through the thickening gloom, he could see infantry moving along the edges of the roadway. Were they Federals or Confederate troops? He had to know. He couldn't just die here on this hillside. He hailed the closest soldier. The man quickly ducked behind a tree. He yelled to a squad of soliders near the road. "Take cover! I ain't jes sure who we got in the trees. Could be bluebellies." The 'bluebelly' instantly disclosed that the troops were Confederate. Wes shouted his situation as the squad advanced. When they freed him from his beloved horse, he found that his leg was not broken but that his knee was damaged. His first question was, "Who's in command?" I'm a dispatch rider, I gotta get to General Jackson's headquarters fast." Volley after volley of rifle fire could be heard from the top of the ridge. Scattered remnants of Confederate troops began to pour back through the woods from the direction of Chancellorsville. Jackson's brave Confederate troops had advanced with more enthusiasm than the southern forces had seen in a very long time. The troopers from the north were now better equipped and better trained. The wild rebel yell was dying on the lips of dying boys from the fields and hills of the beloved south.

Wes cut strips of a blanket to bind his swelling knee so that he could stand the pain of bending his leg. He sought out an officer, and showed his dispatch rider credentials. The mount they furnished him was a skinny mule. Wes mounted, urging the tortured animal to as much speed as he could command. Now and then he would see mounted officers trying to gather fragments of their command to make a stand. Wes inquired as he rode. "Where is headquarters, where is Gen'll Jackson?" A Lieutenant in a tattered uniform motioned toward an open field. The storm of the battle seemed to be further off to the east now. Jackson was to be in conference with

General A.P. Hill somewhere on the road to Chancellorsville. A volley of rifle shots rang out on the road ahead. Wes could see a group of horsemen had come under fire from a low depression in the hills to the right. General Jackson, in his haste to help reorganize the line, had ridden with his signal group toward the lines to the front. Pender's North Carolina brigade had not expected anyone on the road and had opened fire on the General's party. Jackson was hit by three rifle balls. One in each hand, then one that shattered the bones of his right arm. Some of his staff were killed outright, while General Hill was wounded. They spurred for the protection of the woods as the General fell from his saddle. By the time General Pender brought his troops back under control, the damage was done. Enemy fire began to rattle through the trees with charge after charge of grape shot from the cannons, landing in the road. Wes made his way to the confusion surrounding the gravely wounded General. He presented his dispatch case to a Captain Wilbourn, who informed him that the dispatches were too late. He heard the command, "Grab aholt here, solider, help with these wounded." He tried to comply, then fell forward, fainting from exhaustion and the pain in his leg. The fierce battle of that night continued with the command passing into the able hands of J.E.B. Stuart.

Wes awakened the next morning, weak from hunger and pain. He crawled to the side of the turnpike where an ambulance loaded with wounded, dead and dying, stopped to pick him up to haul him to a temporary hospital near Guinea's Station on the Richmond, Fredricksburg and Potomac Railroad. There, on the next Sunday afternoon on May 10, 1863, General Jackson raised himself from his bed, saying, "No, no, let us pass over the river and rest in the shade of the trees." He had crossed his wide river. A great General had given his life for a cause he believed in.

The sudden attack by the southern forces on Hooker's flank was a victory of sorts for the south. So much so, that General Lee planned an attack. He had to have remounts for his forces, food and ammunition. This was to be had to the north and east. The southern battles were being won only by the skill of their commanders. Their soldiers were used to handling arms and riding horses. Spirits were still high among the suffering southern troops. One of the best horsemen in Jeb Stuart's command, Wes Bolt, was unable to ride. The torn cartilage and ligaments of his knee kept him on crutches. He was sent home to his beloved Georgia to mend.

The train ride to Atlanta seemed endless as Wes lay, wondering how his family was surviving this terrible war ordeal. Wes had written home ahead of time to tell them about when he would arrive on the hospital train from Richmond. When the train arrived at the Atlanta Station, he struggled to his feet to make his way to the platform. He was greeted by a thunderous voice crying, "Massa Wes, Massa Wes." Then he saw the white hair of the giant, Tobe. The huge black man gathered Wes into his arms as though he were as light as a feather. Tears of joy streamed down his black face as he gently carried Wes to a waiting spring wagon drawn by two sorry-looking mules. A comfortable bed had been prepared in the bed of the wagon. Wes's heart felt a sudden surge of joy as he realized that the preparations for his comfort were made by his own beloved Adelia. "Yo jes res, Massa Wes, me an these mules gonna have yo home fore yo could say "Tunup greens an ham fuh suppa." The bouncing of the spring wagon lulled Wes to sleep as they left the traffic of the city, traveling on the country roads to the Bolt farm. They camped on the road that night, Tobe told Wes all that was happening on the farm. Adelia's father, Colonel Rodgers, had died of a heart attack at his desk in the legislature, just two months before. They had heard that the Rodgers' overseer had been killed in action at the Battle of the Big Thicket and Mrs. Rodgers was trying to run the plantation with her unruly slaves and what help she could get from resentful poor farmers in the vicinity. Wes began to notice that many of the fields were grown over with weeds and brush. Once neat farmhouses and plantations were falling into disrepair. There were still slaves working in the fields but not nearly so many. Scores of them had either run away to the north, or or were pressed into work gangs to help the war effort at the front. Long before they reached the Bolt farm, they could hear the ring of a hammer on steel. "Thet be Rufus, I ken tell by the music he make on dat anvil. He wukin much too haad, Massa Wes. Dat boy he be as skinny as airy rail in da fence. He think he gotta fix ever thin thet be broke in dis whole state o Georgy." A slender young black boy waiting beside the road let out a yell and ran like a streak for the farmhouses. Long before Wes reached the gate, his family, both black and white, came streaming up the lane with his name on their lips. Wes wanted to run to meet them, but knew he couldn't. He could see Adelia's beautiful chestnut hair streaming in the wind. A chubby little boy ran along beside her as fast as his little legs could carry him. She held a baby in her arms . . . Wes knew that it was Mark, their second child. "God but it was good to be home." Before they met the breathless group, Tobe had stopped the wagon, helped Wes to his crutches. Tobe scooped the baby, Matthew, up from the ground, then handed him to his father. The baby hugged his neck and recited a well-rehearsed speech. "Welcome home, dear father, we love you." Adelia was weeping uncontrollably, the tears splashing onto the face of the infant she held in her arms. Sally reached for the baby as Adelia gathered Wes into her arms. The feel of her strong body against him was the heaven he had dreamed about on countless lonely and miserable nights. Once again Tobe gathered Wes into his arms to carry him into his own house.

Supper that night was grand affair. Cissy had caught fresh catfish from the creek. There were yams, greens, turnips, and ham. Cornbread fresh from the oven was from home-ground meal, served hot with butter and honey. How could there be a war so terrible, still going on only a few days' ride from here? Before they began to eat, Wes heard the gentle voice of his wife begin to intone the twenty-third psalm. "The Lord is my shepherd, I shall not want, He maketh me to lie down in the green pastures, He leadeth me beside the still waters. He restoreth my soul: He leadeth me in the paths of righteousness for His namesake. Yea, though I walk through the valley of the shadow of death, I will fear no evil; for Thou are with me: Thy rod and Thy staff shall comfort me. Thou preparest a table before me in the presence of mine enemies: Thou anointest my head with oil: my cup runneth over. Surely goodness and mercy shall follow me all the days of my life: and I will dwell in the house of the Lord forever. Amen." They all sat quietly, different thoughts running through their minds. Wes relived again the terrible moments on the brushy hillside when the mighty, Big Red, had breathed his last because of men's ideals. Wes whispered again to himself. "Surely goodness and mercy shall follow me all the days of my life."

As they began to eat, Sally voiced her deepest thoughts.

"Massa Wes, whut uv my boy, Wilfred? He ain't able ta write no lettas ya know, he ain't had no learnin. Did you see him, maybe, Massa Wes?" Wes got up from his chair, walked around to her place at the table, then placed his arm around her shoulder. "The last I heard of him, Sally, they took him from my troop and forced him into a labor gang where they were building breastworks. I watch for him all the time, Sally, but I just haven't seen him." Sally wiped a tear, then showed her white teeth in a big smile. "He be awrite, Massa Wes. I pray ta God ever day. God, he hear the prayer o the black folk, too, ya know. My Wilfred, he gonna be awright." They all nodded their heads in a positive thought.

After the meal, Sally and her two teen-aged daughters cleared away the dishes, then they all excused themselves, leaving Wes Bolt alone with his two infant sons and wife who placed only God before him. Baby Mark had long since nursed and gone to sleep, but their eldest, Matthew, was determined to be the center of attention for as long as he was able to keep his little eyes open. It had been a long, painful trip, causing Wes to fall asleep before the youngster did. He felt Adelia smoothing the covers around him as she kissed his face murmuring . . . "Sleep now, my darling. You will be home for awhile and we can catch up on all the love we owe each other." Wes awakened early the next morning to find Adelia more than eager to fulfill her promise. Her lovemaking was more tender and passionate than Wes had remembered. He breathed a prayer, Please, Dear God, why can't this kind of life last?

When Wes hobbled out and about his farm the next day, he found things in a sorry state of repair. Where there once were horses grazing on the lush grass of the meadows, there now were only two old and unkempt mules. These were all that the war effort could spare for them to cultivate their fields with. It seemed to Wes that muscle and determination were all that could be used to hold their way of life together. Wes felt that his injured leg was healing much too fast. He knew that when he was able to walk again that he would be required to return to the front. The news of the conflict was not at all good. The Battle of Gettysburg had been fought in his absence. The south fought gallantly, but was unable to turn the tide in its favor. The north had intensified its campaign on the Mississippi River, Vicksburg was under seige. If this determined force were to fall, it would open the way for the north to cut the bleeding south into two parts.

CHAPTER 15
ESCAPE

Although the New Mexico territory seemed a long way from the fighting, it, too, was to feel the sharp edge of the sword. Clemmy and John Bolt had found their paradise alright, but it was soon to be a paradise in the path of terrible violence. Shortly after finding the ranch-site of their dreams, John saddled his magnificent white Arabian, Aladdin, and rode for the land office in Santa Fe to be sure that he had purchased all rights to the land he was to call home for the rest of his life. Although he could not read or write, John knew that there were lawyers in Santa Fe would could be depended upon to handle his paper work in an honorable manner. Santa Fe itself, was buzzing with war stories of all kinds. Riders from the east had brought news that the war had actually begun. The New Mexico territory was administered directly from Washington, therefore was aligned with the union. The Commanders of several of the frontier forts had resigned to join their comrades who were to ride with the cause of the Confederates. Most had made their way down the Rio Grande to Franklin, later to be El Paso, where Fort Bliss was still under the Command of the southern forces. The union hastened to garrison the forts along the river as a check against the possible invasion of the territory from the direction of Fort Bliss, Texas. Texas had thrown its ten gallon hat into the southern fortunes. Fort Fillmore, south of Mesilla, was garrisoned by union troops and ready. Further to the north, Fort Craig, near Socorro, was manned and ready. Fort Stanton to the east of the Sacramentos was to be the check aginst invasion from the staked plains. Tucson, in the southwestern portion of the New Mexico territory, was a hot bed of southern sympathy. The silver mines there were considered important to both causes. Caroleton's column, which marched all the way across the great desert from Southern California, was to prove to be the saving force for the entire territory for the north. The Colorado Volunteers saved the day in New Mexico, but the stationing of Caroleton's troops in most of the garrisons was the force which prevented the Texans from taking and holding the Rio Grande Valley. Little did John Bolt realize that the stage was being set to force him to take sides against his only son, Wes.

John rode through Glorietta Pass into Santa Fe, where he found a Judge Geer, recommended as honest and very able, in the affairs of the ranchers, who were slowly eating away at the huge land grants left to the descendents of the Spanish Conquistadores. On a chance that there might be word from his family, John went to the Post Office where he found three letters addressed to him from Adelia. The Judge read them to John so that he could in turn tell Clemmy what was in each of them. In the first, there was the positive fact that Adelia was pregnant and that Wes was afraid that he was going to have to go to war. The letters had, of course, been posted prior to the beginning of hostilities. John paid the Judge for the recording of the proper documents with the land office at Santa Fe. Now he and Clemmy were the owners of some of the best ranching country in the whole territory. John reflected on this as he rode The Lad back over the Sangre de Cristo mountains in the direction of the ranch.

The red man, too, had found that the dragoons now were occupied with their own problems, so they had become much bolder in their aggressive raids against the ranches and villages of the territory. There were Cheyenne, Kiowas, Comanche and the dreaded Apache. The Navajos were bothersome, but were more interested in raiding for sheep and cattle than for the outright elimination of the white men.

On this day, a band of Jicarilla Apaches had skirted Fort Union to the west and ridden in search of horses they might steal, or otherwise plunder, which might fall their way. John had gone through the Pass and was winding his way along the narrow road where it flattened out toward Las Vegas. His mind was preoccupied with his children in Georgia, including the thought that he was probably already a grandfather. Suddenly a shotgun blast invaded the silence of the beautiful land. John felt the sting of shot buried in his side and face. The Lad had caught some of the lead as well as the rider. He gave a sudden lunge, then a protesting squeal of pain. John was caught off guard, he began to fall from the saddle, reaching for his holstered pistol at the same time. The sudden lash of a tree branch across his face brought John to the ground with a heavy thud. He had lost his pistol in a tangle of scrub oak when he fell. He sat up in a half dazed condition, then he heard the yelping war cries of the band of six warriors galloping down the narrow road in his direction. He scrambled for the brush at the base of a cliff. Looking back, he could see that four of the warriors were riding down the trail in hot pursuit of the prize stallion. One was mounted on a horse that was limping badly, another who had been riding double with one of the others, approached the spot where they thought the white man had fallen from his horse. One was armed with a rusty muzzle loading shotgun, the other with a lance made from the broken blade of a butcher knife, secured to a long oak shaft. John prayed that they would not find his pistol in the undergrowth. The braves seemed to be confident that he was either dead or unconscious from his fall from the saddle. The one tied his horse as they began to search for him. If he only knew that the others would not ride back up the trail, he would make a stand and fight with his knife, but six men, four on horse back, were just too much, and he knew it. John was wearing high-topped moccasins on his feet which Clemmy had made for him. He retreated as silently as he could into the underbrush at the base of the cliff. A tangle of vines had grown from above and afforded an excellent hiding place. John made himself as invisible as possible by wedging himself back under a ledge of rock. The Apaches started looking for him in earnest now. The one who had riden the limping horse kept looking down the trail into the direction the others had gone. He probably got the idea that there were other white man horses in the direction in which the stallion was running. They began to sweep back and forth in the directon of the ledge. The one still didn't have his mind on his work. He turned, ran to his horse, then rode off down the road. The other was more determined now, he had to have some sort of prize, so his tracking became more deliberate. As he reached the cliff, he began to probe the dense vines with his lance. He was so close, John could smell the stink of his unwashed body. The brave lunged again. John felt the blade penetrate his leg just above his left knee. The rusty knife scraped the bone, then made its exit on the other side. John wanted to scream from the agony of the wound. The Indian pulled the lance back, without noticing the blood it had found, he turned to go back to the road. John knew that the brave would see the blood soon and return in hot pursuit. He crawled free of the trangle of vines in order to give himself room to fight with his knife. John dragged himself after the retreating Indian. The Apache saw the blood on the blade of his lance. He let out a war cry, then whirled. As he did, John's throwing knife caught him at the base of the throat. He fell backward, strangling to death on his own blood. A steady stream of blood was filling John's moccasin, so he sat down to cut his pants leg to make tourniquet. When the bleeding had stopped, John made his way down the road in search of a better place of concealment, in case the other four returned.

Carlos was beginning the construction of a pole fence in the upper pasture, when he heard the shrill whinny of a horse and the pounding of running hooves. He looked up to see the white stallion with his mane and tail streaming in the wind. He was running to the other horses and what he called home. Carlos's heart sank as he noticed The Lad was without a rider. He began to run toward the wagons, yelling while he ran. Carlos reached a spot by a large rock where he had left his rifle. He levered a cartridge into the chamber as he ran. Then he heard the beating of the pony hooves as they came in sight on the trail of the running stallion. Carlos stepped behind the rock, took careful aim, then killed the lead pony in full stride. The falling horse threw the Indian brave into the rocks beside the trail where he lay still, dead from a broken neck. The other three reined into the trees to avoid catching the second shot. By now, The Lad had reached the wagons. Clemmy and Consuela rushed to examine him to try to determine what had happened. When they saw the flecks of blood on the horse's hip, they knew that John had met with serious trouble. Carlos came running. "Ayude me, pronto. Help me saddle a horse." He mounted the hard-breathing stallion, then rode to the pasture where he caught one of the mares. He quickly changed the saddle from the lathered Lad to the back of the Arabian mare. Next, The Lad's bridle, then he was mounted, ready to ride. The young Mexican boy of seventeen was now a man, off to war against the foe who had dared to raise a hand against the man he had chosen to be his idol. He rode back to the wagons where Clemmy was waiting. "Get me a horse, Carlos, fast!" "No time, Senora." He strapped on a pistol and cartridge belt, filled his pocket with cartridges for the rifle, mounted the mare and rode in the direction of the Indian braves. The three, still able, made a fast retreat into the dense piñon forest on the side of a low hill. Carlos knew that they would be no match for the sharp shooting Clemmy, so he rode on up the road in the direction from whence The Lad had come. His sharp eyes began to backtrack The Lad and the ponies. The trail was plain, so he urged the mare on faster. He kept a sharp lookout on each side of the road for any sign of movement. He rounded a turn, he heard his name called from a clump of rocks not far from the road. He rode to John, dismounting. After a quick examination, he determined that his boss was not too badly injured. He stood up, the huge pistol sagging at his slender waist. "Well, Patron, what happen? Them bad Indians scare you so bad you fall off your horse?" John weakly laughed with him. He directed Carlos up the road to where he had fallen from his horse. They found his pistol and began to ride toward home. "Thank God that Injun with the shotgun misjudged his distance. He could of blowed me an The Lad both ta hell. Did The Lad come home, Carlos? Is thet how yu knowed to ride fer me?" "He alright, Patron, got some shot under his hide, jes like you. We dig them out alright, though."

As they road into sight, Clemmy was anxiously waiting. She breathed a prayer when she saw the mare carrying two riders. They helped John into his bed in the wagon, where Clemmy cleaned the knife wound as best she could, applying some of her best remedies to insure that there would be no infection. The grim fear of lockjaw or tetanus was in the back of all of their minds as John's fever began to rise. Four days passed, then his fever began to subside. Clemmy showed her relief by saying, "Reckon there ain't nothin in the whole worl' and New Mexico thet kin kill the likes o' yo, John Bolt." She held him close to her and hummed a Cherokee chant which had been taught to her by her old grandmother, Sun Flower, years ago in Georgia.

Spring came and with it the drudgery of trying to make a ranch of the raw western land. Day and night they struggled to build houses, barns and pasture fences, to hold their precious horses. As summer came on, the mares began to foal. This was the beginning of one of the biggest and best horse ranches in the west. It was a beginning also, for John and Clemmy to be drawn inexorably into the web of war on the side opposite their own son. New Mexico and the Union lost some of their most able commanders. Men such as Ewell, Sibley, Loring, Fauntleroy and Longstreet resigned their commissions, then joined the forces of the Confederacy.

On June 23, 1861, the New Mexico forces were taken over by Major R. S. Canby who had received information that Confederate forces would try to invade New Mexico.

The scorching June sun lay hot on the blistering southern part of New Mexico. The Rio Grande River wound through huge bosques of salt cedar, which quickly gave way to the scorching red sand of the desert. The sun would rise hot and burning on the greasewood, mesquite and cactus land. By mid-day, both man and beast would seek the shade to gain some respite from the ever-increasing heat. Settlements of any consequence were few and far between. This part of the world seemed to be cruel and most inhospitable. Who would want to invade the likes of this? Both Confederate and Union forces alike knew that some part of the war would spill over into this seemingly God-forsaken land. The Rio Grande Valley was to be the highway of invasion. Even now, an impressive Texan named Captain John Robert Baylor, of the Second Texas Mounted Rifles, was riding at the head of an invasion force of several hundred Texas fighting men. It was long road from where they were recruited in the area of San Antonio, but ride they did. In his recruiting efforts, Baylor would tell the men that they were going on a hunting trip. None believed this story. They all knew the ultimate goal. Captain Baylor finally rode at the head of a force of over a thousand men. Many lost their eagerness and dropped out of line somewhere along the seven hundred mile journey. Baylor's forces were welcomed in El Paso, by Judge Josiah F. Crosby and Simeon Hart, two staunch supporters of the Confederacy. They reviewed Captain Baylor's troops. These were hardened horsemen, armed with a rifle, a pistol, and some carried double barreled shotguns loaded with buckshot. This was a volunteer force whose members had brought their own arms as well as ridden their own mounts. They were most eager to strike a blow for the Confederacy.

The now Union Colonel Canby had ordered Major Lynde from his post near Santa Rita, to proceed to Fort Fillmore above El Paso to meet the threat of an invasion up the Rio Grande. He commanded four companies of the 2nd Infantry. Over seven hundred fighting men encamped at Fort Fillmore. Lynde sent a dispatch to Canby immediately, asking permission to abandon Fort Fillmore. He felt that it could not be defended. The water for men and animals was too far away in the river. The weather was so hot that the heat waves began to show and simmer by mid-morning. Captain Baylor now rode at the head of only 250 mounted Texans. He by-passed Fort Fillmore, then occupied Mesilla, to the northwest of the Union forces. Major Lynde immediately mounted a force to dislodge the Texans from Mesilla. The superior union force advanced, sweating and falling as they tried to haul a heavy howitzer through the loose, blown sand along the edge of the desert. Lynde asked Baylor to surrender to his superior forces. Baylor sent two riders out to answer Lynde. Their reply from Baylor was, "If you want Mesilla, then come and take it."

The Texas forces began to fire from their concealment behind fences, thick walls of adobe houses and the protection of trees and brush. The Union forces withdrew and began preparation to abandon Fort Fillmore. Lynde had decided to retreat to Fort Stanton more than a hundred and fifty miles to the east. It was a poorly executed retreat by the forces commanded by Lynde. Some of his men even carried whisky in their canteens instead of water. As they marched across the blazing desert, they became exhausted, falling by the road. The Texas forces saw the dust cloud released by the Union forces and rode to the pass at St. Augustine. Baylor's forces were waiting for Lynde when he arrived at St. Augustine Springs. Lynde surrendered his entire command.

The Texans rode on up the river toward Fort Craig. They were a triumphant and confident lot now. They were well-equipped with the ammunition and guns from the surrendered Union forces. The now General Canby, sent word to his garrison at Fort Craig, below Socorro, to hold against the Texans, to defeat them without further advance. Besides the predicament of the advancing Confederate forces, the Federal forces were being harassed by the vicious Mescalero Apache Indians who had become bolder by the day, now that the soldiers were fully occupied by "white eyes" of their own kind. This was their opportunity to loot, kill and burn, and so they did.

Baylor wrote to General Sibley, former New Mexico Commander, now a General in the Confederate Forces with command of the entire southwest. Baylor complained that he was not well enough equipped to go against General Canby's men. There was a brigade being formed in Texas then to march against the territory. General Sibley had convinced President Jefferson Davis that New Mexico, Colorado and California, must be taken and held against all Union forces. Sibley brought his brigade to El Paso, Texas, encamping at Fort Bliss. His forces had suffered terribly from disease and hardship on the long march from the central part of Texas to the far reaches of the west of the vast state. The General now, in a letter, appealed to all his old friends and comrades in New Mexico, to rejoin him and the fair government of the Confederacy. The Union forces were being out-generaled on every turn. Fort Fillmore had surrendered, the panic was so great that Fort Stanton was abandoned, plus the fact that, now Colonel Baylor had shamed the Union forces at St. Augustine Pass. It was time for Sibley to move his Army up the Rio Grande. This maneuver now had the attention of the Union high command. On February 21, 1862, Confederate troops, 3,000 strong, had advanced up the Rio Grande, past Fort Thorn, were within about ten miles of Fort Craig. Rebel forces rode boldly across the Rio Grande to the west side. The Union forces repulsed them, waded the river in hot pursuit. A hail of sharpshooters' bullets cut into the Union forces, forcing them to retreat to the safety of the fort. A long line of supply wagons hurrying northward, indicated that Sibley did not intend to fight the Union forces in the safety of Fort Craig.

General Sibley sent a detachment northward into the vicinity of San Marciel, to intercept the column. The Union troops, under the command of Colonel Ben Roberts, began firing. Canby had many effective soliders at his command, including such well-known as Captain Selden, Colonel Christopher (Kit) Carson and others. The courage of the Union troops began to fade as they began crossing the river to the west, in the face of heavy Confederate cannon and rifle fire. The Colorado Volunteers, under Carson's command, wore colorful uniforms which the Texans used as a target. It wasn't long until it was obvious that the northern forces were being routed. They retreated to the safety of Fort Craig, leaving behind a huge treasure of food, ammunition, artillery and other war material. The southern forces put them to immediate use, driving in the direction of Albuquerque. They had by-passed the Union strong-point at Fort Craig and were bent on the capture of Santa Fe. Sibley drove his forces relentlessly toward their ultimate goal. They lived off the land of the lush Rio Grande Valley. They used cattle, sheep and hogs for food, they rode the horses of the ranchers and farmers who were hapless enough to be in the path of the onslaught. Word of the relentless advance of the southern forces spread over northern New Mexico like a chill wind from the slopes of the high mountain. General Sibley had written in his report that the Battle of Valverde was the first he had encountered in which the enemy had used double-barreled shotguns when they approached at short range. Wild stories were circulated about the brutality of the Texans wielding their terrible buckshot loaded shotguns. The Confederates advanced on, then took Albuquerque, by March 2, 1862. They occupied the mountain pass to the east, then advanced toward Santa Fe. By now the Union commanders had began to order a scorched earth policy. As the Texans rode, they encountered burning stores of both food and forage. These things were vitally essential to their extended lines. Major McDonald, the Union commander of the garrison at Santa Fe, decided that the city could not be defended. He burned his surplus supplies, then retreated through the pass to the east to Fort Union.

This ominous advance of fighting forces had Clemmy and John Bolt greatly troubled. All of their mares had produced a foal in the summer of the preceding year. They had even bargained for mares of a lesser quality to be bred by their magnificent stallions to produce a better than average offspring. Their horse ranch was sure to be in the path of destruction.

A year had come and gone since our travelers had chosen their promised land at the foot of the Sangre de Cristos. Their choice of a location near the Santa Fe Trail had, by cruel fate, also placed them in the position of having to choose to take sides in a war they had traveled hundreds of miles to avoid. The winter this year had not been too cruel, so their horses had come through without too much loss. Four of the colts had been lost. Three to exposure and one to a hungry mountain lion. After the loss to the lion, Carlos practically lived with the horse herd. His rifle was ever ready to defend against either marauding Indians, or hungry animals.

One of the Arabian mares had foaled a snow-white stud colt which was a perfect image of the magnificent Aladdin who had sired him. The only color on him was the shading of black around his eyes and at his flaring nostrils. The colt had no more than begun to nurse from its mother when Carlos went to Viejo. He was unable to restrain his excitement as he spoke to John. "Viejo, you promise me a colt from one of the Arabian mares." Viejo noded in assent. "I have find him, Viejo. He came last night from the brown mare. He is snow-white like the top of the mountains y he will be the greatest horse in all the territory of New Mexico. "Hold on there, Carlos, ain't ya fergitting his poppa is still here." Viejo smiled at the excitement of the young Mexican boy. "He be greater than all the horses in the country, Patron. His name is Gallo Blanco, the White Rooster. He will fly like the wind. Yes, Viejo, he will be even greater than his papa. Is he mine to train, Viejo?" Carlos's eyes were fastened on the older man's face in anxious anticipation. Viejo extended his hand to the slender youth. "He is yours to own, Carlos." "Gracias a Dios, Viejo! These horses will be my life and I will be the owner of the greatest Arabian stud in all the world. People will see me ride him and they will say. 'Who owns that caballo magnifico,' then others will say, 'It belong to the caballero who is riding him.'" Carlos had already begun to dream about riding the colt through the towns and villages of this great land. "I will teach him to run like the wind, Viejo, then he will be the reason our horse ranch is the talk of the land." They all went to the barn lot to see the new arrival. The colt was up on its legs, nursing from the mare. They looked at, and talked about, the other colts running and playing in the big pasture near the barn lot. As they watched, a rider came from the road to the northwest. It was Ben Williams from his ranch further down the Pecos. As was the practice in those days, anyone who rode to Santa Fe, would stop at all the ranches on his way home to tell all the news and carry mail. There was no letter for the Bolt family, but he had plenty of news. He told of the Texans riding toward Santa Fe. Williams left out not one word of what he had heard about the unrelenting tide of Texans riding across the land. "They aim to take every horse they ride up to, Bolt. They will take the mares and your stud and then they will shoot the colts. If ya got any feed, they aim ta take that, too. Then they will go inta yore house and take what there is to eat. Afore they leave, they set a match to all that is left.'' This was an exaggeration, but it was a fact that the Confederates were compelled to live off the land. They took the food they needed, the horses they had to ride. Their General Sibley, however, had given strict orders that the people were not to be molested or their habitations destroyed. He was trying to convince New Mexico territory that it should be under the Confederate government.

The Bolts and Williams all walked slowly back to the house where Williams was given a generous lunch of beans, beef and chile. When he mounted his horse to ride on down the river, he said, ''I tell ya, Bolt, we ain't got no choice but to jine the regulars at Fort Union ta fight them rebels.'' John with his arm around the still slender waist of Clemmy, she with her head on his shoulder. Carlos, with his sister, retreated into the house. Finally John spoke: ''Clemmy, honey, they ain't left us a choice, have they? Larkin always told me never to raise my hand against a man lest he needed killin. I ain't got no cause to raise my hand to the Confederates, cept thet they aim to come here to the place we have fought fer, and take the horse we brung all this way from Georgy. We can't let em do it, Clemmy!'' Not thout trying to stop em.'' ''John, this ain't our war. We come all this way ta keep from fightin over somethin we never did believe in. Sides, John, we be talking bout fighting the same folks our own flesh and blood son is sufferin with right now. Maybe even some o the Miller boys is with that column which is in Santa Fe rat now. Member how they tuk us in and made us feel as though we wuz ther own? What purpose is God got ta have us kill some folks lak thet?'' Clemmy began to weep softly at the thought of the terrible ordeal they both knew was about to engulf all of them. ''Clemmy darlin, you an Connie gonna have ta defend this here house ranch as best ya kin agin them Injuns. Keep horses saddled at all times in the case ya need to ride fast and far. Iff'en ya see that all is lost, ride fer Vegas, stay there till I come fer ya. Don' try to stand again too great a odds. Them horses an this here place ain't wuth one day o yer life fer as I be concerned.'' He held her close to him as he stroked her long black hair, now streaked with grey. ''I aim to give Carlos his choice o stayin here to keep the place, er riding with me ta Fort

Union." "Ya know the choice already my husband. Thet boy woudn't let ya go alone eff'en ya wuz ta beat him half ta death. Sides, I want ya to look atter each other. Me an Connie will stick close ta the house. We kin keep all the stock in the close-In pastures. Thet way we kin keep a eye on'em. I know thout askin thet you an Carlos aim ta ride out ta help turn the Confederates back." John put his hand under Clemmy's chin to raise her mouth for his long and tender kiss. "I shore love ya, gal, an this here task that has been laid pon us jes tears my heart out. There jes ain't no choice." John turned to the house and called for Carlos. The young man and his sister seemed to have been waiting for the signal. They both emerged quickly. "I saddle the horses, Viejo!" "Ya got a choice, Carlos, ya know thet, don't ya?" "No choice, Patron, we ride out now to Fort Union." As they tended to their horses, Clemmy and Consuela prepared food, also a bedroll for each of them to tie in back of their saddles.

Clemmy included a coat for each of them since the March north wind still blew a chill from the snow-capped peaks of the majestic Sangre de Cristo Mountains. Clemmy prayed, "Don let it be the blood o John Bolt, er Carlos, dear God. Shorly they ain't come all this way jes ta be slaughtered by a bullet from another white man jes lak they be! Put yore hand on em, dear God, so's they kin ride back down thet trail." Consuela too was praying, crossing herself as she had been taught to do at the Catholic school where she and Carlos had spent their childhood. The two men armed themselves with rifle and pistol, then rode off to the northeast. It was March 23, 1862.

At the same time, General Sibley's troops were taking possession of the territorial capitol at Santa Fe. Riders had relays all night from Santa Fe to Fort Union with the news that the Texas column was intending a fast sweep to capture Fort Union before the arrival of the Colorado Column under the command of a lawyer named John P. Slough, and a preacher named Major John Chivington. This column of one thousand three hundred regulars and volunteers had marched over one hundred and seventy two miles in just a little over five days. Slough had heard about the Val Verde defeat as he was marching his troops to the aid of Fort Union. They rested at the fort, then marched out on March 22, bound for Santa Fe and a confrontation with the Confederate forces who had ridden so far, so hard, in their conquest of a vast land populated by so few people.

John and Carlos met the Union Colorado troops, they marched out of Las Vegas on the morning of the twenty-fourth. While they rode along beside the column of horsemen in the lead, a Cavalry Captain greeted them with, "if you aim to be volunteers, fall in back there with the dragoons. Report to Lieutenant Bently." John felt a sudden surge of rage rise up in his guts as he heard the names Bently and dragoons. He wondered, what other indignity could be sent his way? Going to a war he didn't want to fight, prepared to kill other men just like himself, opposing the Army which included his very own son, and forced to be under the command of a man he despised.

The force ascended, then descended the mountain pass and approached Pigeon's Ranch. There the tired troopers hastened to quench their thirst and then fall to rest in the shade. Little did they know that the Confederates had already reached that point in their advance, placing their cannon and rifle squads in concealment. When the Union forces had relaxed their guard, the Confederate forces started pouring cannon and musket fire into their ranks. The Union officers were gallantly trying to rally their men, to get them into line. When the weary Texans felt they had the Union forces totally off balance, they attacked for hand to hand engagements. As the battle raged, the Union forces began a hasty retreat back toward the safety of Fort Union.

During the fierce engagement, Slough ordered two companies of cavalry under the command of the preacher, Coloney Chivington, to advance around a mountain to reconnoiter the Confederate rear. Chivington observed the Texas supply wagons at the place called the Stone Corral, about eleven miles on down the mountain from the battle at Pigeon's Ranch. Captain William H. Lewis led a attack against about two hundred troops guarding the supply wagons. Among them rode Carlos and John Bolt. They had been given a position at the rear where the dust was the thickest. Their eyes and nostrils were filled with the flying dirt as they rode. They soon found themselves at the head of the charge. This, of course, was due to the fleet-footed Arabian horses they rode. John caught a glimpse of Carlos, aiming a pistol over the crook of his arm as he rode. He could feel the heaving sides of his white stallion speeding into the face of the returning fire from the Confederate wagon train. John levered round after round into his rifle as he fired at the now retreating Confederates. He could see men falling, horses down. Some riders rose again to still fight, while others lay where they had fallen, never to rise again. He felt the presence of another rider just to his left, then he looked into the sweating face of Lieutenant Bently. They both brought their mounts to a skidding stop when they saw that they had over-ridden the wagons to emerge on the other side. John had emptied his rifle, then was reaching into his saddle-bag for more cartridges. Bently maneuvered his sweating horse in front of The Lad. "I aim to have that stud, Cracker. Just make up your mind that you have done volunteered him to a good cause." The lieutenant unsheathed his sabre. Bently was so intent upon what he was saying to John that he failed to see an enemy soldier point a pistol and fire. The round caught Lieutenant Bently square between the eyes, his head exploding like a squashed melon. John tried to get a shot off at the retreating Texans, but the enemy had fled into a patch of juniper, where he was out of sight. Bolt wondered, was the lieutenant drawing the sabre to end John's life, or was he still in pursuit of the enemy? That question would never be answered. When the Confederates at Pigeon's Ranch, who really had the situation well in hand, heard the firing in their rear, they spread the word that their old enemy from the Battle of Val Verde, General Canby, had marched his forces up the Rio Grande and was now at their backs in overwhelming force. The Confederates retired from the field thinking that they had lost the battle.

There were several other bloody skirmishes in the Glorieta area, but the burning of the Confederates supplies was the turning point. The Texans retreated back toward Santa Fe and Albuquerque. The Confederate forces were so badly scattered that they were forced to retreat in a disorganized route. Some returned to the Duke City by way of trails on the east side of the Sandia Mountains. They joined the forces holding the Tijeras Canyon Road. When they had regrouped to the south and east of Albuquerque, they tried to cross the Rio Grande. There, troubles were multiplied, wagons, cannon and mules became stuck in the sand and water at the river's edge. Try as they may, in their haste, the tired soldiers were unable to release their mired supplies. They cut their traces, then, it was every man for himself in their headlong flight to Fort Bliss at El Paso. John and Carlos made their way back toward the Bolt Ranch as fast as they could push their already tired mounts.

When they neared the ranch, they could hear the sound of an occasional rifle shot. Both urged their horses to a fast run, a cold chill ran through them. Someone was after their horses, and Clemmy and Connie were making them hard to get. As they entered the top end of the valley, they began to fire their rifles into the air to let both friend, and foe, be aware that more contestants were joining the fight. They could see a part of their herd of mares being run toward a break in the rail fence at the edge of the valley. Some mares were separated from their colts, other colts were running along-side their mothers as fast as their legs could carry them. Carlos let out a scream of anger, he could see the Arabian mare in the lead being drive to the forest of pinon, juniper. The snow-white Gallo was running with his neck stretched, his young legs flying. The little stallion was making a valiant effort to keep up. John yelled: "I'll check the house, you follow the horses. Stay behind . . . Don't try to come too close with them Injuns." Carlos could not hear, for he was already reining toward the horses and riders fast disappearing into the trees. His already jaded mare was closing the gap between him, and six Jicarilla Apache braves, who were riding hard now, to take their spoils back into the hills and canyons of the higher range. Carlos knew that they would ride for a cleft in the rimrock to the north, so he rode as hard as he could urge his mount up the steep, brushy hillside. The Jicarillas knew that there was but one rider in pursuit so they did not make an effort to stand for a fight. They concentrated on driving the horses before them. John, riding in the other direction, reached the ranch buildings, dismounting in a shower of dust. The white stallion stood with his head down, his side heaving with the effort to get enough air into his lungs. John ran toward the house, yelling as he crossed the bar ground of the ranch yard. "Clemmy! Clemmy! Where in hell are ya?" "Here John! Here in the barn loft." John changed directions, then could see Clemmy standing in the opening of the hay loft. She still held her rifle at ready. "Apaches are steelin the mares, John!" "I know, honey, I know. You alright?" Where is Connie?" The Mexican girl appeared beside Clemmy. "Aqui, Senor Viejo, aqui." She also held a rifle which she had been firing from the other end of the barn loft. Her eyes widened as she searched the barnyard for Carlos. She almost screamed her anxiety. "Donde esta Carlos?" In his concern for Clemmy, John had momentarily forgotten Carlos in his headlong pursuit of the retreating horse thieves. He tried to be reassuring, although he was not sure. "He went after the horses, an he is gonna need some help. Is there a horse in the corral?" "In the barn, John!" Clemmy was descending the ladder, she directed her husband to where she had saddled and bridled a pair of horses, just in case she and Connie were forced to make a run for safety. "Need cartridges, Clemmy. Get em fast." She had a buckskin pouch of unspent ammunition slung around her shoulder, she threw it to John, he was tightening the cinch on one of the stabled horses. "They come here early this mornin, John, me and Connie heard the big stud soundin a challenge to them Indian ponies. They be six o em, John. We kep em off to a distance, but they been at us all day. They got the fence down on the upper pasture jes afore yo come in. They got some o our best stock, John. I tried hard to hit some o em, but they wuz too fer away. Me and Connie wuz afeared ta leave the ranch buildins ta try fer a closer shot. We ain't shore some o em did'n circle around ahind us. Still ain't." John led the horse outside, swung into the saddle. "Take The Lad inta the barn, tend ta him. Stay inside an keep looking sharp. I aim ta help Carlos bring them horses back." He slammed the rifle into the saddle scabbard, lashed the brown Arabian mare that was Clemmy's horse into a fast run as he crossed the pasture to the opening, made by the retreating Apache. He soon picked up the trail, riding as hard and fast as the brush and tree covered hills would allow. The sun was getting low, he neared the jagged notch in the rimrock at the north side of the wide valley. The stillness of the afternoon was shattered by three rapid shots from a pistol, somewhere up ahead. There were two quick answering shot from rifles. The vicious whine of a ricochet bullet sang its deadly song somewhere off to the right. John's eyes darted in all directions in an effort to take in the action so that he could join the fray. Short yelping war whoops could be heard straight ahead. John used the reins to lash the mare to greater effort as he headed for higher ground. From his vantage point, John could see the horse herd being urged toward the break in the rimrock. Four braves were dashing back and forth behind the horses, yelling, waving their rifles over their heads in an effort to keep the horses moving. Two other were dismounted, firing from cover at the sparse protection of some rocks on the edge of a small ravine. Carlos had recklessly closed with the would-be, new owners of his precious Gallo. The other eight or ten mares, with colts, and the huge draft stallion, were important too, but the white colt was his. Some of the colts had failed to keep up and were calling pitifully for their mothers to wait for them. John knew that if they could not gather them in time, they would be mountain lion dinner before morning. John rode in a skirting sweep to get behind the position he knew to be occupied by Carlos. The mare his boy was riding had literally done her very last effort, to bring Carlos to the rocks where he could get some protection. Carlos then cut the cinch on his saddle, removed the bridle to let the exhausted mount stagger in the direction of the others she knew. He felt that the Indians would not make too great an effort to do away with him. He was on foot now and did not pose too great a threat to them getting away with their prizes. They still could not resist the urge to kill this white man. It would make them look so good back at the rancheria. Besides they could use his saddle and weapons. The two were converging on Carlos when John made his appearance. He encountered the one to his right. The brave was so intent on his effort to kill Carlos, that he failed to see John in time to get off a shot. John swung his rifle to his shoulder, fired one time, killing the Indian instantly. Carlos had directed his attention to the new action, changing his position to counter what he thought was a new threat. The other brave saw his chance, then tried to force his pony to trample Carlos into the dirt. The young man whirled with the quickness of a cat. His action caused the pony to shy away. The young Indian warrior was thrown from his mount and crashed heavily into Carlos. They were both momentarily stunned from the impact. They recovered, then began what they both knew was a struggle to the death for one, or both. John could see them fighting with all they had, but could not shoot for fear of hitting the wrong target. The combatants hit with their fists, kicked, gouged, used knees and elbows, they struggled to reach their knives to put an end to their opponent. The Indian hit Carlos in the face with his fist, causing him to release his hold and roll away. They both came up with knives in their right hands. Carlos clearly had the advantage now, for he had spent countless hours under the patient coaching of the grey-haired man he called Viejo. The Jicarilla lunged for the chest, Carlos moved just enough to let the knife point pass his heaving torso. Then his knife hand darted for the throat. The fight was over. Carlos lay back gulping air into his lungs.

John was already riding to join the battle with the four who were now almost to the notch in the rocks where they could hold pursuers back while the horse herd was being driven to the safety of the high mountain meadows. There the Indian forces would be strengthened with more of their own kind. John was cautiously aware that these Indians had rifles. The Apache had also followed the battles of the previous days very closely. When a soldier was downed on either side, the stealthy Indians would grab what arms and ammunition they could, and retreat to the safety of the scrub oak and piñon clad hills. They were well-armed, but not so well schooled in the use of the arms they had stolen. John rode hard in their direction. Carlos saw him leaving, he ran for the Indian pony, swung aboard, following as fast as the poor beast could carry him. John rode like a mad man as he realized his prized draft stallion and several of the mares might soon be ridden to death by the hard-pressed Indians. The light was beginning to be bad, he lashed the brown Arabian to greater effort to beat the stallion to the cleft in the mountain. He rode literally through the four Indians who were pressing the horses toward the pass. John arrived there first. He wheeled the Arabian so fast she could hardly keep her feet. He dismounted to begin firing as fast as he could work the lever of his rifle. He saw a rider slump forward, then fall from his running horse. The other three tried to shoot from the backs of their running mounts, but the shots went wild. They soon had had enough, they faded into the gathering gloom of the piñon and juniper forest. John mounted, then rode to the big stallion. He began to talk to the huge beast in his soothing southern drawl. The stallion stopped. His nostrils flaring in a effort to breathe in more air. He was lathered and mad. The sound of the familiar voice began to calm him. John rode along-side the big stud, slapping him on the withers. "Now looka here, big hoss, ya'll got a job to do. Best ya git on with yer work. Getten dark now, big man. You git them ladies and their youn'uns headed back fer tha Bolt place.'' The big animal was sure of the voice now, so he nickered softly. John was already riding back down the mountain toward the inviting valley far below. The big stallion raised his great head, released a long whinny which echoed through the rimrock walls. Anxious mares began to call to their colts as they sought the company of the great Percheron stud. The cries of the little ones which had been left back down the trail could be heard in the gathering night. From the darkness John heard, ''Viejo, quidado . . . careful.'' ''Where ya been, Carlos? the party is done over.'' Carlos rode the Indian pony alongside as they watched the big stallion gather his harem for the trek back to the safety of their pasture. One colt was lost, causing the mare to be greatly troubled. Carlos and John decided they could not look for it this night for they were still not too sure of the safety of the ranch itself. They fell in behind the horses; pushed them toward home. Carlos had already made certain of the safety of his milk white colt he had named El Gallo. ''Did you see that Gallo run, Viejo? That colt ran faster than his momma. One day, Patron, he gonna outrun The Lad. Then one day he be the best race horse in this whole country. I teach him everything, Viejo, you see.'' They rode in silence for a while. Each absorbed in his own thoughts. Finally Carlos spoke in his soft, Mexican accented manner. ''Viejo, this Indian I fight did not care to die any more than I want to die. He fight like a devil. He fight for his home, Viejo. Just like I fight for a home. I know how that Apache feel, Patron. We ride on his land right now, Viejo. His wives and children are hungry. When a man have his back on the wall, then the only thing he do is fight to survive. I deed not want to keel him, Patron, but he were taking my Gallo and his momma. Gallo, he be the only thing I own in the worl, so I fight til I die for heem. I fight for you too, Patron. You, my Viejo, the only one I ever know.'' John grunted and nodded his head. He, too, was reflecting on what his life had become since he had left his home in Georgia, so that he would not have to fight another man's war.

If it is a question of a man going to war, then he will try to avoid it, but if the war comes to the man, devouring what he considers to be his or his loved ones, then he will fight until he dies. The face of his own young son came to John in the darkness. He could hear Wes now as he had told them: "Go on out to the territory, Momma and Poppa. This is not your war. I gotta stay here, though. This farm is mine now, and I have a wife whose father is part of the system, the heritage of the south. Yep, Poppa, this is gonna be my war, and I will be fightin for something I really don't believe in. If someone is going to change my way of living though, I don't believe he has the right to do it. I'm gonna stay, Poppa and Momma. I will most likely fight." John's heart felt as heavy as lead as he remembered the flying bullets and busting shells of the day before in the skirmish at Glorieta. He wondered, with dread if his own beloved son was still alive. "Damn this way of living, anyway." This he said aloud, provoking a one word reply from Carlos . . . "Si."

Even as they rode back to their ranch in the north-east part of the vast New Mexico territory, other events in history were taking place that would leave the mark of a heavy hand on this part of the world.

General Albert Sidney Johnston, a former Texan, had resigned his command of the Department of the Pacific in California and had returned to be named a general for the Confederacy. General Sumner, for whom Fort Sumner was named, was transferred to California to take command in Johnston's place. An Army was organized in California, to be called the California Column, which was to be transferred overland to relieve the threat of any Confederate thrust to take over all the western portion of the country. This Army was placed under the command of the then, Colonel James Henry Carleton. This man was quickly elevated to the rank of General, setting about the monumental task of moving an Army across the vast stretches of desert between Fort Yuma on the Colorado, and the Rio Grande in the eastern sector of the New Mexico territory. While that vast Army was on the march, the Texans had already made their thrust into the vital Rio Grande Valley. They were repulsed at Glorieta, thence had returned to Texas while the troops under General Carleton were marching toward the battle area. When the California Column reached Fort Thorn on the Rio Grande, east of Cook's Peak, it was August 7, 1862. Shortly afterward, he took Fort Bliss at El Paso on the Rio Grande. Carleton was then assigned as commander of all of the New Mexico territory. Since the Confederacy did not bring the war back to Carleton, he decided to make a war of his own. He began a campaign to eliminate the threat of Indian depredations into the towns and ranches of the west. In the process, Fort Sumner at Bosque Redondo on the Pecos, was established as a reservation for the Mescalero Apache, Jicarilla, and Navajo Indians. His ruthless treatment of the red men almost caused their extinction, but relieved the pressure of Indian raids on the people who had settled in the territory. As this small war was being waged in the west, a greater and bloodier one was beginning to grind the southern forces to pieces in the east.

CHAPTER 16
TO FIND A FRIEND

In the summer of 1863, Wes Bolt was still limping on his badly injured knee. Orders came, nevertheless, for him to join his unit at once. Grant had engineered the final surrender of Vicksburg on the Mississippi. With this thundering defeat, the Mississippi River was opened up as a new highway for the pincer movement which was squeezing the life out of the Confederacy.

Wes was wearing a uniform which Adelia had reinforced from the inside with patch after patch. His boots were carefully mended by Tobe who had used rawhide sinew and patches to make them wearable. When he reported to the Command Post at Atlanta, he found that his entire company had been ordered to the Chattanooga front to be under the command of General Bragg, new Commander of the Jefferson Davis Army of the Cumberland. The Battle of Missionary Ridge and Lookout Mountain was beginning to take shape. By now, many of General Lee's most able commanders had fallen on the field of battle. More than twenty percent of his high command had been decimated. The remaining officers, even the command of the northern forces, wondered how the ragged, hungry armies of the Confederacy could keep fighting with the fierce spirit which won them the respect of their enemies.

Wes was again given a mount and the assignment of dispatch rider. His troubled knee was still so bad that he would find it necessary to bind it with any kind of rags he could find before mounting his horse. This was turning out to be a particularly rainy time in the vicinity of Chattanooga, Tennessee. The roads would sometimes be covered with as much as a foot of water. Men and beasts on both sides were suffering agonies. The whole morass of cold, rain and mud became a horrible, painful nightmare to Wes

Bolt. "Form a line and stand, boys, fall back and regroup at the creek, take a message to the Colonel, ride hard to headquarters, form a line at the river, carry your wounded, no fires tonight, then form another line on the other side of the ridge." On and on the mind-shattering conflict raged. When he was fortunate enough to have the luxury of a tent, Wes would huddle in the shelter from the rain, with his mind on his little family in Georgia. He tried valiantly to make even a trace of sense as to why he was here helping to kill men just like himself. Men who marched to a different tune, but bled and died all the same when their bodies were cut or blown apart.

After his successful campaigns against the Confederate forces along the Mississippi River, General Ulysses S. Grant became Commander in Chief of the Northern Armies. General William T. Sherman became prominent in command and was assigned to head a pincer movement to the sea, thus cutting the staggering south into two indefensible sectors. Losses on both sides were terrible in the ensuing battles, but Grant drove his northern forces on with a new determination. Grant coordinated the advance of all key Union Armies at the same time. Spearheads developed toward the Shenandoah Valley, Richmond, Mobile. Then General Sherman launched a campaign to destroy Atlanta. He was a thorough, relentless general with Thomas, McPherson, and Schofield as his most able assistants. He built his supply lines as he went. By the fourth of May 1864, Sherman's Armies were poised for the spring into Georgia. The mountains of Georgia were beautiful this time of year with a profusion of flowers and greenery.

The Confederate Forces under the command of General Johnston were in line waiting for their final chance to turn the despised Yankees away from their heartland. Wes had been under fire so many times now that he was considered an old hand. All those who had been fighting since the first of the war were old hands, although Wes was in his early twenties. He wore a sergeant's stripes now, so the officers considered his calm attitude a comforting pillar for some of the mere boys who helped to make up the Army of the Confederacy. General Joseph Johnston's Confederate armies rallied to make a stand to hold the railroad complexes at Catoosa, Red Clay, and Dalton. The southern General fortified the pass called Taylor's Ridge, and Buzzard Roost Gap. On

May the seventh, the northern Fourth Corps arranged for the battle to begin, then started a slow advance toward the dug-in southern forces. The constant pressure and skirmishing caused Johnston's forces to fall back. The odds were just too great. Southern soldiers fought to exhaution. Among them was Wes Bolt. He was familiar with this part of northern Georgia. He had been here many times on horse-trading jaunts with his father. He was now fighting for his life on the farms of the very people he had visited as a boy. He would see a farmhouse, remembering the good meal he had there. The memory even more vivid now that he was hungry and never without pain in his injured knee.

The beauty of early spring and summer was everywhere on the land, yet the grandeur was being defiled by men hurling objects of destruction at other men, then leaving them to die in the streams and on the back roads of a beautiful country.

One early morning Wes was riding a dispatch to the rear, or at least what he thought was the rear, when he was confronted by a squad of cavalry in blue uniforms in the middle of the road. He wheeled his mount to take to the woods, but the poor beast did not have the strength to make it up a vine covered embankment, the horse fell heavily, throwing Wes to the ground with a sickening thud. The world turned black as he lost his senses. He was awakened by dismounted cavalry soldiers who seemed concerned about the extent of his injuries. Wes seemed to be looking through a blood red haze at the bearded face of a blue uniformed sergeant. "Wake up, Reb!" The sound came weakly to his pain-tormented head. "Wake up, Reb. You gotta take a walk down the crick ta join your friends." Wes sat up. There seemed to be nothing broken, so he rolled over, getting to his feet. His weapons had already been take from him. The sergeant spoke again. "You are a prisoner now, lad, so don't try to do anything we will all regret." Wes had no will to differ with this positive statement. He walked down to the road with his hands in the air. He knew that the war was over for him. They had already taken his dispatch case. A rider had gone to report to the Union Commander. Wes limped ahead of the horsemen, to a clearing where a farm had once produced its bounty for some Georgia farmer. There were hundreds of southern soldiers of all ranks, and condition, already sitting or standing along the banks of a little creek. The wounded were laid in the open field, to be attended by their comrades as best they could. Hundreds were being herded into the clearing by mid-afternoon. The news of a Confederate change in high command began to circulate. General Johnston had been replaced by General John B. Hood who had given the southern cause an arm at Gettysburg and a leg at Chikamauga. Johnston's officers felt that this was a grave mistake on the part of President Jefferson Davis. It might have been. Atlanta fell like a fiery torch.

Wes had been confined as a prisoner during the long hot summer. The battle for Atlanta had raged up into the fall. General Hood retreated northwestward, hoping that Sherman would follow. Instead, Sherman retreated slowly to the Chatahoochee where he encamped and began to prepare for his great march to the sea. Many of the southern soldiers from Georgia would escape from the prison concentrations, then just wander back to their farms in the hills and valleys. Little effort was made to recapture them. Wes had planned many times with other Georgians, to escape to his farm and family to the south of Atlanta. His injured knee would just not allow him to run. He stayed, suffering in the cold and hunger of the prison encampment. The entire southern army was being wracked by desertions from the ranks. The demoralized soldiers just felt that all was lost anyway. Others were just as determined to fight and die for a lost cause. Wes would hold onto the memory of his devoted wife and two children, grit his teeth, then swear to God that he would not die. That he would go home to start a new life after his hell on earth was done. He wasted away to skin and bones as he hobbled around the cantonment with the other wretched souls from the south.

In November of 1864, General Sherman began his march to the sea. He had dressed his army down to nothing but the very best. Only those who were capable of marching great distances were chosen for this huge operation. The marchers threw away all but the bare essentials. Their orders were to live off the land, then destroy whatever they could not use, so that the enemy could not possibly raise the will to fight behind them. The order read, "Make fifteen miles per day, corduroy the roads where necessary, destroy whatever property as designated by the Corps Command, and to consume or destroy everything eatable by man or beast." As the Sherman march began, all slaves deserted their masters. Many went to the northern forces to reveal where hidden stores where to be found.

When the foragers reached the Rodgers plantation, they found that it was deserted, except for the big house. There they were met by two aged house servants and a resolute matron who warned the blue clad soldiers that they were on her property and that they would meet with resistance if they advanced into the yard. The order quickly went out to burn the place to the ground. The livestock was quickly gathered from the outbuildings, then the torch went to work on one of the grand old plantations of the south. Slaves gathered in groups to watch the flames spread. Their plight, too, was grave. They now had no one to look after their welfare and see that they were fed. The fire had begun to eat away at the mansion, Mrs. Rodgers advanced to the front window, fired a shotgun blast at three soldiers who were applying the torch to the garden gazebo. The bird shot stung them to hasty retreat, but a blast from several rifles caused the woman's face to disappear from the now glassless window. They never bothered to enter the house to see if she was dead. The two grey-haired black servants ran from the house. They later made their way to the Bolt farm where they told Adelia of the fate of her strong-willed mother. Her heart labored under the strain of sorrow she now bore. She had not had word from her husband for many months now. She could see the smoke rising from the burning plantation where she had spent her happy childhood. Adelia knew that the foragers would be at the Bolt farm before the night was over. All hands at the Bolt farm, both black and white began to scurry about in an attempt to hide as much food and as many of the farm animals as they could, before the dreaded foragers reached them. Tobe and Cissy hurried the mules into the thick brush along the creek bottom. They knew every trail to make the job easier in the gathering darkness. Sacks of beans and peas were stashed in hollow logs and trees. Live chickens and pigs were released from their pens. It was intended that they could gather them later, after the dreaded Sherman march had passed.

Adelia had instructed all the blacks to pretend that they had just been liberated and were happy about the prospect of being free. Two of Sally's teen-aged daughters had already gone off to a liberation meeting in the county seat. Such meetings were being held openly now by groups of slaves being lectured to by other blacks, who had spent some time in the northern sanctuaries of the Union Forces.

The sun rose the next morning and was shining brightly when they came, one sergeant and three privates in a spring wagon. The giant Tobe had told Adelia that he would never leave her side. His determination could not be swayed, so Adelia had placed him on the front proch with the boy Samuel, from Sally and Rufus's family. She had coached them carefully. They were not to make a move, no matter what happened, unless she called upon them to do so. She knew that if anyone tried to defend her on the farm, that all would be lost. A few could possibly be defeated, but it would only bring more with harsher punishment for the resistors. Two soldiers with rifles at the ready were posted at the edge of the farmyard. The sergeant and the other soldier started toward the two houses where the blacks lived first. They were all made to leave the house and stand in the yard. They had strict instructions not to re-enter. Rufus was instructed to carry all food left in the houses out and place it in the spring wagon. He obeyed without a protest. They all seemed to be happy that the day of jubilation was finally here. There was very little to load into the wagon. The sergeant grabbed Rufus by the hair, then threw him to the ground. "Where did you hide the rest of the provisions?" He had placed his foot on the throat of the complacent Rufus. The black began to beg. "Naw suh, Cap'n, we ain't got no mo. We hain't had nawthin on dis place fuh a lon lon time. We is starvin, Cap'n." The sergeant's heavy boot applied pressure to Rufus's throat. Little did he know that Rufus could have broken his leg, then killed the other soldier in a flash, if he had been forced to do so. He bore the pain, then when the pressure was released, he began to beg again. "Please Cap'n we jes be po black folk. We ain't got no food ta keep body and soul togedder." The sergeant kicked Rufus in the ribs. "If you are lyin to me, I am to kill all of you." Rufus stayed on his knees begging. "Let us go, Cap'n, ain't we suffered enough already?" "Ya look dam fat ta me, an I ain't seen no darkies wearin clothes as good as them you got on. Now get back to the house and stay there." Rufus scurried back to his waiting family, then entered his house. He took a double-barreled shotgun from beneath the loose boards in his bedroom floor, then stood by the window where he had a clear view of the two soldiers at the wagon. The sergeant went to the larger house, where Adelia was waiting to see what could happen next. He used the butt of his riffle to smash the door down. Tobe and Samuel, on the porch, seemed disinterested in the rude actions of the Yankee soldier. When the door burst open, Adelia, now pregnant with her third child, stood to face the intruder. He backed through the door. "Come on outa there, woman." He yelled at her in a rough voice. The two little boys began to cry, clinging to their mother's patched skirt. "Git, I said!" Adelia held her head high as she went through the door onto the porch. The sergeant used his left hand to rip her bodice from top to bottom. Adelia did not flinch as her ample, milk-white breasts shone in the morning sun. "Well, now, looky here, we got us an aristocrat! This here ain't no ordinary Georgia Cracker. Where is your man?" Adelia, still standing erect without a trace of shame, replied, "He is to the north somewhere, fighting Yankees." "Well now, he should be here to see his woman with her tits shin'n in the morning sun." A gurgle of rage escaped from the throat of the huge Tobe, who had moved closer to the sergeant. The younger black took hold of Tobe's hand and said. "Uncle Tobe ain't got good sense, Mr. Soldier. He be kind of simple-minded. Here, Uncle Tobe, set down and be quiet." Tobe sat, but the boy could feel his steel hard muscles tensing beneath his homespun shirt. The sergeant extended his hand as though he would caress the exposed bosom before him. Adelia began to pray in her soft gentle voice. She quoted from the twenty-eighth psalm. "Unto Thee will I cry o Lord, my rock, be not silent to me, lest if Thou be silent to me I become like them that go down into the pit. Hear the voice of my supplications, when I cry unto Thee, when I lift up my hands toward Thy holy oracle." Adelia raised her hands and eyes to the heavens. The only source from whence she could expect mercy. The soldier with the sergeant said, "Leave her be, Sarge. Can't you see she ain't no tramp to be handled like thet. We ain't had no order to be this way with people. This is a lady, an she don't deserve to be treated like a whore." "Shut your damn mouth, Perkins, you think you are in command here?" The private shrunk back at the angry words and look of the non-com. Nevertheless, he continued in defense of Adelia. "I aim to report this to the lieutenant if you don't ease off. He never told us to abuse nice folks, jes to take what they have." The sergeant wavered at the mention of the higher rank. "Perkins, I aim to have your ass fer this. Your life in this here Army is beginning to get hard." Perkins didn't waver in his resolve to see that the lady got just treatement. The seargeant looked into the house. "Clear them cracker brats outa there, woman, I am gonna burn this hog pen to the ground." Adelia ran to pick up her youngest, she led the eldest into the yard. The soldiers then set fire to the house she had wanted to keep for Wes to come home to. She could not contain her sobbing as she made her way to Sally's house where she was immediately covered, and comforted. "How much more can we stand, Sally? Please God, how much more? Wes, oh Wes, please come back to me, to help me. Please come home to us, we need you so." She felt that he heard her, then she slept in the arms of the strong black Sally. Sally was praying, too, that her Wilfred would come walking up the road to lift the leaden burden she carried in her heart for her first born.

The southland burned, groaned and suffered while the war ground to an end. It had been the hardest of all hard winters when General Lee surrendered his southern forces to General Grant on April 9, 1865. All prisoners of war were released within a few days to start their journey to, God only knew what. Officers were allowed to keep the horses they rode, while enlisted men gained whatever transportation they could afford. Mostly walking. Wes set out to the south as soon as he could see the light of day. He limped along the roads he knew from his childhood. Now and then he would leave the road to see if he could find anything to eat. Salad greens, a frog, maybe a fish in a small pool of a creek. He ate anything he thought would sustain his life as he struggled to join his family. Hundreds just like him were lining the roads on their way home. In his weakened condition, he was able to make only about ten miles per day. Anyway, he was headed home. He would make it, no matter how long it took.

Wes skirted Atlanta to the west and kept on the side roads. There, at least, he could occasionally find a scrap of food to keep his tortured body going. One evening, just as the sun began to set, he caught a large king snake that had tried to cross the road in front of him. He killed the creature, then thrust it beneath his ragged shirt. He followed an over-grown path to a tumble down abandoned farm. The sun began to set, it also started to rain. The chill of the cold rain caused him to shake all over. He made his way to the pig shed which was the only shelter left standing. Wes crawled under the sagging roof, then began to gather dry sticks to make himself a fire. He skinned and cleaned the snake with his bare hands, as best he could. When the fire had begun to burn with enough heat, he skewered a piece of the snake meat on a green tree branch, then began to roast it over the fire. The anticipation of something in his hungry belly made Wes want to hurry the cooking process. He knew the snake had to be cooked, or he would not be able to keep it down. While he roasted his supper, a great cloak of loneliness settled over him. It was a dark night, the only things to remind him that he was still alive in the world, was the sound of night birds in the trees. Now and then, he could hear the rustling of small animals scurrying through the undergrowth. He was tired, his body ached for the comfort his own home. He said aloud, "I will make it home! The war is over now, so there ain't nothing that will keep me from seeing my wife and boys." He didn't even know that his wife was expecting another.

The meat roasting over the fire began to smell good. He leaned closer to the fire to see if his meal was ready to eat. An agonizing moan came from the depths of the dark shed. The sound startled Wes. He fell back from the fire, from his long months as a soldier, he reached for a sidearm. There was none, so his hand closed over a large stick he had gathered for firewood. The sound came again. This time it was a groan. The sound of a man in great distress. Wes took a burning stick from the fire, then made his way toward the back of the shed. By the dim light of the torch he could see the shape of a man lying with his back to a crib, in which they used to feed hogs. Wes call softly. "Who's there?" A feeble black hand raised from the man's side. In a weak, raspy voice, the black man ask, "Will you come closer, stranger? I be dyin here. I be ready to die, but I jes do'n wanna go thout my kin knowin where I be. My Momma gotta know somehow." Wes moved closer, then smelling the revolting stink of the man's unwashed body. The skinny wretch before him wore a tattered southern uniform jacket, a pair of pants so worn they could hardly hang to his tortured body. His face was covered by a growth of black beard. Wes spoke softly to the pitiful shape against the crib. "Maybe you don't need to die here, soldier." The man's eyes opened. "I wuz a good soldier, Mister, till I lost my arm at Chancellorsville." Something about the black wretch bothered Wes. His manner of speaking, the sound of his voice. The torch had burned out, so they could not see each other in the blackness of the shed. "Do a dying man a favor, stranger. Tell Momma and Poppa thet you saw me. Tell em I was good soldier who fought fo his fren as long as I had the strenk ta stay on my feet." The voice faltered, then began again. "I was growed on a farm bout two days good walking to da south o here. Go tell Momma at the Bolt farm thet her boy, Wilfred, died like a good soldier." The shock of the man's last sentence stunned Wes into silence. He put his hand out to feel the man's skinny chest. Then Wes began to cry out the agony that was inside of him. "Wilfred! Thank God I found you! Speak to me again, Wilfred, You ain't gonna die now, Wilfred. I will take care of you. I will take you home, Wilfred." "Wes . . . ? Wes, thet sound lak you, awright. I jest couldn't be shore. Fraid I jest done wore out right here in dis here hog pen." "I won't listen to more of that kind of talk now. We are going to go home." Wes put his arms under the thin shoulders to pull him toward the fire. It was then that he became aware of the stump of the right arm. His dearest friend's arm had been blown away by a blast of grape shot. The black man groaned in agony, Wes dragged him to the fire. Then, more sticks were thrown on the coals to help warm them both. "I got some chicken roasting here, Wilfred. We are gonna have a banquet." Wilfred smiled weakly through his tangled beard. "Thet ain't got the shape o no drumstick, Wes. Sides, I ain't hongry." "Well you are gonna chew, and you arc gonna eat this here meal. Now don't go talking about dying any more. Talk about living! We are gonna be eating your Momma's cooking again, so square around here and have your supper." Wes put pieces of the roast snake into Wilfred's mouth. Soon he was chewing and swallowing the tender meat. They devoured every last morsel of the meal. "Thet fire shore feel good, Wes. Wonder effin I could make it on home wid you?" "No wonderin, Wilfred. We are going home as soon as you can git on your feet." "On my feet it be, Wes. I hain't had no shoes fer nigh onta two year now." They both laughed for the first time in months. Wilfred began to shake from the fever he was enduring. Wes lay down beside him on the side away from the fire. "God almighty, Wilfred, you stink like a boar hog.'' Wilfred began a prayer of thanks. ''I aim to pray again, dear Jesus. This time I ain't askin. I wanna thank ya, Jesus fer bringin Wes ta me. Now maybe he can help me git on home to Momma, Poppa and the res of the fambly.'' They slept fitfully for the rest of the night.

The next morning as the sun rose on the beautiful Georgia hills, Wes got up, built up the fire, then made his way across a small meadow to a sluggish creek. There he was able to take a stick with which he killed several frogs. He even found a small turtle. On his way back to the hog shed, he crossed a garden patch. The former owners had evidently left in a hurry. There were still turnips in the ground. Now he knew they would live. Before the day was over, Wilfred was sitting up with his back against the shed wall. By the end of the second day he was up, walking around. Wes walked him to the creek, where they both washed themselves in the clear water of the stream. ''We start home tomorrow, Wilfred.'' Wilfred shook his head. ''Cain't make hit now, Wes. Need bout nother week for I kin git to the road.'' ''You got two good legs you can walk with. I only got one that works real good. We can help each other. Now . . . by the grace of God, the Bolt farm is goin to see a couple of skinny soldiers marchin down that lane. One black and one white. One will be swinging two arms, tother two legs, by God we are going home.'' A broad grin creased Wilfred's black face. He lay down to sleep. He had made up his mind he was going to be there marching in that lane that led past the blacksmith shop. Next morning, they gathered turnips to munch on as they walked. The skies were clear, the air was fresh. Their progress was slow, but they were going in the right direction. As they walked along the roads, people would come to them to inquire about loved ones who had not made it home as yet. Perhaps they never did. The good people would give then cold water to drink, and share their meager fare with them. The closer they came to their home, the lighter their hearts became. They rounded a turn in the road, then they saw the remains of the once magnificent Rodgers plantation. Families of former slaves were camped under the trees. They were waiting for they knew not what. All at once a cold hand of fear gripped the heart of Wes Bolt and Wilfred. They both realized that the same thing could have happened at the Bolt farm. They tried to quicken their pace, but they were just too tired and weak to hurry. When they reached the clearing, they could see the Bolt farm still standing, the only house burned was the one where Wes was born. They could see washing on the clothes lines, smoke rising from the chimneys of the two small houses left standing. They turned into the lane, then started past the smithy. The huge bulk of Tobe could be seen in the shade of the shop roof. He was there, trying to restore the wreckage left by the marching soldiers who followed Sherman.

Tobe raised his white head to look at them although he had seen hundreds just like them in the past few weeks. Wilfred yelled, "Uncle Tobe!" The grey-haired man threw his hammer down and ran to them. He raised his great black arms into the air and shouted. "Glory be an hallalulyer!" He began to shout at the top of his lungs, "Hit's them!" O glory, hit's them! O glory!" He ran to them . . . picked them both up as though they were children and started walking toward the houses. His shouting had gotten the attention of everyone else. They all came running. The tearful reunion didn't last too long. Both the weary travelers were faint from the exertion of walking day after day on the well-traveled roads. They were both hustled to bed. Wilfred was already experiencing the tender care that only a mother can give. Sally was heating water to give him a bath. At the same time food was being prepared for both of them. Before Wilfred drifted off into a troubled sleep, he suddenly realized that there were members of the family missing. "Momma, where is Poppa and the girls?" Sally could not hide the shadow of pain which crossed her kindly face. "Hesh now, Wilfred. They be awright. I tell ya all bout em when you have yoscf some sleep." In the other house, Wes could not get enough of holding his two sons, trying to find out all about them at once. Matthew was four years old now and had a great deal to tell his Daddy. He had been saving up for the time he would come home. Mark was still not too sure just how to treat the new situation where his Mother was getting too much attention from someone he still considered a total stranger. Adelia was trying to do everything at once. She would work a moment, then hurry back to the bedside. Wes reached out a hand, tenderly patting her on the fat tummy. "Looks like you are pregnant again, honey. Seems like you are that way all the time. At least you are trying to repopulate Georgia." She blushed, but held his hand in place. "Feel the baby move, honey. This time, maybe we could have a girl. Anyway, this is what happens when a soldier comes home from the wars.'' She leaned over the bed to be closer to her beloved. ''I knew God would send you home to me, darling. You seem a lot worse for the wear, but you are here just the same.'' The hot food and tender care caused Wes to doze off to sleep. He was not disturbed until the sun was well up the next morning. Tobe had already run his trot lines at the creek, bringing in a string of blue channel catfish to be their lunch. Grits and fresh pork was their breakfast. They were able to find some of their pigs in the thickets of the creek bottom. Tobe had thought that this was the ideal time to butcher and prepare a feast. The warriors were home at last!

CHAPTER 17
FALLEN ANGELS

After they had eaten, Adelia told Wes of the horrible death of her Mother at the hands of the Union soldiers. Then she began to get Wes up-to-date on the story of Rufus and the two missing teen-aged daughters of Rufus and Sally. Adelia's gentle voice began: "After Atlanta fell, the slaves all refused to work. They would roam the roads, gathering in groups to discuss their newfound freedom. On Sundays, they would gather in great crowds to hear freedom folks from the north tell them about the wonderful things that Mr. Abe Lincoln had done for them. Although Rufus and Sally's teen-aged daughters had never been slaves, they were young and impressionable. They were caught up in the excitement by the newfound freedom of other black people. One Sunday evening they had had a heated discussion with their family. Marabelle, the eldest, was nineteen, Floralee was just sixteen. Marabelle said, 'Poppa we talked to the nicest man at the freedom meetin today. He is wearin beautiful clothes, has a diamon ring on his finger, an drives a horse an buggy the likes of which you ain't neva seed. He even got a gold tooth in front, Poppa, an he wears a silk top hat. He tole me an Floralee that we is free as the birds now, an we kin git a job an live like white folk.' Easy going Rufus cut in with, 'Ya ain't neva been no slave, so whut you talkin bout?' 'We tole thet ta Mr. Absolom, and he said thet we was all jes Mr. Bolts' niggas, an thet we ain't had no freedom till jes now.' Rufus had gotten up from his chair, raised his hand to strike the girl for what she had said. Sally stopped him, then she tried to reason with the girls. 'Don' you go lisnin' to no talk lak dat. Yo hear yu Momma?' The girls had been so well propagandized by the freedom talker that they defied their parents. 'Mr. Absolom says he know there are places in the big cities where girls lak us kin make lots o money, an we ain't got ta wok in no fields, neither.' By now Sally and Rufus were in a rage at their wayward daughters. They tried to reason with the girls about the wonderful life they had right here on the Bolt farm. The girls sat in stony silence. Their eyes defiant. Then Sally had sent them to their room without supper. The next morning, Sally and Rufus had heard a galloping horse come to a stop on the road. Their two girls, dressed in their finest Sunday clothes, were getting into the back seat of a two seated buggy, drawn by a high stepping bay horse. They threw their bundled possessions into the wagon, then settled themselves into the seat. Rufus ran from the house, yelling in desperation, for the two girls to wait for him. On the seat of the spring wagon was a big fat, black man with a high silk hat. He wore a white shirt with a black suit. Long before Rufus could reach the road, he had whipped the horse into a gallop. The father of the two young girls was left in the dust by the road, weeping in frustration. The dregs of humanity, no matter what color, were already feeding upon the misery of those who had been so long oppressed. Rufus fell to his knees to pray. "O my Gawd! Whut gonna happen ta my little girls now? Please Gawd, make em see some sense an leave dat evil man. Make em git down fum dat wagon an come home ta the folks whut love em and want ta keep em fum harm." His fervent prayers were not answered, the wagon grew smaller, turned the bend in the road in the direction Sherman's soldiers had gone. Rufus hurried back to the house. There he desperately ran to the pasture, caught one of the old work mules, bridled him, swung aboard the animal's bare back. Sally ran to her husband. "It ain't possible ta ketch up to dem on dat po ole boneyard mule, Rufus. Jes ain't no use a tall." The heartbroken Rufus got down from the mule, hung his head and wept out the misery that was in his heart. When he could weep no more, he looked at his sorrowing wife. "Sally, we tole them girls lots of stories bout Savannah. We tole em o the fine big house. We tole em o the stores which sold all them things from across da ocean. I reckon they thought they wanted to go see fer their selfs. I be goin' now, Sally. I gotta fine my two baby girls an bring em back here ta home. I don know whar ta look but I reckon I kin go ta Savannah ta see effin they be there. Maybe they could be wokin in some white folks fine house by the time I get thar." In his sinking heart, Rufus knew better.

Rufus left the farm to begin the over two hundred mile walk to Savannah. As he trudged, the grinding miles of the Georgia roads, he would ask anyone who would listen if they had seen his two young daughters. The more he asked, the more he became aware that there were hundreds of black girls who were following the northern troops. Most of them were being watched over by cruel vicious pimps, both black and white. Rufus was afraid that he knew their fate, but he trudged on in the hope that he might possibly find them. By the time he reached Savannah, he was out of food, his clothes were in rags, his shoes were long since worn out.

The war was almost over, Savannah had fallen to the devastating sweep of Sherman's soldiers. Thousands of blacks were wandering the countryside not knowing what to do. They had always been looked after. Now there was no one but themselves to care whether they lived or died. Rufus was in that miserable stream of humanity. He begged for food, took it when possible, or worked for a meal when he could. He wandered along the riverfront, with the dim hope that he would catch a glimpse of his daughters. The places were teeming with solidiers, sailors, and the regular scum of the earth which frequents the waterfront cities. Each time Rufus would try to enter one of the honky tonks to inquire about the girls, he would be rudely driven out by a team of bouncers put there for just that purpose. One evening he ran from them to the rear of the building where he lost them in the early shadows of the night. He hid behind some trash barrels to rest. While he sat there, two young black girls emerged from the back door of the second floor of the building. They were dressed in flimsy, tight-fitting, brightly colored gowns. Rufus could see that they had nothing else on. They began to smoke cigars which they had evidently stolen from customers. One of them spotted him in the circle of trash. "Whot yu doin' dere, Pop? Dat bouncer ketch you, he gonna break yo haid." They both giggled. Rufus looked up, "Ain't meanin' no harm ta nobody. Jes lookin fur someone." "Who yu be lookin' fur, Pop?" Rufus quickly told them the the names of his daughters, where they were from, how long they had been gone from home. One of the girls began to talk in a subdued voice. "We ain't neva seed no body by thet name here, Pop. Once you gits in ta one o these places, you can't leave. No matta how bad yo mout yern ta go home. We is fum Calhoun County, ourselfs. All da jint owners knows whut girls wok whar. They jes don be no way to run away. Some girls tries it sometime. When they ketch em, they bring em back and give em a good bustin. The onliest way a gal lives dees jints, is effin whe gits da sickness. She get da sickness, den dey take huh way to do hospidle an nobody eva sees dem again.'' Rufus thought, ''My God, slavery ain't over, after all, an probly ain't neva gonna be.'' The girls had turned and gone back through the open door of the second story. Rufus was hungry, his feet long since without shoes, were bleeding. He stumbled into the main street along the riverfront. He could hear the bawdy music, the raucous laughter, the profanity of the gutter, as he pushed his way through the throngs of humanity in the street. When he reached the outskirts of town, he noticed that he was going north. He looked at the stars in the sky as he mumbled, ''Dear Gawd, my gals is dead. Dey both be dead. Pray Gawd dey didn' hatter suffer too much.'' A sort of peace settled over his tortured soul.

The road began to rise away from the riverfront, Rufus noticed that he was traveling the very same highway they had taken when he left Savannah so many years ago in the wagon he, Tobe and John Bolt had made with their own skilled hands. He remembered how John Bolt had made the black man's love for his faithful, Sally, into a beautiful dream by taking him with him on his way to build the farm he had dreamed of from the time he was an unwanted boy traveling with the horse trader. He remembered the giant Tobe panting and sweating in his effort to catch up to the wagon. Yes, he remembered, then smiled. A vision of his Sally crossed his mind, the faces of his children were there. He wondered if his oldest boy, Wilfred, had been killed in the war. What of young Wes Bolt? Would the world ever become a place to live in again? He suffered days and nights as he made his way back to northern Georgia. The war had ended, Wes and Wilfred were at home when Rufus dragged his tortured body past the smithy, toward the home he had built with his own two hands. He was greeted with tears and kisses. When he learned that the two soldiers were back at home, he actually felt happy again, after so long a time.

Wes recovered much faster than Wilfred. His black friend felt that most of his life was past. After his body had mended sufficiently, Wes went for a walk with him one summer evening. He, Tobe, Adelia and Cissy had managed to get some crops in the ground. They were beginning to grow, making it seem that the whole world was on the mend again. Whippoorwills called their mournful songs in the underbrush, cottontail rabbits scurried for a hiding place as the two men strolled down the fence row. "Wilfred! You an me gotta make this farm good again. The land is still here. All it is going to take is some hard work." "How kin half a man hep yo, Wes? You be pulling all de load. No way thet could be a fair change." Wes stopped to look at his friend for a long interval. "Wilfred . . . you have always been the best horse groom in the state of Georgia. You will be that again! Tell me, and tell yourself you will." Wilfred started to grin as he thought of their present plight. "We got two bony ole mules, Wes, think they need some o my expert grooming? Good thin they got a hide, cuz thet sho is all they got to hole theirself's togedder." "You are a better man with one hand, than most are with two. Now promise me you will stop being sorry for yourself, an git on with the business of living." Wilfred extended his good left hand. From then on, they worked the farm from what they called can, to can't. From the time they could see in the morning until they could no longer see at night and things began to grow. Tobe rebuilt the blacksmith shop. Not to its former size, but to a size that did all their work, as well as taking on some of the neighbors' tasks. Not many horses were being shod, but wagons had to be repaired, hand tools made and sharpened.

Now that the war was over, mail service was being established all over the land. The Indian wars were in full swing in the western reaches of the broken nation, but mail did manage to get through. Every month, Adelia would write a long, newsy letter to John and Clemmy, in care of the Postmaster at Santa Fe. They were not even sure that the couple was still alive. Adelia wrote anyway. Some didn't make it, but some did. One day there was a letter in return. It was written by Connie in childish simplicity. It served the purpose just fine. They now knew that John and Clemmy were indeed alive and doing well. Their horse herds were growing, the market was excellent. The westerners were overjoyed to hear that they now had two grandsons. Another boy was to be born to Wes and Adelia Bolt. It was now Matthew, and Mark.

The Bolt family, separated from east to west, began to prosper again. The pieces of broken lives were being fit back into place.

Wes Bolt of Georgia, watched his sons grow with the other things on the farm. They managed to trade some of their land for some livestock. Four mares produced four strong colts. Two young sows produced over a dozen little pigs. It began to seem that there could be a happy world again. Then the vicious nature of men began to pierce the flimsy facade of normalcy. Nightriders, under the guise of protector, began to strike terror into the hearts of any black who tried to better himself. The blacks on the Bolt farm, earning their way with toil from morning until night, were to be a prime target.

CHAPTER 18
THE INDIAN AFFAIRS

After General Carleton's California Column reached the Rio Grande, the Confederacy had no plan to try to retake the vast reaches of the New Mexico territory. The General took up headquarters at Santa Fe. There he became alarmed at what might happen to his well-disciplined troops if they were to just sit idle. He must keep them busy. Since the war effort had taken most of the attention of the soldiers up to this time, the Indian tribes had begun to make serious depredations into the ranching and farming communities of the river valleys. General Carleton chose this opportunity to keep his troops busy, then at the same time, teach the savages a lesson they could not forget. His aim was to subdue them, or destroy them. The Indians, no matter how fierce the tribe, were no match for the hard-riding cavalry. The soldiers' horses were of better quality, they were shod, allowing them to travel over rocky ground for days at a time. The soldiers were well-armed, as well as well-disciplined. On the other hand, the Indians were never really organized. They fought each other as well as the white men. They had few guns and very little ammunition. Their hiding places and rancherias were scouted out by rival tribes.

On September 6, 1863, General Carleton wrote to the War Department in Washington, that he was beginning a campaign against the marauding Navajos. He established that they were to be moved from their canyon vastness along the Rio San Juan, to the bleak prairie area of the Bosque Redondo on the Pecos River, near Fort Stanton. This was a distance of four hundred miles. A column under the command of Colonel Kit Carson was equipped and dispatched to the Navajo country near Fort Defiance. Carson had orders to destroy anything that the Indians might use for food. He was to take the Navajo horses and sheep. These were to be returned to the cavalry posts for dispostion by the directors of Indian Affairs for the territory. The long walk started. Navajos by the thousands were herded toward the Pecos. Hundreds died on the way. Navajo and Apache were to be forced to live together in a way of life they had never known.

The wretched Indians began to congregate at the Bosque. Riders from the south would stop at the Bolt Ranch to tell of their plight. Clemmy's very soul would cry out for them. After all, she was the daughter of a full-blooded Indian. Why must these proud people be ground into the dust from whence they had come? She made a vow that she would help these most unfortunate human beings. She remembered the bleakness of the place called Bosque Redondo. The Indians' hearts bled to return to their beloved Canyon de Chelly, Moqui, Window Rock and other canyon homes they and their ancestors had established so many generations ago.

Carleton gave his soldiers order to kill Indians wherever they were encountered. They were to be given no quarter. Complete capitulation was their only choice other than death at the hands of the soldiers. John Bolt was among the citizen soldiers which were commanded by the ruthless general of the territory. He could not help but feel a strong antagonism for the Apache. After all, hadn't they tried to take his life and his possessions on more than one occasion? He wanted to insure the safety of his horse herds, so he saddled to ride with a company of soldiers to the south of his ranch, along the eastern slopes of the Sandia Mountains. They rode as far south as Tijeras Canyon, then doubled back again toward the high country to the north.

The fall of 1863 was turning to winter while they scoured the sage, piñon, juniper and pine forests of the eastern Sandias. A band of Navajo who had been trying to hide in the forest, were flushed out of the brush, then encircled. The women, young and old, threw themselves over the bodies of the younger children in an effort to afford them some protection. The braves were fighting valiantly against a foe that had them far out-horsed, as well as outgunned. Twelve of them were killed. The women and children made ready for a trek to the south to Bosque Redondo. John Bolt then swore that unless the Indians came after him, or his possessions, that he never again would raise a hand against them. John was a fighter, but this was no contest. When he rode back to the ranch to tell Clemmy, she stared into the darkness and wept for her people. This brave, half-Indian woman believed sincerely, that if someone or anyone made war upon her, or her loved ones, she had a God-given right to fight back with her last ounce of strength. To push these forlorn people to the depths of destruction just because they were Indian, was something she found revolting. Because of this, the name Carleton would always stir a wave of anger inside her. His harsh administration of the government of New Mexico affected many people in the same manner. Letters and petitions began to bombard Washington to have him removed, still the relentless war against the red men became an obsession with him. He continued to push them to the very brink of destruction. The cavalry needed horses so the Bolt Ranch took advantage of the situation to become the horse-trading center of the northeastern part of the territory. John Bolt, though ignorant from the standpoint of education, was far from stupid. Horse trading at any level, was a game with him. A game in which the unmindful seeker of horseflesh, would come out on the little end of the deal. Clemmy and Viejo Bolt knew the advantage of having their prize horses seen. There was not a get-together anywhere, that they were not there, riding the fine Arabians they had brought from Georgia. Their work teams were entered in pulling contests, natually always the winner. There was no match for the huge, magnificent Percherons. John Bolt's shock of snow-white hair, in contrast to Clemmy's which was black as a crow's wing, caused them to stand out in any crowd. There were turkey shoots which Clemmy always won. Knife-throwing contests in which John had no competition, except for his own corboral, Carlos. Viejo was hard put to score more points in the target than this scar-faced, lithe bodied young Mexican. Carlos had demonstrated his prowess in a fight too many times to be challenged by the rough and ready ranch hands of the area. Everyone knew that he was corboral, top hand, of the best horse ranch in New Mexico. His ambition was to be better at everything than anyone he knew, except his beloved Viejo. The fact that John was his superior was a thing to be expected. As the ranch grew and prospered, they were obliged to add more buildings, corrals, stables, fences, etc. . . .

Young Mexican caballeros began to notice the rare beauty of

the shy Consuela. They dared not be too bold, lest they provoke the wrath of her brother. He watched over her like a hawk. His reputation as a fighter was her guardian.

The Indians were being bled to death, and the Confederacy did not venture into the territory again, so most of the ranchers could concentrate on making the most of the fruitful land. Fields and orchards began to bloom in the peaceful valleys. There were long summer evenings when Clemmy and John would climb the hillside above the river to survey their domain. It was a magnificent sight. Rolling, grass-covered hills and valleys stretched away to the south and east. To the west and north, the towering Sangre de Cristo mountains lent their majestic, forest-covered beauty to an almost perfect setting. The world would have thought that these early pioneers would have felt that their world was complete. It was far from so. Their hearts were heavy with the worry of what was happening to their own flesh and blood, as well as their dear friends back in the home of their childhood, the red clay hills and valleys of Georgia. If they could only have seen the destruction, they would have probably saddled up and ridden back over the very roads they had traveled. They would have wanted to help. But, what good would two more broken hearts have been?

When the war finally wound to its tragic end, they began to scheme different ways they might persuade their family to join them here in this near paradise. Little did they know that a force far greater than they could exert was already forming in the backward minds of some of the red-necked bigots of the south. The horrible deeds they were dreaming up, in the name of protection, were to be the shame and scourge of the already bleeding agony that was a defeated Confederacy. These deeds were to cause more roots to be torn from the land, then scattered to the four winds.

CHAPTER 19
A VICIOUS LIE

The sun rose over the Wes Bolt farm in Georgia, just as it had for the centuries past. After Rufus had returned to the farm, they had devised a system for getting the place back to production. Tobe was beginning to feel his age now, the wounds and strains of his slave days were to be felt in the form of twinges of rheumatism. He had lost the rest of his teeth, also his hair. A fringe of snow-white ringed his bald head. Rufus was also beginning to show effects of the long hard days in the shop. Their task was to begin again, just as they had when they first built the smithy at the front gate of the Bolt farm. John was the inspiration then. Now it was his only son, Wes. Thus the work was divided. Wes called everyone together one morning to outline his hope for the future. It was a very good plan, it could have worked. Tobe and Rufus would be in the blacksmith business again. They would trade their work for anything they could get that would make a farm bloom. There was little money to be had. They would shoe a mule for a pig. Shoe two, for a coop of hens. Welded steel rims of the neighbor's wagons for a heifer calf. As they would trade for the animals and produce, Wes and the one-armed Wilfred would figure ways to put it to the best use. They would either plant produce for seed, or take it to town, to trade with the merchants of the county seat. Samuel, the youngest son of Sally and Rufus was a gangling teen-ager. He worked with the best of them. He knew no hours, he was available any time of the day or night. No chore was too unpleasant for him. At night, Adelia would hold class for those who wished to read and write. Wilfred was her best student. He had a burning desire to learn to read. He wanted to own his own farm one of these days, so read and write he must. Slowly but surely, the Bolt farm again was to be looked upon as one of the best in the county. The coming of success, as always, brings out the people with nothing better to do than to hate, grumble and start false information directed at the ambition. Post-war south was a steaming cauldron of discontent anyway. Great bands of the ignorant would gather together to form night rider clubs, supposedly to keep the newly freed slaves in line. This, at any rate, was their cause.

Wes and Wilfred took a wagonload of produce to town to sell, or trade. They were early, with very few already at the market place. When they rode in, they were greeted by a trader at the market. Gig Martin had long been their friend. "Hey Wes, Hey Wilfred. Reckon ya done brung me some more o them scrubby wild hogs fer trade." He laughed as he pretended to look into the wagon. "Git down you fellers. I done got some coffee boiled. We kin sup up a cup as you cheat me out'n my last dime." Wes tied his mules then they all three went to the produce shed. Martin poured scalding hot black coffee into some tin cups. They visited and drank, while two other wagons came into the area. A lanky, bearded farmer sat on the seat of the first wagon. Two young men, his sons, dressed just as the father, overalls, wide suspenders, and floppy hats, were walking along beside. They waited for the other wagon to come into the yard. Two other men were with it. The first three greeted them. Then Martin hailed them from the shed. "Mornin' Turlocks 'n Hastys. This looks lak a real good mornin' fer Gig Martin. I need to trade, an you neighbors is here to do it." The five were standing now beside the lead wagon. "Come on over," Martin invited, "Coffee's on an I got more tin cups." Turlock turned to Martin. He shouted, "We don't aim ta drink no coffee from a cup you lettin thet nigger slobber in." The three in the shed bristled in anger. Then Martin could see his business being greatly harmed by the possibility of such talk getting around. His voice was concilatory as he said, "Now Wilfred don' mean no harm, do you Wilfred? Thet be his cup and he aims ta take it back ta his wagon ith him. Don't ya, Wilfred?" The one-armed black man looked to Wes for advice. Wes was seething with anger. He shouted at Turlock. "That cup belongs to Gig. He was kind enough to give us coffee from it. Now we aim to do our trading and get on back to the farm." Gig Martin, was beginning to get very nervous as the belligerent farmer marched toward the shed. "Now, ya'll, I don' hanker ta have no trouble here in my trading lot. I don' aim ta try ta settle this here quarrel. I got ta git the constabule. This could git downright serious." At the mention of the law, the five stopped their advance. This time, Hasty found his voice, "Gig! We don't wanta ever see you cater' in to no nigger again. Specially one o them uppity ones from the Bolt farm. Bolt don' have no control over them niggers he got out there. They, accordin ta what we hear, be gittin real dangerous. You don't control em Bolt, then there be other people in the country who will!" Wes stood his ground. "These people ain't mine to control, Hasty. The war ended with all the blacks being free. They come and go as they please. Now if it is a fight you are wantin, then me an Wilfred are here to help you start the music." Gig again entered a plea for peace. "Please neighbors. Don't start no hooraw here in my yard. I gotta call the constable if you do." The belligerent farmers backed away. "You got the word, Bolt. You ain't so high an mighty thet you cain't be brought down. You keep them niggers under control." They turned their backs, then walked away. Wilfred selected a strong club from the wood box by the stove. "I aim's ta even this here rukus up a bit." Wes put his hand on his friend's shoulder. "Let it slide, Wilfred. We got work ta do, and we won't be able ta do it with our hands all bruised." The tension eased, so they started their trading with Gig Martin. Their assortment of produce brought them a reasonable price, putting them in better spirits, so they guided their team of mules back down the road toward home.

As harvest time drew near, young Samuel became interested in a girl who lived on a share-crop farm which had once been a part of the vast Rodgers plantation. That huge land holding had long since been divided up into smaller farms, then sold for back taxes. Poor blacks were then allowed to move onto the land, build a shanty, then farm the land for portion of the crop they could produce. Their only equipment, for the most part, would be one mule and a plow. From then on it was pure hard labor which produced a bare existence. Work they must, and survive they did. When Samuel's own long day was done, he would eat his supper, then cut through the fields to where Honey lived with her mother, father and three little brothers, in a two room shanty. He was allowed to talk to her until the mother and father grew tired and told Samuel it was time to go to bed. Samuel was allowed to touch her hand as he left each night. The thrill of that touch would linger with him all the way home through the open fields. He would dream of it again on the following day. The older people on the Bolt farm would tease him without mercy. The very next night when Samuel was returning from his visit, he decided to cross the field of a family of poor whites who lived between the old Rodgers place and the Bolt farm. It was the time of the harvest moon. Samuel's long lanky figure was silhouetted against the bright night sky when he passed the farm house. He could hear people singing on the front porch. His heart was light, he hummed the song as he ambled toward home.

The very next day, the whole countryside was buzzing with the vicious lie that a black boy from the Bolt farm was seen looking into the window of a white woman. As the huge fabrication passed from mouth to ear, it became even more distorted. Tempers began to flare. They all needed a cause to vent their misery. Veiled threats of, "burn the nigger," began to circulate about the country roads and lanes. It seemed that everyone was hearing the monstrous lie, except those innocents on the Bolt farm. When the chores were all finished that evening, Samuel went his happy way toward the home of his new-found love. His evening was even more complete when Honey's mother allowed them to walk a way down the lane, hand in hand. The young black boy just knew that the whole world was made for lovers like him and Honey. When he left for home, his mind was as high as the bright moon which was rolling through the partly cloudy Georgia sky. His feet seemed to fly, he climbed over the rail fences, then skirted the fields laden with cotton, corn, beans and other farm crops. All at once he heard a shout. "There he is, git him!" Suddenly, men with rags tied around their faces began to run toward him. Samuel's heart stopped beating when he saw them come. He heard one of them shout, "Stop you black bastard." Then he heard the hiss of buckshot passing near him. The flash and sound of the gun put him to flight. Samuel ran as he had never run before. He took to an unharvested corn field, running down the rows. He could hear his tormenters close at his heels. Cursing and shouting seemed to come from all directions, the young man ran for his life. He emerged from the corn field, then made his way toward the bottom land along the creek. He knew that if he made the protection of this bushy area, no one could catch him until he was safe in his own farmyard. His feet pounded the earth of the fields, he could feel the blackberry bushes tearing at his face and clothes. It didn't matter, he knew he must reach the safety of the cane breaks and brush along the creek. He crossed the road, then saw men on horseback galloping toward the Bolt place. His breath came in great laboring sobs, as he reached the safety of the brushy creek bottom. There were trails he could run, that he knew every twist and turn. He had been fishing with Uncle Tobe so many times that this was his second home. He crossed a fenced row, then knew he was on home ground. Somehow he knew he was safe. Samuel ran to the safety of his own house where he sobbed out the story of his escape. Sally held her young son in her arms while he denied the awful thing they had accused him of. He had heard someone yelling to another, that they were after a nigger who had tried to rape a white woman. "I did no sich thing, Momma! I jest went ta see Honey. She is black, Momma. I ain't never even spoke to no white woman, cept to Miz Adelia. I wouldn't do no awful think lak dat, Momma." "Course you ain't done nothing, Samuel. We done learned you a heap better dan dat. It jes be some o them vile po white trash whut think they got to tawment us black folk. White folk ain't all good lak da Bolts, son. They be some of the bestest in the whole worl." Wilfred had gone to awaken the Bolts to tell Wes what had happened. They were all up and dressed when they heared the riders enter the lane. There were seven or eight of them. Some carried torches. When they reached the barnyard, the torches and moonlight revealed that they all wore masks over their faces. The leader of the group spoke, Wes recognized the voice of the eldest Turlock son. They shouted toward Wes's house. "We come ta git thet rapin nigger, Bolt. Hand him over an there ain't nobody but him goin ta git hurt. You been warned thet one o yore niggers wuz gonng git out'n line. Well one o em has. We aim ta take him Bolt. When we git through with him, there ain't no nigger in this here county dare look at another white woman agin." From the shadows of his porch, Wes said, "Turlock you git your scum off my farm as fast as them horses can carry you. There ain't nobody gonna take a soul from the Bolt farm this night or any other time as long as I am still livin. Now turn an git your ass out o here." One of the riders spurred his horse in the direction of the barn. He threw a torch into the loose hay inside the doorway. The roar of a shotgun blast came from the direction of the smaller house. Rufus stood in the doorway with the gun still smoking. The shot caught the rider in the back as he hurled the burning torch. He screamed. The horse also stung by the shot, gave a great leap, dumping the rider into the dust of the barnyard. He landed heavily, then lay still. Other riders converged on him to offer assitance. They took their wounded, making a hasty retreat toward the road. When they passed the blacksmith shop they set it on fire. Some threw their torches on the roof of the shop, then they galloped in the direction of town. There were two on either side of the injured rider . . . the Bolt families grabbed buckets, pans and brooms, then ran to the barn which was now burning where straw had been scattered in the vicinity of the horse stalls. There were no animals in the barn as there would have been in the past, when the farm was the show-place of the county. Now they fought to save their precious barn along with its stables and ample storage space. Neighbors who had been afraid to come out of the darkness until the riders had gone, now rushed to help in the losing battle. Before long, they knew that it would only endanger lives if they continued the battle. Wes called to the weary fire fighters to meet him at the house. It was a bedraggled sad troupe which gathered at the front porch. There, they all were given cool well water to quench their thirst. Wes Bolt spoke in a hoarse, bitter voice. "Neighbors . . . what you have seen here at the Bolt farm tonight ain't never goin' to happen again with out people being killed. Our boy Samuel is a good boy. We know he never tried to look at anybody, er harm em in any way. I want you neighbors to spread the word that the next time the night riders come onto the Bolt farm, they better come shoot'in. We aim to protect what is left of our farm, and of our dignity. Thank you all fer com'in ta help us when we really needed to know that there were still decent folk on the face of the world." With that, Wes turned to his wife, put his arm around her, then walked into his house and shut the door. Adelia began weeping softly. "When is it all going to end, Wes? We try to be good people. We help, we respect our neighbors, we pray to God. We fought for what we thought was right. Will the insane killing, the wickedness ever stop?" Wes held her close to him, smoothing her beautiful hair. He could feel her body tremble with the fatigue and anger she was trying to hide. They went into their own room where they held each other close, talking, then loving each other into the morning hours.

When morning came the next day, Adelia was unable to get out of bed. She calmly told Wes that he should drive to town for the doctor. The anguish and physical strain of the night before had been just too much. Their third child was about to be born. Wes rode one of the old mules. Urging the poor animal to its utmost. He left the tired animal in town so that he could ride back with the doctor. The doctor's buggy was pulled by a high-stepping gelding with a gait which literally ate up the miles. Even at his best, Wes thought the doctor should urge him to greater speed. By the time they arrived back home, the sun was about at mid-day. They rushed into the house to find Sally rocking and singing to a small bundle she had cradled in her arms. She smiled broadly. "Whar yo been, Mistah Wes? Yo done miss out on de comin heah o yo youngest boy." Wes looked anxiously toward the bedroom door. One word was all he could manage. "Adelia?" "She be fine, Mistah Wes. Yo be some quiet now cuz she an young Luke Bolt dey both be sleepin." Wes sank heavily into the nearest chair. "Thank God again. Seems I always got something to thank Him for." The doctor asked Sally to put the baby on the table where he could examine him. He chuckled to himself as he went about his business. "Seems I ain't got much to do here." Sally swelled with pride as the doctor praised the way she had been so efficient at the birthing of a baby. Adelia had already named him Luke. Matthew, Mark, and Luke Bolt were a new generation to help a nation recover from the terrible wounds of war.

Tobe patiently set about making repairs to the roof of the blacksmith shop. Some of their precious tools would have to be retempered, but for the most part, the shop would be able to function again within a few days. The barn was a total loss. It was still burning when they had finished their breakfasts the next morning. A neighbor stopped by during the early hours of the evening to inform them that a doctor had gone to the Turlock farm to treat one of the boys. The doctor could understand the broken leg and collar bone, but the buckshot imbedded in his back was a little hard to explain. When Wes heard of the injuries of the night rider, he knew in his heart that they had not seen the last of the trouble which would be directed against them.

Little did it matter that the young black boy, Samuel, was totally innocent of the charges circulated about him. In the minds of the white community, even the most sensible, it began to grow into what they began to believe was the truth. Crimes were committed against whites, then blamed upon the blacks. Soon there was a panic of fear circulating the countryside. The people with whom Wes had made enemies, were quick to seize upon the opportunity to make the Bolt family into a bunch of monsters. They stayed strictly on their own farm. When Samuel wanted to go see his newfound love, Honey, he was escorted there and returned to the safety of the Bolt fence. Their property soon became an armed camp. Work for the blacksmith shop began to dwindle. Now they knew that everthing they needed to sustain them, must be produced right on their own place. At night they would see riders on the main road carrying torches. Others were sighted in the woods along the creek bottom. Livestock not guarded closely, was found dead and multilated. The war was supposed to be over, but there was a state of war existing right here in the quiet countryside in northwestern Georgia. The armed camp was not invaded, but the embattled family was living in a state of constant fear, wondering what would happen if they were suddenly rushed by a large group of night riders. They sought help from the local law, only to find that there was little solace from that quarter. They were advised to get rid of that young nigger that was causing all the trouble. Wes left the constable's house with a bitter taste of anger in his mouth. When he returned home, he was entering the lane by the blacksmith shop when the mail carrier greeted him from the back of a slow plodding mule. "Hody, Wes. You folks ain't had no mail for along time now, but I got a letter here fer ya." Wes took the envelope from the curious mailman. His hands began to tremble as he tore it open and began to read. The mail carrier waited to see if Wes intended to share the news from the letter with him. The New Mexico territory return, had him very curious. When no information was forthcoming, he queried, "Everthin all fine wit the folk in the territory?" Wes slightly nodded his head, then began to walk toward the house. The clear concise writing of Consuela started out by telling them that they were all in good health. After that, Wes began to be at ease. It was a long letter, filled with a description of the Bolt horse ranch. All the quotes from Clemmy and John would start with, tell them that, then continue with the message they wanted to impart. The last page was a quote from his father. Connie started with, tell them that, I want them all here with us in this fine country. There be plenty of room son. Yore Momma an me got a hurtin in our hearts ta see all o yo. I know yo got a fine farm there in Georgy, my boy, but there be so much unused land here, that we air able ta git ya one o the finest spreads you ever could see. You could farm and raise horses jes lak yo Momma an me. We ain't too long on the farmin though. Yo could bring Tobe n' Rufus n' all their fambly. Mayhap you could sell the farm fer enough to git a good start here? I hear tell the travelin ain't too bad now. The Injuns had all been pushed back to the high mountains. I reckon there still be some trouble through Comanche country in Texas. Them devils is hornet mean, an now they be jinin up with their renegade Mexicans fum down across the Rio Grande. Yo could be real keerful ta jine a big train when yo start across the west part of Texas. They be folk on the way here by the thousands now. Com on iff'n yo can, son. Then there was a long, tell them from Clemmy. She longed to see her grandchildren and the son she had left so long ago. She promised Adelia that she would personally help to build them a fine home of rock and pine logs. Wes gathered all the families together early that evening to read the long letter to the whole group at one time. When he came to the part about the possibility of them leaving Georgia, for the territory, Tobe's eyes began to stream tears. "Glory be an hallalulyer. We gonna git ta see Massa John afore I die. Glory be an thank yo, Jesus." The old man looked to the west. "Massa John, we gonna be on da way soon, Massa. All we needed wuz fuh yo to tell us ta come on ahead. Praise da Lawd, Massa John, we is done on our way." To see the giant old man so happy caused the rest of the gathering to feel a surge of sadness. They all knew that in their present state, there was no way they could pull up stakes to go to the west. Their wagons were not the proper type, plus the fact that their livestock consisted of four mules. Two of them so old that they were named Skin, and Bones. These two could be expected to drop dead before they reached the Georgia state line. They all tried to talk at once about the wonderful opportunity this would afford to get them out of their miserable state of seige in the state of Georgia. Uncle Tobe would chuckle, clap his hands, then begin to chant, "We is on our way, Massa John. Yo gonna have a blacksmith one mo time. I is da bes blacksmith man in da whole lan, Massa John. Now I gonna be da bes in da whole wile wes.'' They all feared the old man had lost his mind. Wes put his arm around the still muscular shoulders. ''Uncle Tobe, it may be quite a spell before we will be able ta travel fer the promised land. Could be a year, or two, the way things is working for us right now.'' The old man could not be persuaded. It was twilight time now, a chill had set in. The old man went to a nearby tool shed where he selected a long-handled shovel. Then he made his way to the path that led to the creek. His step was light, he began to praise the Lord again, talking to his beloved friend, Massa John. They watched him go, then Wes motioned for Samuel to follow. They all feared that the shock had been too great for him. His own wife, Cissy, had a worried look on her wrinkled face. ''I would a goed wid he, cept he ack lak he wern't hankerin fer no company.'' When the old man went out of sight down the path to the creek, Samuel followed at a discreet distance. Before Tobe reached the creek, he turned to his left, walking down a little used path. He had stopped singing now, he had become more cautious as he went. Samuel was hard put to keep from being seen, and still keep the old blacksmith in sight. Tobe disappeared into the shadows of a huge oak tree Samuel lay in the rush, watching. Tobe went to the base of the huge tree, then paced five long steps from the trunk of the gnarled old oak. He began to chant a strange ritual remembered from his days back in Africa. A chill went up the spine of the young man watching from the concealment of the brush. Tobe began to dig as he chanted. Samuel guessed he must have dug at least three feet before he leaned down into the hole to remove a small wooden box bound in brass. The box was a work of art, crafted by the very hands which now held it. Tobe continued the slave chant, he replaced the disturbed dirt he had taken from the hole. The old man stayed on his knees with the box before him. He then looked up into the moonlit sky and began to pray. ''Lawdy, Lawdy, I done prayed ta da moon, and I done pray to da sun. Dey done belong to yo. I thank yo God fuh Massa John. He save dis fambly agin, Lawd. Yo tell him tonight dat ole Tobe done make it possble fuh all o us ta go ta where he be. Thank yo, Gawd, and Jesus too.'' The big man got up from his knees, then started up the path toward his cabin. He sang as he walked. ''Good News, chariot a comin, good news chariot a comin an we don't wanna be lef ahind." As he passed Samuel's hiding place, the boy could see the tears streaming down the wrinkled black face. "Yass suh, Lawd, tell Massa John we is on da way." The old man went into his cabin, closing the door. Samuel went to report what he had seen to the rest of the people. It was a restless night for all of them. The excitement of the letter, then the strange behavior of Tobe, made them lay awake and wonder. They were all up at their regular early hour the next morning. Tobe told all of them that he wanted to talk to everybody right after chore time, this very morning. The morning work went fast, since they were all anxious to learn what was in the box as well as what Tobe had to say. The sun was beginning to warm the countryside when the old man sat down on his porch, lighted his pipe, then waited for all of the others to gather around. There was a look of total contentment on his black face, he puffed his cob pipe. They waited. He would talk in due time. Finally he knocked the ashes out of his pipe against the heel of his workworn shoe. He began: "Long time ago, me an Rufus come ta dis place wid yo Pappy, Wes. Wern't much here then, jes a ole shack da preacher had live in. Rufus, he and Sally an da baby, Wilfred. Massa John he got ta lookin ovah da fence at a purty lil Injun gal name Clemmy. Dat was the Bandy place yonder." He waved his calloused hand to the north. "Twern't long till da Bandy place were part o dis here fahm an Miz Clemmy were Miz John Bolt." The old man chuckled to himself as he remembered. "We all wuk togedder. Dug dis nice fahm right outen da bresh. Me an Rufus, we blacksmith, whilst Massa John raised dem fine hosses o his'n. For long money commence comin. Massa John, he tuck his pay in gole. Den when da spences be paid, he divide dat gole three way. Hit were forever more a nice thing whut Massa John done fuh me an Rufus. I all da time gittin my enjoyin fum going fishin an listenin to da whippoorwills playing in da bresh down by da creek. I needed nothing cept ma clothes an sumpun ta fill my belly. I make his here box, and I commence throwing dem gold coins inside. Da good Lawd musta knowed we be needin em some day. I ain't got no way o knowin how much dey be, but I know da good Lawd done give me nuf fer ta see Massa John agin." Tobe filled his pipe once more, Cissy went into the house to fetch a burning stick from the fire place for him to light up. He puffed contentedly for a little while, then stood to offer the box to Wes. "I know you a good man jes lak yo pappy, Wes, take dis here box o gole money an take us all ta da heaven place whut Massa John done tole us bout. You and Miz Adelia had da book larnin, so's yo knows how ta handle dat money. When da bad times come, I hid it good so's dem Yankees don' git dey hans on it. We going to da promis lan, Mr. Wes. Yo make da plan, an we all hep." He began to rock and sing. "Good news chariot a comin . . . good news chariot a comin an we don' wanna be lef ahind." They were all caught up in the rhythm of the spiritual. Soon they were all clapping their hands and singing. When the excitement had died down, Wes cautioned them all to be very careful not to disclose their plans to a soul. In the presence of all, he carefully counted the gold coins, mostly twenties and fifties. With paper money at such a low value, he knew the small stacks of gold coins before him would get them a dozen sturdy horses for four each on three wagons. Adelia wrote a long letter to the western Bolts to let them know they would soon be on their way for a reunion of the family. The thoughts of rebuilding the farm in Georgia, were a thing of the past now. All efforts were concentrated on the great adventure. The pressure on the Bolt family because of Wes's devotion to his black friends began to intensify. They lived in constant fear that the threats of violence demonstrated in other parts of the county, would travel to their very door like a giant dragon, ready to devour them in a cloud of fire and smoke. With this in mind, they determined to start their new journey from Atlanta, rather than from their own farm.

Before the stars began to fade in the eastern sky the next morning, Wes, Wilfred and Samuel set out for the capitol city. Wes carefully stowed a double barreled shotgun beneath the spring seat of the wagon. They rode in silence for a long while. The two older men were on the seat, while Samuel sat on a pile of sacks on the floor. When the sun began to rise, Samuel stood up, leaning between them. The mules plodded along, Samuel was the first to break the silence. "I ain't goin ta no New Mexico, ya know." Wilfred turned his head sharply. "What yo sayin, Samuel? Yo knows we is all gwin ta New Mexico in one big fambly." "I ain't goin', Wilfred! I done made up mah mind." Wes laughed softly "You haven't been hit by the love bug that bad, have you, Samuel? I think I am readin somebody named Honey into this picture."

Samuel stammered out his embarrassment. "It be thet bad, Mistah Wes. Me and Honey done talk bout dis a long time. We done made plans ta have the pahson say the word over us, then we aim ta head out'n here. We may go up noth, all da way ta Pennsylvany. I could git me a job up thar, an den nobody gonna be talking bout burnin me up no mo." "Ya done tell Momma bout dis crazy idee?" Wilfred looked hard at his younger brother. "There be no use botherin Momma an Poppa bout dis here plan, Wilfred. I jes turn nineteen an I kin take keer o me an Honey jes fine. I aim ta do my share ta start y'all off ta da wes. Den iffin ya could let me have dees po ole mules an dis here wagon, me an Honey could fine a place in da sunshine, whar da good Lawd could let us live like we is human people." The young man lowered his eyes, a pained expression came over his dark face. "We'll talk about it more, Samuel." Wes held the reins in one hand, then he patted the boy's shoulder. They rode in silence again, each one concerned with his own thoughts. They rode into Atlanta where they rented an acre of land with a small house and barn, on the outskits of the city. This was to be the secret assembly point for the expected flight to the promised land. Wes and Adelia had labored hard over their plans. Everything they could think of was written down. There was an order to things. The first purchase made was a long bed, sturdy wagon, with a team of magnificant mares in new harness to pull it. Feed was purchased for the two old mules, while Wilfred was made comfortable in the ramshackeled old house. It was Wilfred's lot to stay with the new staging area, while Wes and Samuel rode back to the Bolt farm in the new wagon. This was the rig which was to carry their belongings back to the jumping-off place in Atlanta. While they had been away, feverish preparations were being made at the farm, for them to depart. Tobe had salvaged his precious blacksmith tools from the wrecked smithy. He had carefully retempered those which had suffered in the fire from the night riders. He then built sturdy oak boxes for them to be stored. Cured hams and bacon sides were being packed in barrels to serve as food on the long trek. Boxes of fresh food would be used first. They tried to be sensible about what to take along. But decisions were difficult. After all this had been their home from almost the beginning of their lives. More than one load would have to be hauled to Atlanta. There it would be distributed into three wagons. Each family would have their own.

There was constant flow of conversation about what they expected to be ahead of them. Although they had read of it, no amount of speculation could prepare them for the endless miles of road they would travel before they came into sight of the Bolt ranch near the Santa Fe Trail. Two trips, with the wagon heavily loaded, were made to Atlanta before they were satisfied that this was all they could take. Wes had afforded the luxury of two fine saddle horses for himself and Wilfred. On the final evening before departure for all the families, Wes told Sally of Samuel's determination to stay with his beloved Honey. She called to Samuel, then held him gently in her arms. She recalled the time, years ago, when she and Rufus were about to be separated forever. They were slaves then, which made their helplessness even more acute. "Samuel, my son, I knows jes how yo feels bout dat leetle gal. My boy Samuel an me is goin ta ax Mistah Wes ta hitch up da spring wagon. Den he gonna drive us ober ta da Rodgers plantation. We gonna git dat Honey and fotch huh back wid us. A preacher gonna say da words ovah yo at Atlanta, den she goin all da way ta Massa John's place. I knowed all lon bout da two o ya. I done talk ta her Mammy an her Pappy. Now let's go git her!" They did just that, with Wes riding with them to be sure that there were no new incidents with troublemakers along the way. After a tearful farewell, a new member was added to the Bolt expedition.

CHAPTER 20
FACE THE SETTING SUN

The next morning they all left in the wagon, except Wes, who stayed behind to sell the land and what was left of the once proud, prosperous Bandy-Bolt farm. When the family rode past the Rodgers plantation, Adelia wept at the ghostly sight of the burned mansion where she had spent her childhood. She bid a silent farewell to her mother and father who had in their own way, given their lives for a cause they thought to be right. As they were riding, Wes Bolt strolled in the other direction to the graveside of his grandmother, Little Dove, and his grandfather, Will Bandy. He was torn with the sadness of leaving this place which was carved out of the brush and timber by his pioneer grandfather. The love story of Will Bandy and the little Cherokee girl named Little Dove brought tears to his eyes, he removed his hat, then looked to the morning Georgia sky. "Sleep well," he murmured, "the land is yours, it will always be." With that he returned to his own farm where he saddled his horse for the ride to the county seat where he spread the word that he was taking offers for the Bandy-Bolt farm. It was several days before he finally got an offer he could accept. The sale was made, with the local bank being made the receiver of payments in his behalf. Wes then rode to Atlanta where he found that his efficient wife, Adelia, had already made the division of their goods to be placed in the three wagons. He stood silently to watch her. He marveled at how such a kind, gentle woman could command so much respect. He silently thanked God for a woman like this to raise his three sons. No matter where their fate would take them, he knew that as long as he had a woman like Adelia to be at his side, his life would, indeed, have meaning. Wes was young yet, but now the father of three healthy boys. What would fate hand them in this far-off land they were almost forced to flee to? They all talked of how fortunate they were to have a place to run to. After all, there were thousands of people now pulling up stakes to travel in the same direction. A great many of those were running from hardship, to final despair.

The ravages of total war had demanded a heavy toll. It seemed that a whole nation was looking westward to a new land which was there for the taking. Little did they know that it was not to be taken easily.

Wilfred came to stand with Wes where he was resting against a rickety wooden gate. ''Wes,'' Wilfred began slowly, ''We seen a heap togedder here in Georgy.'' Wilfred's eyes were fastened to the horizon in the direction of the rolling hills to the west which cradled the Bolt farm. ''Hit be tearin at ma guts ta leave here, my friend. Cept ya ain't got no way of knowin how I long ta git ta whar we be goin. I aim to have a place o my own, Wes. I will stand on these two good feet, an thar I will live til I die. I jes gotta feel free in my soul, Wes. Don't know jes how ta tell ya how I feel. No matter how pore hit mout be, Wes. I wanna pint ta what I got an say 'this here be all mine.' I gotta have the paper ta show it's mine. I wanna be able ta spit right in the eye of any two legged bastard whut mout think he can step on me. I aim ta git me some o thet New Mexico! Then I gonna git me a good woman an make me a bunch o little citizens whut kin hole up they haid in thet new lan.'' Wes could see the anticipation shining through Wilfred's black eyes. ''We ain't even had no las name, Wes. We has jes allers been called the Bolt niggers. Well, I tole Pa thet our las name now be Larkin. Thet be the name o the fust man whut own my Pa. He wuz a good man, Wes. He was the one whut come ta be the only Pappa John Bolt ever wanted ta claim. I don' reckon he be too upsot bout us taking his name. Fum now on, I be Wilfred Larkin. Samuel and Ma and Pa, they be Larkin too!'' Wilfred clenched his only fist, then raised it to the sky. ''God be mah witness!'' Wes extended his hand. ''Let me shake yore hand, Mister Larkin.'' Wilfred showed his white teeth in a wide grin. ''Miss Adelia done showed me how ta write my name, Wes.'' Wilfred took a stick to draw his name in the dust of the yard. When he had finished, he stepped back to admire his new accomplishment. ''Thar she be, Wes!'' His pride was too apparent to conceal. ''Now, spose we give a han ta the others an git this train rollin tords my new farm." They went back to their tasks with renewed determination. Wes never ceased to marvel at how the tireless Adelia could carry her infant son in one arm and accomplish so much with the other.

Wes and Adelia read all the papers and magazines they could get their hands on about the happenings in the great move westward. A few mornings later they both saw the same ad at the same time. An Atlanta newspaper showed an advertisement on a back page. There was a drawing of a modern steam paddle wheel ship. It carried full sail, with the giant paddle wheels amid-ship on either side. The caption urged customers to book passage to the Texas coast aboard the steamer, Admiral Marcel Le Claire. This magnificent ship was named for a famous southern blockade runner who had gone down with his ship during the recent conflict. From the ad, they learned that there was branch office right there in Atlanta. Wes and Wilfred hired a horse and buggy the next day to search out the steamship office. They learned that they could, indeed, book passage on this modern vessel. There was room for their wagons, teams and families. Their passage was booked all the way from Augusta, Georgia, on the Savannah River, to Corpus Christi Bay on the Texas gulf coast. Their passage along the Savannah was to be in great river barges which were guided by a steam driven paddle wheel boat.

Their spirits were high when they boarded their loaded wagons to leave for Augusta to the south-east of Atlanta. They allowed themselves six days time over a well-traveled road to the river town. A cold, drizzling rain had set in, typical of Georgia for the early winter months, causing the roads to become a sea of mud. Wes Bolt guided the three wagons with great anticipation. He felt their world could be nothing but better from this point on. They had practically given away their home and farm here in Georgia, but on the other hand they already had a good headstart on most other travelers. Poppa John had begun to make a place for them in the vast rangelands of New Mexico. Rufus, Sally, Wilfred, Samuel and his new wife, Honey, were the passengers of the second wagon. The last was Tobe and Cissy.

When the long drives through the vast ranges of Texas and New Mexico would be reached, Samuel would volunteer his help in the handling of the wagon bearing Uncle Tobe's possessions. At

Augusta, the travelers helped to load their caravan aboard great wooden barges. The horses were blindfolded then made to respond to the reins and voices of their drivers. The sight and smell of the riverfront activity was just too much for them to cope with. The loading and blocking of the wagons, boarding and tying of the teams was a long, tiresome task. The steady rain was cold, soaking them to the bone. By nightfall they were all secure. The barge captain advised them that he would leave with the first light the next morning.

After a restless night, they were awakened by the river boat, powered by a single steam boiler amidship, coming alongside the wharf to start the barges on their journey downriver. Beds were made atop their other possessions in the three wagons so that a minimum of loading and unloading was required. Adelia made sure that her little boys were all comfortable before she looked after the want of herself and her husband. Sally was constantly watchful to see if she could be of assistance to the small ones. The wooded banks of the Savannah River began to glide by, the sun put in a half-hearted appearance. At every bend in the river there were vast woodyards which catered to the steam powered vessels now crowding the waters of the rolling river.

All the travelers were wide-eyed with anticipation, wondering what new scene would present itself at the next bend of the river. Their own escort steamer would stop now and then to take on more fuel to feed its hungry boilers. The barges would load more cargo, until the inexperienced aboard were sure they could not carry the weight, thus going to the bottom of the muddy water. Old hands assured them that they knew exactly how much they could load and still be safe. The stops seemed interminable to the travelers.

Darkness the first day set in early with the leaden skies beginning to weep once more, the barges were nudged to the shore to be tied to great pilings set along the banks of the river. When all was secure, the crew abandoned the steamer and barges to hurry up the high bank to a small village composed mostly of taverns and eating establishments. Several travelers from the barges went with the crew, but the New Mexico-bound voyagers huddled into their wagons to prepare for a long restful night.

Adelia was reading from the Bible, by lantern light, when they heard Rufus softly call from beside the front wheel. ''Wes, could I have jes one word wid yo?'' Wes invited him into the wagon out of the chill of the night. When Rufus was under the protection of the canvas, Wes could see the sad expression on his lined face. ''Wes, we gonna be in Savannah by tomorra. Me and Sally bin talkin. We heard the music fum up on da hill, an it remin us'n o our two gals whut rund away ta Savannah. Whut I need ta ax, Wes, do ya think we could see clear ta spen one extry day in Savannah so's me an Sally could try one mo time to see kin we git some word bout our little gals? Seem a shame ta be here in Savannah thout makin one more try.'' Wes patted the black man's shoulder. ''We will take whatever time you think we need to, Rufus. This time, we will all be look'in. Surely, if they are here, then we will find some word about them.'' ''Thank yo, kindly, Wes. Seem we jes gotta try one mo time.'' Wes could see the sorrow in the lined faced beneath the thatch of grey hair. Rufus still mumbled to himself as he left the wagon to go to his own.

At first light the next day, they could see that the barges out in front of them had been loaded with cotton bales until the very top sides of the vessel seemed level with the muddy waters of the Savannah. The day wore on and the barges loaded with cotton and other commerce were nudged into the share near a jetty with a steam-powered crane which was standing by to lift the merchandise to the shore; great drays pulled by long teams of mules, stood by to transport it further down-river to the deep water docks where ocean-going vessels waited to sail it to all ports of the world.

They waited for what seemed to be an endless time for the barges to be unloaded. When they were empty, they were shuttled to the other side of the river where they were to be loaded again for a trip up the river this time. Finally, the overworked paddle wheeler maneuvered its way to the rear of the vessel holding the Bolt entourage of horses, wagons and people. They were shoved into shallow water, there a ramp was put over the side for them to begin to disembark. They too, were to go further down the river where the ship of the star line they were to board was tied up at a huge wooden pier. Unloading was no easy task, so the sun began to set when the tired travelers came ashore where they could make camp to prepare their supper. At this point along the Savannah, great gangs of stevedores lived in row after row of board shanties along the high banks of the river.

When night had fallen, the lights of their lanterns looked like long strings of fireflies in the dark of the night. The river work gangs would gather in large groups, then sing the songs they had learned from years of labor on the shore of the mighty Savannah River. Pangs of loneliness for their own home gripped the hearts of the travelers as the voices of the singers reached them in the night. Early morning saw them on the high road along the northeast bank of the river. While they traveled, they began to smell the salt air of the Atlantic. They rolled eastward, they asked directions to the pier where their ship of the star line was to be tied up waiting for cargo.

The first sight of the ocean-going ship held them all in fascinated wonder. The newest addition to the Star Fleet was a gleaming white from bow to stern. Gigantic paddle wheels were mounted, and covered, amidship while tall spars still graced the modern steam-powered giant. A black smokestack at the center of the ship told where the steam boilers were located. The vessel was tied to the pier and a huge cargo door was open at the side. They halted the wagons on the crowded street, then Wes dismounted to go into the office of the Star Lines pier. When he approached the counter to present his tickets, the center of attention was an oversized portrait of a beautiful woman hanging behind the clerk who was examining tickets. The caption beneath the portrait read, "Jeanine Le Clere, Owner of Star Lines." Wes was fascinated, first by the beauty of the woman, then by the suggestion that a woman could be the owner of such a tremendous business as a steamship line. He was till gawking at the picture when the clerk interrupted him with a gruff, "Well Mister, you gonna let me see yore tickets, er air ya gonna stare at thet picher all day?" Wes was so startled, he jumped to attention before the skinny, mustachioed clerk. "I got my tickets right here, Mister, I bought'em in Atlanta at your office there." The clerk rudely snatched the tickets from Wes's hand then began to examine them for an assigned place on the ship. Wes had bought cabin class tickets for all the people in the party, then space below decks for the horses and wagons. The tired-looking clerk spat a long stream of tobacco juice in the general direction of a bucket behind the counter. "Where is the rest o your fambly at,

Mister?'' Wes waved a hand in the general direction of the wagons. ''They are with the wagons.'' The clerk snuffed his nose, then spat again to empty his mouth enough to talk. ''Yore tickets is in order, Mister Bolt. Unhitch yore teams when yo git em pulled out onto the pier. We will have our stevedores doin all the work o loadin. The teams o horses, an the wagons is goin ta be loaded on the third deck down. All the folks is goin ta be on the second deck. All top-side passengers is fust class. Now roll em on ta the pier.'' Wes left the office with one more glance at the portrait. He motioned the others to drive the loaded wagons out onto the pier. The horses snorted and shied as they began to feel their feet on the unfamiliar hollow-sounding boards of the wooden structure. It took some handling to get them all near the ship. The teams were then unharnessed, with the harness hung to the sides of the wagons. One by one the huge draft mares were led through the cargo door of the gleaming white ship. Other teams and wagons were already stowed in the dark depths of the lower deck. Rows of ship lanterns lighted the work of the stevedores who skillfully stabled the horses and blocked the wagons to keep them in place during the voyage. When the precious teams were all tended, Wes led the group up the gangplank to the upper deck, where he proudly presented his tickets for assignment to their cabins. They had chosen second class to try to save money. This was supposed to put them on the second deck down. Wes and Adelia led the troop up the plank and across the rail. Wes carried their second son, Mark, and he held the hand of his eldest, Matthew. Adelia carried the baby, Luke. The others trailed behind. All were a bit apprehensive when they walked on the unfamiliar feel of the deck of the great ship. Wes presented the tickets, then he and Adelia were instructed to follow a purser to their cabin. The ticket taker then asked, ''Mister Bolt, are you the one who bought fare fer the niggers?'' Wes turned on the man, then answered a bit too loudly. ''I bought tickets for all of us. Paid the same price in gold for every last one. There are ten of us in all. Now show us to the cabins we paid for.'' ''You an the Missus and kids kin go second class, Mister Bolt, all niggers is third class. The line will refund the difference in your tickets.'' Wilfred stepped to the front. He looked the man straight in the eye as he said, ''Now looka here, Mister, we done paid the price and we aim ta git our money's worth.'' A burly seaman wearing white trousers and a blue pea jacket walked up to the ticket taker's side. He stood with his feet wide apart, the better to display his powerful body. His face was red from exposure to the weather. A round sailor's tam topped a shock of flaming red hair. He folded his arms in front of him, pulling himself to his full height. The weight of his shoulders was unmistakable, the pea jacket strained to contain his paunchy belly. He addressed the crowd which had begun to gather. "I be first mate, Tullus, of this here ship. There is a rule laid down by the Capin o this here ship that no darkies is to be allowed in first er secon class. Now thout further delay, either git on board as we say, er git on shore." Wilfred started to advance toward the mate. Adelia laid her hand on his good arm. She spoke calmly, "Go where they show you, now Wilfred. Help the others. We have such a long way to go yet. We must get there together." Her calm voice carried such significant meaning that Wilfred relaxed and motioned the other blacks to follow. He and Samuel were seething with anger. They also knew the terrible consequence of being left behind. When they parted, Wes let them know that he would find them as soon as Adelia and the little children were settled in their cabin. The second class quarters proved to be quite comfortable on the new ship. Wes left Adelia with the children while he went in search of the others. He found that third class was on the same level as the stabled horses. Only the engine room amidship separated the blacks' quarters from the tethered horses on the cargo level. Wes was appalled at the sight, but knew they had no choice in the matter, whatsoever. They went to look after their possessions. There they decided that Wilfred and Uncle Tobe would stay with the horses and wagons while Rufus and Samuel would look after the the two women. The blacks were free people now, but still slaves to custom.

As the men stood by their possessions, a crew of sailors came down the ship's center aisle. Led by none other than the first mate. Tullus was laughing loudly at something he had just told the seamen. They all joined in as though Tullus was a very funny man. Suddenly Tullus spotted the one-armed Wilfred leaning against a wagon wheel. The mate straightened up and held up one hand, then pointed an index finger in the direction of the slightly built Wilfred. "Now looka here," Tullus began, "it be the uppity nigger whut didn't take ta going below with tha other black uns." Wilfred stood away from the wagon wheel. By then Tullus was in the midst of them. Without another word he lashed out, to brutally slap Wilfred across the mouth. The force of the blow knocked Wilfred to the oaken deck which was covered by a mixture of straw and horse manure. Wilfred was monentarily dazed by the suddenness of the blow to the face. A trickle of blood began to ooze from the corner of his mouth where his teeth had pierced his lower lip. He shook his head to clear his vision. Wes could see the giant, Tobe, making his huge hands into fists. Wes knew that it would take one blow from one of those calloused ham-like hands to lay the bully Tullus low. Perhaps for a long time. Wes quickly said, "Stand easy, Uncle Tobe, you must stand easy." Wilfred had begun to try to rise. Wes knelt beside him. "Stay down, Wilfred." Wes knew he had to command the situation completely, or all would be lost. "Stay down, Wilfred, for God's sake stay down. Wilfred's burning black eyes looked into the face of his friend. His voice came in hoarse whisper. "Yo want me to eat horse shit, do yo, Wes? I am a man, an by God, I aim ta stand like a man." "You must stay down fer all o us, Wilfred, I'm beggin you." Wilfred slowly nodded his head. Tullus began to chuckle. He turned to the other seamen. "A horse shit eating nigger on board, lads." The others laughed half-heartedly. Wes stood before Tullus. "You got the top hand, now, Tullus." Wes hissed. "We paid our fare with gold, we are passengers on this here ship. You are a employee of this steamship line. Now you ease off, or I will go to the Captain with our problem. If that ain't enough, then I will go to the owners of this ship. Now you stay clear of me and my friends. When we git to dry land again, Tullus, then either me or Wilfred, one armed though he is, will meet you with anything you may choose. An by God we will try to kill you." the steel in Wes's voice could not be mistaken. Tullus knuckled his forehead and mumbled, "Sorry, Mister, me and the lads was jest havin a little fun with tha darkie. No offense ta you, sir." With that, Tullus, with the seamen, made a quick retreat back to the aisle, then out of the hold. Wilfred began to sob in abject frustration. "I eat horse manure an you have to fight my battle fer me, Wes. When, O dear God, will I ever be a man who kin stand fer his own?" Wes put both hands on Wilfred's heaving shoulders. "This ain't the time now, Wilfred. One of these days, when we get to where we are goin', then we will start all over. The big job now is for all of us to get there." Tobe nodded his grey head in agreement. He started to pat the nearest horse on the shoulder he began to sing softly, "Good news chariot a comin, good news chariot a comin an we ain't gonna be lef ahind." The tension eased as Wilfred wiped the blood from his swollen lip.

They learned later that day, that the ship was not to depart until the tide changed in the early morning hours of the following day. With this information, Wes made arrangements for himself, Rufus, and Sally, to go ashore to search for word of their two lost daughters. All the next day they tramped the muddy back streets of Savannah, asking in all the likely places about the possible whereabouts of two young black girls who had followed the troops of General Sherman to this city by the sea. The answer was the same everywhere they went. Hundreds of young black girls had been promised the world, then used, then thrown away as though they were some broken toy with no further value.

The evening shadows began to lengthen, the searchers started their trek back to the ship. The people of Savannah had suffered at the hands of the northern soliders, so had the proud city. Many once stately buildings still stood in charred ruins. Every business which had any semblance of potential aid to the southern war effort, had been unmercilessly destroyed. One burned out establishment which caught Wes Bolt's eye was down near the water front. A sign bearing the name, Larkin Wagon Works, hung precariously from one pole of what had once been a decorative archway entrance to the wagon factory. The name instantly rang a bell in Wes's mind. This was the Larkin who had been the benefactor to John Bolt when he was a small boy. The others waited while Wes made inquiry as to the whereabouts of the former owners and operators of the Larkin Works. A black family living in the partially burned office portion of the establishment knew nothing of the fate of the Larkins. The only answer Wes could get was that they must have died in the war, or gone away somewhere. Wes wanted to take some good news of Tony Larkin to John Bolt out in the far off territory. Now he resolved to just not mention the subject unless he happened to asked if he had heard anything. The desolation of the wrecked, burned factory would always be another memory of the horror he had lived through as a soldier for the south.

They went back to the ship, then to bed, with Rufus and Sally resolving to consider their precious young girls as casualties of the same war which had brought the south to its knees in agony. Sometime during the early morning hours they were awakened by the jarring movement of the great ship. A paddle wheel tug had come alongside to move the vessel out into the deep water of the river delta. Soon the steam engine of the ship began to work. From then on, sleep was out of the question. They began to feel the swell and fall of the Atlantic, the ship made headway toward the south. Wes got up from his bunk early, dressed quickly so that he could go up on the deck to watch the land of his birth fade into the early morning fog. The sky was leaden with rain clouds, so the coastline was already obscure. Wes felt a bit queasy in the stomach, so he made his way toward the bow of the ship, where he found a place at the rail. There he could watch the great ship knife its way through the heaving swells of the Atlantic. The fresh cold air blowing in his face made him feel better. He was deep in thought, wondering what it would be like when they disembarked in Texas. A voice at his elbow startled him. "Morning traveler, takin some air?" Wes turned to see a tall, handsome man in the uniform of an officer. The seaman extended a strong hand to Wes. "I am Captain Bert Halladay at your service, Mister. What might be your name?" The man had strange accent which Wes did not recognize. Wes felt ill at ease in the presence of the Captain of this ship. "I'm Wes Bolt, sir. I have booked passage for myself and party to Texas." "Oh, yes, Mister Bolt. I have been intending to look you up. I want to make excuses for the rude behavior of my first mate on the first day of your arrival." Wes was surprised that the captain knew of the incident. He had certainly not mentioned it to anyone in authority. The captain read the expression on the face of the farmer. "I bloody well know everything that happens on this ship, Mr. Bolt. That is my business. I would get rid of that blighter, Tullus, if he weren' the only man I know who is as familiar with this ship as I am. He has a working acquaintance with her from stem to stern. Please accept my apology, Mr. Bolt." "Quite alright, sir, we just want to live in peace." The captain looked toward the shore. "I can jolly well appreciate that, sir. After all you people have been through, peace should be the uppermost thought in your minds. I have been a seaman all my life, and a captain for the past three years." Wes estimated the man to be no more than forty-five. "I took delivery of this beauty in Liverpool for Mrs. Le Clere, herself." The captain placed his elbows on the rail. He seemed preoccupied as he continued to talk. "Now there is a woman! She is getting up into the years, but her mind is still as sharp as the sting of the lash. She has the figure of a woman in her thirties." The captain paused. Wes interjected with, "I saw her portrait in the shipping office; she is a beauty." Captain Halladay spoke again. "The Admiral went down with his ship during the blockades, but not before he had piled up a fortune in banks in England and France. I was first officer on one of his ships, so I made it a point to call upon Jeanine every chance I got. On one of her trips to London, I convinced her that I was the man to take command of her prize ship. When it came off the ways, it was mine. She knew that I had the knack for making a fortune for her as well as myself. Her husband was a sharp trader and she wants another. I intend to marry her, Bolt. There is a woman who could take care of all my needs. She told me she had only two loves in her entire life. I don't know who the other lucky bloke was, but I am going to take the place of both of them." Wes was a bit embarrassed at this kind of intimate talk about a lady. The captain straightened, then slapped Wes on the shoulder. "Nice to make your acquaintance, Bolt." He strode away in the direction of the wheel house. Wes wondered if the captain would be successful in his desire to marry the wealthy owner of the shipping line. He need not have wondered, for it never happened.

Before the day ended, the sky began to clear. The morning of the second day found them under bright sunny skies. Hundreds of sea birds seemed to travel with the ship, making its way to the warmer waters off the Florida coast. Their passage through the Keys was sheer delight for everyone. Their first port of call was to round the Peninsula of Florida, then to Tampa Bay. There, additional cargo was to be loaded for the trade along the Texas coast. These were pleasant times, now. Wes would help Adelia with the children for trips to the top side, where they would stroll around the deck to take in the sunshine. Now and then they would see the coastline in the distance. The black families were allowed to come on deck too, but only in designated locations. There, they would gather to talk, laugh, sing, roll dice, and just generally get acquainted. Wes spent a great deal of time on the cargo deck. Tobe, Rufus, Wilfred and Samuel would help him look after the horses, then they would sit for hours making plans for how they would set up their new blacksmith shop and farm in New Mexico. Of course, they did not imagine the vast distances of rangeland, without any sign of human habitation. The pictures in their minds always resembled rural Georgia with its small towns and farms.

CHAPTER 21
GOD REST A GIANT

The ship stayed in port in Tampa Bay for some time while they unloaded certain cargo, then took on something entirely different. Extra fuel was then hauled aboard to sustain them on the extra-long trip across the Gulf of Mexico. There, the sails of the vessel would come into play, to help power it through the calmer seas of the Gulf. The voyage was dampened by only an occasional rain squall which caused no real discomfort or hazard to the ship. The travelers had been aboard for over two weeks, when they began to see great flocks of brown pelicans, gulls and other sea birds. The coast line was sighted early in the evening, but the captain announced that they would not attempt to go into port until light of the following day. Great islands of sand formed a sort of reef in front of the Texas coastline. They would be piloted through a channel by a local man who knew the treachery of the shifting sand bars.

Adelia devoted almost all of her time to the care of her three small boys. Sturdy little Matthew was going on five, Mark was three, and the baby, Luke, was just four months old. The washing of their clothes was a task shared by Sally, since she had no small ones of her own. Attention to the unloading of the wagons, teams, and the saddle horses was a task left strictly to the men. When the wagons were put onto the pier, the horses were brought around to move them to a wagon assembly point on a high ridge above Corpus Christi Bay. By the time the Bolt party was all ashore, night had begun to fall. Campfires of mesquite wood began to appear to keep off the cold of the foggy evening. Wes asked Wilfred to go with him to some of the other camps to see if they could move out to San Antonio the next morning. There were four freight wagons ready to leave at daylight. Others asked to trail along, then soon there were eleven wagons in all, ready to hit the road to the Alamo City, more than a hundred miles to the northwest.

It was hardly light when all wagons began to roll up along the banks of the Nueces River. After they left the sandy land and fog of the coastal plain, Texas was a sight to behold. The sky was a bright turquoise blue above the great expanses of mesquite trees and scrub oak. The river bottom was a winding serpent of leafless wild pecan trees, rosebud bushes and a host of other timber. The sun rose out of the foggy horizon like a giant fireball which brought to life huge flocks of water fowl. Sometimes it seemed there were so many that they would hide the sky. The travelers felt that truly, God had made a wonderful world. It was a well-traveled road they were on. Since it was a main line from the rich inland farms and ranches, to the Gulf. This second migration of the Bolt family saw them spending Christmas in San Antonio.

The great war was over, so thousands of people were trying to put their lives back together. During the conflict, vast herds of cattle were left to run loose and unattended. They became as wild as deer, roaming the rich brushlands of Texas. Ranches were being re-established by combing the brush for these cattle, then branding them with the red hot iron of the rancher lucky enough to rope and throw one not already branded. It was through hundreds of miles of this exciting untamed country that the travelers would venture. After their Christmas celebration, then a few days of rest, they joined a train of fourteen wagons to travel through the Indian country to the west and north. The rolling hills and valleys to the west of San Antonio posed no problem to the caravan as it made its way to Kerrville. This bustling cowtown was the last outpost of any consequence between there and Fort Stockton beyond the Pecos.

This was the land of the still fierce Comanche, the dreaded Comancheros and bands of outlaws who would rendezvous in Mexico near Del Rio, then ride like satan's own, until they encountered suitable prey to pillage and burn. Then they would take what they could carry back across the Rio Grande into the safety of the wild mountains and canyons of Mexico. The wagon trail extended east to west across a plateau which was scarred by a thousand ridges. Each day those ridges became rockier. The flinty hardness of the stones they rolled over ate away at the horses' hooves as well as the steel rims of the wagons. When the blacksmith skills of the Bolt party were learned by other members of the train, there were never-ending tasks to do. Tobe and Rufus spent many long evening hours helping some other traveler shoe a lame horse, tighten a wagon rim or fashion new parts for those which had broken. The skies remained clear for the most part, however, a bitter cold wind constantly blew over the plateau. The canvas covers of the wagons were protection, but not nearly enough. To make things worse, an epidemic of whooping cough began to sweep through the wagon train. There was a wagon master named Simms who tried valiantly to keep the infected wagons separated. His efforts seemed in vain. Adelia's two boys began the symptoms. Their eyes reddened and their coughs became more intense. Then the baby, Luke, began to cough. They all three would cough until they were exhausted. When they had used all the breath in their lungs, they would take in more air through their mouths, a wheezing whooping sound would emerge from their tortured little bodies. Sally rode night and day in the Bolt wagon to help Adelia with the terribly ill children. The Bolt children were sturdy and strong, so they were able to survive. The train was forced to stop four times to bury other small children in the rocky ground along the wagon track.

After days of traveling, the Devil's River was a welcome sight. Horses, mules and other livestock had been without water for two days, so, as they began to suffer, they became unruly and hard to handle. A two day rest was called so the people and animals could rest along the banks of the small stream. The wagon master estimated that there were still over two weeks to travel in this rough land before they would reach the Pecos. The roughness of this inhospitable land did not improve. In fact, it worsened as they traveled westward. This was a much worse track than Clemmy and John had traversed to the north of them. The struggle began again with everyone trying to help the other.

This was an unusually dry January on the high plains of Texas. The grass had first frozen, then turned dry and stemmy. The only trees were gnarled mesquite which seemed to grow almost as thick as the grass. To make things worse, they began a constant watch, for now they were in Indian and outlaw country. The wagons were circled at night to serve as better protection. All were awakened in the middle of the night by the restless panic of the animals. To the north of the wagon track, they could see a red glow in the night sky. Simms was up shouting for the others to harness up, to be ready to roll. He met with the men of the party. The bearded face of the wagon master was grim as he held the hurried conference. "Tain't no use sayin not to worry. We are in a hell of a fix. This is a Comanchero trick. They use the fire to scatter the train. They gonna be following the fire to see if there is anything left after the blaze has done its work. Them mean buzzards will look fer anything that's left. The idee is, we gotta stay together and make a run fer it. Pray to God the wind changes afore it forces us to turn south. Thet be the case, we try to pick a high ridge thout much trees on it. Thet way we might could fight the fire enough to keep it off'en us. Stay together behind my wagon an whip them teams. Don't nobody fall behind. Now move em out!" The men left the conference running. Their teams were in the traces in record time. Simms knew the Comancheros would not be foolish enough to be out in front of the fire, therefore, there was no immediate trouble from that quarter. It was fortunate that the animals could see much better in the dark than the humans, they kept to the track despite their nervous-looking to the north. The sky was just beginning to lighten in the east when animals of varied descriptions began to cross their path. The panic was obvious, they bounded to the safety of a place without fire. Deer, antelope, bobcats, wild turkeys and a great variety of birds passed without as much as a glance at the wagons. People in the wagons began to be crazed with fear. Adelia began to pray as she held her three little ones close to her. She tried valiantly not to show the panic that was holding her heart like a huge hand. God seemed to be answering the prayers of the travelers, for the lead wagon had reached a wide mesa, or table top, of land. The going was much easier. They could smell smoke and see the fire now, traveling with the speed of the wind. Ashes and smoke began to cause them discomfort in breathing.

When the sun rose, the wind began to shift from northerly, to directly out of the west. Soon the fire was no longer a threat. Simms placed riders out on the outskirts of the train. He expected an attack at any time. The strength of this particular wagon train must have discouraged the raiders for they never put in an appearance. They once spotted a line of riders off to the northwest, but they quickly disappeared — into the tangle of mesquite forest. There were more days of toil and hardship as the travelers made their way into the west. The weather was still dry and cold on a Saturday morning when they reached the escarpment above the Pecos River. The wagons came to a halt, everyone looked for miles into the western horizon. Little Mark stood on the wagon seat between his mother and father. "Where is New Mexico, Papa? I can't see it yet." They tried to point out to him that it was way beyond the river, then past the big blue mountains in the distance. Then Grandpa and Grandma would be there waiting for them. The little boy remembered that spot forever.

A full day's work was ahead for everyone. All wagons had to be let down the steep slope, one at a time. The passengers walked. Reaching the Pecos River was like an oasis in a great desert to the weary travelers. They could see miles of flat sandy land now. After the rocks of the plateau, it would seem like a grand highway. Simms told them that Fort Stockton would be the next rest stop, the wagons were circled near the river so that people could wash clothes, as well as bathe themselves. It had been a long dry trip from Kerrville. Men on horseback scouted the area for signs of hostile raiders, or Indians.

They found none, so their spirits rose to the greatest heights of the trip. Fresh antelope meat was brought in by some of the men who had gone on a hunt. A square dance was the attraction in the center of the compound that night.

There couldn't be a river that Uncle Tobe would not try for catfish. He was up early the next day, with Cissy following along to keep him company. He took a shotgun, then made his way to a marshy place along the river where he killed a mudhen to use for bait. After carefully stringing the flesh of the mudhen, including the intestines, on his hooks, he tied one end of the line securely to a limb on the bank, then let the long line drift downstream. The multiple hooks were bound to be a banquet for some unsuspecting catfish. He chuckled to Cissy as he worked. "Maybe ole granpaw catfish in dis here ribber, Cissy. He wait fuh ole' Tobe ta come cotch him on dat long line. Mayhap some o his granchillen, too." Salt cedars grew thick along the banks of the Pecos, where the old man set his lines. He was sure the murky waters would yield them their supper that evening. "We go take us a nap now, Cissy. Fore long we come back ta give thet line a tug. We see den does old granpaw catfish keer ta be our suppah.'' Fishing was the greatest delight in the life of this ugly battered giant. He took Cissy by the hand, they made their way back out of the cedar thicket to where the wagons were circled. ''Time come soon now, Cissy, we see Massa John agin. He be my boy, Cissy. He da fustes man to say to me, 'I loves yo.' He were not a man den, he were jes a leetle feller. He ride my back lak a hoss one day, den he squeeze mah neck an he say, 'Tobe I love yo fo evah.' Dat wer a long time ago, Cissy, but I reckon he still do.'' Cissy squeezed his big hand. ''Course he do, Tobe, yo is a easy man to love, cuz yo heart be as big as yo is.'' Tobe gave a toothless smile, then said, ''I gonna res a spell whilst ole granpappy catfish hab dinnah. Den I go down ta de ribber again ta tell him howdy.'' He threw his big grey head back and laughed. ''Howdy dere, granpaw catfish . . . howdy.'' The day of rest wore on until the sun began to set behind the escarpment the travelers had descended. Tobe roused his wife for their walk back down to the riverbank. They strolled along over the dry ground, talking of things to come and wondering about the names of the different trees and shrubs. The trot line had been set at a bend in the river where a deep hole caused the water to gently swirl. When Tobe tugged on the line, there was a answering tug from the depths of the pool. The black face lighted up with delight. ''We done cotch him er dem granchillen or his'n.'' Tobe untied the line form the limb, then began to pull back toward the bank. Two fourteen or fifteen inch catfish flopped onto the bank. Cissy was also excited. She chortled in delight. ''Suppah be almos ready, Tobe, peer lak dey be more on da line.'' Tobe gave another strong tug on the line. The ugly head of a giant catfish came to the surface of the roily water. The head was easily eight inches wide. Long, whisker-like feelers extended backward from the sides of the gaping mouth. Tobe jumped up. ''It be him, Cissy! I done kotch him way out here in da wilderness. Say howdy ta old granpappy, Cissy.'' Tobe laughed and leaned over the river edge, put his hand in the mouth of the creature, then yanked him on to the bank. The catfish would weigh easily twenty-five pounds. The line then yielded another smaller one. The former slaves were so excited about the catch of the great fish, that they failed to see the Comanche brave silently close in on them. Before they knew he was there, the Indian lunged with a wooden shafted lance. The Indian's intense hatred for anything that represented trespass on his territory had caused him to be brave beyond all caution. The lance point entered Tobe's huge chest, then the shaft broke off with a sickening crack. Tobe swung his great calloused fist with such force, that the Indian's jaw bone broke, and his neck snapped. The Indian fell to the ground, dead. The big eyes in the scarred, wrinkled, old face showed the mortal wound which had been inflicted. He dropped to his knees on the river bank, extended one hand toward his horrified wife. Then he said, "Cissy, dahlin, tell Massa John." Then he fell backward into the swirling waters of the Pecos River. Cissy began to scream in long agonizing shrieks. Men with drawn weapons came running from the wagons. When they reached her side, Cissy could not stop screaming. She could only point to the swirling water. Wes Bolt read the story before she could talk. The dead Indian, broken lance shaft, and the absence of Tobe told him that his lifetime friend would never be seen by them again. Wes folded the big black woman into his arms, put her grey head on his shoulder, in an effort to comfort her. He asked, "Shall we try to find him, Cissy?" "No, he daid, Mistah Wes. Kain't nobody fetch him back now. My Tobe he don gone on." Great river of tears streamed down her shining face. With great difficulty they did find him, then at sunrise the next morning, they buried the scarred body of a man from Africa, in the sandy soil of the Pecos River Valley. When Wes finished his marker, it read simply, "Here lies a real man, His name . . . Tobe Bolt." Adelia read from the Bible, "Be merciful unto me, o God, be merciful unto me: for my soul trusteth in Thee: yea, in the shadow of Thy wings will I make my refuge, until calamities be over past." Cissy began to croon . . . "Good news chariot a coming, good news chariot a coming, an Tobe were not lef ahind." The big black woman walked to the grave. "I tell him, Tobe, honey, I tell Massa John. We see yo by n' by." With that she turned to take her place in the wagon. Young Samuel and his bride, Honey, were her guardians now.

The wagon train began to roll toward Fort Stockton. From there, they would have an escort of cavalry soldiers all the way to Van Horn's wells. They were leaving Comanche country, only to find themselves in the lands still contested by the fierce Apache. There were no better soldiers in the world than these Indians. They were out-gunned, out-manned, but still fighting. Their adversaries were buffalo soldiers, black men, of the U.S. Cavalry, recruited for lonely garrison duty in the reaches of the territories. The job they did, was to go down in history as "well done."

Near the first of March, this wagon train made its way into El Paso. This thriving city on the banks of the Rio Grande, afforded them a chance to buy provisions for the final journey up the Camino Real, King's Highway, to Santa Fe. Wilfred had ridden with the troopers, a great deal of the time on the way to Van Horn's well. He struck up an acquaintance with a corporal named Clanton. One evening at the campfire, Clanton had asked Wilfred what he intended to do with his life. Wilfred didn't hesitate to tell Clanton of his lifelong dream. "I aim ta git me some ground. I'll get me papers thet says it be mine. Then I aim ta make thet my home for the res of my life." Clanton spoke quickly, "Wilfred, the govmint got some fine lan in the Valley of de Rio Grande whut they gonna let black veterans homestead on." "Thet be da place I gonna head fuh, when I git out." Wilfred sat up to pay more attention. "Shore nuff," Clanton declared, "It be in the valley afore yo gits to Las Cruces. If yo be a veteran, den maybe we could be neighbors." "I be a veteran awright! This empty sleeve say I got real close ta da wah. I be riding dat way, Clanton, I foh shore as hell, gonna take a look." His mind was preoccupied as the Bolt party's three wagons rolled up the Rio Grande for their final destination. A blast of cold air blew in from the northwest, but they felt they were so close to home now that the discomfort was really not too great. The threat of Indian attack up the Rio Grande Valley had been greatly reduced by constant pressure from General Carleton's troops during the recent war. A line of forts was now manned all the way from El Paso to the Duke City of Albuquerque. The winds of March were blowing a steady chilling blast. Great billowing clouds of dust covered the travelers. They had never seen anything like this in their lives. It was a frightening experience. until they were reassured by other travelers that it was just a little ole duster, which would blow over in day or two.

Great flocks of water fowl were making their way north up the winding stream. Years of changing course had caused the valley to be scarred by bosques, or small forests of Tornillo bush and salt cedar.

When they reached the area in the valley which Wilfred had been told about, he would leave the wagon train for hours at a time to ride through the sand hills, topped with scrub mesquite which were common to the area. There were great coveys of big blue quail and other wild fowl. Wilfred would become so excited at the possibilities of farming this rich valley, that he would keep the others awake for hours everynight just talking about how he intended to come back here one day. They made camp near the village of Mesilla. The town was built around a square where all manner of travelers would gather to trade horses, mules and cattle. They would talk of Indian attacks which would still occur now and then as the wild Apache grew more and more discontented with reservation life. Soldiers from Fort Stanton, further up the river, mingled with the townspeople. This was one of the important centers of the New Mexico territory at that time, a favorite stopping place on the long road from Santa Fe into Mexico.

Although our travelers were still a long way from their destination, they had fallen in love with this wild, dry, country. The air was so clear, with skies so blue, that a person could see for over a hundred miles if a mountain didn't get into the way. They pressed on with an urgency now. They were still over three hundred and sixty miles, or so, away from their reunion with the rest of the family. It was to be the end of March, before they were directed to the winding road down the small river that led to the Bolt Ranch. Long before the party arrived at the headquarters, they were spotted by Mexican Vaqueros attending a spring roundup at the north end of the range. A rider left the group, then spurred his horse to a run to bring the news of the long expected homecoming of the rest of the family. The rider dismounted from his horse before it stopped in the yard of the ranch. "Senora! Senora! Son aqui!" The young Mexican cowboy was as excited as the rest of the family were to be. Clemmy came running from the house, followed closely by Consuela. "Donde estan, Martin?" Connie addressed the boy in Spanish. Where are they? "Una hora y media mas in El Camino, Senora." The boy gestured wildly toward the north. An hour and a half more to the north. Martin recovered his sweating horse then left at a run back up the road from whence he had come. Clemmy, her grey-black hair flowing in the wind behind her, ran to a triangle of steel hanging from the verandah roof at the ranch house. She took a long piece of metal, hanging there for the purpose, then began to pound the triangle with all her strength. The loud clanging sound attracted John and Carlos who were tending a large herd of horses in the upper pasture. They, and other ranch hands, came as fast as their mounts could carry them. The triangle was the alarm to come at once. It could be an Indian raid, yet John just knew in his heart that it was the joyous news of the arrival of his long-awaited family. He raced Carlos to the ranch house. When they saw Clemmy and Consuela standing in the yard, they knew there was no danger. Clemmy was already having her gentle mare saddled. Connie elected to stay at the house so that she could start to prepare a great feast of welcome. When her horse was ready, Clemmy, John and Carlos rode at a gallop in the direction of the approaching wagons. Clemmy's light brown face was beginning to show the ravages of the sun, wind, and time. Her still magnificently beautiful features were now showing lines about her eyes and mouth. Her long flowing hair was streaked with silver. She still rode erect, which showed her figure to be comparable to that of a much younger woman. Her husband, riding beside her, was clothed in a buckskin jacket with his silvery grey hair streaming below a flat-crowned felt hat. His bright blue eyes stared straight ahead from his intense, weather browned face. A half smile parted his lips. This uneducated man from Georgia was considered to be the top rancher in this part of the vast New Mexico territory. Their adopted son, Carlos, was as lithe as a mountain lion, riding the horse he was mounted upon as though he were a part of the animal. He playfully rode behind Clemmy's mare, slapped it a resounding whack on the rump. He threw his head back to laugh when the mare leaped forward. The livid scar on the side of his face was a terrible blemish on an otherwise handsome man. "Hurry, Abuelita, little grandmother. Your nietos, grandchildren, will be much older if you don't get there soon. They may scold you for being so late." They rode steadily at a gallop until they sighted the three covered wagons. The wagons stopped at the sight of the oncoming riders. Everyone dismounted, riders and wagon passengers as well. Carlos reined his horse to a stop at a discrete distance while the reunion of the family took place. There was not a dry eye. They all embraced, all trying to talk at once. Clemmy's first interest was her own son, whom she had left when he was such a young man. Clemmy wept for the first time in a long while. She tried to gather her family to her all at the same time. Then John missed the presence of the giant Tobe. He asked, "Whar be Tobe?" There was a sudden silence. "He ain't sick is he?" John became anxious, he noted Cissy standing alone. "Cissy, whar be Tobe?" The large woman lowered her eyes but couldn't speak. Wes broke the spell. He looked his father in the eye. "Paw, Tobe didn't make it all the way. He got killed by a Comanche at the Pecos River. John Bolt's face suddenly became a mask of grief. His blue eyes filled with tears, he walked away from the group to a large Ponderosa pine away from the road. He stood with his back to the rest of the family, he thought of the great black giant who had once gathered him into his huge hard arms to soothe his battered young body. They were kindred souls then, the great slave from Africa, and the small boy who had been put adrift in the world to make it without the benefit of a mother or father to guide him. John remembered for only a short moment, then blew his nose loudly, and turned to join the others. He would help to make this a joyous occasion.

A great fiesta was planned at the Bolt Ranch, with people coming from as far away as Santa Fe and La Vegas. The great distances through the prairies and mountains caused them to have to bring their own bed and camping equipment. A whole steer was barbecued over a bed of oak coals. Whole young goats were roasted over a slow fire, as only Mexican people knew how. On the night of the fiesta, there was such a great crowd that the dancing had to take place in the yard of the ranch house. The music was a Mexican band from Santa Fe. Not too much in tune, but loud enough for everyone to enjoy. The new members of this vast community were really overwhelmed with the friendly manner in which they were accepted. The bitterness of their recent experiences in far off Georgia were soon fading to nothing more then a picture of the past. Many a romance blossomed at this great ranch fiesta. There was horse-racing in the afternoon, with the prancing white stallion, Gallo, owned by Carlos, taking all the honors. There just wasn't a horse in the territory to beat him. Viejo Bolt, as John was known, would never pit The Lad, Gallo's sire, against the prancing younger stallion. He would always just laugh and say, "Some day, Carlos, me and The Lad are gonna kick a bunch o dobe dirt in your face." A round of friendly betting began. Everyone wanted to see the great Arabian stud, Aladdin, sire of hundreds of fine horses in the territory now, pitted against his famous son, Gallo.

Viejo enjoyed the back-slapping and bantering carried on by his many friends. When the excitement was at a high pitch, Viejo mounted the porch steps to announce in a loud voice, "I jes ain't got tha heart ta do this ta Carlos, I done see all the young fellers bettin on Carlos an the rooster. I know The Lad would feel bad bout taking em down ta sich a great defeat. There jes ain't no way we gonna do that ta poor Carlos." The taunting and speculation lasted up into the night, but no one ever knew if the great white stallion could outrun his offspring.

Tired revelers began to leave the Bolt Ranch the next morning after a gigantic breakfast of chili beans, beefsteak, hotcakes and ham. The Bolt fiesta was never forgotten, for many of the new romances which blossomed that night ended in marriages which helped to raise the population of the rich land.

The ground work for the establishment of the Wes Bolt rancho was already done by Viejo and Clemmy. The younger man's ranch merely became an extension of the one already established in the name of Bolt. The one-armed Wilfred would take leave, now and then, to ride to the lower Rio Grande Valley. A community of black people had sprung up there, so he was determined to become a part of it. He had worked diligently to learn to read and write. This advantage he used a great deal as he began to put his dream together. He stayed that spring and winter, working with Wes to establish the new ranch. One winter day, he rode with Wes to tend stock on the open range. "Wes, I ain't cut out to be no rancher. I gotta see the land bein' turn over wid a plow. I got me a hunert and sixty acres o thet land by the Rio Grande. Hit ain't a thing now, Wes, but salt cedar, bosque, an sand hills. It's mine, Wes, an thet is the way it gotta be fer the res o my life, whether it be a long life er a short one. I gonna set on thet lan, Wes, an God hep any man, any coloah who try ta take hit fum me. Dis here one han gonna wok hardah dan any two haned man dat eber rode up da crick." Wes looked at his friend and saw true happiness in his face for the first time since they rode together as young boys. "I'll help you, Wilfred! Maybe Paw could spare some men, come spring." "Don't need no hep, and don' want ho hep! I gonna stan on my own damn boots an piss atwix em on my own damn lan. They be black women there now, Wes. I gonna fine me one which wants ta hep me raise a passel o kids.'' This was the first time Wes had ever heard Wilfred speak of wanting to be married. Wes thought that, at last, the loss of the arm in the war had ceased to trouble him. ''This here mare I ride is a thorobred, Wes. I got her bred ta thet Gallo o Carlos. I aim to take ta four Percheron mares what belonged ta Unkle Tobe. Dey all bred already ta da big stud. Unkle Tobe's wagon will be my home till I got me a dobe shack built.'' Wilfred raised his face to the cold New Mexico sky. ''Yes, Wes, by the grace of the almighty Gawd, this land gonna be my home.'' Wes laughed aloud, wheeled his horse, then lashed it with his long reins. He yelled back over his shoulder. ''I always been the best rider, Wilfred. I'll wait for you at at the barn.'' Wilfred wheeled his mare, he let out the rebel yell. The race was on. The mare under Wilfred's light form, pulled away from Wes before they reached the barn lot.

Before spring set in, Wilfred piled all his belongings into the wagon to leave. His younger brother, Samuel, now with a pregnant wife, approached Wilfred down by the corral. ''Wilfred, I gotta talk fer a spell.'' ''Shore Sam, you jes talk away.'' Samuel, in contrast to his brother, was a big, very strong young man. He shuffled his boots in the dirt as he began to express what was on his mind. ''Wilfred, me an Honey done talk to Momma an Poppa. We tole em we jes gotta go some place to make a home. Dey din cotton to da idee too much, spec'ly wid da baby comin. Dey done give us dere wagon and team, cuz I tole em we gonna go anyway, somehow. I jest want yo ta understand, Wilfred.'' Wilfred put his good arm around the young man's broad shoulders. ''I knows zacly how you feel, li'l brothah. When I pulls away fum these mountains, I gonna spec ta look back ta see Sam an dat pregnant Honey in a wagon ahind me. Dey be plenty room by da ribber, so cotton fahm, here come da Larkin brothas.'' Soon their plow began to bite into the rich land in the river bottom below old Mesilla. It was their land and remained so. Their father, Rufus, was content to set up a fine blacksmith shop on the Bolt ranch. There he worked, when the spirit moved him, which was seldom.

The obtaining and holding of ranchland in the New Mexico territory in the early days following the Civil War was not an easy task. Immigrants of all descriptions and character were pouring into the west along the famed Santa Fe Trail. Some were bound for points further to the west, but there were those who had grown tired of the constant travel, they decided to just settle where they were. Most were broke, tired and hungry. With very little to sustain them, they would steal cattle and horses from the local ranchers and farmers. For this, they were dealt with harshly. The Bolts were a helping hand to many of them, sending them on their way with fresh provisions and repairs to their wagons. Schooling for her children was most important to Adelia. She worked tirelessly to see that they were educated enough to cope with the expanding populations. When there were no schools to attend, she made her own, welcoming the children from the neighboring ranches to attend. Her boys were growing strong and healthy. Their toys were those which were made by Uncle Rufus, in the blacksmith shop. Pets were wild burros captured in the hills, a magpie which had fallen from its nest, a prairie dog which had been drowned out of its burrow at a very early age. These creatures they lent a helping hand, then made them a part of their lives. Horses, cattle, hogs and other livestock were part of their bringing up. They learned to respect the dangers of ranch life and were taught how to cope with it.

CHAPTER 22
THERE WERE THREE SONS

The personalities of the three boys were as divergent as brothers could be. The eldest, Matthew, was his father's shadow. He had grown to be a powerfully built young man. His shoulders and arms were very muscular. His fair complexion caused the freckles on his face to stand out as bold as the brown spots on a turkey egg. He was slow to anger, but a force to be reckoned with when he did become aroused. Matthew's red hair caused him to stand out in a crowd. He would be a man totally dedicated to ranch life. Mark had inherited the gentle nature of his mother. His hair was black, his hazel eyes were accented by his quick smile. Mark's favorite reading material was the Holy Bible. He was no sissy by any means, yet, New Mexico was to benefit from his gentle nature. Adelia would laughingly refer to her youngest, Luke, as a holy terror. She would tell the other boys, "Go find Luke and tell him to stop whatever it is he is doing." These boys were constantly looked after by an adoring Carlos. He referred to the three boys as mis chavalos, my young ones. While they were growing up, they felt that all their hurts, and problems, could be solved by Carlos. Their constant association with him, caused them to learn a valuable attribute. They all learned to speak Spanish at a very early age. Following the Civil War, the vast reaches of the New Mexico territory was divided into Colorado, Nevada, Arizona and New Mexico. The Gadsden Purchase of 1853 was supposed to have left the existing Spanish land grants in the hands of the families who occupied them. This proved to be chaos for many Spanish descendents. Their records were in far off Spain. Some of them were not too secure as it proved to be. Only a very few of the old Spanish families were able to hang onto the properties which were their heritage. Greedy land speculators managed to wrest control of some of the vast grants, break them up into smaller parcels, then sell them off to new owners.

When Matthew reached his eighteenth birthday, the state was in a turmoil. Gunfights brought on by the age-old sheep versus cattle feud, would spring up like the lighting of a match. The Lincoln County wars were being fought in the Sacramento Mountains of the southern part of the territory. The newspapers were full of the accounts of the outlaw, Billy The Kid. Through all of this, the Bolt empire was being built. There were serious setbacks from time to time. The weather was the most formidable foe. Viejo Bolt used to say that if the weather did not freeze everything to death, it would dry it up, bake it, and then blow it away. The acquisition of a huge rangeland to the south and west, in an area of rolling hills and mesas prompted them to look for more livestock to populate the land. The horse ranch was a big success. Now it would be cattle. Letters were dispatched to the Miller family in the northern hill country of Texas. Through bargaining with his old friend, El Viejo bought five hundred head of female cattle. They were to be gathered by the Millers, then driven to New Mexico, up the Loving and Goodnight Trail, to the upper Pecos. After long planning sessions, it was decided that Carlos would select ten vaqueros to ride with him to fetch the cattle. Matthew, and Mark, were to be in charge of the remount horse herd. Viejo and Wes were to leave for St. Louis to buy the bulls necessary to upgrade the cattle to produce more beef. Martin was to oversee the ranches, under the guidance of Adelia. When young Luke was informed that he was far too young to be on a cattle drive, he protested angrily. He saddled a horse, then rode like a madman out into the prairie, where he cried out his frustration and disappointment to the wind. From that time forward, Luke Bolt always had a driving urge to prove to everyone that he was very much a man. This was a boy wanting to grow up too fast.

It was early winter when the different missions took place. Viejo and Wes rode to the northeast where they would catch the train at Fort Dodge, then travel on to St. Louis where they were to purchase their bulls. The bigger party rode down the Pecos on their way to Texas. It was a great adventure for two boys, also Carlos who would ride again through the Pecos where John Bolt had rescued him and Consuela when they were greatly in need. The cowboys rode hard on the way to Texas. They would travel at least thirty miles each day. No new country they saw, in their opinion, could equal the beauty of their home near the towering Sangre de Cristo Mountains.

Carlos carefully took a tally of the cattle gathered by the Millers, then they strung the herd out in a long line reaching for the setting sun. Trailing the unwilling cattle was hard, dangerous work. It taxed men and horses to the very limit at times. The Mexican Vaqueros knew no fear when they were mounted on a good horse. This was the life they had known since they were children. The cattle moved slowly, but they moved. By now, other herds had made their way up this same trail. This caused the grazing to be poor, so the driven beasts suffered from hunger as they were forced westward. When they finally reached their own rangeland, they found the buffalo grass dry and brittle, but still nourishing enough to sustain the cows until better times in the spring.

The return of all the travelers was an occasion for another great celebration. Adelia pressed each of her brood to her ample bosom, then she thanked God for their return to the safety of the Sangre de Cristo. Viejo and Wes had returned with the new bulls at least two weeks ahead of the cattle drive. Spring was late in coming which resulted in the loss of some of the cows they had driven so far from Texas. When it did finally arrive, it was one of the most glorious springs seen in years. The buffalo and grama grass grew tall while the spring roundup got under way.

Matthew and Carlos were checking the horse pasture one noonday, when they noticed a section of the rail fence down. Carlos dismounted from his stallion, Gallo. He examined the loose ground beyond the fence. "Look like four, maybe five, caballos come through this morning" . . . Carlos was still reading the hoofmarks as he talked. "Matthew, you stay to fix the fence. I gonna ride on after these which are loose." He swung lightly into the saddle as he talked, then went out of sight into the piñon and cedar forest. Matthew thought nothing of it as he replaced the downed rails. This was not the first time Carlos had ridden after strays. Besides, this was spring roundup time. Everyone had a job to do. Carlos had ridden in the direction of the notch in the rimrock. This was the same direction he and Viejo had taken, years ago, when they were in hot pursuit of Apache thieves who had stolen the big stud and their precious brood mares.

Night fell, there still was no alarm. Matthew told his father about the hole in the fence. ''Carlos will come ridin in in awhile. Them horses probably run for a spell when they found they were free. This was not the case, however. A great black curtain of fear decended over the Bolt Ranch. Gallo came at a gallop into the feed lot where his stable was. The reins were still across his neck, he was lathered and spent, there was a great deal of blood on the pommel of the saddle. The alarm was sounded for all hands. They were to be ready at first light. Viejo would not allow them to ride into the black of night in such rough country. He feared for the lives of others. Through the night a thunderstorm began to grumble and flash over the ridges and mountains. A steady spring rain swept in, which lasted for over an hour. They all knew that tracking would be made almost impossible.

When the search began, the men stayed in their saddles for endless hours. Carlos Martinez Bolt, was never seen again, alive. He was not forgotten in that part of the country though. His sister, Consuela, would tell her many children, countless stories of the hard-fighting, hard-riding, Tio Carlos. Any time a Bolt rider ventured into the high country, he would always be on the lookout for some sign of what might have happened. Even two years later, Luke Bolt, now fifteen, rode into the high country looking for stray Bolt cattle. He was an unbelievably handsome boy. Already tall for his age, his shoulders were broad, his arms well-muscled. His flat crowned hat partially concealed a tumble of curly black hair, and yet his eyes were as blue as those of his grandfather. When he smiled he showed straight white teeth. He rode lightly in the saddle and was alert to everything that went on around him. His horse was laboring up a steep trail when he heard the tinkling of a bell. He dismounted quickly, leading his horse to the edge of a meadow where the bell was sounding. A breathtakingly beautiful scene lay before him. The meadow was summer pasture for a herd of sheep. A camp wagon was sitting at the edge of a little brook. Luke led his horse deeper into the shadows of the spruce trees. A grey bearded Mexican sat on a horse near the grazing sheep. Luke recognized him as an older soldier called Sargento. He was head herder for the De La O sheep ranch, one of the few Spanish grants which had managed to survive. The old man had been a soldier under the command of Colonel Kit Carson. He was speaking intently to a young girl who stood on the ground in the morning sunshine. Suddenly the old one reined his horse to ride away, down the trail Luke Bolt had just ascended. Luke watched the young girl, she leaned over to pet one of the sheep dogs which had come to her. He could tell from the distance that she was about his age and unusually pretty. Luke walked toward her out of the protection of the trees. When she looked up, she was momentarily frightened. She made a motion to grasp a shotgun which had been placed against a tree. She then recognized him, so stood her ground. She was dressed in high topped boots, a divided riding skirt and man's shirt which seemed to be having trouble concealing her firm young breasts. The color of her skin was like ivory, her full beautifully shaped lips were slightly parted, revealing white even teeth. Her small waist line was accented by a heavy leather belt with a huge turquoise buckle. Luke, in a mocking gesture, removed his flat crowned hat, making a low bow at the same time. "I'm Luke Bolt," he said, as his glance covered her from head to toe. A sudden mountain breeze whished her hat from her head, allowing a tumble of raven black hair to fall to her shoulders. Luke looked into her large brown eyes. "I know who you are. Everyone in this part of the country knows who the Bolt family is." "How come I have never seen you before, pretty little sheepherder?' Luke's tone was insolent. "It's because you never notice anyone but yourself, Luke Bolt. There are a lot of girls at school in Santa Fe who talk about you all the time." Luke grinned broadly at the compliment. "And what do you say about me?" "I say nothing at all about you, or anyone else." Luke extended his hand to touch her hair, his fingers momentarily brushed her velvet smooth cheek. A sudden thrill coursed through his strong young body. A thrill such as he had never felt before. She stood perfectly still. Luke moved closer to her. "Ya know something . . . I ain't never kissed a little sheepherder girl before." The truth was that Luke had never kissed any girl before in his entire life. Her big eyes narrowed in anger. She still showed no fear. She raised her chin even a little higher. He noticed that the corner of her mouth quivered, ever so slightly. His eyes drank in the softness of her throat, then descended to the crease between her firm young breasts. She took a deep breath, then said softly, "Luke Bolt .. . I am Graciela, the daughter of Don Alexandro Silva

De La O. My ancestors were on this land before yours ever crossed the Mississippi River. We are a very proud family. If you try to shame me, I would be left with but two choices. One would be to tell my father and brothers, who would ride to the Bolt Ranch to avenge our honor. The other would be to kill myself. That I would do before I would cause terrible anguish to innocent people in your family and mine. When she lowered her heavy eyelashes, single tear rolled down each of her cheeks. Young Luke Bolt felt a surge of hot blood rise to his face, a mantle of shame spread over him like a huge dark cloud. He turned quickly, then mumbled half aloud, probably wouldn't have been any fun anyaway. He swung into his saddle, spurred his horse across the meadow . . . scattering sheep in every direction as he rode.

Luke rode into the ranch stables just as the evening sun had made its curtain call behind the distant mountains. The ranch hands gathered in the adobe bunkhouse, while Luke, after tending his horse, walked up to the front of the comfortable ranch house. He was still troubled about the encounter he had had that morning in the meadow of the high country. He resented the sudden slashing of his ego, yet the haunting beauty of Graciela De La O kept nagging at his memory. His mother, whom he knew to be the greatest cook in the whole wide world, had prepared her usually delicious supper. They gathered at the huge ranch table, where they were being served by a young Mexican woman. When they all began to eat, Mark announced that he had something to tell the whole family. He looked anxiously at Adelia who obviously had already heard the top of his expected announcement. He began, "Paw, I have been a good hand here on the ranch, and I love all of you with all there is in my heart. What I aim to say is that although I will miss all of you and the ranch very much, there is just something that I have to do with my life." Wes began to listen intently, he glanced questioningly toward his wife. Adelia merely waited for Mark to continue. Mark's voice had suddenly taken on such a serious note, that they all had stopped eating, their eyes fastened on the second son. "What I'm trying to say, Paw, is that I want to leave the ranch." He timidly proffered an opened letter to his father. Wes took it without looking at it. "Go on son! We will hear you out." Mark took a gulp of water, then continued. "I asked Momma and she said it would be alright for me to write to the

Methodist School in Denver, to see if they would take me in to study for the ministry.'' Mark sat back in his chair, waiting for the momentous news to sink into the minds of his father and two brothers. Matthew was the first to speak. He exploded with . . . ''Well, I'll be damned!'' Then added quickly . . . ''scuse me, Mark, I didn't mean . . .'' The older brother suddenly felt that he had sinned in the presence of the clergy. Luke exploded with . . . ''Now how could you want to do such a stupid thing as be a preacher? We got all the work we can do . . . right here on this place.'' Mark froze his brother with a cold stare. ''This territory needs ministers who have some education, Luke. I intend to come back to build a church in Santa Fe, or Albuquerque.'' He looked back again at his father who had been sitting silently looking at his plate. Wes spoke softly, ''Well, Mark, everybody don't all want to be Catholic. There gotta be some chicken eating Methodists, too.'' He smiled broadly at his second son. A wave of relief spread over the young man's face. Wes continued: ''Every man has to choose to do what he thinks is right. If he don't then he will spend the rest of his life thinking he should have. Now I remember a time when Viejo asked me to leave a farm in Georgia to come way out here with him. I made my own choice at that time, an by all that's holy, Mark Bolt has got the right to make his.'' Adelia smiled broadly, her kindly face showing the pride she felt in the family she had dedicated her life to. She raised her husband's hand to her lips to kiss it. At the same she extended her other hand to her second son. Luke slapped his brother on the shoulder. ''Well brother . . . if that is what you want, then I'm with you. Still can't see why we need a preacher in the family, though.'' Matthew blushed beneath his red hair. ''I will, one day, Brother Mark. You can say the words at my wedding.'' They all began to tease Matthew about some father coming with a shotgun. He said shyly, ''A man has gotta marry some day.'' Wes shook the hand of his second son. ''Tomorrow . . . you go up to the big ranch an tell Viejo and your Grandma Clemmy. They are gonna be right proud of you.'' They really were!

CHAPTER 23
SUNRISE, SUNSET

Two years had rolled by since the new bulls and the herd from Texas had arrived at the Bolt range. Dodge City, Kansas, had become a boisterous cattle shipping point with vast herds being driven up from Texas. The gold and silver mines of Colorado began to boom. There became a constant demand for the quality beef, and superb horses produced on the two Bolt ranches. This was a land where boys were not privileged to stay boys for very long. Since the disapperance of Carlos, Matthew had become the authority everyone looked to for direction.

It was beginning to be the fall of the year, a time when this segment of the Santa Fe Trail took on its most beautiful mantle. The skies were clear and blue, the air was beginning to be cool, the late summer rains had promised the ranchers an abundant supply of feed for the winter. It was this time of year that a great fair and fiesta was to be held in Santa Fe. All those who were able to travel would be in the territorial capitol by September twentieth. It was to be the big event of the year. Fair time was on everybody's mind. Preparations were being made at the greatest and smallest of homes and communities. The most exciting events were to be the horse races. During those days, everyone loved fine horses. Descendents of the mighty Aladdin were to be shown and raced. The fastest on the ranch was being trained for the great mile event. Riders from the south were bringing news of an unbelievable fast mare from the lower Rio Grande Valley. The rider for the big race, in the company of the most trusted caballeros, took the show horses tied to the tailgate of feed wagons, then left for Santa Fe. The whole family was to follow in light buckboards. Those who could ride, of course, did so. One of those was the handsome, dashing young Luke Bolt. He had saddled a coal black Arabian stallion. In the saddle aboard this magnificent animal, Luke felt like a king. He had promised a friend of his, Tim Pain that he would stop by Apache Canyon, where Tim lived on a small ranch, so that they could ride to the fair together. The family stayed on the road which skirted the high country to the south. The going was easier that way. As he rode, Luke felt that those who had never experienced an early morning in northern New Mexico had really not lived at all. When Luke drew near the summit at Glorieta, he could see a team of horses hooked to a light wagon standing in front of the stage station. There, a grey-haired old Mexican man was straining to load a heavy trunk into the back of the wagon. Then a young woman emerged from the front door of the tiny station. "Sargento . . . espere te." Luke recognized the voice instantly. His heart leaped to his throat, it seemed to choke him. It was Graciela De La O. He had heard that she had been away to El Paso where she was learning to be a teacher. Luke leaped from his horse, then literally threw the trunk into the wagon. The old Mexican bristled, "Es mi trabajo, joven. It was my job, young man." Luke nodded his head to the old man. "Si Don Sargento, dispense me. Yes, excuse me." Graciela was standing very still, watching him as he turned. He approached her . . . "Graciela, I have been . . ." he stopped and shuffled his black boots in the dust of the road. He began again . . . "Graciela, if you could only know." His voice trailed off again. She whispered softly . . . "I do know, Luke . . . I do." He could smell the perfume of this, the most exciting woman he had ever seen in his life. She had been in his thoughts since that time he had been so rude to her at the sheep camp. Luke was ill at ease. He removed his hat, then brushed at the dust on his shirt. Graciela looked up at him with her big soft brown eyes. Luke thought that he read in them the same way that he felt right at the moment. "Graciela, do you suppose that we could?" She stepped near him. "Oh, Luke, there is so much between us, but maybe some day . . . quien sabe?" With that she turned to join the old man on the wagon seat. Luke watched the wagon until it turned a bend in the winding road. He mounted his horse, then while he rode he kept hearing the delicate Spanish accent ringing in his ears . . . "Maybe some day . . . quien sabe?" When he joined Tim on the west side of the pass, the poor fellow thought that Luke had been stricken with some sort of strange disease. He was just not his regular self. They spurred their horses into an easy lope. They were on their way to the fair.

While these gay crowds rode toward Santa Fe, the world was beautiful. A haze impending autumn lay over the Sandias to the south. First frosts of fall had already colored the slopes of the Jemez to the west. A thin layer of wispy white clouds were trying to avoid the highest peaks of the Sangre de Cristos to the north. Buffalo grass waved in the cool September breeze. Young Luke Bolt should not have had a care in the world. However: the words of Graciela kept coming back to him. "Oh! Luke there is so much between us, but perhaps some day . . . quien sabe?"

Since they had caught up with the main party, Tim could no longer stand the melancholy mood of his best friend. He spurred his horse to join the group of happy caballeros, and vaqueros who were laughing and joking in anticipation of the wonderful things they could do at the grand fiesta. Luke rode up behind the carriage which was carrying his grandparents, parents and Consuela. The happy chatter from this, now pleasingly plump Mexican lady, seemed like the drone of a pesky bee to Luke. Connie knew all the gossip from ranches for miles around.

Riders approached from the opposite direction, so the carriage pulled to the side to give them, at least a fair share of the road. It was three gentlemen, dressed in the fashion of Spanish ranchers. Their elegance reflected the fact that they were from the families of the rich. Horses and saddles were the very finest, adorned with, what Luke Bolt thought was, a disgusting amount of silver. The three doffed their flat crowned hats as they rode by the ladies, their attitude was gracious, they bowed low in their saddles. They didn't as much as give Luke a glance. He was not particularly interested in them, either. Connie looked back to see if they had traveled sufficiently far that she would not be heard. She was bursting to tell what she knew. She began. "The won in da meedle," Connie's accent would never improve, "He is Reynaldo Perez de Garcia." She nodded to the south of the Sandias. "They have such a beeg land grant. It reach way down into the Manzano Mountains. They are lawyers, so they make sure the land belong to them. Reynaldo, he practice law in Santa Fe right now. The family, they run the great rancho." Connie took a second breath to continue. "I know something else, too, Right now, he ees ride to the De La O rancho. They probly eenvite heem because Graciela suppose to come home today from El Paso." Luke suddenly stiffened in his saddle, a hot surge of blood seemed to rush through his entire body. Luke swore to himself . . . "Damn him, God damn that Spanish lawyer to hell. He wouldn't dare pay attention to Graciela. He must be at least twenty-five. Graciela was no more than eighteen." How could this old man be going to call on her." Luke's blood was boiling. He wanted to wheel his horse, dash down the road, then challenge this man to a fight. Knives, guns, fists, anyway at all. Luke was not a fool, so that insane thought passed quickly. Connie rambled on, but Luke paid no more attention. His thoughts were completely awash with the tragic thought that someone, beside Luke Bolt, might get the attention of Graciela De La O. What if that Spanish son-of-a-bitch, might even touch her? Question after question bombarded his poor jealously crowded brain. Why did this sudden threat, to his thoughts of Graciela, have to be everything that woman could want? He was rich, handsome and intelligent. Besides he is Spanish, and that was sure to influence the De La O family. What gave the bastard the right to be the owner of such a vast chunk of the New Mexico territory? After all, hadn't the Spaniards taken it from the poor Indians? Their horses, steel tipped lances and guns made it no contest, when they took the land from its original owners. Luke tried to justify his own ancestral right to be there at the moment. After all, his grandfather had bought the land with hard-earned money. Then they had all worked hard to keep and improve it. Right then, it seemed to this hot-blooded young man, that the land was for those with the might, not necessarily those with the right. Luke knew in his heart that there would be a challenge and that it would have to be met.

Matthew, too, was preoccupied. He rode with a special posture on this glorious day. His muscular body was straight, his gaze constantly to the southwest. Something was definitely on this young man's mind, too.

They topped a high ridge as the road turned to the north. There before them was the Rio Grande Valley. Nearer to Santa Fe, the river wound through rather deep canyons, then the valley flattened out into the wide area of bosque with salt cedar, cottonwood, tornillo and mesquite dominating the scene. They could see the

Camino Real, the oldest road on the North American continent where it extended as far as the eye could see, in the direction of Albuquerque. The other terminus of the road was Mexico City. The Spaniards established the King's Highway as far back as the sixteenth century. The road was marked by dust clouds from the many travelers in either direction. Most were on their way to the great fiesta in Santa Fe. The others continued on, while Matthew sat his horse with his gaze fastened on the ribbon of highway. His mind went back to the crisp fall day they had ridden away from the ranch on the way to pick up cattle in Texas. He was seventeen then, two years ago, but already a seasoned ranch hand.

While in Texas he had met a girl. She was three years older than he, yet he fell hopelessly in love with her. Since that time they had been exchanging a steady stream of letters in both directions. Only his sweet and gentle mother, Adelia, shared his secret. He had asked the girl to marry him. Instead of consenting right then, she had asked him to wait two years until he was absolutely sure. Matthew smiled broadly, reined his horse back into the road to gallop after the others.

The huge fair was designed for the exchanging and selling of livestock of all descriptions. It served its purpose well the first day. The second day was to be the great horseracing events. The greatest spectacle of all was to put the riders and mounts against the best of the territory on a winding course laid out through the rolling grassy hills to the south of the town. Spectators would line the hillsides along the finish line. The starting time was to be at one in the afternoon. The entered horses began to come to the finish line. The Bolt ranch champion was a sleek brown Arabian, to be ridden by one of Connie's young sons. Saddles were sheep skins cinched to the horses' backs, short stirrups made up the balance of the rig. The Bolt stallion was the favorite among the betters, nevertheless, there were rumors of a racing mare which had been brought up from the lower Rio Grande Valley. She was said to be the fastest in that part of the country. All eyes turned when the valley mare was ridden to the line. She was half-thoroughbred, and half Arabian. The rider was slightly built black man with only one arm. The pony horse beside the mare was ridden by a giant of a black man. They paraded their horses while anxiously looking into the crowd. They sprang from their mounts when they saw the grey heads of their Mother and Father hurrying toward them. Wilfred and Samuel embraced their parents, Sally and Rufus. The boys held their parents close to them as the tears streamed down their faces.

The starting trumpet sounded, so they left hastily with a promise to see them after the race. They would then show off their respective families. Wilfred, too, was married and had a child. Wilfred spotted Wes at the starting line. His face broke in a wide grin. "Sorry, Wes, me an da lady here aim ta be kickin dirt in your stud's face." Wes was overjoyed to see his lifelong friend. He shouted: "If the mare had a rider, Wilfred, then I might be worried." Wilfred waved his brother away when he approached the line. All horses in the race were to be at the line at exactly five minutes after the first warning. Those under control would have the advantage of a fast get away. At the pistol shot, Connie's boy, on the Bolt stallion, an excellent rider, had his mount at the line at precisely the right moment. Wilfred had wheeled his mare and was coming to the line as the shot rang out. It was a wild stampede, with the Arabian stallion taking the lead, he leaped away from the start. Horses and riders jostled on the narrow track, straining for a place at the front. The spectators watched as long as they could see the action from this vantage point. Then they crossed the ridge where the finish line was to be. The race was no contest except for the Bolt stallion and the brown valley mare. When they came down the stretch, the stallion was still a length ahead. Wilfred began to talk to the mare in his own gentle manner. Then, when they were nearing the line, he strained forward to shout in her ear . . . "Now! Yaaah!" The sleek brown mare seemed to take wings! She leaped foward! In a few strides she had passed the stallion, streaking for the finish line. This horse race was talked about for years to come in northern New Mexico. Matthew, anxiously made all the family promise to be at the stage depot at precisely four thirty. That was the time the coach would arrive from Albuquerque. He had a surprise they must all be there to see.

The Bolt clan made a large group at the stage depot that afternoon. When the vehicle did arrive, the passengers were most anxious to get down from the infernal vehicle. They were covered with dust from head to toe, all were obviously very tired. The last to alight, was a slender, full-bosomed young lady. She was clothed in a grey dress, the fashion of the day. Long sleeves covered her arms and a skirt fell to her ankles. Matthew was standing besides his grandmother, Clemmy. "It's her, Grandma . . . It's Linda!" The girl had removed a scarf and hat, allowing a tumble of golden hair to spill about her shoulders. Clemmy gasped, "Glory be! It is Linda! Little Linda Miller." Matthew was already at her side. He enfolded her in his brawny arms, then awkwardly but tenderly kissed her dusty mouth and face. Linda had come all this way to marry Matthew Bolt. She came alone, since her only brother had fallen with the Texas Battalion at Glorieta, right here near Santa Fe. The entire Bolt crowd gathered around the tired but happy girl. At that moment they heard Adelia exclaim: "Mark! Oh! My son, Mark." A tall young man with a face the carbon copy of Adelia Bolt, pushed his way into the throng. Mark had come in answer to a summons from his older brother. Something about someone needing a preacher. Mark was just what his brother had ordered. The family made way for Clemmy and her husband. Her hair was all grey now, her skin was wrinkled like parchment. Her dark eyes were still bright, but now spilling over with tears. The old lady clasped the girl in her arms, then whispered, "God sent ya back ta Clemmy. I have always love yo, my chile." She then turned away, calmly taking a corn cob pipe from her pocket. She lighted it, then she took the arm of her husband. They strolled toward the busy square of Santa Fe. At length Clemmy spoke. Very quietly she said, "John, my whole worl be complete now. I be ready, any time, ta cross my river." John's only reply was . . . "Over there we will be together forever."

www.ingramcontent.com/pod-product-compliance
Lightning Source LLC
Chambersburg PA
CBHW020430030726
47495CB00006B/1733
* 9 7 8 0 8 6 5 3 4 1 1 7 3 *